AT WHAT COST, SILENCE?

AT WHAT COST, SILENCE?

A NOVEL

KAREN LYNNE KLINK

SHE WRITES PRESS

Published 2023
Printed in the United States of America
Print ISBN: 978-1-64742-603-3
E-ISBN: 978-1-64742-604-0
Library of Congress Control Number: 2023907942

For information, address:
She Writes Press
1569 Solano Ave #546
Berkeley, CA 94707

Interior Design by Kiran Spees

She Writes Press is a division of SparkPoint Studio, LLC.

I dedicate this book to Billy,

And all the boys who walked in their mother's dresses and heels

Down the streets of their neighborhoods if they wished,

And all those who loved whoever they wished.

You know who you are.

Thank you.

"It would be like hearing the grass grow and the squirrel's heartbeat,
And we should die of that road which lies on the other side
of silence."

George Eliot, *Middlemarch*

Characters

Blue Hills

Paien Villere, Creole papa from New Orleans – m. Isabelle Beaumont, Lucien's birth mother who dies in childbirth en route from Virginia
Madeleine Fortier Villiere, his second wife and children's maman from Savannah and France
Lucien Beau Villiere born June 1831, eldest son from first marriage – m. Joanna Camden, from abolitionist family
Adrien Denys Villere born August 1841, first surviving son of Madeleine and Paien Villere
Bernadette Louise Villere born July 1842, his sister
Jule Villere born August 1844
Abigail Villere born September 1846

Marcus Holland, overseer, Paien's good friend and Isaac's papa
Betta Holland, his wife, Isaac's mama, and Madeleine's personal lady's maid
Isaac Holland, their son, and Adrien's supposed "brother" and close friend
Esther Davis, cook
Simon Thatcher, butler

Hartwood

Randloph Hart, father
Lucretia Porter Hart, his wife
Jacob Hart, eldest son born September 1832 – m. **Porscha**

William (Will) Hart born January 1841
Lily Hart born September 1843 – m. **Andrew T. Garrison**

Colt Alvaro, half Tonkawa and Jacob Hart's companion

PART I

Chapter One
Blue Hills

$\mathcal{B}$ernadette

Women do as we are told in a world run by men.
I did what was expected of me. Managed the plantation, married young, and loved my husband as much as I was able.

Now I have a family of my own and, having attained a certain age, realize that perhaps my love for my brother was greater than acceptable. Maman doted upon him, and I might have been jealous except her attention on Adrien gave me more freedom than most young ladies of our place and time, and for this I am grateful. Adrien remained a staunch supporter of my most unusual endeavors, even though such often brought him trouble with Papa.

I believed I knew Adrien well; nevertheless, he kept a secret from us all, though not so dangerous a matter as Papa's. Such deceptions run in my family, as convention and our survival demanded them.

No one knew the true me. No one but Adrien.

Chapter Two

Adrien

I am haunted by my past.

Even today, a grown man with battle scars, I am nearly as pretty as my sister, disgustingly so.

In torment of escalating secrets, I grew up alongside fine English- and German-made furniture, our slaves, and hypocrisy. Only later did I learn of deceptions from those with whom I lived.

Isaac, my dear friend, brother, and companion since babyhood, slept with me—played with the same top and toy soldiers. We listened to the same stories Maman told on endless, sultry afternoons on the green velvet sofa.

We shared fears and dreams.

"You little goose," my brother Lucien said, "he's a slave, not your brother."

Papa had to say for me to accept it. To point out Isaac's darker skin. Dark as Betta, my mammy and Isaac's mama, and Esther, our cook. Papa said they were all our Negroes, all those I had thought were . . . I do not know what I had thought. "Our people," he said, not "our slaves," and we always said, "please" and "thank you" when they did for us.

How naïve to have to be told.

Walking across the carpet with his head and shoulders lowered, Papa made the floor creak: *Slaves must be heavy to have. Not the same as horses and dogs and Maman's silver.*

I understood little regarding slaves, or Negroes, or coloreds, as most said, not wanting to admit to the more damning term. If I could keep the word silent, unspoken, then, in my mind, the belief was of no consequence. In any event, it was of no consequence to me.

I learned that keeping secrets was merely conforming to normal family behavior.

꽃

Texas, 1849

I was about to do murder. I had practiced for weeks. Measuring gunpowder, driving powder down with a ramrod, shooting old cans, chunks of wood, and, finally, vaporizing grasshoppers.

Isaac lay to my left and his papa, our overseer, Marcus, to my right. We had crept here in the dark to sprawl under the trees and thick brush behind the henhouse, whose pale, gray boards appeared to glow in the light of the moon that had just risen behind us. Deep blue shadows stretched across the yard and up the boards in contorted vines. The silence was peppered with soft peeps of tree frogs and the occasional call of a night bird. The hot July day had cooled into balmy night, and a capricious breeze reached us from the river a mile east and lifted my hair.

In case the breeze changed, we had rubbed ourselves with wild garlic that grew along nearby Oak Creek to mask our scent. Our own garlicky smell did not quite cover the powdery odor of the hens that had bedded down earlier. We might be lying here on our stomachs unmoving for hours; hence, I had chosen as comfortable a position as possible. But after what seemed hours, my legs ached. I wriggled my toes in my boots, turned my head to relieve a crick in my neck, and twitched my fingers, fearing numbness.

Suddenly, there he was, to the left of the henhouse, having somehow slipped inside and out again without waking the sleeping hens.

Having been given first shot by Marcus, I breathed in, out, and sighted along the barrel as the wary coyote hesitated, a hen hanging from its mouth, one forefoot raised in perfect profile. Moonlight showed the critter's ribs protruding through its ragged fur. Starving, yet so clever and wild, belonging right here on our plantation before any person. Before any of us. His head swiveled and yellow eyes stared at me. Through me. Breathless, I could neither move nor blink, much less pull the trigger. When I did blink, the critter was gone.

Neither Marcus nor Isaac uttered a word.

I relaxed my trembling fingers, lowered the rifle—a fine Cub Dixie with a walnut stock—a gift from Papa on my eighth name day. An entire year later, and I had once again played the fool. I rose, pointed the barrel toward the ground as I had been taught, and slunk my way to the main house where I would empty the powder and clean the bore. Isaac followed, as always. I had again proven I was only good at shooting cans and grasshoppers.

And I would have to tell Papa.

You may wonder how a boy nearly nine years old and raised in Texas could consider killing a raiding coyote murder. Dear, sweet Maman. How I loved her, though I later grew to resent her, avoid her, and lug guilt upon my back for doing so.

She had been raised alongside her closest confidante, Betta, in Savannah, Georgia, to stories told by her family's Negroes, stories of talking animals—in particular, the trickster Br'er Rabbit. She raised me and my younger sister on those same stories. Hence, my head contained many worthless thoughts for a young man on a Texas plantation.

I scrubbed the mud from my boots on the edge of the porch and stood on the thick Turkish carpet of the parlor, facing Papa. The light from the lamp on the corner table and the dying fire on the hearth left his face in half darkness. No matter, I knew well this particular look.

My heart raced from shame. I had again disappointed him. He would not yell as some did; Papa never found raising his voice necessary. Not with our people, and not with his family.

"Don't forget to remove the shot from your gun," was all he said as he turned away.

I crossed the hall and, chin down, headed up the stairs to my room, not noticing my older brother, Lucien, until I was nearly upon him at the top landing. He would not move aside, and I brushed his arm getting by.

"Failed again, did you?"

How my blood rushed as I grasped the Cub rifle tight and pictured swinging the weapon at his head, followed by my fist. But by the time I reached high enough, he could knock me across the hall. He had lingered here at the top of the stairs like a vulture, waiting for his chance to pounce.

"For once, can you cease goading me?"

"Why should I? You repeatedly give me reason."

I should have walked away. Instead, I struck high with the rifle and, as he made to grab it, I lowered my head and butted him hard.

His *oof* and thump into the wall was highly satisfying. Maman's voice calling my name was not.

Lucien's bent legs and wheezing breath were well worth my sore head and dizziness. I caught Maman out of the corner of my right eye, hastily joined by Papa at the bottom of the stairs.

"Go to your room, Adrien." Not the first time I had heard such a statement from Papa—in that same disapproving voice.

Two disappointments in one evening.

I slunk my way to my corner room above the library. Ignoring my heart about to jump out of my chest, I emptied and cleaned my rifle over a pile of newspapers, which gradually got my rapid breathing back to normal. The tail of my mind considered the welfare of the Aubusson rug beneath my feet. I kept my emotions in check long enough to wash my face and hands in the bowl on the dresser left earlier by some house slave. Likely Mintie. The water had cooled, but she had thought to bring this fresh bowl after removing the old one before supper. I must remember to thank her.

I dropped to my knees at the east-facing window, tucked aside the linen curtains, and pushed up the bottom casement to let in whatever slight breeze might find its way from the Brazos River a mile away, detecting mercurial odors of willows and fish. The moon rose high overhead and floated among the leaves of the pecan tree that grew higher than the house. More than once in the night, Isaac and I had climbed out onto its branches to sit and dream. Not tonight, though. I expected Papa.

When younger, I had thought my brother like Papa when he rode with him to the tobacco fields every morning. Though he paid me scant attention, I tried copying him. Until he began calling me a cussed nancy.

I clutched the windowsill.

Why? Because I was small? I liked *nice* things? I thought too much? At the wrong time? If I had shot that coyote without thinking—

A knock—the door swung open—my stomach lurched.

Papa was dressed in black but for his white linen shirt and satin brocade waistcoat. The glow from the kerosene lamp next to my bed made the ruby pin in his cravat wink, and my room shrank in his presence. I sprang to my feet.

He strode forward, laid a hand on my shoulder, and released an immense sigh.

"Do you recall once before when we talked about your temper? You were still in the nursery."

That talk had changed a great deal about my home, my family, and nearly everyone I knew. I had learned my companion from babyhood, whom I slept with and loved as my brother, was a slave. Fancy that.

"When you explained about Isaac?"

"Exactly," he said. That long-ago evening, Lucien had called Isaac a pickaninny and shoved him against the wall at the top of the stairs.

Papa sighed. "You must learn to control your temper, Adrien. Your temper will cause you trouble. I know, as I have the same temper."

"You have a temper?" I had never seen any sign of it.

"I do. I regret the terrible things I have done by allowing my temper to get the best of me. Which is why I have had to learn control."

"But Lucien—"

"Nothing Lucien does will be solved by losing your temper." He took a step back, sat on the edge of my bed, and waited for me to do the same.

"Think," he said. "All the times you have been angered by Lucien, has losing your temper solved anything? Even once? Did you feel better afterward?"

I peered down at my feet and picked at a thread in the quilt.

"No, not after." I looked up and had to say, "It felt good during, though."

I swear I saw a sparkle in his eyes, but his mouth tightened all severe-like. "Were those few moments worth what came after?"

"I suppose not."

He stared at me, saying nothing.

"No." They were not worth this—his and Maman's disappointment.

He leaned forward and put a hand on mine. His calluses scraped my knuckles. "I have spoken to Lucien. This abusing of one another has got to stop. It is no way for brothers to behave. Tomorrow, you will remain in your room with no breakfast or lunch and consider how to control yourself."

After Papa left, I changed into a bedgown and crawled under the covers. Would Lucien stop his taunting? I would likely give him too many opportunities to resist.

❦

I was nearly nine years old that summer night, rather puny, with scant interest in knives, guns and scrambling in dirt with other boys. Though old enough to shoot coyotes, rabbits, and other defenseless critters, the idea repulsed me. Alas, Maman's stories. Perhaps I should have considered the poor, helpless hens.

Isaac, my Negro "brother," was supposed to sleep on a pallet at the foot of my bed, but I convinced him to join me in my German-made four-poster once cold, wet winter set in. No one knew but the girl who brought water, emptied the chamber pot, and laid the fire early every morning. Mintie would not tell. On punishment nights (mine, not Isaac's) he bedded down with his folks in their cabin out back.

I had grown up with women. While my older brother, Lucien,

hastened off with Papa to work in the fields, I was kept home with Maman, my sister, Bernadette, and our house people.

At night curled up with Isaac, thoughts hung around in my mind like moss on trees.

Our two-story house nestled among the trees lining Oak Creek on the west with a great old oak that shaded visitors' horses in front. During hot days in summer, the double front and back doors to the porches were left open to let the southeast breeze from the Brazos River flow through the house.

When five after breakfast I often stood in the eight-paned double doors on the front porch and watched Papa and Lucien ride off with Isaac's papa, Marcus, our overseer.

One morning, as Papa and Lucien rode off, I felt Maman's palms on my shoulders.

"Where do they go?" My hand shading my eyes, I squinted at their silhouettes disappearing down the grassy road past the horse barn and into a pink-and-gold horizon.

"Our tobacco takes work," she said. "All our people work the fields, care for the animals, the buildings, and the crops. Every living thing plays a part. And you must trust me and your papa to teach you to be a gentleman." She sank to the floor, her skirts ballooning. "Do you trust me and your papa?"

"Yes, Maman."

"*Je t'aime, chéri.*"

"Is Papa a gentleman?"

"He most certainly is."

"Then I will be a gentleman too."

I watched Papa. I watched him from the back door on evenings when he returned to the porch with dark circles under the arms and back of his shirt. He tossed his wide-brimmed hat on the wall hook and collapsed on a chair while our house man and butler, Simon, pulled off his muddy boots. Simon polished Papa's boots every night. Lucien took the second chair and copied Papa.

Papa removed his shirt and leaned over a metal tub, scrubbing with soap, while Simon stood by with a towel. Papa sometimes turned his head, hair dripping, and winked at me. My heart would leap. Then Papa set off upstairs to change, trailed by Lucien.

At breakfast and supper, I watched Papa drink his coffee. I watched how he held his spoon and fork and knife. I watched him wipe his mouth with his napkin. I watched him hold Maman's chair when she sat and when she rose from the table. Papa placed his hand ever so lightly against Maman's back when they moved together. He opened doors for her as she entered a room.

Papa's head nearly reached the tops of the doorways. Sometimes he carried me on his shoulders and would have to duck.

Our people smiled and nodded, curtsied and said, "Yes, sir." Visitors listened when Papa spoke, they shook his hand, said, "Yes, Paien," and women smiled, their eyes sparkling. Even Marcus, a tall man himself, and bigger, stood slightly behind and to Papa's left.

The sound of Papa's voice drew me, as did the tread of his footsteps. Mostly, he walked away.

Chapter Three

Paien

Paien Villere continued down the upstairs hall to his bedroom and tapped on the door to his wife's room.

"*Entré, mon amour.*"

Dressed in her nightgown, Madeleine sat at her mirrored dressing table bathed in the golden light of the glassed candle. She turned to him, lips on the verge of a smile.

Betta tucked her chin with a pursed lip grin of her own, ceased brushing her mistress's long, auburn hair, and curtsied before leaving by the hall door. Paien strode forward, lifted her hand from her lap, and placed a kiss on her palm. Her walls were painted in muted rosebuds and green leaves above cream wainscoting, nothing too frilly, including the rose quilt on the bed. Two open windows allowed a breeze to carry in the fragrance of climbing roses planted out front years ago. Full of contradictions and surprises, she wore lavender scent, had their people make lemon soap, and insisted on wildflower expeditions every spring, not allowing any to be picked as they too soon died.

"Is our son settled?"

"Quite," he said, settling in the stuffed armchair opposite her. They often conversed before he retired to his room unless she invited him to stay—which she frequently did. He was a fitful sleeper, tormented by unruly dreams.

He looked forward to Sundays when he could spend the entire day with his family. As no Catholic churches existed in Washington County, he read from the Bible early Sunday morning for his family and his people. He read mostly from the New Testament for he preferred the love and forgiveness of Jesus Christ to the ruthless and unmerciful God of the Old. He wished in his every thought and by every deed that he might be forgiven.

On Sundays he gave passes to those who wanted to visit neighboring plantations. Other coloreds came visiting Blue Hills for his readings and the fine spread he provided at noon. Afterward, his people played music and sang with an enthusiastic spirit he and his family enjoyed. He often sang along under his breath.

He had struggled with his decision to cease having more children—but the danger to his wife had won out. Thank the Lord modern ingenuity afforded an alternative to abstinence. Those new French "safes" were purported to be more reliable than silk or skins. Madeleine was no prude and enjoyed their coming together every bit as much as he did. *I am most fortunate in this regard.*

"You appear rather too self-satisfied to be contemplating our son's display of temper, my dear." The intensity of her gaze was causing a familiar stir he could not ignore.

"I was thinking of the three children you have given me."

She laid her hand on his. "They are rather special."

"If only Adrien had not inherited my temper."

"He is bright for his age, although a mite impulsive." She relaxed, took a deep breath, and squeezed his hand. "It would help if his papa were more often home to guide him. He dotes on you so, Paien."

"I wish I could be in more than one place at a time."

"You have mentioned how Marcus knows as much about tobacco as you. Why can you not leave him to oversee the work and remain home with us."

He kneeled next to her chair and gripped its back beneath her hair. "Tobacco is a demanding taskmaster, my love. I've turned over land for a fourth field. Each one requires constant care until summer's end, then there's curing. We've earned a reputation for the finest tobacco in the area, perhaps in the state. I dare not slacken now."

Soon, soon he might take his ease.

His wife faced him and placed a palm on his cheek, her voice low with concern. "Lucien."

"He has never given you cause—

"No. Of course not." She rose from the chair and continued as he rose from the floor, "It is not his fault. Stepmothers can be challenging, and there is that, other."

Good Lord, if that boy so much as . . . "What has he done?" He couldn't bear to imagine anyone hurting her in any manner, not even Lucien who had become a relatively tall, top-heavy ox of a fellow.

"He has done nothing untoward of which I am aware. It is merely this notion I have that he has never gotten over the loss of that woman, the one you found necessary to sell. It was partly my fault she was sent away."

"You were having your lying-down pains, about to bring Adrien into our lives. Rosanne brought what happened upon herself. And Lucien knew it."

Sweat formed at the nape of his neck, trickled down his back. He must not reveal the truth of that affair. Madeleine would see a different man, one unworthy, and she would be correct; he might lose his entire family.

"Perhaps. But the heart does not always follow the mind's logic. Lucien was a child."

She had again taken his hand, and he must be careful not to squeeze hers too tightly. They caught one another's eyes. Her trusting eyes. He ached to tell her everything. He could not.

"Adrien has neither an available father nor an older brother to show him the path to manhood."

She had removed the pin at his throat and began loosening his cravat. Her mood called for one more thing he chose to discuss. He placed his hands tenderly at either side of her waist while she unbuttoned his waistcoat. She was ahead, in dressing gown only, and this was a game they often played, undressing one another.

"Adrien lacks a physical outlet, a focus for all that energy," he said, looking past her at a painting by Claude Lorrain. It was a reminder of her parents. "That old horse is no longer enough. He needs a younger animal. I'm considering giving him that get of Maximillian's. Miguel, our hostler, can geld and halter-train him by Adrien's birthday in August, and the responsibility for the rest of his training will do Adrien good."

"You truly believe ten is old enough to take on a young, half-trained animal?" She traced her finger down his chest, which never ceased to make him shiver.

"Most Texas boys are riding decent horses by his age." He reached inside her gown to caress her back.

"Texas again. Are we not here to bring civilization to this place?"

He held her wandering hand and brushed his lips over her palm. "Of course, and we are. But such isn't accomplished in a year or even one generation. We can't make changes if we stand apart from those around us, my dear."

"Such as our neighbor to the north?"

"Randolph Hart carries a great deal of influence in this county. Besides, aren't you and Mrs. Hart friends?"

"She is a dear, but her husband. . . ." She fingered the top button of his trousers, pulling him close. "I suspect he abuses her, Paien. You need not look at me that way. You have not seen her as I have. Twice she has explained away bruises as falls, and once she sent a man here to cancel a visit, saying she had become ill. She was not ill at all, unless her illness was caused by that man."

"He has not approached you—"

"Of course not. He is always the gentleman around me. Rest assured; I would never let a man treat me in such a manner." At that, her hand was on his most private part, reminding how she treated *him.*

"I have never cared for the man, but we fought Santa Ana together. Though I despise the shameful way he treats his people."

"*Voilà,*" she declared as he rose, stepped out of his trousers and underdrawers, her hands clasping his buttocks.

"He is one man, my love." *Dear God, she did like to control a conversation.* He lifted her, carried her to the four-poster, straddled her lovely figure, and untied her gown slowly through the tiny eyelets, the silk ties dangling between his fingers. She often said how she loved his long, gentle fingers, the way he teased, until the teasing and gentleness were no longer necessary or wanted. *She was not one to keep her needs to herself, thank God.*

"One man too many of that sort," she said, raising her arms above her head and meeting his eyes. "Adrien's tutor must assure we have at least one son who shall be a true gentleman *and* attend a fine college. N'est-ce pas?"

"I walked into that, didn't I?" *She was also deft at rearranging the subject when it suited her purpose.*

And she gave him such a lovely smile.

Drifting off to sleep afterward, his thoughts traveled over the earlier discussion with his son. *He is so like Madeleine, yet too much like me in temperament. Dear Lord, don't let his temper lead him where mine led me.*

To this day, he couldn't say what part of that cursed night years ago had been loss of control and what had been calculation—calculation in order to protect his family. He would do anything to protect his family.

Chapter Four

Isaac

On a warm August mornin when he was a young'un, Isaac learned his true place at Blue Hills. He sure nuff didn't expect such a mornin to turn out the way it did.

Him and Adrien—Isaac talked more like Mama than he did Papa or Adrien cause he didn't much care—was always sneakin off somewhere to see what they could find. They had to sneak cause Adrien's mama kept him closer than a sow her piglets. They got good at slippin off. Not sayin the mistress was bad company or nothin, specially as mistresses go, she was right fine. But they was boys, and sittin listenin to stories left them with the wigglies after a while.

When they was small they dearly loved explorin the kitchen out back cause of what Esther fed them—biscuits and cake warm from the oven. Many a colored said Esther was the best cook fer miles about. White folks said it too.

Twarn't long afore they had to go a more distant piece to escape gettin hauled back to the house. The kitchen garden was full of all manner of bugs and lizards and snakes. His papa showed him right quick how to tell a poisonous snake from a safe one like them garden snakes. He and Adrien liked to catch 'em and chase the gals in the quarters. You never heard such squawlin bout a little brown snake.

They got to playin with other boys too—those not yet old enough to work in the fields—runnin bout the cabins and into the trees and the creek when it got hot in the afternoon. Throwin stones and themselves into the water, clothes scattered on bushes, and them free as birds. Laws, was the missus wrathy the day they got home barefoot and muddy. They'd ditched their shoes when they got together, and Adrien forgot where he left his. That evenin Adrien got a switchin from his papa, and Isaac got a sermon from his, which was bout as bad as a switchin. Adrien said his switchin was nothin much as the marse held back, what with his mama cryin and takin on so the whole time. It was days and days afore they could sneak off after that.

Never did find those shoes. Adrien said he didn't mind, as runnin together was worth any amount of switchin, even if it was worse next time. Though he was more careful of where he left his shoes after. Adrien said he didn't want to upset his mama again, which Isaac spect was true. Many a time they'd bring their mamas a flower or a pretty stone found in the creek or somewheres. They'd find stuff for little sis Bernadette too.

It was their secret that they still slept together in Adrien's new room cause they was still brothers, no matter what anyone said.

After Marse said he should sleep on the floor, Isaac huddled under a rough wool blanket on his pallet at the foot of Adrien's bed. That ol hearth fire died down to nothin but a few glows.

"Isaac?" A whisper from the dark! No haint, but Adrien.

"I's here," he whispered back.

"Are you all right down there?"

"My feets is a bit chilly."

"Do you think you might come up here and keep me company?"

"Marse, your papa said I should bed down here."

Seconds passed. Isaac shivered, teeth chattering.

"I think it is wrong you should be cold down there while I am warm up here."

Oh, Lord. Adrien was gonna do contrariwise from Marse, his papa. This was some scary, but darn if his bones warn't shakin more from cold than fright.

"I order you up here, Isaac. So it will be my fault if anyone finds out."

Order me, huh? Fast as Br'er Rabbit, he sprung from the floor and dove under the covers next to warm Adrien.

"Dang, you *are* freezing," Adrien gasped, clutching him close.

"Some," Isaac chuckled into his brother's neck.

"I will sleep with you on the pallet when it gets warm," Adrien said under his breath. "Then everything will come out even."

That sounded right.

Which is how they got back to their old habit. When nights turned warm, Adrien came down to spread out on Isaac's pallet where there was a good cross breeze from the two windows. Leastways, that was their reasoning.

Then came the spring mornin they overslept, and Mintie the house girl caught them.

She come right in the door. They was a little slow while she stood danglin a big pot of hot water. Adrien stood first, tryin to be straight and tall in his nightshirt; he was straight but no taller than Mintie. She was taller, really, and older.

"You must keep silent about this, Mintie," Adrien said, narrowin his eyes and fixin them on her most intently. "If not, you will cause trouble, and Papa will wonder why you did not catch us sooner. Do not say a word and we will keep it our secret." Marse had brought Mintie in from the fields the year before as she was clean and biddable. She was thirteen and would likely be swayed by such a "suggestion" from Adrien if he put it to her in the "right" way.

"Yes, sir, young Marse, I not say a word." She bobbed a curtsy, hurried to light the fire, poured steaming water into the pitcher on the table, gave him another curtsy, and scurried from the room.

"Mintie, take that as an order," Isaac said, gazin at the closed door. This was the first time he had seen Adrien tell anyone what to do: *give a slave an order. His order that other time didn't count. Did it?*

"Papa said I am old enough to know my place just as our people must. And Mintie *took* that as an order."

Isaac dangled his arms and bowed his head, attempting to hide a crooked grin. "Oh, yes, Marster, ah knows ah speak de bad Gullah, but ah tries to do betta, ah surely does."

"And I nearly wet my drawers," Adrien said, and jumped him. They wrestled and tumbled across the floor.

If Isaac counted happy days, these was the happiest.

Mistress Villere was teachin them the days and months and how to count, so Isaac knew this day was in August and early mornins was cooler than them hot afternoons. Adrien was learnin to ride that ol horse Betsy then too.

He and Adrien got all excited cause of goin visitin the neighbor Hart plantation. Hector would drive them alls over in the Rockaway right early after breakfast and spend the night. John, their blacksmith, had strengthened the wheels and undercarriage so it could handle East Texas roads. Marse couldn't go for all the work, so it was just the missus and chillun. Dang if at the last, Isaac had to rush upstairs to say goodbye to Mama. He figured she was in the missus's room clearin up after all the packin and such. Sure nuff, he found her there and ran over to hug her skirts, as high as he could reach.

"Bye, Mama," and he spun for the door, runnin on out and downstairs hearin her callin his name. Didn't dare stop as he was sure the carriage was bout to leave.

When he got back out the door, they was gone. They didn't wait? Left without him? His insides dropped. Whole body felt like lightnin was gonna come out of it. All tight and burstin. Betrayed.

Mama came down behind and took his elbow, and he jerked his arm free.

"I didn't know you thought to go along," she said.

He felt ever more bad from the low-down tone of her voice. Couldn't say nothin.

He fisted his hands so hard they hurt.

Mama came round and squatted in front. Sun risin over her right shoulder, wet eyes gleamin in her shadowed face. That took thunder outa him. She clasped his arms, raised his hands, and held them long side her own. They was brown-colored, browner than Adrien ever got.

"You and Adrien be milk brothers," she said, "but that not the same as true brothers. I be mammy to both you babies, him on one tit and you on t'other, but his birth mam be Mistress Madeleine, mistress of this house, and his papa be our marse. You is better than a field colored, but you is a house colored like me, and you never be white, no matter Adrien call you brother."

"Some in the quarters be white as Adrien."

"They got white blood and colored blood too, like you and me and your papa. Plus, white folks dress better and speak better and read and write, so white folks always tell us apart, even if some look like they do."

Missus Madeleine was dressin him bout as good as Adrien—leastways good as Adrien's everyday getups. Right now, he wore a coat as fine—well, nearly as fine—as the one Adrien had on when they left. And Papa spoke better than those other coloreds; he spoke like Marse and the rest of the family. Was that why Papa was overseer? Plus, he was big. Bigger'n ever colored on the place but John, their blacksmith. Papa knew bout tobacco too.

Right then, Isaac figured he got to get smart, speak better, and learn to read and write.

A couple days later, Adrien came home and said he didn't know Isaac was not to go, and Isaac forgave him.

"I decided somethin else while you was gone." They sat facing one another on his pallet at the end of Adrien's bed. He had on his serious face, so Adrien knew he was aimin to speak serious words. "I needs to get an edication. I needs to read and speak good as you. Papa will help, but he's not round much, so I'm askin you to help me."

"I *was* gone, but you *were* not."

"Huh?"

Adrien grinned a second, then looked him in the eye. "I was. You were. If you want to learn to speak proper."

Isaac rocked, "Yaaah. I was, you were."

"There is more, if you are ready."

"I sure nuff . . . am."

Mostly, he had to pay attention to how Adrien and the white family spoke. And his papa. When Adrien got his tutor, he left his room door ajar so Isaac could sit in the hall and listen in on his lessons, lessons they later studied together in secret. No one knew, except Bernadette. She often studied with them, even if she was a girl.

Came the morning when six-year-old Adrien came rushing back from outside, past Isaac at the front door without a how-de-do, and upstairs to his room. Course Isaac had to rustle himself up after him only to find a surprised Bernadette already leaning at his bedside with Adrien face down on the counterpane and mumbling into it.

"I cannot hear a word with you speaking that way," Bernadette said.

Adrien turned his head sideways. "Because you should not. I am cussing. I am cussing Lucien. He hates me."

"Why?"

"I don't know why. I followed him to the barn to help, and he pushed me into the wall and called me, he called me names, a name."

"What cuss words you learn?" Isaac said.

"Oh, Isaac," Bernadette said.

Adrien slowly turned over and sat up, dangling his legs over the bed and rubbing his head. "My head hurts."

Bernadette gently touched the back of his hair. "There's a little lump back there!"

"I told you he pushed me."

"You didn't say how hard. We should tell Betta, or Maman."

"No. It would just cause trouble. I am always causing trouble. No matter what I do, I am always wrong."

"Not to me." Bernadette sat next to him and gave him a hug.

"Me too," Isaac said, taking two firm steps closer.

Bernadette sat back and clapped her hands together. "I have an idea. Let us be blood brothers like that book." She undid the broach at her bodice.

"But you are a girl," Adrien said, watching her.

"I am a blood sister, then. Give me your finger." She took his finger, the broach. "We swear to always support one another and always tell one another the truth of what is in our hearts."

"Do you want to be part of this, Isaac, or not?"

"I surely do."

"Then put your finger in here.

Chapter Five

Bernadette

My family was unusual, though I don't know as anything explains their behavior entirely.

My papa never spoke of his relatives in Louisiana, and this was a matter of contention between him and Maman. Dear Maman never knew his reasons for silence, and it was many years before the rest of us learned, to our regret.

Maman named our plantation Blue Hills for the hillsides covered in bluebonnets every spring. Maman and Uncle Charles Fortier, who lived in Galveston and was Papa's tobacco factor, referred to their mysterious early childhoods in France as full of Troubles. Troubles conjured frightening notions in my young head, dreams that haunted me and my brother when we were small. Maman believed she could bring civilization to Texas. All civility had been butchered in France, and she would see it restored in Texas. She insisted her children speak "properly," never using contractions, and began teaching us to read, write, and behave like ladies and gentlemen before we were three years old.

Firstborn Adrien felt the brunt of her will and her love.

Everything came to my brother first, as he was nearly a year older than me, and boys were more important.

After Papa gave Adrien the old mare Betsy, he gave me Patches the pony. I learned to ride sidesaddle, and my skirts often tangled with my boots. Being led around and around in a circle by Ruth was dull. "Faster, Ruth, please."

"I mustn't, miss. You might fall off, and there'd be the devil to pay."

Truly. Ruth never went faster than a slow walk.

I followed Adrien about like the wagging tail on one of Papa's dogs. My brother petted me in rather the same way: "Do not stand so close to the stove when Esther is cooking; Bernadette likes the ginger ones best."

Best was when Adrien, Isaac, and I cuddled with Maman on the green sofa in the parlor to listen to stories of Br'er Rabbit and fairies and princesses and knights.

Once I convinced Adrien to take me with him and Isaac to the kitchen garden. When Maman found out, that was my last excursion for several years. Perhaps the mud on my shoes, skirts, and hands compelled that decision.

"Young ladies do not play in the muck," Maman declared as I accepted a clean dress from Betta. Betta had been with Maman since they were girls, as far back as Savannah, before they moved to Galveston.

"But I want to be like Adrien." My lower lip extended in the smallest pout as Maman lifted a dress over my head.

"Adrien will be a young gentleman, but you will be a young lady."

"I do not wish to." Muffled by all the ruffles as they were lowered over me.

"You were born to be a young lady, *chérie*. You might have been born a poor field mouse or a rabbit to be chased down by one of your papa's hounds."

My head popped out from the neck of the dress; Maman's expression was ever so serious. Too serious, surely. "Maman."

Maman's hands cupped my face. She placed the softest kiss on my forehead—the scent of lavender floated about me.

"You must consider how fortunate you are, *mon amour*. You have the most beautiful dresses and shoes. You will have a lady's education. And one day you will marry a fine gentleman and have a family of your own."

I was not sure I wanted those things, but one thing would be ever so nice. "Maman, might I have a girl of my own?"

"Betta birthed Isaac at just the right time, *chérie*. Ruth is your girl."

"But Ruth is not a girl. Ruth is old. And I must share her with Jules and Abbey."

"Perhaps, one day, you may have a girl of your own."

Which meant never.

❧

I was five when Mr. Archibald T. Clarence arrived from Connecticut— one of those horrid words that did not spell as it should. A state back East, in the North. Maman had searched for months to find Mr. Clarence—in secret. Which meant Papa had not been aware of such a search. She kept these sorts of secrets from him. About how women behaved with men in general, as men held all the power in this world. "A man is often run by ego and something else you will understand one day."

What did Maman mean?

I had expected an old man with gray hair, but I was reminded of Ichabod Crane in the Washington Irving tale; he was so tall and thin. There the resemblance ended, for his features were even, he smiled often, and he had a lovely baritone voice, though words came out of his mouth rather strangled and short—a northeastern way of speaking, Maman said.

Too young to join my brother, I slipped into Adrien's room nearly every evening after supper to review the day's lessons with him and Isaac.

Adrien and I did not care for mathematics, whereas Isaac sailed happily through anything concerning numbers. "Did you notice nine is a magic number? When you multiply by nine and add them, they also make nine."

"Interesting," Adrien murmured and continued reading *Peter Parley's Winter Tales*.

❧

I must have a glass of milk. Counting sheep was dull but did not remove my thirst. I had had one small glass with cake for supper. *Do not be piggish, Bernadette; only one piece and only one glass of milk.* That had been hours ago. Here I was in bed, and my throat was dry as last week's biscuits. Water would not do. I would surely have to get up and use the necessary under my bed. *I may as well have milk.*

I threw off the counterpane, slid off the bed, pushed my feet into slippers, and pulled on my dressing gown. *Brrr.* If I had a girl, I could send her down to get the milk and stay in bed.

The room was awfully dark. I turned to the table next to my bed, lit the candle, and placed the glass over it. Maman had warned us about carrying candles around without the glass. "Let us not burn the house down."

No one in the hall. How quiet, but for a night wind soughing in the eaves. I felt my way down the stairs, my free hand sliding along the cool banister.

Would our butler, Simon, be in his chair in the hall this time of night? He must sleep, surely. My candle made a bobbing circle around my feet on the carpet, but the light it threw did not go far enough down the dim hallway to see much. Surely Simon would have said something by now if he were there. Goodness, the house seemed different in the dark.

There were no such things as ghosts. There were not. No one had died in this house.

Voices. I nearly turned to hurry back up the stairs. But they were coming from the indoor kitchen at the end of the hall, and one voice was Adrien's. I took a deep, relieved breath. He must be hungry or thirsty too. Perhaps one of our people was there with him—Simon? The door was ajar as I approached. No sooner there than there came a clanking *crash* that made me jump.

Lucien: You stupid goose, now see what you've done.

Adrien: You . . . you bumped it—

Lucien: Don't try blaming it on me, you little Miss Nancy. And clean that up. I'm going to bed—

That was all, for I turned, rushed upstairs down the hall and back to my room to blow out the candle and huddle under the covers, dressing gown and all.

What had happened? Lucien had sounded so awful and angry. And frightening. To tell the truth, I was never entirely comfortable around him. He usually ignored me. He ignored Adrien. Except tonight. And other times I had heard similar confrontations.

I should have helped Adrien. He would have helped me. I am a coward. I ran.

I grasped the quilt close and drew myself up tight, so tight I shook. I mashed the fist-enclosed quilt to my eyes. *I will not cry, I will not. I will not be a coward. I will never run from what I fear again. Not ever.*

Chapter Six
Hartwood

Jacob

Jacob Hart had been anxious to return home to Hartwood and the colt he'd bred that would eventually sire a line of superb mounts. Mounts that would once and for all prove to the old rip that horse breeding was as fine a way to make a living as growing cotton.

When Jacob was thrown out of Baylor University in Independence at fifteen, he recalled the old reprobate's remark: "Managed to get yourself tossed out, did you?" Practical experience and advice from the young Tonk his father had hired as his companion gave Jacob all the knowledge he required. Having been a Comanche captive for half his childhood, few knew more about horses than Colt Alvaro.

Catchfire needed discipline and hard riding, and Colt was the only one who could approach him besides Jacob. But even Colt didn't dare ride him.

Dew still slicked the grass when he returned from a satisfying ride on the young stallion. Jacob was reflecting on his escape from that dull school and what sort of distraction he might create for summer and fall. Mother expected Mrs. Villere and her brood over this morning. Not one for family gatherings, he avoided them at all costs. Hartwood provided plenty of room to avoid anyone, with its Greek Revival monument of a house, its numerous outbuildings, gardens, and cotton fields.

He had strolled up the stone path through his mother's wildflower garden profuse with purple foxglove, asters, and yellow daisies, in the back door, ordered up a late breakfast of sausage, eggs, cornbread and coffee, and was on his way to the stables when she called from the front veranda. *Damn, caught.*

"Jacob! Thank God."

He ambled over so she needn't yell. A lady should not have to raise her voice like that. He squinted at her from under his wide-brimmed hat.

"Mrs. Villere's son is missing. He is only seven and not in the house. Fetch a few slaves to search the grounds, will you?"

"Of course, Mother." *Good Lord, now he'd have to find some child.* He spied a woman standing in the doorway behind Mother. *That beauty is Mrs. Villere?* He stepped to the right to see around his mother and get a proper look, nodded, and touched his hat. "I'll find him, Mrs. Villere. Don't worry." *Tarnation, how did I miss her?*

He spun—*older ladies ain't so bad*—and spied one of the slaves pushing a wheelbarrow across the grassy, dandelion-dotted yard. "Enos, round up some men to look for a young white boy who's wandered off."

Enos lowered the barrow. "I seed a white boy headin for the stables jus a while ago, Marse."

"The stables?"

"Yes, suh."

Shit. Just my luck, he'll go near Catchfire's stall. He set off at a trot.

His heart beat fast as he entered the barn, and not from exertion. Several curious heads peered over the tops of their stalls, and he heard a low murmuring—*damn*—coming from Catchfire's stall. *Blazes!*

Stay calm. Don't spook either of them. Heaven forbid that woman's boy gets trampled by my horse. He crept to the stall and regarded the scene within. The child stood at the stallion's head near the rear of the oversized stall, talking nonsense. Catchfire had his head down so the boy could caress his nose with one hand while stroking his neck with the other.

"His name is Catchfire," Jacob said, his tone low and calm. Catchfire jerked his head up and eyed him, ears forward.

"It is?" The boy turned. Jacob saw the most engaging black eyes and classic face—Mrs. Villere's son. *Intriguing how a woman's line ran as true as a fine horse's.*

"He is the finest horse I have ever met. Even finer than Papa's Maximillian."

"You think so, do you?" *Such diction in one so young.*

"Absolutely."

Now to get him out of there without fuss. "How about you let him rest and join me? I'll show you our other horses, and we can go for a ride after lunch."

The boy came to the front of the stall, and Catchfire snorted and tossed his head. Jacob's heart nearly stopped. The boy calmly turned. "It is all right, Catchfire. I will be back again soon and bring you another apple."

Jacob held his breath until he had latched the door again. *Jesus, the boy has no idea. Likely that's what saved him, the little fool.*

Mrs. Villere swept down the aisle, arms wide, followed by his mother. "Adrien, are you all right?" She bent low, skirts ballooning around her, and reached for him.

"Of course, Maman."

"You must never wander off alone. I was so worried. Promise me you will never do so again."

"But, Maman, nothing happened. I am fine." The young fellow gave her reassuring pats on her back.

"Mrs. Villere, if I may," Jacob said, stepping forward. "I'll be glad to watch over the boy whenever you visit. I had planned on taking responsibility for Will's education, anyway."

"You had?" His mother said from alongside Mrs. Villere. Her head with its blond locks was cocked in the most charming manner.

"Of course. Will should learn to ride better, shoot, and any number of manly things. And I believe his reading is suffering. Our library is full of material of which he hasn't begun to take advantage."

"My goodness, I had no idea you had any such thoughts." Her hands were folded stiffly at her waistline.

"Don't you think I should consider his education? Beyond what he learns at that school in Washington? Father certainly hasn't."

"Your father is busy running this plantation," she said, tucking her chin.

How quickly she turned the subject from Father's laxness. He could not fathom why she defended the man, considering how he treated her.

"What do you think, Madeleine?" Mother had turned to Mrs. Villere. "Would you accept Jacob watching over Adrien whenever you are here?"

"Jacob is somewhat young, but Adrien might benefit from an older brother figure, as Lucien is always off working with Paien." She turned to her son and said firmly, "Only if Adrien behaves like a proper young gentleman."

"Please, Maman. I will be ever so good. Truly I will."

How emphatically he speaks, practically raising on his toes.

"You will not find it necessary to teach my son reading, Jacob, as he studies with a tutor five mornings a week. And Adrien has ridden nothing but calm, well-trained animals. You must promise to never let him out of your sight."

"Of course, madam. I will keep my eyes on him." *I certainly shall. He's surrounded by too many skirts.*

⁂

The year 1849 was good for cotton, corn, and tobacco. Three steamboats were tied to the wharves in Washington at once to load bales and hogsheads for the trip down the Brazos to Galveston. Plantations along the river settled in for a fine, fat fall and a satisfying winter.

An October wind rattled the leaves, and it smelled of rain the blustery evening Jacob heard a horse in the drive and hurried to the front door. He stepped onto the veranda, saw lather pouring down the mare's sides, and his father sliding from the saddle and tossing the reins to the boy who had come running up. The old tyrant would ruin a good horse in order to get home a little faster.

"Fetch my saddlebags," he said as he passed, trailing the scent of sweat and tobacco smoke. Jacob had expected no other greeting.

Thank God, their butler had also heard the horse and held the door open as the old reprobate strode in.

"Lucretia," his father yelled, moving on through the marbled entry hall toward the carpeted stairs. "Where is that woman?"

Mother came hurrying down the hall.

"Welcome home, dear. Supper will be ready shortly, and I have Caesar preparing a hot bath."

"Bring supper to my room. You bring it, not the girl. And wear that pink dressing gown." He spun on his heels. "Don't forget those bags, Jacob. I'll want to look at those papers while I eat. And send up some of that brandy. I've had enough of that cheap whiskey Marshall Holman serves." He turned and stomped up the stairs, fist gripping the walnut banister.

Jacob stood a moment watching him, the bags dangling from his fist. He wanted to throw them at the bottom of the stairs. Then he felt his mother's uncertain fingers on his forearm and glanced down into her porcelain face.

"Do as he says. It does no good to defy him, as doing so only makes him worse." She gently touched the scar at his hairline. "As you well know."

He lowered his head, dropped the bags, and took her hands, kissing the back of one.

"My dear, gallant son."

"Hardly, Mother." He studied her, so pale, so guileless and accommodating. She still thought him the towheaded boy of six who had brought her all his secrets.

She lowered her arms, lightly clutching her waist. "You have become nearly as tall as your father. You are my rock, and William and Lily adore you." Her right hand hovered at her graceful neck, and she cocked her head. A blond strand slightly struck with gray curled there. He recognized a typical flirting habit, in this case, one meant to make him agreeable—she likely had no idea she was doing it. "There are compensations." She need not say for what.

"I'll see that William and Lily have supper and are put to bed," he said.

"He'll want to see them after he eats." That tucked chin again.

"I'll have them ready for bed."

"What would I do without you?" She was peering down at the carpet.

"You would manage." He bent to pick up the bags and headed up the stairs.

I hate him. One day I'll be older, and then we'll see. The old reprobate. We'll see then.

⁂

September a year later, seventeen-year-old Jacob was an inch taller, but little else in East Texas had changed. Cotton grew, and riverboats ran the Brazos which flooded with rains and receded with the change of seasons. His father replaced old candle and whale oil lights throughout the house with the new gaslights. Jacob missed the smell of beeswax but not the odorous whale oil.

He spent more time with young Adrien Villere, as planned since that morning over a year before. He reminded himself to treat the youth like any fine thoroughbred, as the boy was inclined to stand on his dignity, take the bit, and run if one wasn't careful.

Adrien reined in, huffing from some hard riding after Jacob and Catchfire, who halted to let him catch up. "You sure like to push a fellow," he said.

Jacob grinned. "More likely pulling from where I sit." He patted the stallion on the neck as it pranced beneath him, not even winded. After a few months of riding double on Catchfire, Adrien had graduated to riding solo on full-grown horses, and by fall he was straddling half-wild broncs as though he'd been born on them. Like most Texans, the youth was a natural rider. Thank God, he'd gotten Adrien free from his mother's skirts in time. Madeleine Villere was a beautiful woman, but she'd nearly turned this one into a popinjay.

Besides, he loved to watch the boy's eyes grow bright and his chest rise with excitement.

If only he were older. But he will be one day.

"Look at that sky." Adrien gazed off west, where clouds turned shades of azure, pink, and purple.

The boy had an eye for beauty. "That sky is telling us it's time to head home."

"Wait a minute longer, will you?"

Jacob leaned his forearm on the saddle horn. Catchfire could find his way home in the dark. Jacob was patient. Years patient. His chance would come.

Chapter Seven

Bernadette

I loved visits to the grand house at Hartwood once we were old enough to run about the rooms on our own. When I was small, though, Maman and Mrs. Hart settled on the shady north veranda garden room at Hartwood Plantation while little Jules played on the floor at their feet. Maman rocked a crib with baby Abigail while two colored children pulled on lines rotating ceiling fans for our comfort. For soon-to-be-seven me, all this rocking, gossiping, and sitting was dull.

I attempted to drag five-year-old Lily Hart on the latest excursion with Jacob, Will, and my brother. Drag was the correct word because Lily preferred to stay inside, where she might remain clean and pretty in her ruffled, lace dress.

"There may be birds and butterflies and maybe kittens in the stables." I knew nothing of kittens, but such might get Lily to come along.

"I would rather look at pictures." We had pored over the pictures of women and children repeatedly, for it took ages for new copies of *Harper's* and *Godey's* to be delivered this far west. I kept her company for ever so long over those boring pictures but could do so no longer.

"I am leaving, Lily." I stood, brushed at my dress long enough to give Lily time to decide, and held out my hand. Thank goodness, Lily accepted it.

When we reached the paddock, Lily's brother, Will, was leaning against the fence alone.

"Where are they?" I shaded my brow and peered about. April morning sun was quite bright. I should have put on a bonnet.

"One guess," Will said, turning to us in exasperation, booted toes kicking the grass.

"Not again." I felt like pouting, as my brother was off riding that horrid horse with Jacob again. Maman said pouting was unladylike.

Lily's shoulders sank in disappointment. She leaned against me, and I settled my arm about her. "It is all right, Lily. Look there. I see them." I pointed to where a horse and rider burst out of the yellow-blooming huisache trees lining the field at the far end of the drive, sending yellow blossoms scattering like angry bees.

They came on, running full out before slowing to a trot within a couple hundred yards, the red stallion arching his neck and snorting as he halted fifteen feet away, displaying his prancing profile. Will stepped between us and them, stretching both arms as if to protect me and Lily. Jacob held Catchfire in firmly, and Adrien clutched Jacob's waist from behind, grinning. Previously my brother had ridden in front, enclosed by Jacob's arms. He could fall off much easier from behind, could he not? The smell of horse sweat and leather wafted over me.

"Did you see? Did you see how fast we went?" Adrien was all quivering excitement, black hair stringy with sweat, gulping breaths between blurted words. He slid to the ground, so close to those high stomping hooves that my breath caught.

"Oh, Bernadette, how we flew! Jacob says I might have one of Catchfire's get if Papa approves. Do you think he might?" His dark eyes were wide, wild, and shining. He turned to Jacob. "Are you going to walk him and give him oats? I will come help if I may."

"Hello, y'all," Jacob said. "Join us if you like, and then we'll head in for lunch."

Will lowered his arms. "We'll go on in now. Mother and Mrs. Villere likely wonder where we are."

Jacob led the horse off to the barn. My brother was full of withheld energy, reaching toward the older boy, pulling back, excitedly chatting, going silent, speaking again, practically jumping up and down. Lily was trembling, and neither Jacob nor Adrien had noticed. I absently stroked Lily's hair.

Maman would not want Adrien riding that horse. But if I told, Maman would not let us play with Jacob, and he was fun when he was not riding that horse. He recounted stories of the Greeks and Romans and took us on the most wonderful excursions. Jacob made history and biology fun. My brother would never forgive me.

I never told Maman what we did.

⁂

Spring ushered in an early sweltering heat that began the end of April and wilted the bluebonnets by the third week in May. By June, afternoons had turned unbearably hot and muggy.

"I'm thinking the boys should know how to swim, considering how close we live to the Brazos. I'm sure you're aware how often the river and creeks around here flood."

Our Blue Hills house was high on a bluff a mile from the river, but who knew where boys might run? Clever Jacob slipped such thoughts into a person's mind. Accordingly, he encouraged Maman and Mrs. Hart to agree with his suggestions.

My tummy fluttered when I found myself saying and doing what I would never before have said and done. Most were challenges. Only Maman would not have allowed me to accept such challenges if she had realized.

The afternoon Jacob drove the four of us in a bouncing buckboard to a swimming hole in Indian Creek, our parents had left for a meeting in nearby Washington, which was once the capital of Texas. Papa or Marcus went to Washington every week or so to pick up mail, supplies, or food we did not grow ourselves. Sometimes Papa took the entire family on holiday, and we stayed overnight and ate at the Alejandro Hotel and visited the wharves and riverboats that took our tobacco downriver.

Jacob tied the horse as we crept down to the languid creek. Leaves fluttered and birds chirped as I inched into cool, green water in nothing but my chemise and drawers. Wet sand slurped around my feet and toes. How I shivered with delight as water inched up my legs, and

I slipped in deeper up to my chin. Oh, how cool after the ferocious heat!

"Paddle," Jacob shouted from farther out. "Like a dog, like I showed you. And kick your feet!" And he showed me again, lifting his arms and paddling the air.

So I did. I kicked and splashed, imagining myself a steamboat, and I paddled, laughing, alongside my brother and Will, who wore only drawers. Gloriously refreshing. I had never known such freedom, my limbs so light. I bounced on the sandy bottom, waving my arms, lifting my feet and floating. "Come in, Lily, it is wonderful."

"No. I will stay here in the shade. I do not want to get wet." Stubborn Lily. Sometimes not even Jacob could stir her, and she adored her eldest brother.

Will shifted toward his sister with a mischievous expression.

"No, Will." I put a hand on his arm. "Let her be." I caught his eyes. "Please?"

He grinned and threw himself backward into the water, splashing. I spun and splashed after him, blinking droplets from my lashes.

How many seven-year-old girls swam in a creek?

A week later, I tied my skirts around my limbs with twine and climbed a tree. What a heady feeling, high above the ground, looking down at the grass and bushes. We three perched in the branches like birds.

"Come up, Lily, just to the lowest branch. I'll come down and help you."

"No, I do not wish to."

I could see the top of Lily's glossy blond head. She would not even look up.

Will sat next to me and sighed. "Lily, you are such a goose."

Adrien dropped down from the branch above. "Do not call her that."

Will glanced up, surprised. I was surprised myself.

"Sorry. Just do not. All right?"

"Sure."

Adrien continued on down to sit alongside Lily—one black head and one blond.

"I didn't mean to," Will said in a low voice. "She's Father's little darling. I suppose it's not her fault. I'm the odd one born between her and Jacob. She's so pretty with her blue eyes and blond curls, and Jacob's the same, only handsome."

"Why, Will, what do you mean?" I asked. "I find blue eyes rather cold. You have the warmest brown eyes, and your face is nice. I do not believe you are the slightest bit odd."

"Truly?"

"Truly."

His face turned pink, and he lowered his head, swinging his feet.

I shivered inside. I had made him blush. My, I had never known such power.

Chapter Eight

Paien

The benevolent winter of 1850–51 turned into a spring furious with heavy rainfall, sending the Brazos raging over its banks and filling every creek, ravine, and crevice with torrential flows. Powerful wind might blow down a large tree whose roots no longer grasped waterlogged earth and mist-filled hollows. Riders must search for stock that had wandered to become trapped in sucking mud.

Paien usually transplanted his tobacco seeds from their beds to the fields in April, but this year doing so was impossible. Nearly May, and the rain showed no sign of letting up. Early each morning, he shrugged into his wool overcoat and rode out with Lucien and Marcus to check mud-covered fields, help with stock, mend broken fences, and clear clogged drainages. Emergencies abounded: a tree pulled loose from its soaked roots and trapped someone; a horse and rider slipped and fell.

This was an opportune time for another venture—one of which only he and a few others were aware.

When Paien remained home, it was either unusually quiet or unbearably repetitive with the same succession of notes played over and over, or the same tune, as Madeleine was teaching Adrien and Bernadette to play piano. Paien retreated with the latest newspaper to an old chair on the back porch where one of the smaller colored children would interrupt his reading by begging a treacle from his trouser pocket where he hid them for such occasions.

Once delightful silence descended upon the household, it was because "Adrien is taking lessons with his tutor, and Bernadette has joined them." Madeleine refused to let her children ride or even step outside in such inclement weather.

The second week of May, the sun broke through a hazy sky, turning it cerulean blue by midafternoon. High on a ridge, Paien halted Max, his black stallion, looked across the wet, green hills, and took a deep breath of damp air. Swirls of pale mist trailed from the draws and disappeared as he watched. A blackbird trilled from the long sparkling grass to his left. Max's ears pointed forward.

"Do you understand what I feel, my friend?" He sat quietly, then stretched his back, making the saddle creak. "Moments like this make everything worth the effort. This and my family." Max flicked one ear and pawed the ground. They moved off down the ridge to a fence line where Lucien bent mending a broken post.

He waited a week for the land to dry enough to plant seedlings. The lowland remained full of rushing creeks and standing pools, though the sun blazed hot the rest of May, signaling attacks of malaria and cholera.

Betta declared Blue Hills was safely high above the river where cleansing breezes blew such devilment away. Paien no longer minded her references to spirits and signs. As long as those signs were positive and brought no strife upon Blue Hills, as Rosanne's delusions had. His breath grew short. He steered clear of any thoughts that wandered down that dark path.

He finished transplanting by the first of June, a month late. God willing, his luck would hold. Last winter he had invested sizable profits in northern stocks, some of which were supplying dividends that he planned on pouring into new seed for a third tobacco field north of the house. Twenty-three children in the quarters were nearly grown, and he could purchase six more people to replace those he would retire—to sit about and entertain the little ones. Better folks came here to Blue Hills than some other places he knew.

Much of his success was due to Marcus Holland. He had bought a beaten Marcus from his owner in Virginia and ridden to Texas with him years before when they were in their twenties. Marcus had taught him about tobacco. Marcus had been with him when Lucien was born. Marcus had helped him bury Lucien's mother after she died. They knew one another as no one else did, not even their wives.

He was thrilled when Marcus and Betta took a fancy to one another and married, and at Blue Hills, they were married properly, as all were when they asked.

Life was good. He tried not to be irrationally concerned when life was too good.

Then July staggered in gravid with heat.

Chapter Nine

Adrien

Maman, Bernadette, and I were drinking iced lemonade on the veranda where we could catch the breeze from the river when Papa and Lucien came cantering up the drive from the fields in early afternoon. Papa was out of the saddle, hat in hand, and a pallid look on his face such as I had never seen.

"Yellowjack has come upriver from Galveston," he said, "and Lucretia Hart is ill." Maman's face took on the same pale expression as she raised her palm to her mouth.

"I've told Marcus to keep all our people from leaving the grounds. Our hands too. We'll keep to ourselves until this illness runs its course." He clasped Maman close. "We'll be fine."

This time, Papa was wrong.

Yellowjack reached the quarters that night, and the first to succumb were the eldest and youngest.

Despite Papa's protestations, Maman insisted on going to the quarters to help. "Betta and I had the fever in Savannah," she said. "We will be safe." She and Betta hurried off, carrying blankets and baskets of food and fresh water from the well.

"I also had yellowjack as a boy in New Orleans," Papa said, "and will do what I can. Y'all must listen to Ruth and give her no trouble. Lucien, you're now the man of the house. Treat Horace, Simon, Mintie, and the others as I would. Watch over your brothers and sisters. If anyone becomes ill, send Simon to fetch me."

Left behind with Lucien? *Will I see Papa or Maman again? Is*

Will all right, and Jacob and Lily? I was all muddled inside; my chest throbbed, or maybe it was my stomach.

"Let's go up to the nursery." Ruth pulled Abby and Jules toward the parlor door. "I'll tell y'all a story."

"I can read my own story," I spat, fists at my sides. I was too big to be read to.

As she left the room, Ruth gave no indication she was impressed by my remark, but I could have choked on what I said with such bitterness. Bernadette bumped me. I saw her disappointed expression, her withheld tears. I stared at my feet.

"I am going to listen to her story," Bernadette said, and made her way up the stairs.

Isaac stood next to the piano. I spun at him, thrusting my arms about like a mad puppet. "What are you waiting for?"

"I's a slave. I has to wait on you."

"Stop it, Isaac." He veered to avoid my flailing arms.

"Stop what, Massa?"

I ached to punch something. I stood; he stood; we were nose to nose. *Temper, Adrien.* I spun the opposite direction and flopped onto the sofa, fisting my eyes.

"Dang it all."

Isaac perched next to me. "Yeah."

I got the notion to grasp his shoulders but did not. He put an arm round me. My eyes grew wet. Stopped that right fast.

We set a spell.

The following morning, I lay in bed, though birds sang in the pecan tree outside my window the same as every dawn. *Why bother? I must remain inside anyway. Besides, it is so hot, and the ceiling will not stand still.* I had to use the bedpan and stumbled out onto the floor, reaching under the bed. *Why is the pot so far beneath?* I could not get hold of it, as the thing kept wiggling out of reach. How odd. Finally managing, I sat rather than stood. *So tired. Just lean here on the bed for a minute, only a minute.* People, white, black, brown, and red haunts, floated in and out of the gloom, forward and back. Dark horses thundered around and over me beating, drumming my ears, my head. Hot, so hot. *I have been bad. Bad to Ruth. Lucien knows I am bad. I am gone to hell.*

I do not recall much of the misery or the hours or days I fought in the plains of that bleak place and am glad for it.

Diffused sunlight lit the top of Mintie's white-capped head when I raised the heavy, sticky lids of my eyes. The sheet was damp beneath my fingers. I blinked, for the light made my head ache. "Mintie." Was that a scratchy old bullfrog trying to speak?

She jumped from her chair. "Young master, you is alive."

"Where is Maman? And Papa?" My words harsh whispers. I swallowed, which hurt.

"They is all at the graves."

My heart jerked. My eyes burned. "They are not—"

"Oh, no, sir. Your mama and papa is fine. Your mama spend all hours here with you and Miss Bernadette—" Mintie brought her hand to her mouth, her head down to her shoulders, lowering her voice to a loud whisper. "Miss Bernadette sleeping right over there, and we's got to keep quiet so's not to wake her. She over the yellowjack like you." She fussed at the sheet and pulled it around my shoulders, which forced me farther into the pillow. "You go back to sleep now so you gets your strength back, and I has some nice chicken broth when you wakes up."

Why was everyone "at the graves"? My eyes were heavy, all of me was heavy, and sleep was escape from hurt.

Next I knew, soft yellow light came in the window, and Papa sat carefully on the bed and told me we had lost Abby, Jules, and Ruth to fever. Lucien fought it off, but Mrs. Hart had succumbed. Papa was gray under his eyes. "Your maman is sleeping. She couldn't sleep until she saw you and Bernadette recovering. We are all so relieved." For a brief moment, he placed a cool hand on mine, stood up, glanced at Bernadette, and walked from the room as though carrying all of Blue Hills on his back.

Lost? My little sister and brother were lost? Ruth was lost with them. To heaven? Was I to accept they had gone to heaven? Little children and good people went there to be with God. Did our people go there, as well? Slaves thought so, didn't they? They prayed the same as we did. They didn't believe they were slaves once they were in heaven. If they were not slaves in heaven, how was it proper for them to be slaves on Earth?

I awoke sometime in the night to find Maman bending over me, her hand stroking my forehead. "My son, my precious son," she whispered. "Go back to sleep. I did not mean to wake you. Sleep now, sleep."

In the morning, had she been there, or was it a dream?

❧

As weeks passed, the weather remained hot and sluggish. We left the doors open so the breeze could sweep through the hall. Papa and Lucien returned to the fields, for tobacco would not wait.

I slept four days before dragging myself from bed and downstairs for a bath. The house was empty and quiet. Simon filled the tub, and I dozed in the warm water. As it cooled, shivers forced me out. I shrugged into an oversized flannel shirt and crept into the hall. Bernadette hobbled down the stairs in her dressing gown and slippers. She and I had not spoken since the sickness began. My legs turned to mush. I grabbed onto the hall chair where Simon usually sat, to keep from collapsing to the floor. "Bernadette," I whispered. We fell together onto our knees, holding one another and sobbing. I was not the least ashamed of crying.

❧

I was sure I would never be happy again when, a few weeks later on a warm evening at the end of August, Papa said, "Come outside. I have something to show you." Maman placed her needlepoint on her chair and followed.

On the grass in front of the veranda, Miguel, his grin showing from beneath his dangling mustache, stood holding the reins of a young chestnut gelding with three white-stocking feet and a new saddle on its back. I neglected to breathe.

"Did you think we forgot your tenth birthday?"

"Papa." My voice broke in a strangled sigh. Everything spun away but that horse. I ran down the steps, remembering to slow the last ten feet so as not to spook that lovely fantasy. Surely, he was not real, as perfect as I could imagine. He arched his neck as I came near and raised a hand to stroke his velvet nose. He was real, after all. "Does he have a name?"

"Name him whatever you like."

"Troy. His name is Troy." Jacob, Will, and I had been reading Greek stories, often orating passages in the original Greek. I ran my palm down his neck, over his back, down his legs, then walked around to his other side. I continued stroking and talking, looking him over as Jacob had taught me. I bent under his neck, reached up, and caressed his velvety ears. I checked the cinch, leaped into the saddle, and took the reins from Miguel, who smiled up at me. The slightest signal from my bed-weakened thighs, and we were off.

We went like blazes across the drive, down the road, between the stables and pasture, to the smithy, and back around the big oak in front of the house. Neither Papa, Maman, nor anyone at Blue Hills knew of the hours I had spent on young horses dashing about the Hart plantation with Jacob. Maman would never have let me. Riding a fine animal of my own was the best thing that had ever happened to me. How could I possibly feel so good after feeling so bad? Papa had done this, and Maman.

Both appeared startled when I pulled up, eyes wide and mouths half open. Then Papa grinned. "You never learned to ride like that on old Betsy."

I leaned forward to pat Troy's neck. "Jacob taught me." I turned to Maman. "I did not want to worry you."

Maman's expression was one of anxious perturbation, and Papa drew her close under one arm. "Now, Madeleine. Nearly every Texas boy Adrien's age rides like that. If he's spent that much time learning on the sly, I'd say it's obvious he loves horses. You don't wish to take that from him, do you? You 're an accomplished rider, yourself. Now you'll have a companion."

"Very well." Maman leaned into Papa and hugged his arm. "I know when I am outnumbered." Shading her eyes from the early morning sun, she peered up at me from under her hand. "Still, do not assume I condone such behavior from here on. You will not go behind my back again. Is that clear?"

"Yes, Maman." I did not plan to. But one's plans sometimes go awry.

❧

Though I now had a good horse, it was made clear that I was to remain with Maman, not join Papa.

I will read every book in the library. I will learn everything Mr. Clarence and Jacob can teach me until Papa no longer ignores me.

I returned to piano lessons and learned more Spanish from Miguel. Will and I continued our Greek studies with Jacob. Hartwood was less than an hour's ride north on a fine horse like Troy.

At ten, I had finally become a true son of Texas: an excellent rider, a darn good shot, and my first kill was Bre'r Rabbit. Papa let me pick a pup from one of his hound's litters, and Courage stuck to my side like a tick.

I commenced riding to Hartwood in the company of only Isaac. Will, Isaac, Courage, and I followed the twisting creeks of both plantations and nearby areas, hunting and trapping frogs, squirrels, rabbits, and possum, scaring up porcupine, weasel, or skunk. Whatever we discovered ended up in a stewpot.

Jacob's Tonk friend, Colt, showed me how to take animals in the "proper way," with respect and thankfulness to the spirit of each kill. I skinned and used every part and found more satisfaction from the first rabbit turned over my campfire than from any meal on our linen-covered table.

Two mornings a week before lessons, I accompanied Maman on

her mare. Once or twice a month, Bernadette joined us on her little pony. I was too young to realize how important these rides were to Maman. I thought of what *I* wanted, *my* yearnings, how I spent *my* time. Too late, I learned the penalty for indifference to the desires of those we love.

Chapter Ten

Adrien

In May 1853, Mr. Clarence informed us he planned to return East to marry his childhood sweetheart. After discussion with Maman, Papa told me that in the fall I was to attend school south of Washington with neighbors' sons and daughters.

Having met those sons and daughters during Sunday visits, both at our home and theirs, I was not inclined to the idea. One fellow's remark rang like the nancy harangue Lucien had spat at me: "You don't really read that namby-pamby stuff, do you?" Other sorts of remarks worried me more, since Isaac would accompany me: "That colored of yours is a mite uppity, ain't he?"

Since Hartwood Plantation was an hour's ride closer to school than Blue Hills, Mr. Hart graciously invited me to stay with Will on school nights. Late Sunday afternoon after dinner, Isaac and I would ride along the Brazos River Road to Hartwood and return Friday night. Isaac and I had become used to long rides as we had been all over Blue Hills, even outside its boundaries exploring up Oak Creek and east to the Brazos. We watched the steamboats going up and down the river, and sometimes a captain blew his whistle when we waved to him from shore.

Bernadette wanted to join us, but Maman put her foot down. No *jeune fille* should ride so far in the company of two young boys. My sister owned the darndest notions for a young lady, though I did not blame her. My dear sister had good reason to be downcast. Hopefully, my promise to pass on everything I learned to her and Isaac would lift her from despondency.

❧

If only I had been wrong about school.

The three-year-old, cedar plank school building kept out rain and boasted two small glass-paned windows facing the road and one on each side that let in a fair amount of light, despite numerous live oaks and a few pecan trees outside. The one room was barely large enough to hold seats and desks for the twenty-five students who showed up most days. I believe our teacher was relieved when certain fellows who were prone to misbehavior remained home. Mrs. Weber, mousy brown hair elaborately curled in tight ringlets at her temples, was quick and accurate with her wood ruler, as many an unruly fellow soon learned to the grief of sore knuckles. But she seldom ventured forth beyond the schoolroom, particularly on rainy days when a colored boy was assigned to keep the stove near her desk filled with firewood.

Boys taunted me: "Go play with the girls, Miss Adrien."

I was cursed. Blighted with perfectionism. Even my name was a joke. What was wrong with good diction? With dressing well, admiring poetry and music?

Everything in Texas.

A whack from behind drove my hat to the ground.

"Oops." Shad Campbell lurched past on my left. Shad's chum, Clay Thatcher, brushed by on my right. Snickering, the two swaggered down the path.

"Couple of chumps," Will said to their backs as he bent down to snatch my hat.

The bigger one, Shad, turned and smirked. "Aww, gawsh. Wittle boy can't stand up for hisself." He elbowed his friend, and the two strode on.

"Thanks, Will. But I don't think . . . shit." Hands shaking, I slapped my hat on my head. Dang it.

Will sighed. He glanced at me sideways from under his own hat.

Even my best friend expected something from me—a decision of some sort. But people expected opposite things. Maman insisted that gentlemen did not resort to violence to settle their problems. Besides, I had never hit anyone in my life, and Shad Campbell and Clay Thatcher were bigger than me. Fighting either one would be stupid.

On the other hand, everyone else declared that real men settled their differences with their fists. Though my brother's nancy taunts never physically threatened me. Unless one counted the time Lucien shoved me against the stable wall.

The next afternoon when I collected my wool jacket from its peg at the rear of the room, the lining was covered in mud.

I hated school.

Chapter Eleven

Bernadette

I scarcely noticed finches chirping outside the open window as Eliza coiled a braid at the top of my head. The soft morning breeze drifting in that window belied the anxious clasping of my hands and tightening of my tummy. "Do get on, Eliza." Eliza was attempting to take Ruth's place. I had become used to doing for myself and had little of Maman's patience.

"Yes, miss. A few more pins an we be done."

How fine to be like my brothers and not spend so much time preparing for the day. Thank goodness, at eleven a corset was required only for company. According to Maman, such was one benefit of living on the frontier, though Papa said true frontier lay farther west.

Preparations complete, I scurried next door to my brother's room before he could escape downstairs.

Lingering barely a moment after tapping on Adrien's door, I pushed it open a couple inches. "Adrien?" Without waiting for an answer, I shoved it wide and stepped inside. He was standing before the wardrobe in trousers and shirtsleeves.

"You are up and ready early," he said, straightening his collar and turning toward me.

"I should like to speak with you before going down."

"Speak then." He turned away, reaching for his coat on the bed. My, he was gruff.

I stepped into the room. No point in beating round the bush. I folded my hands together at my waist and said in my most resolute voice, "You must tell me what is wrong."

Jacket in hand, he hesitated, turned, and studied me with an aggravated expression.

"What makes you think you may make demands on me?"

Had I ever seen him so upset? At me? His chest was rising and falling rapidly—brows knit, black eyes flashing—my heart skipped a beat; I nearly stepped back. Then my own fire lit. How dare he? I fisted my hands at my sides and stepped forward.

"We made a pact years ago—in case you have forgotten—you and Isaac and I after Lucien shoved you into the barn wall. To always remain truthful, to be one another's support, and not keep secrets no matter the circumstances."

Goodness, how forcefully I had spoken, for he backed and sank onto the bed, letting his coat slide to the floor. I had the upper hand and dared not succumb to the threatening giggle. I stiffened my shoulders and stood as tall as possible, Maman's lessons in deportment standing me in good stead. "Or have you decided to go back on your word?" How pleasant to look *down* upon a male person. How dear he appeared, though, all astonished and confused. And how satisfying to have the upper hand. Best to take advantage now. I turned and sat next to him, taking his hand.

"Tell me what has got you so disheartened and angry."

His hand flopped like a dead fish in mine. "That school." He peered down at his feet. "Not the school. Two fellows. Me, really. It is me, Bernadette."

That same hand came alive to grasp mine tight, and he stood and pulled me to the mirror on the wall over his dresser.

"Look at us."

I saw two olive-toned fine-featured faces as nearly alike as two peas in a pod, which was what Maman's maid, Betta, would say, though Adrien was a boy and practically a year older than me at twelve years. Both with deep-set dark eyes and matching black, glossy hair. Mine coiled in a braid at the top of my head and his hung in waves to his shoulders.

"You see the problem?" he said.

I saw myself squinting as I peered into the glass.

"I look too much like you," he exclaimed in exasperation, throwing his hands in the air. "Look at this," clutching at his hair, pulling it, he spun and headed for the door. "Come, you have shears in your sewing basket do you not?"

I hurried after him to my room. "Yes, but why?" Then I realized what he planned to do. "Adrien you cannot. It will upset Maman. Your lovely hair. You must not."

We were in my room where he had found my basket on the dresser, withdrawn my silver shears, and raised them in the air like some lost treasure. Or, in this case, a sword.

"You have no idea, Bernadette, what it is like with my name and the way I speak and dress and"—he grabbed a handful of hair— "this," and cut off a five-inch shock. How quickly it dropped to the floor.

"Adrien!" I raised my hands but could do nothing with them. Clutch his arm? An outrageous idea. Bending over my dresser mirror, he cut another handful that landed on the back of my silver brush.

I said the first thing that came to mind, rather weak, I must admit. "Other men have hair to their shoulders."

"But they have manly faces. They do not look like a girl. And they cut their hair with Bowie knives, not with fancy shears in the shape of a stork's bill."

"You do not look like a girl." I dared reach for his arm, but he jerked away and continued, snip, snip—locks of hair fluttered to the floor. He did not bother to look in the mirror but cut with a terrible vengeance.

"Close enough."

I must talk him out of this . . .mood. Bowie knives, of all things. He read too many of those cheap novels. "You will grow out of it, the same as Maman says that one day you will grow taller."

"Which does not help me now."

❧

"It was too long," Adrien said. He had made it to his chair at the breakfast table before being spied by Maman.

Her hands at her mouth, her brown eyes round as two porcelain teacups, "*Mon dieu!* What have you done?"

"Good God," Papa said, "you look like a hen mauled by a fox."

Mintie entered the dining room and nearly dropped the silver coffee tray.

Across the table, Lucien snickered from behind his hand.

Mintie, attempting to hide a grin beneath her lowered head, managed to reach Papa's side and begin pouring his coffee as he said, "You will eat breakfast, and afterward Betta will see what she can do with the mess you have made." He glanced at Maman at the other end of the table. "Furthermore, you will never do anything like this to your person without first consulting your maman or me beforehand. Is that understood?"

"Yes, sir."

"Sit and eat."

My brother was silent throughout the meal. Under the circumstances, I was not satisfied that I had received the entire story. This evening was our time for studying what Adrien had learned during the week. I would wait until tonight. It should not be difficult to enlist Isaac's help. After all, he was the other member of our pact.

Chapter Twelve

Adrien

My family gathered before a cozy fire in the parlor: Papa in his favorite chair reading his paper; Maman across from him on the sofa doing needlework. Her needle projects were endless. One could not lay one's head back in a chair without resting it on fancy flowers or vines that our people washed and replaced every fortnight, ostensibly to protect the furniture from hair oil. To say nothing of the tea cozies and doilies for every dish.

We had canceled our Saturday study night as Isaac's folks wished him to spend the evening with them.

I kept reaching up and fingering new coolness at my neck. Hair tips curled around the backs of my ears.

Papa said from behind his paper, "You would be interested in this, *chérie*. A Women's Rights Convention was held in Ohio for the fourth year, and similar conventions have been held in other cities, as well."

Maman continued poking her needle and thread through the fabric on her lap. "And does the article state the subject of these conventions?"

"It appears these women, Jenny Lind among them, hmm, and some men believe women are equal to men in all things."

"My goodness. Who would have thought?" Maman continued with her needle.

From the floor, I watched Papa lower his paper to his lap, raise a brow, and tuck his chin. Papa's sparkling eyes fixed on Maman. The corner of his mouth raised ever so slightly. Maman continued her work a second or two before her own eyes raised and met Papa's. She gave him a most charming smile.

Bernadette, who sat next to Maman on the sofa, her face deep in her book, looked up and said imperiously, "I do believe those women are quite brave, Papa, to stand up for what they believe." My sister was not one to hesitate if she had something to add to any conversation. None of my family were. Perhaps that was due to Maman's family having to flee France as a result of the Troubles there. Papa declared revolution and its aftermath were in her blood.

Lucien, from his chair at Papa's right on the other side of the kerosene lamp, proclaimed, "They are fools. No proper southern woman would engage in such unladylike behavior."

"I'm sorry, Lucien," Papa said, "but I must agree with your sister. One should always stand up for one's beliefs, no matter how foolish that stand might seem to others. The more berated the cause, the more courage it takes to fight for it."

I clutched my book and looked at the pages but did not see the words. I might tell myself fighting was stupid. But must I stand up for myself, for who I am? *Do I possess that sort of courage?*

I can jump on Troy and ride down a ravine, jump a fence, do any number of things that might cause injury. Because I have some control and know what I am doing. But if I were to, do this, stand up for myself, I am bound to lose. It would be a sure thing. Another matter entirely.

Chapter Thirteen

Bernadette

I had made ready for bed and nearly lost my nerve but was resolved. Something would surely occur to one of us if we faced this together.

I must merely consider those courageous women in Ohio, and I could do anything.

So here I was, outside his door in my dressing gown and preparing to knock. Considering his earlier mood, I dared not give him a chance to turn me away, so I tapped three times, turned the knob, and walked right in.

Goodness. He stood before the bed in his nightshirt, aghast at my presumptuous entrance. That new haircut gave his head such a sleek appearance, and his eyes seemed unusually large and dark.

"What if I had not been dressed?"

"But you are. Sort of." He looked vulnerable in his nightshirt. He was still smaller than most twelve-year-old boys and thin. Which made me feel more confident and determined.

"Earlier, I passed Isaac on his way to spend the night with his folks, and I thought you might be lonely." I stepped farther into the room, passing my hands behind my back and squeezing them together. "Betta did ever so nice a repair on your hair."

He pulled a stray strand behind his ear before he flopped on the bed and settled against the massive headboard. "Come on. You may as well come in and say your piece."

Oh, good. I went hastily around the bed and crawled up next to him. "Like the old days." We were at that age, or nearly. *This is likely the last time, and I will remember it.* I gave a sigh and arranged my gown around my legs. When much younger I often crawled into bed with him and Isaac where they cuddled, read stories (Adrien did), played games, and sometimes got so rambunctious (I loved that word) that Betta had to hurry upstairs to shush us.

"Somewhat," he said with a sigh and sidelong glance, hands flat on thighs.

I fiddled with the lace hem of my gown, watching my fingers with feigned interest.

"I expect you think I am snooping," I said, "but I am doing as we promised—you, me, and Isaac. Whatever trouble you are in, I still love you, and I will support you, no matter what. I want to help, even if you think I am only your sister." I continued looking at my hem as I finished this statement and then fixed my eyes on him with the gravest intensity I could muster. *He is dear to me. Dearer than anyone, save Maman and Papa. My, what a surprised expression on his face. How many times have I surprised him today?*

"Bernadette, you must keep reminding me how special you are." He leaned forward and held me tight. I grasped him back and recalled the last time we had done so, that terrible summer soon after we discovered one another well and alive in the hall.

Holding one of my hands and stroking it with his thumb, he said, looking down the bed at his feet, "A couple fellows at school are, well, tormenting me. I must fight them to end it, and fighting is stupid." He let go of my hand and folded his arms around himself. "But I have no choice."

"Because of what Papa said tonight? About standing up for yourself?"

"Yes. Well. Partly." He drew up his knees and grasped his legs, bare toes curling into the counterpane. "Promise me you will tell no one, not Maman and not Papa. Such would make everything worse. I must prove myself, do you see? Otherwise, this treatment will never end."

"Does Isaac know?"

"He will." Adrien grinned. "I will need someone to haul my broken self onto Troy afterward."

"That is not funny," I said, shoving him.

"Will shall be with me. He can make sure only one fellow comes for me at a time." He scratched his head. "I hope any fighting will happen early in the week, but will you help me keep this from Maman? If I come home bearing evidence?"

"You mean like bruises?"

"Or whatever."

He was practically as fine-boned as me and not much taller. How could he punch anyone? His fingers were meant for playing piano. If another boy punched him? "Oh, Adrien."

"Bernadette. Do not look at me like that." He clutched my hands and sat up straighter. "You must help me be strong. Promise?"

"I promise."

That night I prayed extra for him. The next night too, and I would the following and every night until he came home. I had to pray for myself too—that I would not tell Maman or Papa. Adrien would never forgive me if I did.

Chapter Fourteen

Adrien

"Have you ever been in a fight?"

"Only with you," Isaac said. From Troy's back, I could barely see him floating to my right through the morning mist coming up from the river. Shandy, the mule he rode, was white as the mist. I wanted to get an early start to Hartwood so I wouldn't accidentally reveal my trouble. Removing myself from the scene ought to keep Bernadette silent.

"I mean a proper fight."

"Who would I fight with?"

I heaved a deep breath. "I must fight some fellows at school."

"Ssshut." Isaac sat up almighty straight, forcing Shandy over closer as the mist hushed voices and figures.

I looked on down the road with what I hoped was insouciance. "They are likely going to pound me good. They will think I am a lick-finger if I do not fight them."

"You want I should stand with you?"

With me? What an idea. A colored boy standing with me facing two white boys. My eyes burned with tears. I blinked.

"I will need you to take care of Troy, make certain he is ready to ride afterward."

"Sure," he said flatly.

Our heads nodding with our mounts' movement, we looked at one another, knowing what we were not saying.

I said nothing to Will Sunday evening at Hartwood, and Monday morning, nothing untoward happened. Lunch break I glanced at Shad, then Clay, from the corners of my eyes.

Monday and Tuesday passed.

I could barely sleep.

Wednesday was the same.

From his inquiring look, Will suspected something was up, but he said nothing.

By Thursday afternoon, the thought of having to worry all weekend had me practically jumping out of my skin. After dismissal, as everyone poured from the schoolhouse in an escaping tide, Shad Campbell bumped my arm hard enough to scatter my books to the ground. "Aw," he said, "did nancy dwop his books?"

At "nancy," past and present collided and turned the world red and black—withheld anger rose to fury that consumed me beyond reason.

Next, I knew, Will was helping me up from the ground and I had to breathe through my mouth for all the blood in my throbbing nose. My ribs hurt, my knuckles hurt, and Mrs. Weber was turning aside and saying, "Go on home, now. All of you."

"You moved darn fast else your nose would be broken," Will said.

"I did?" He held me under my left shoulder as we stumbled along where our mounts stood beneath the trees. Isaac hurried toward us.

I half-recalled a fist sliding away from my face, an awful punch under my ribs and grabbing onto someone and rolling in dirt or grass or both. I recalled driving my fist into Campbell's middle. The red, raw rage had taken over, that which Papa had warned me. The rest of the fight returned in bits and pieces in the following days: punching, grabbing, rolling, clods of mixed grass and dirt flying.

Strange how the anger had left nearly as soon as it had begun, with the first jab or grab.

The pain was terrible but not as bad as the dread beforehand. Plus, there was an unforeseen result.

When we returned to Hartwood, Jacob, a smile pulling at the corner of his mouth, took one look and said, "If you must fight, you'd better learn how." Thus, began other sorts of lessons entirely.

I worked with him before school in the morning and after school before supper. Being sore was something I must get used to—time to toughen up.

"You're not in college learning to box like a gentleman," Jacob said. "You fight to win, any way you can. Especially when your opponent is bigger than you." He showed me how to block, feint, parry. Also, how to clinch and jab—things that were definitely not gentlemanly.

Strange. Instead of balking in the face of Maman's disapproval, I gloried in finally taking action, even in being sore and exhausted. It was as though Jacob had set me free, the same as he had when he taught me to ride. Except I was inordinately aware of my desire to please him. And his splendid good looks.

Wednesday the following week, I took on Clay Thatcher. There was plenty of grasping, pulling, and gouging. Fortunately, I did not have strength to do substantial harm with the underhanded blows Jacob taught me, but my willingness to take a licking and ability to do damage eventually won acceptance and friendship from Thatcher. His pal, Henry Carlyle, came along, and others followed. We were soon tussling and smacking at one another constantly, with no one intending any actual harm. This kind of physical contact with another boy was acceptable, and to my surprise I loved it. Before, there had been only Isaac, and for obvious reasons, we had been circumspect.

The most difficult part of the entire affair was dealing with Maman, who nearly pulled me out of school when she discovered my black eye, swollen lip, and scraped hands. School brawling was one of the few times Papa supported me—dare I say, against Maman?

As a result of this grappling, a new concern arose. At night while attempting to drift off to sleep, I replayed the grasping and fellows' smacking at me, and how it felt when I did the same. I had never engaged in such actions, particularly grabbing at anyone's backsides this way. Isaac and I had approached the physical thing as children do—as a matter of exploration. I now considered my feelings in an additional, different sort of light, one that left me with a fluttering dread.

Chapter Fifteen

Adrien

I imagined all sorts of scenarios, something I might have done that would have led to a different outcome. If Maman and I had begun our usual morning ride earlier, later, taken a different trail. If I had not been preoccupied with my repulsive predilections, what happened would not have occurred.

Dew had sparkled lush spring bluestem and switchgrass, wetting the fetlocks of our horses as we passed the kitchen garden on our left and neared the rears of the house-peoples' cabins. Insects darted every which way through bars of sunlight filtering through overhanging leafy branches of sycamore, cottonwood, and ash. Sparrows fluttered through the underbrush, and Oak Creek burbled and glittered on our right. We could not have asked for a lovelier morning, and on the return ride, Maman's mare and Troy were breathing easy.

I had completed an entire year of school without bringing disgrace upon my family. I may even say I adopted a certain wary boldness with young ladies that enabled me to dismiss, spurn, or otherwise ignore unwanted impulses. We often threw our arms around our best companion, as Shad and Clay frequently did, as Will and I sometimes did—even put our heads together and murmured secrets in one another's ears. I ached for more, though I wasn't sure what *more* was.

"I seldom see you," Maman said from my left. "You are at Hartwood with Will or at school, and when home, you are off elsewhere with Isaac. You are growing up fast. I appreciate your spending this time with me."

"I enjoy our rides together, Maman." I did enjoy them, but I was always considering what might happen afterward—fishing with Isaac, exploring with Will, or—*Should I have been born in Greece hundreds of years past when love among boys and men was normal, even heroic? What was that sort of love, exactly? I ached to hold someone close, to nuzzle—*

"Saying so is gentlemanly of you, Adrien. You are much like your papa in that respect."

"He wishes I were more like him in many respects." *True. But I should not speak so. My mind was wandering again.*

"Your papa loves you, as I do."

Why does he never want me with him? I glanced down at my hand fisting the reins, my stomach tightening. *Lord, what a mood.* "Lucien said I don't contribute to Blue Hills, and he is right. Papa never takes me with him to the fields or anywhere else. All I do is go to school and play." *Because of Maman.* As Lucien was under Papa's purview, I was under Maman's, the same as Bernadette.

At thirteen, I was nearly a man, yet they treated me like a child. If I urged Papa to give me some task or responsibility, perhaps he would do so, at least in summer. I needed a chance to prove myself capable of more than schoolwork and shooting defenseless rabbits.

Maman rode on ahead down the trail, her back moving effortlessly with her mare. She was an excellent rider. Earlier we had raced down the road from the north field head-to-head. It had been necessary to push Troy to keep up with her.

"Do you ever consider that Lucien antagonizes you because he is jealous of your position?"

I might retch, the way my stomach churned. *What?* "*My* position?" *Impossible!* I practically stuttered, replying, "He's always at Papa's side; he will inherit Blue Hills."

She stopped her mount, waited for me to come alongside, and reached over to place a hand on my arm. "But he works hard for that—"

"Oh!" she said, jerking in the saddle and slapping her neck through the net of her hat, sending her sorrel mare spinning.

Troy danced in sympathy. "Maman?"

"I am fine." As always, even during a nasty situation, her diction was perfect. "Something bit me. Good gracious, it stings. I expect a bee got trapped under the net. Betta will have something for the sting. She helped me once before when we were young." She signaled her mare forward, then turned toward me. Her eyes and mouth opened wider. "My. I cannot seem to catch my breath." She gasped. "Adrien?" Bending, her hand came to her throat as she swayed and began to slip sideways from her saddle.

My God! Blood racing, I flung myself from Troy. Her horse side-stepped. She slid, fell into my arms and we collapsed to the ground.

Her eyes were enormous, her face pink. "I cannot," a short gasp, another, "I —" Her mouth moved, but no words came forth. Her throat was swelling!

Heart beating savagely, I yanked off her hat. She clawed at the French lace of her blouse. I ripped the highest buttons apart, lifted her head and shoulders onto my lap. "Help!" I screamed. "Help!"

She kicked and jerked in my arms, mouth open wide. Her tongue, swollen beyond belief. Her face, pale, wide eyes staring up at me, pleading—

Maman! She could not breathe! *How could I get air into her? How?* I stuck a finger in her mouth to force her tongue aside to let air in, to no avail.

Someone came running—Simon.

I grasped one-handed at his trousers. "Simon, help her! Save her!" Simon would do something, he must. He had been a trusted servant since we were little.

One of her hands clutched my shirt, the other squeezed my wrist so hard my fingers went numb. Her wide eyes found mine . . . then . . . she quit kicking. Her hand, her fingers loosened and slid away. Her face lost color. She stared past me. I could not turn my eyes from her face. Could not move. Failed to breathe. Something kicked me in the chest. No.

Simon stammered, "Oh, young massa, young massa. She done

this. That Rosanne. I been dreamin o' her. I knew trouble comin and she back to her old devilment. Oh, lordy lord."

I hauled her up higher into my arms. I would warm her. *No no no.* "Maman," I whispered into her ear, caressing her cheek. I rocked her. "Don't go, don't leave. I did not mean it. Please. Whatever you wish, I'll do it. Just stay." I whispered, I rocked her, I rocked and rocked and rocked and . . .

Chapter Sixteen

Isaac

Master Paien, Isaac's papa, and his mama took the body—hard to think of her that way—to the springhouse on Oak Creek under the hill. June grew hot by midmorning, and the springhouse stayed cool enough to keep ice, even in August. For a fortnight, anyway.

Isaac ran to Oak Creek where Adrien would be, where no one else would look because only he and Adrien knew of their special place. He crab-walked to get through the brush tunnel, then hopped from one rock to the next across the creek. After a couple of turnarounds and through tangled sumac, he arrived at their clearing.

In dappled shade, his back against the gray-and-white bark of a sycamore, Adrien sat head down, arms hanging over pulled-up knees. Leaves and twigs hung in his hair, reminding Isaac of a half-built bird's nest. Adrien didn't look up, not even when Isaac crawled through the dry leaves and squatted next to him.

"Horace fetched Doc Hayes," Isaac said. "He said your maman was as, asfix, she couldn't breathe."

"I knew that." The words sounded muffled and dead between his arms.

"He said it was probably an insect bite. She was allergic."

Adrien turned to him, face flushed and twisted, black eyes rimmed in red. "That's it? She stopped breathing because of a bug?"

"He'd have to do an autopsy to learn more, but your papa said, no."

Adrien stared wide-eyed at him, before turning away, leaning, and retching over the leaf litter. Mostly clear liquid. He wiped his forearm across his mouth, rubbed his hands on his trousers, then hugged his knees and rocked. "I should have done something."

He rocked like some crazy old man, with leaves, twigs, and a bit of spider web in his hair. Mumbling the same thing repeatedly.

"Shucks, Adrien." His own stomach tightened. He wiped a hand across his mouth and poked his friend in the arm.

"If Lucien or Papa had been there, they would have helped her." Adrien turned to him and said miserably, "They would have, don't you think?"

"Blazes, no one could have done a thing once it happened."

"I was always running off somewhere when she needed me. What if God took her in atonement for my selfishness?"

"This is all about you, huh? What about Bernadette at the house all by her lonesome? Your papa is all taken up in his grief. You think Lucien's going to concern himself with how Bernadette feels? She lost her mama too. Though it appears to me you forgot all about that, you been so caught up in your own self."

Bernadette was the one person his friend adored as much as his mama.

After swiping the back of an arm across his nose, Adrien sat there silent in the leaves. Then rose to his feet. "You always were too clever for a Negro."

Relief flooded Isaac. This sort of response was familiar territory. The two often mimicked what they saw as aberrant adults.

"Look out white boy, or I gives you a bloody lip."

"You could try."

"Not today. Your sister needs you whole."

With that, they returned to the house. Together.

❧

Isaac stood between his papa and mama among the rest of the house colored. The heat made any sort of lying-in impossible. Early that morning, Paien had sent riders to a few neighbors, including the Harts, who had arrived for the sunset burial.

Sweat drooled down the middle of Isaac's back and pooled beneath the belt line of his trousers. He never imagined standing here at the family cemetery so soon. Only a few years since yellowjack went through the county plucking folks from their lives like cotton from the boll.

How strange, white folk dressed in black surrounded by black folk dressed in white. White duck was what all field colored wore, as no one bothered to dye what they worked and played and slept and died in. White except where it was stained all the colors that wouldn't come out in the wash, colors of dried blood, Texas mud, green grass. and the tarry brown of tobacco.

Who was he, a thirteen-year-old colored boy in black top coat and trousers? With all these house colored next to his family? All wore cast-offs from their white folk. Not new every year like field colored got, but better. So why didn't he feel better?

He felt old anger, old frustration, though he was more fortunate than most. He could read and write better than many white boys his age. He would never be parted from his family because Master Paien was Papa's friend.

All through prayer, field slaves swayed and hummed in harmony, knew when the master was done, and sang.

Sisters, won't you help me bear my cross,
Help me bear my cross?
I done been wearing my cross,
I've been through all things here.
Cause, I want to reach over Zion's hill.
Sisters, won't you please help bear my cross
Up over Zion's hill?

Master Paien threw a handful of dirt into the open grave. Lucien, a young man grown, threw another, then Adrien and Bernadette. Adrien had insisted on helping dig the grave with the field colored. Isaac watched him without letting on—saw his trembling hands, the taut, thin line of his mouth. His friend was wound up tighter than a fiddle string.

Adrien kept an eye on his sister, one arm around her waist, guiding her. It had always been so—Lucien off with his papa, Adrien left behind with his sister and mama. The mistress had doted on Adrien, and he had done anything to please her.

The white family turned away, moved down the hill to the house.

"Papa, I should go see if Adrien needs me." Isaac looked up at his papa, tall and distinguished in his own fine suit taken out of their cupboard for the funeral.

"Don't make a nuisance of yourself. He may want time alone."

"I won't." He was off and running through the mixed grasses and bluebonnets.

�֍

Down the hill, past the smithy, through the pasture, and round the house to the back porch. All was quiet, too quiet. He stood looking down the long hallway. He'd never been inside when no one else was about. The double back door had been left wide open, and bugs got in, but so did air, which was more important this sweltering time of year. He and Adrien had wondered what the hall looked like when it was the dogtrot—before they were born. They had tried to imagine the house without the second floor, no carpet and no doors. All manner of dogs and chickens and bugs must have passed through from one end to the other.

With none of the family about, it would be strange to go in any farther than here at the back double doors, so he waited. He could go upstairs to Adrien's room—his room, too, as often as not. But everything felt different. Without the mistress, it *was* different. She had been good to him and so important to his mama. He had hardly seen Mama since the mistress's death.

She was first to arrive in the doorway behind him. "Bless you, boy," she said. "Here, take these and help me light the lanterns. You do the hall, and I'll get the parlor."

She hurried off almost before he could blink. Jings, he didn't often get to hold a whole box of new safety matches, as he used a strike-a-light to start fires outside, or flint and steel, as did all field colored. Boxes of lucifers were kept on the mantel, but no one carried them around, as they lit at the least bit of rubbing. Funny stories passed around regarding fires begun in someone's back pocket.

Stars pictured on the cover of the box disappeared in the fading light. He hadn't been aware of the growing dark, how open doors had become gray rectangles against the dim hall.

He lifted the glass chimney, set it on the carpet at his feet and lit the wick. A single flick of his wrist snapped yellow fire into being, and its sulfurous smell tickled his nose. Tucking the burnt match into his shirt pocket, he wiped his hand on the front of his trousers and replaced the chimney. Mama had told him to wait until the chimney warmed before turning the flame up. He had no sooner finished than Master Paien, followed by his sons, Bernadette, and guests made their way through the front door and into the hall.

"Don't light all the lamps, as we'll all be retiring soon after supper. Our guests have ridden hard to get here."

"I'm not hungry, Papa." Adrien turned toward the stairs.

"We'll all eat what Esther places before us. I won't have anyone coming down ill. We'll sit together with our guests in the parlor until supper."

"Yes, Papa."

Isaac ate in the outside kitchen with the other house slaves, then quietly went upstairs and waited in Adrien's room. The room was warm this night. Isaac was perched on the north windowsill gazing at stars, braving mosquitoes, and catching the breeze from the river, when he heard Adrien enter. He pulled the door closed and sat at the desk chair to remove his boots. Isaac slipped off the sill, hurried to his friend's side, and dropped to his knees to grasp the heel of one boot, pushing at Adrien's hands. "My job," he said, and pulled.

"Christ," Adrien whispered.

Your mama wouldn't care for such language, Isaac thought but didn't say it. Not this time. He pulled the other boot off. Looked up at Adrien looking down. He swam in those black, glistening eyes, something deep in them, and in himself, made his heart thud in his chest.

Adrien stood. "I am tired," he murmured, gazing off somewhere unknown.

Isaac wondered what it would be like to lose his own mama and stopped himself in the middle of wondering. He didn't care for such a thought.

Isaac sprawled down on his pallet, listening to Adrien brush his teeth and use the necessary beneath the bed. Every sound was loud, even the creaking floorboard, as the other boy padded across to join him. He lay down facing away, and Isaac didn't move or speak. He took a deep breath and let it out, maybe louder than normal.

Adrien turned to face him. Isaac couldn't see much as no moonlight shone in the window, only stars. But he could hear his friend's low voice.

"Bernadette's alone. I was thinking I should go stay with her tonight," Adrien murmured.

"Yeah?"

"What do you think?"

"Yeah."

"Wish you could come with me."

"Yeah. Well." Isaac smiled. "I'm too old now."

Isaac watched him close the door softly as he left. Adrien needed her as much as she needed him.

Isaac swallowed, drew his knees up, held them to his chest, and blinked in the dark. Too old now to be part of the threesome they were. Not only a boy, but a colored boy. That was the truth of it.

Chapter Seventeen

Bernadette

N o-o-o! I was falling, flung—sky, trees, a yellow-and-orange blur, and ground a solid thump on my right shoulder followed by the rest of me. I lay in grass and dry gone-to-seed wildflowers trying to draw breath. Lord. I must move, get up. He dared not think I was injured. Of all times for that stupid horse—

"Bernadette!" Adrien wasted no time getting to my side, on his knees, his hands shaking, reaching for me, face as pale as Maman's company china.

"I am fine." I sat in the grass. I was not fine. My shoulder hurt and, *ow*, my hip and, pushing him away, I dared not let him see how much hurt.

I offered my arm. "Help me up." I brushed at my riding skirt, hiding the limp in my right leg. "Thank goodness, my skirt did not get dirty." I must get Adrien's mind off injury.

With such a white face and grim mouth, my brother appeared about to lose his breakfast. I must fix this, and fast, or he would never take me riding again.

"Adrien, look at me." I held both arms out and turned, stifling a wince. "See? It was not your fault that rabbit took off under the nose of my horse."

"Oh, I don't know bout that." Isaac leaned forward on the neck of his mount and fell into his mama's South Carolina Gullah. "Br'er rabbit said to hisself, 'Here come the marse of that hound always chasing me, and I'm gonna fix him good.'"

I brought my hand to my mouth and snickered, which ladies were not to do. My shoulders shook, and I laughed, relieved at Adrien's smile. It had taken weeks to get him to take me riding, and only after I told him how dreadfully melancholic I had been since Maman's death. He could sally forth into these glorious October afternoons with Isaac, but what might *I* do? I was losing my mind, confined to the house.

He had one condition. We would never ride where he and Maman had ridden that day. I understood. Riding together would be healthy— as long as nothing untoward happened.

And the first time, my horse threw me.

"Then why was it my horse that shied, and not Adrien's?" Hands on hips, I peered indignantly up at Isaac.

"Adrien took more fright than you," Isaac declared, heaving in his saddle with a cackle.

Adrien made his hands into a stirrup to help me remount, and I clenched my teeth when I swung my leg over the saddle. Thank goodness, Papa had not insisted on a sidesaddle.

"Shall we head back?" My brother rode his horse alongside mine.

"Absolutely not. I want to ride up by the north barn."

He still looked brittle. His color had not entirely returned, and his eyes were shifty. Isaac came up along my other side, and we cantered to the top of a grassy hill where vegetation lining Oak Creek meandered off to our left. We stopped to let our horses breathe after the climb. Pale blue sky met distant clumps of trees and golden hills, not a cloud in sight. The ground sloped down to a huge old oak and the north drying barn.

"Have you ever heard of someone named Rosanne?" Adrien said, idly tossing the ends of his reins against his limb.

"I haven't," I said.

"Me, neither." Isaac leaned forward, forearm resting on the pommel of his saddle. "Who is she?"

"That's what I'm wondering. Simon mentioned her."

"Maybe you should ask *him*," Isaac said.

"I did, and he denied knowing anything about her."

"You sure you got the name, right?"

"I think so."

My brother squirmed in the saddle. "It was not," he said stretching his back, "the best moment when I heard it."

I reached over and put my hand on his. "Not important then."

He met my eyes. "I guess not."

I must break his mood. "Last one to the barn is a scalawag," I said and dug in my heels.

"Berni, no," Adrien yelled, but he was already behind as my mare took off down the gentle slope. How glorious to gallop, the wind in my face and hair!

I was past the oak before either caught up. The aches were worth my triumph. I hoped I would feel the same tonight.

❦

Two weeks later, Adrien, Isaac, and I were lying among last summer's high grass peeking through golden seed-topped stems, Adrien's hand on a trembling Courage. Must be anticipation, as I trembled, myself. Two pairs of wool stockings inside Adrien's castoff boots kept my feet dry, though the dawn chill of early November soaked through my brother's castoff trousers, and I breathed the odor of damp wool, dog, and earth.

Despite the wool gloves, my fingers were turning numb lying here waiting, for what, I did not know. Adrien declared we must be absolutely silent if I wished to see something special.

I forgot my discomfort when a gray fox slipped out from under the brow of the hillock not twenty feet away. Sniffing the air, it turned, slid through the tall, dead grass to the top of the knob, and checked the air before disappearing beneath the hillock. I gasped, Adrien squeezed my hand, and out came the fox again, followed by one, two, three fox kits. At first, they were tentative, then one hopped at something unseen, and the other two were soon leaping at one another. *How dear. If only I might play with them. I must ask Papa to tell Marcus not to shoot them. Only he would know I was wandering about like a boy. That would never do.*

Observing the little ones, I forgot my discomfort. Then Courage whined. The mother fox, lying quietly watching her charges rose and chased them back under the hill, disappearing after them.

Adrien sat up. "Well, that is that."

"May we come see them again?"

"I do not think so, Berni."

I loved how my brother had begun calling me Berni this morning when I had dressed in his trousers.

"The kits were probably born late last spring, and she will likely move them since we have discovered her den."

I sat up, curling my legs to my side. Foxes, like coyotes, were considered pernicious creatures and harmful to our chickens. "Would you ask Papa to tell Marcus not to shoot them?"

Adrien took a deep breath, rubbing his head. "I . . . ." He raised his eyes to mine. "If I do, Papa's suspicion that I am weak will be confirmed. I cannot do anything to disappoint him. We left extra early so he would not discover I brought you along." He stood and offered to help me up. "We better start back."

Mashing my lips, I refused and rose on my own. Land sakes, this was not fair. I dared not ask since I am not supposed to be out here. These darn boots were so big and clumsy I couldn't keep up. I tried to and fell.

"Here." He returned and offered his hand again. "Isaac and I will help."

I snapped at him. "I can do it myself." *I need neither of them.*

"Bernadette." He was standing before me, fists on hips.

"I will be more careful. I will not fall again." *Tarnation.* My breath was coming short and fast, making trails of steam in the cold air.

"We have to walk faster."

I raised my chin. "You go on. I will be right behind you."

He mashed his lips together, spun, and stalked off toward the house.

I stomped after him, Isaac trailing silently behind me.

I was not stomping by the time I saw Adrien waiting by the

kitchen garden. I was exhausted, and my legs and feet hurt. The entire morning was fun until, until we saw the fox. Until my brother refused to do as I asked. He always did as I asked, until this one time he did not. *This one time.* My brows came together hard enough to give me a headache, and tears threatened. I blinked fast. *Oh dear. What have I done?* I wanted to collapse to the ground and curl in upon myself. Instead, I grasped Adrien's upper arms.

"Adrien, I am sorry. I have behaved shamefully, especially after you took me along this morning. Will you forgive me for behaving so selfishly?"

He studied me with a wrinkled brow, taking my hands. "Of course, I forgive you, but I fear we are late. Let me help you." He put an arm about my waist, nearly picking me up. He had grown in the past year and was stronger than he looked. Isaac reached around from the other side, and they lifted me off the ground. I wanted to laugh in relief, as they practically swung me between the two of them, and we followed the path past the outdoor kitchen, up the steps, across the back porch, and through the double doors into the hall.

Where Papa waited.

My smile fled as Adrien and Isaac lowered me to the carpeted floor.

Papa had never appeared so tall. Taller than his six feet. Arms at his sides, his dark brows were low over his glaring black eyes. "You may leave, Isaac."

"Yes, sir."

As soon as Isaac left, Papa peered down at me. "Where have you been?"

Papa was calm, cold calm. I clutched my hands behind my back and looked down at my feet—in mud-caked oversized boots. On the carpet. I swallowed. "On an excursion."

"An excursion. What do you call that getup you are wearing?"

Call it? Um. "An excursion outfit?"

"Is that the sort of thing young ladies wear these days?"

"I thought—" Adrien said.

"I did not ask you."

"No, sir. I mean, yes, sir."

"Betta." He spoke loud and sharp and made me jump.

Betta appeared as if by magic.

"Get my daughter out of those boots and into a bath. See she dresses properly."

"Yes, suh." As Betta bent to rid me of the boots, Papa continued, "It is abundantly clear you need a lady's maid and companion to keep watch over you. Either that, or I must send you East to some ladies' school, as Randolph has planned for his daughter."

"Please, Papa, do not send me away. I could not bear to be gone from my family for so long. Not after Maman—" I could not continue. The look on Papa's face stopped me.

"A lady's maid, then. When you have completed your bath, go to your room." He put his hands behind his back and took a deep breath, releasing it slowly. "Adrien."

Betta had taken my hand and was pulling me from the hall. "It is not his fault, Papa. I pestered him ever so much to take me along, truly I did, and—"

"Enough. Adrien is a year older and should know better. One of the few duties you have, Adrien, is watching over your sister. She is a young lady, is she not? Not some little brother to run around with you and Isaac in the bushes. I thought you understood that. Now I must hire someone to take care of even this."

Papa's voice faded into muffled sound when Betta closed the door of the indoor kitchen.

Later, Betta brought oatmeal and tea to my room and informed me I was to remain with no dinner or supper until the following morning and to think on proper behavior for a lady.

"What happened to Adrien?"

"Marse tell him the same, Miss Bernadette. Except for the lady part. Then he get a strapping.

"Your papa been grievous, though he hide it better 'n most, but his grief make him testy. Though you young, you needs think about takin your mama's place hereabouts. You and I need do some talkin when you ready, sooner better than later. I helps you all I can, but you got to take up the lady reins of this plantation house afore your time."

Betta placed the breakfast tray on the table next to my bed and hurried out. Papa was cold furious, the worst type of angry, certainly so if he gave Adrien a strapping. Years had passed since the last, which had upset Maman so. Our people would be on tenterhooks until Papa got over this. Maman had cured him of low moods soon after their beginning, but without her, there was no telling how long this one would last.

I sat beneath the counterpane and hugged my knees. Take Maman's place? *How could I, at twelve?* Tears flooded my cheeks. Proper young ladies were supposed to learn how to take care of their home and husband once they got one. *I do not want a husband. Not yet. Maybe never.*

What would Maman say? Take a deep breath and consider your choices. Write them down with consequences of each. Nothing is as terrible as you think.

Maman had given me and Adrien journals on our last name days, and I had never written in mine after the first day. I scrambled out of bed and fetched the journal from beneath my petticoats in my dresser drawer. I copied lessons and wrote letters on a bed desk. That would do for my journal. Many ladies learned to read and write, but most did not learn about history, math, and the sciences as Isaac and I had. States had laws against Isaac learning to read and write, but was Texas one of them? Isaac was already better at math than Adrien.

Maman was correct. Once I wrote my thoughts in my journal, I was sure Papa would never make me marry so soon. Though Papa and Mr. Hart had fought together in the war for freedom from Mexico, they were not friends, not like Will and Adrien, nor like Lily and I. The end of the pen in my mouth—what were they, exactly? *I had never considered this. I will pay attention from here on.*

Maman had been composed, always managed despite any upset around her: *What would Maman do?*

Betta is right. I have been caught up in my misery and neglected to notice Papa's. I must do my best to be the mistress of Blue Hills. The more I am needed by Papa, Adrien, and Lucien, the less chance Papa will send me away to school. I must become indispensable.

Chapter Eighteen
Hartwood

Lily

"Bernadette doesn't have a maidservant following her every-where," Lily Hart declared to her father on a Wednesday morning at breakfast. At eleven, Lily presumed she was grown enough to go about without the company of her girl, Mae, who, at fourteen, was merely three years older.

"You will be a lady," he said. "Paien Villere is not paying the fortune it will cost me to send you to finishing school in Charleston. You want to go to Charleston, do you not?"

Father always brought up Charleston to put her in her place because he knew how desperately she wanted to attend Madame Talvande's French School for Young Ladies.

Hartwood was exceedingly dull. Since Mama died of the yellow fever, there had been no parties, no excursions or picnics, few interesting visitors, and no one with whom to exclaim her way through the latest issues of *Harper's Bazaar* and *Godey's Lady's Book*. Bernadette wanted to read the stories and cared little for fashion.

Adrien was no longer fun. When not teasing, his manner was offhand. He displayed more devotion to that dog of his.

Adrien and Will previously let her and Bernadette join them in their games. After Jacob introduced them to Homer's *Iliad* and other Greek tales, she loved playing Helen to Adrien's Paris. He stole her off to Troy—the second-floor sewing room—while her husband, played by Will, followed with his army—three of the youngest house boys—to rescue her. Paris went to war for her! Only they killed Paris. Then Adrien and Will became other heroes, and they died as well. Heroically, of course. They would never finish killing off one another with those stupid wooden swords. She became irrelevant to their games. She had been irrelevant ever since.

Who cared? She didn't. Foolish boys' games. She was growing up and would soon become a lady. They would see. Especially Adrien. Just because he could speak French, Latin, and Greek. She would too. She would paint lovely pictures and play piano better than Bernadette. He would notice her, then.

"You are pouting, Lily. It doesn't become you." Father always pointed out her laxities.

She stared at her plate of cold biscuits that rose like oozing islands above grease-streaked white gravy dotted with shiny globules of pork sausage.

"May I please be excused?"

She glanced at her father. A great dollop of cream gravy clung to his beard at the corner of his mouth. "You may," he said. Gravy hung there, undisturbed by speech.

She dropped her napkin on the table and sped by Jacob on her way out the door. She ran down the hall to the indoor washroom and upchucked into the nearest bucket. Thank goodness it was clean and empty—or had been. Mae appeared at her side with a damp hankie and a cool glass of water. She must have been waiting in the hall.

"I cannot abide greasy sausage," Lily said, returning the empty glass to her servant.

"No, miss."

"Ham is acceptable, well-smoked and lean, but not that disgusting —ugh." She shivered from head to toe. "I'm going to the music room to practice. Bring me a pitcher of water and a cup of hot tea."

"Yes, miss."

She would practice scales until that dreadful sausage went right out of her head.

No one had to tell her to practice, as she was determined to play piano better than anyone when she arrived at Madame Talvande's. Father had purchased the finest piano in the county, if not all of Texas, and their slaves kept it gleaming. The constant humidity meant a man had to come up from Galveston twice a year to tune it, but fortunately there were also a couple other pianos to tune on his journey upriver, as well as the one at Blue Hills. Mr. Wittenberg said he would tune their Bösendorfer as often as they wished, it was such a fine instrument.

The drawing room was quite large, if a little gloomy, as Father insisted they keep the drapes closed so the sun would not fade the exquisite Persian carpets and the furniture imported from England and France. She perched on the piano bench and settled herself, smoothing the folds in her skirts, until Mae returned with her tea. Mae fetched a small box of lucifers from a pocket in her apron and lit the oil lamp that rested on a doily directly above the music folios.

Lily was so engaged in the first part of a Bach Polonaise that she nearly lost her way when long fingers settled on her left shoulder. Her heart jumped. It was Jacob. Father announced himself from a distance. Will never touched her from behind or without her acknowledgment. Only Jacob did. She stopped playing and dropped her hands to her lap.

"Soon you will play better than Adrien," he said. "Better than Bernadette."

"I expect to be better," she said. "I practice more." She leaned forward the littlest bit and felt his hand slide away. She watched his tall figure cross the room to perch like a tomcat in a teacup on the Queen Anne chair in front of the draped window.

"I doubt Adrien has practiced lately, what with the death of his mother," he said. "Texas boys have no business playing piano." He leaned back, crossed ankle over knee and dangled his long arms over the chair.

She looked at her hands in her lap. "Why should you care?"

A heartbeat of silence. *How long can he sit in that dainty chair? Will it give way?* She had to mash her lips together to keep from giggling.

"I don't," he said. "You want his attention. But you won't get it playing piano."

She felt heat rise from her neck. Her nails dug into her palms. Would she never learn when to keep her mouth shut? "Has Will left for school?"

"He wanted to make sure you were over your . . . illness. But he was already late, and we both heard you playing. Was that bit of theater another excuse to avoid going yourself?"

"It was that awful sausage."

"You got over it soon enough."

She began playing scales.

"Look at me," he said.

She raised her chin and looked right into those cold blue eyes of his and would not look away no matter what.

"That's my girl. You have brains in that head and ambition beyond your years. Only eleven, and already all this isn't enough. You'll need more than a pretty face and that fancy school to get what you want. There's another sort of education available if you will accept it."

Oh, pooh. Perhaps her expression gave her away.

He smiled and stood. The chair seemed fine.

Pulling the drapery aside, he looked out the window. "Mother was lovely, wasn't she? And had a fine education at one of those boarding schools in Virginia and played Chopin. What did it get her?"

This beautiful house and what it contained. The lovely clothes, servants, parties. And Father. Lily's room had been across the hall from Father's and Mother's. She had buried herself beneath the bedcovers when she heard thuds and sobs that sometimes came from Mother's bedroom. Mother would remain in her room indisposed for days, occasionally a week, receiving no one.

She could not forget the night that fourteen-year-old Jacob interfered and received a black eye and a broken arm for his pains. Mother had begged him to never interfere again. When Jacob was sixteen, he had slaves move her bedroom to the far end of the house. Father never said a word. Fortunately, Will's room had always been farther down the hall. He hadn't grown suspicious until he was nearly twelve, which was when yellowjack took Mother away.

Did Mother have a choice?

Lily shifted on the piano bench. *I will never, ever let a man treat me like Father treated Mother. I will absolutely die first.*

Jacob was still staring out the window. Was he looking for something specific or waiting to hear what she would say?

"In September, I will leave for Charleston," she said. "What sort of education?"

"One of which only you and I must know. An education for which Randolph and your new teachers would thoroughly chastise you. One that, if you persist as I think you will, may prevent you from being totally ruled by such as our ignominious father. Such an education will give you something with which to occupy yourself."

He had her. They both knew it. But she could not guess what he meant. She would not beg him for an answer. "You only call Father by his name when he is not present," she said.

How his eyes sparkled. "I do believe," he said, "you may have every man in the county begging for your favors when you return."

Oh! She turned back to the piano. If only she had a fan. Time to hide behind a fan, to flutter it and glance up with only her eyes showing. She crossed her ankles and tucked her feet beneath the bench. When he made her feel like a child, she hated him. She was looking at the keyboard but could hear him moving across the room until he stood not two feet away. She smelled his aftershave.

"Books," he said. "Not schoolbooks, not silly romances, but books about the real world, not some fool's wish for the world."

"Books?" She couldn't help the disappointed tone in her voice.

Such an expectant look on his face. "Books no young lady dare read. Not according to proper society. But you can, and, afterward, we'll discuss them. Then, if you can assure me that no one snoops through your correspondence once you are in Charleston, I'll mail them to you."

How intriguing, though she had never been one for reading.

He put a hand on the edge of the piano. "A bargain. If, by the end of summer you don't wish to continue, we'll stop."

A whole six months. Seven or eight books? She could manage that, especially if those books held secrets she was not supposed to learn.

Chapter Nineteen
Blue Hills

Adrien

"*Blam, blam, blam!*" Feathers flew everywhere in diffused dawn light. The chilly December air smelled of briny earth, pond, pine, and now, gunpowder.

"Blazes, Slick, we'd have waited all morning for you to shoot."

Burly Clay Thatcher was our gallant leader—able-bodied, devil-may-care, reckless, and prone to misbehavior—the ideal of a wild Texian. Will, as second-in-command, was "sound on the goose." Reliable, not one to say much, he had kept us from grief more than once. Me? No longer unacceptable Adrien, but Slick. I fast-talked us out of trouble when Will's suggestions were not followed or failed. Women loved the manners and French accent I poured on rather thickly whenever we deemed needful.

Will, Clay, and Henry Carlyle were up and out of the fog-shrouded gully we hid in, leaving me, my unfired shotgun, and footprints behind in the red, sticky mud around the pond. Our prints joined those of the cows, deer, and other critters. Salmon and lavender water reflected the dawn sky, and patterns made by tiny striders skated among the reeds. The wood ducks were magnificent: green-crested head over a dark face with white stripes on both sides of its throat and reddish chest. I could not shoot one.

At thirteen, I was nearly a man by Texas standards. Yet I loved poetry, playing piano, reading, and gazing at birds in sunrise skies. To say nothing of my regard for Isaac, who was the fifth member of our group, assigned to hold horses while we went about our doughty deeds. Hunting was merely my excuse for glorious dawn wanderings about the hills and oak-thick ravines in the cool, birdsong air of our East Texas country.

I thrust myself out of reverie, rose, and followed the others.

A soaked Courage dropped the duck at my feet and shook pond water over us. Eager brown eyes gazed up at me. He had fetched rabbits, squirrels, and quail before, but this was the first time he had retrieved a kill from the water. "Good boy." I caressed his head, scratched behind an ear, then took up the beautiful bird and offered it to Clay. "Here. This is yours. My mind is not on hunting today." I settled my gun, pointed down in the crook of my other arm, and continued fondling Courage's ear as he leaned against my knee, dripping water onto my boot.

"Do tell," said Clay, and spat sideways into the reeds. He could hit a grasshopper at nearly three feet. I had seen Jacob hit the center of a spittoon at four.

"I need to take care of (*what do I call it?*) a vexation." Best to settle the Rosanne question that had been bedeviling me for months.

"By all means, do," Henry said with a snickering sideways glance.

On the ride home, I remembered to stuff my saddlebags full of boughs and cedar branches in lieu of birds, and Isaac gathered a few for his parents' cabin. Bernadette had insisted we decorate the house for the holidays: "Maman would expect it." That statement settled any issue, at least as far as Papa and I were concerned.

I had practically fallen out of my chair the first night she had lit Papa's pipe for him the way Maman used to. His eyebrows raised, and the pipe nearly came loose in his hand. "Thank you, Bernadette." It took three tries to catch his tobacco before the match went out. Papa was patient.

A couple weeks before, I had caught her and Betta with their heads together. "This be women business, young Marse," Betta said, dismissing me with a turn of her head. Fine. I was not interested in women's business. I shied from recalling the last time my sister showed interest in *my* business. I would not again bend for a strapping.

Berni's face lit up when she saw my arms full of greens. "You are back early. How lovely and fragrant!"

"I'll hang them. Or whatever you want." I stood in the hall, needles and cedar up to my chin.

Betta walked in and spread old newsprint at my feet. "Drop 'em here Marse, afore you have 'em all over the carpet."

"You are the best brother." Berni hugged me. Then, "Ew," raised her arms and peered at the bodice of her blue day dress.

"Oh, Lord. Sorry. I am afraid I got into some pine pitch. I brought home cedar and fir, though, so the rest should be okay."

"That pitch make a plumb fine salve, but take some doin to get off clothes," Betta said. "You both best change afore it attach itself to anything else."

"I am sorry, Berni."

"I dare say, in payment, I shall keep you busy all morning helping me decorate." Grinning, she lifted her voluminous skirts and spun toward the stairs. She was true to her word, and I followed her around the rooms much as one of our people might, fetching and carrying.

We finished in time for supper. Betta included extra candles and colorful holly berries with the greens, and the house did look festive.

"My, you have brought the outside in," Papa exclaimed when he and Lucien came through the back door.

Supper's enticing aroma added to the scents of cedar and fir. Esther had prepared a delicious meal of smoked ham, beans, and collards, along with her famous pecan pie for dessert. I did not want to interrupt an excellent supper by asking my question too soon, so I waited until Simon served tea.

"Papa, may I ask you a question?"

"Seems you just did." Papa wiped his mouth and put his napkin next to his plate. "Go ahead, Son."

I nearly changed my mind, as Lucien, Berni, and Papa became still and attentive.

"Who is Rosanne?"

Lucien, directly across the table on Papa's right, stiffened and blurted something crude under his breath.

"Where did you hear that name?" Papa said, his voice low and fierce, white-knuckled fingers gripping the edge of the table.

Had the roof fallen in? I barely got out, "Simon."

"When?"

Lord save me. "When Maman . . . he said Rosanne, said it was her fault, she caused—"

"Son-of-a-bitch." Lucien bellowed, and leaped from his chair, knocking it over.

"Lucien!" Papa planted his hands on the table.

"Confound it, Papa, I won't stand for it. Not from Simon and not from this no-account nancy!" Lucien threw down his napkin, spun, barged around the table and out the door.

Papa began to rise from his chair, hesitated, and slowly settled, both hands gripping the edge of the table as though to keep him from collapsing beneath it. No one spoke for several moments. I dared not. My heart thudded against my chest; I had never heard Lucien, nor anyone, speak to Papa in such a manner.

Papa said, "I might have avoided this confrontation by telling you about that woman sooner, but I never expected to hear her name again. I hoped, prayed, I would not." He glanced across the room to the painting of Maman and us on the wall, took a breath, and continued.

"Rosanne was the personal slave of my first wife, Lucien's mother. She was Lucien's wet nurse when Isabella died shortly after birthing him. Rosanne raised him and practically ran this house until I brought your maman, Betta, and Simon here from Galveston. Rosanne felt her place was usurped."

Taking another deep breath, he straightened his arms and sat back in his chair. "Rosanne practiced magic—voodoo, it was called in Louisiana. Some folks credit such nonsense. She caused problems among our people here at Blue Hills, and her reputation spread among nearby plantations. Lucien was nine when I sold her." Papa's eyes focused elsewhere before including the two of us again. "He was devastated."

"If either of you have further questions concerning this matter, ask them now, for I never want to hear her name again. Bernadette?"

"No, Papa."

"Adrien?"

My heart banged in my chest, but I had to ask. "Why did Simon believe she caused Maman's death?"

"Simon and Betta, some of the other slaves believed she was jealous of their position in this house and was responsible for everything bad that happened here, including your maman's miscarriages."

Miscarriages? What miscarriages?

"Your maman was overjoyed when you were born healthy. We both were. It was no wonder she doted on you, Adrien. Our people believed our fortunes improved because Rosanne was no longer around." He stood and regarded each of us. "I will never hear that woman's name again after this. Am I clear?"

"Yes, sir," Bernadette and I said in unison.

Papa dropped his napkin on the table and stiffly left the room, leaving me with a baffled longing for something I could not define. His anxious look and trembling hands at her name kept me frozen in place.

Nobody came to clear the table. Bernadette looked small opposite me, that smallness belied by her voice when she spoke.

"Oh, Adrien, why must you choose the most inopportune timing for such, such a disturbance? All these months and you ask that horrid question a week before Christmas. I have tried so hard to make everything perfect for Papa, and you ruined it."

"Perfect?" I could not stop myself. "Nothing will be perfect again."

The moment the words were out, I wished I could swallow them, choke on them. My Lord, the way her face scrunched up and tears came into her eyes. I nearly fell over my own feet scrambling out of my chair, around the table and on my knees before her.

I grasped her hands. "Berni, do not listen to me. You are right, I am an idiot. You are so good, like Maman. Truly you are, and I ruin everything. You have made Papa happy. Surely you saw how content he was before I asked that question. How do you put up with me? You must—"

"Enough, Adrien, please, you are giving me the hiccoughs."

This was obvious enough. Time for Betta's remedy. Still on my knees, I pulled a glass of water across the table. "Drink this slowly while holding your breath." I waited while she did so, holding my breath with her.

After putting the glass down, she gazed at me appraisingly. "You can get up now."

"Are you sure?"

"Oh, do." There was that old, bemused hint in her eyes, thank goodness.

I sat on the edge of Papa's chair, facing her. "I truly am sorry. My remark was totally uncalled for."

"Papa will not sell Simon, will he?"

"Of course not." I hoped saying so made it true. "I have never heard of him selling anyone." Simon was a young man when we were children. He suffered the brunt of our games and silliness with good humor and carried me pig-a-back everywhere. I could not imagine the house without Simon at his customary place in the hall or ushering in guests. He was our majordomo, butler, guardian, and playmate, all in one.

No, Papa would never sell Simon. He would get a good dressing down. I doubted matters would come to worse than that.

Was it how shockingly the memory of that woman affected Papa that he never noted what Lucien had called me, or that the name-calling was of no significance to him?

It mattered little considering the eventual disaster.

Chapter Twenty

Bernadette

Early this morning, Adrien pulled me out of bed, down the stairs, and out the back porch in gown, slippers, and Papa's overcoat snatched from the hall. Guiding me over to the trees lining Oak Creek, he declared, "Look."

Night's rain-frosted plants had become a magnificent, sparkling fairyland. Every tree, bush, fern, and vine glittered in the early dawn sun; a spider web spangled with tiny diamonds. He held my hand as cold wet seeped into my feet, and I scarcely dared blink as sunlight gleamed and shimmered the magic away to drip onto the ground.

Alas, later that morning, my composure was breached when I had to hurry upstairs upon one pretext or another as some bauble reminded me of Maman and a past Christmas. Upon reaching my room, I soaked my pillow like a dribbling baby. I blew an unseemly honk into my handkerchief before getting myself in hand. *This will not do, not if you are to be mistress of Blue Hills.* I rose, wiped invisible wrinkles from my skirts, and strode from my bedroom door and down the stairs.

That afternoon's Christmas dinner may not have been as sumptuous as previous years, but the ham, gravy, pheasant, cranberry sauce, squash, greens, corn, rolls, pumpkin, and pecan pies were delicious.

As we finished, the fire in the hearth died down to hot coals. Simon laid on another log—only one, rightly judged as the room yet felt warm from plenty of victuals, candles, and kerosene lamps set about.

Esther carefully placed one of Maman's crystal wine glasses on the table before me, then Papa, Lucien, and Adrien. A German glassmaker had cut delicate vines and roses on each before they were brought to Blue Hills in boxes filled with straw. Simon followed, pouring red wine, a first for me. Papa must intend for me to have wine. Hands in my lap, I glanced at Adrien to my right. His brows rose with a shrug, indicating he knew no more than me.

Simon paused behind Papa, Betta and Esther on either side.

Papa fingered the stem of his glass. "I trust y'all have been avoiding speaking of your maman, but it is time to end such grieving." Papa's eyes drifted around to each of us as he spoke. "I want to remember her, and speak of her, of all the splendid times when my wife, your maman, was with us. She made this house the fine home it is. She gave me children of whom I am proud." He pushed his chair back on the carpet and stood, raising his glass toward the painting. "To Madeleine Fortier Villere, the former mistress of Blue Hills."

Adrien stood, raising his glass, followed by Lucien, who turned to face the painting.

Thank goodness I was not expected to stand, as the wine was warm going down and warmer flushing up into my head. I hardly tasted it for all the feelings rushing about every part of me. I nearly did not hear when Papa continued.

"I also toast my daughter, Bernadette, who is fast following in her mother's footsteps as the new mistress of Blue Hills."

Fortunately, my glass was on the table by then, or I might have dropped it. Adrien grinned before taking a drink. Even Lucien was smiling. The warmth that flushed my face and down my neck was not entirely due to the wine.

And Papa. He did appear truly happy, and that happiness reached his eyes. This Christmas had turned out much better than I hoped. *Please let this moment last and last.*

Chapter Twenty-One
Hartwood

Jacob

After concluding another unpleasant dinner, Jacob sat at the far end of the table facing his father. Randolph Hart's shadow loomed across the damask tablecloth, impeding the fancy patterns created by soft January light seeping through lace curtains draping the window behind him. After Jacob's mother died, Randolph insisted his son take her chair where father wouldn't have to turn to give Jacob his orders. He could detect the least sign of hesitation or defiance.

How absurd to eat breakfast, dinner, and supper at a table that seated fourteen when there were often only the two of them—or four, when Will and Lily were home.

Randolph appeared a southern gentleman in a silk brocade vest and frock coat, his skull made even larger by thick graying hair. His trimmed mustache and beard adorned a chin his detractors declared thrust forward like the prow of an old warship. His close-mouthed smile, rarely encountered unless he got the best of someone, concealed yellow, tobacco-stained teeth.

He raised a linen napkin and wiped a corner of his mouth. "I suppose you haven't heard from Alvaro or you would have told me."

"The boy must have run farther than expected." Jacob said. "But he won't outrun Colt. He's the best tracker in the county."

"So you say. You should've gone with him."

"I trust Colt. He'll bring Gabriel back." Colt Alvaro had been his companion since boyhood. If he couldn't trust him, he could trust no one.

"He'd better, or you'll go after him on your own hook. That nigger's worth too much to go scot-free."

The double doors to the hall opened and Henry, their butler, announced, "Scuse me, suh. Mista Alvaro be here, suh."

"Speak of the devil," Randolph said, shoving his chair from the table. He opened the top button of his coat, sat back, and snapped the fingers of his right hand. A mulatto boy standing in the shadows immediately stepped to Randolph's side and flipped open a humidor. Dormancy reigned while Randolph chose a cigar. The boy clicked the lid shut and lit the tip of the cigar. Randolph took a long draw, raised his chin, and sent a cloud of smoke spiraling above his head. "Send him in."

During this performance, Jacob had raised his empty cup of coffee and pretended to drink—a habit he had developed in the presence of the old reprobate—to be doing something, anything, at such moments.

Tipping his head and shoulders, Henry retreated, and a rangy, beak-nosed man who looked anywhere from thirty to forty replaced him. Long, black hair tied with a leather thong at the nape of his neck, he gave the impression of someone uncomfortable within a house. He took one step into the room, gripped a ragged, dusty, wide-brimmed hat with white-knuckled fists, and stood straight as an arrow. "I found your man south where Doe Run meets the Brazos. He's outside, unharmed."

"A fellow of few words and to the point," Randolph said, an elbow on the arm of his chair and fingers rolling the cigar. He spit into the brass spittoon on the floor to his right as his gray eyes slid to his son. "You will discover where Gabriel hid that first night and who helped him. He was on Blue Hills land, and it was a Blue Hills nigger who hid the bastard, but I can't go to Paien Villere without words from Gabriel's own mouth. I must have names. But don't kill him. The son-of-a-bitch is too valuable."

Not like the runner you beat to death years ago in Galveston, eh?
Jacob clutched his thighs.

"What are you waiting for? Another cup of coffee?"

"No, sir." Jacob motioned to Colt, and the two hastened from the room.

❧

Colt had stripped and splayed the boy belly down on the ground, ankles and wrists strapped with leather to four posts pounded into the trampled dirt. Colt could be depended upon. The two had been cohorts since Jacob befriended him when Colt was twelve and Jacob two years younger—after Colt escaped from the Comanches. Colt was a Tonkawa, and the Tonks were here on the Brazos when Randolph Hart arrived; they were here when the Mexicans arrived before Austin.

Jacob stood at an angle from the boy's feet, arms folded at his own chest, legs apart. *Boy*, Jacob called him—at twenty-seven the young man displayed cruelly before him was older than Jacob by four years, and in excellent condition. Fine musculature, skin the color of mahogany and glossy with sweat—in January.

Jacob could practically smell the man's fear. If *he* could smell the heat from the fire in the nearby smithy, the sharp tang of hot grease and iron, so could the man in the dirt.

It was called a slut: an iron bar punctured with holes that allowed sizzling grease to make its way into tender flesh.

His father expected Jacob to be good at this dirty little chore. He went about the job patiently, methodically, and thoroughly. Hartwood enslaved didn't need chastising more than once. No man, or woman, forgot what they learned under Jacob's hand.

He crouched on his heels a foot from the curly head and spoke in a confidential tone only the two of them could hear. "You stayed at Blue Hills the first night. At least one slave there hid you. Speak one name. No one will blame you. Paien Villere will not. He won't even beat the one who helped you. If you tell me now, I will stop. Your choice."

A tongue wet full lips, but no words came forth.

Jacob ran caressing fingers across shoulders that trembled at his touch.

An hour later, and Jacob was sweating the same as the man at his feet.

Didn't the man believe he could stop this? Punishment had its limits: Twenty lashes, the slut, and twenty lashes, followed by the slut and twenty more lashes. He stopped at intervals to let them know what was finished, what was to come. Contrary to most, there was no audience. He made punishment an intimate dance between himself and the punished. Only Colt Alvaro stood nearby, watching in silence in case he was needed. He never was.

The hot iron, the sizzling grease bubbled skin, popping dark flesh. Twenty lashes slashed open neatly laid furrows across his back. All Jacob's urging brought forth nothing but screams, moans, and spittle.

Twenty more lashes, and he dropped the end of the whip into a bucket filled with pink water, drew the braided leather through his gloved hand to remove the ragged, bloody flesh. His right arm and shoulder ached. Twisting the whip into a loop, he crouched near the grayed face running with sweat. One palm at the man's neck he murmured into his ear.

"Gabriel. You see, I have called you by name. You are a fool if you believe the name you keep is worth so much. You think this is all? We've hardly begun. I will have my supper while you and the flies get acquainted, then we'll continue. It's amazing how annoying those little buggers can be on one's open flesh. Consider how easy it would be to end this. One name. One place. You could whisper it in my ear."

This foul duty had ruined his appetite.

᭞

Jacob was patient. His father was not.

"You've got nothing? I thought you'd have him squealing like a pig. What the Sam Hill you been doing out there? You off your feed?"

I am now.

"Doing what?" Will said, entering the dining room. Adrien and Lily trailed after him.

"Plantation business," Randolph said, turning and heading for his place at the table. His tone was familiar to all and brooked no more questions.

As Jacob sat at the opposite end of the table from his father, the room took on warmth at night it lacked during the day. Light from mirror-backed kerosene wall lamps and two sets of candelabras flashed off the silver. This evening's addition of Will, Lily, and Adrien might help to dispel the sick anxiety that had settled over him like muck from a hog pen. He looked forward to school nights when Adrien stayed at Hartwood. The boy had proved to be both intelligent and ingenuous—and willing to tackle any adventure Jacob suggested.

Good-natured Will generally found something interesting or exciting about his day to share, and Jacob watched Lily's inquisitive blue eyes dance from Will to Adrien to him and back again, but not at Randolph, despite her being Father's little darling. The old reprobate planned that her marriage would be his next step up the sociopolitical ladder. He was oblivious to the fact that she avoided him like a hen would a fox.

Jacob remained an ear for her complaints, a shoulder to sob her woes upon, and a chest on which to pound her frustrations.

He caught Adrien's black eyes and held them. The boy no longer smiled as he used to when their eyes met, not since losing his mother. Danger lay with a boy that alluring.

He found himself torturing the soft linen napkin in his lap. At this moment, he wanted not one of the three near him.

❧

Colt had lit several pitched torches so Jacob could see what he was about. The entire area stunk with blood and sweat and fear. The flies had got themselves off with the onset of dark.

He laid open bone with the last, and the man passed out—had to be revived by a pail of water.

Jacob stared past the edge of the torchlight where he caught a glimpse of a trotting coyote, its tongue dangling—brought close by the smell of blood.

Jacob turned. "Give me a name," he growled. And struck. Ten lashes flung blood and bits of flesh. *Speak!*

"Give. Me. A. Name." A raspy roar. *Speak. He commands. Father commands.* Blow after blow. *God damn you!* "Name." The word came out a hoarse wail—

Colt grasped his arm and Jacob staggered like a drunk. Colt held him up. He was covered in sweat and gore, gasping for breath.

"The man is out and feels nothing," Colt said. "You'll kill him."

Jacob blinked, mouth open, chest heaving. *Kill him.* He turned, took five strides toward the house before opening his hand, dropping the whip, upchucking his supper, and kept going—through the rear door, up the servant's stairs and down the hall. Outside Father's bedroom sat his personal slave on the floor who stumbled to his feet, a gaping expression on his face, as though he might block the door, but stepped back as Jacob pushed his way inside, and there were Father and a young dark girl together in his bed.

Jacob, covered in sweat, blood, and pieces of flesh, declared, "He will not speak."

"You." Father flung aside the counterpane, stood, aghast, eyes glaring, lips twisting and spitting from his beard. "Get out." Louder, "Get out!"

Jacob closed the door, leaving blood on the knob and stains on the carpet, and walked down the hall much more slowly than when he came, a grim smile on his mouth.

❧

Open double doors threw a rectangle of hazy February sunlight across the cypress planks of the Hart carriage house. Jacob and Adrien were barefoot and in trousers only, skin gleaming with exertion. Their fists circled before them, ready either to punch or grab, depending upon perceived necessity, both shuffled sideways in unison. Jacob jabbed, and Adrien slid away into Jacob's left cross and went down. He pushed against the floor, leaning on his arms, shaking his head.

Jacob held out his hand to help him up. *Another match or so, and I won't wait. He'll be ready.*

"You had better react faster next time," Jacob said, grinning from one side of his mouth. "In a real fight, no one'll give you time to recover." *He's got to learn to defend himself against anything.*

The boy wiped blood from his lip with the back of his hand. Knees slightly bent, chest pumping, he circled around Jacob.

Jacob followed him with his eyes. Saw withheld anger, determination not to be caught the same way again. He had nerve, and he wasn't stupid.

I must play my cards right and not rush the thing. He will be worth the long haul. Funny how fathers can be blind and careless, even Paien Villere.

Chapter Twenty-Two
Blue Hills

Paien

Since arriving in East Texas with his first wife in the summer of '24, every February Paien liked to check on the new seedlings. He could have left the task to those who kept the fires. He trusted every man, or he wouldn't have the job. But he preferred this phase of growing tobacco more than any other. There was promise in the rows of bright green shoots pushing out of damp soil. The new leaves were harbingers of his own family line—his children and his children's children—who would have a life of which his forebears could not have dreamed.

He enjoyed the welcome greetings of his people when he cantered up through the rising mist on Max. He loved the sweet smell of turned soil and burning cedar and pine. He took his time walking around every bed, peering beneath their thin linen covers, surveying the rows, sharing a mug of hot, spiced cider with their caretakers—names and families of whom he knew as well as his own.

He joined Marcus and three men at one of the fires. They stood like statues in the rising sun as the fires crackled, popped, and sent pale smoke spiraling skyward in the still air. Each held a mug and stared into the flames in companionable silence, inhaling the scent of burning cedar and hot spiced cider.

Paien heard the sound of two horses cantering down from the north. He could tell by the carefully blank expressions on his companions' faces that whoever it was, was not welcome.

He turned as the riders pulled up.

"Morning, Paien." Randolph Hart swung down from his gray stallion.

Paien forced a smile, switched his mug to his left hand, and offered his right. "What brings you out this chilly morning, Randolph? How about a mug of cider to warm your bones?" He nodded to the other figure, Randolph's overseer, Jessup Briley, a squat, beefy man he had never cared for from somewhere in West Texas.

If Paien Villere were superstitious, he might have assigned meaning to the fact that Randolph found him outside the north drying barn next to the big old oak this morning. There were so many other places he might have been—any of the other barns, in the stables checking on the mare in foal, or one of the fields. But the north barn and field were closest to Hartwood.

Randolph had no idea they had hid Gabriel here two entire nights. Then Paien's heart took a leap. Unless Gabriel had given them up.

Randolph passed a fast glimpse around the others and said, "No thanks. This is not a social call." He turned and stepped away, making it clear that Paien should follow where they could speak together privately.

Paien handed his cup to Marcus. This wasn't the first time he'd been put in a subservient position by Randolph Hart, and it likely wouldn't be the last. There was little he could do about it, the man being his nearest neighbor and of some note in their far-flung community. Their wives had been friends, and their sons and daughters still were. Not to mention their practically inviolate history of having fought side by side in the War of Independence from Mexico. When Paien joined Houston's army in the summer of '46, Randolph remained behind to make sure both their young families were safe. When so many East Texas families fled before Santa Anna's soldiers, he had kept them safe and hadn't joined the fight until outside Harrisburg.

Randolph wasted no time once they moved away from the others. "I expect you read about that runaway we caught a few weeks back."

"I did, though a couple days later than folks in Washington. I thought perhaps you made sure word got around to discourage such a thing from happening again." Marcus had told him of the vile matter before it was written up in the *Brazos Farmer*.

"You mean the questioning."

Questioning. Paien folded his hands behind his back where Randolph could not see the tension with which he was fisting them together. "The paper did not say much about that, only that the fellow would not admit to having any help."

"That's why I'm here. He had help, and it came from one of your niggers. My tracker trailed him straight as the crow flies to your land."

"I'm sorry to hear that, Randolph. Where exactly did the trail lead?"

"He lost it on Oak Creek north of your place, but picked it up again farther south. That was in January, those nights of freezing rain. He must've laid up somewhere on your land and someone helped him. I'd surely appreciate it, Paien, if you would get to the bottom of this."

"I'll do what I can. Though I expect Marcus would have already told me if he heard anything." *Thank God the man kept silent.* Relief, followed by guilt for Gabriel's condition.

Randolph inhaled and narrowed his eyes. "You ever consider that you trust that overseer of yours a mite too much? You always been too soft on your niggers. You got to keep a tight rein, same as you would an unruly horse. These coloreds got no more sense than children, but they are damn stronger." His neck and face turned pink, going toward red.

Might he suffer from apoplexy? If so, might Jacob be better or worse? Better the devil you know.

"I recall a couple years ago that boy from Independence escaped down the Brazos right through here," Randolph said. "Too many niggers are running to Mexico, and if they think they can get away with it, by God, we'll rue the day, that's all. We'll rue the day." He spat to the side, snatched his sweat-stained plantation hat off to wipe a hand through his gray hair, and rammed the hat back on again.

I'm not the one who's had six run on me. "I'll see what I can learn, Randolph, and let you know."

"Well, I guess that's all I can ask."

Thank the Lord, it is.

As the two rode away, Marcus came to his side, and they watched them disappear over the hill.

"I wonder why he waited this long," Paien said, eyes on the horizon.

"Maybe he was weighing the importance of your good will against the value of his Negroes."

"I doubt it. Perhaps he hoped I would come to him first." Hands clasped behind his back, Paien pivoted toward Marcus and said, "A test. Once I learned of his problem and his solution, how would I react? 'Soft' with my 'niggers' as I am."

"Do you think he suspects?"

Paien scowled, mouth twisting into a smile. "If I were from the North, perhaps. But a white man from Louisiana? Such a thing would never occur to him."

"Even so."

"Yes. Even so. We cannot always depend upon someone like Gabriel keeping silent." A dark cloud passed over Paien's mind, thinking of what happened to the man, despite how they had helped him escape. "Tell John of Mr. Hart's visit, and that there will be no more 'possum hunting' for a while. I'm going to check the seedlings at the south barn."

John Beaumont had been their blacksmith since their arrival in '24 and could be trusted with anything, including hiding runaways.

Marcus nodded, turned to move away, and hesitated.

Paien said, "Something else?"

Marcus glanced off to his left, crossed his arms, lowered his head, then looked up at Paien's face. "I haven't wanted—" He took a breath. "This is about Adrien, if I may speak."

What in God's name had any of this to do with Adrien? "Go on."

"Adrien's been seeing a good deal of Jacob Hart. I thought you should know."

He gazed at Marcus, whose steady brown eyes met his. Paien turned aside, looked off into the distance, and stroked his jaw. Why did his youngest son seek Jacob Hart's company? Wasn't the younger brother, Will, Adrien's friend?

"All right. Thank you, Marcus."

He would not ask Marcus anything more. Marcus and his people were aware Jacob was "skillful" with Randolph's slaves. Of course, Adrien wasn't acquainted with this particular skill in the same way women weren't, and a good many "upstanding" white men weren't. Or perhaps, more accurately, they would never admit such a thing went on.

Enslaved were privy to everything that occurred with their own, well before anyone else. They were privy to what occurred under the roofs of their white masters as well—proof of the pudding—as when Marcus found it necessary to tell him what was going on with his own son. How ironic that he should suffer such a thing. There was no going back. There was never any going back, even if he wanted.

He waited until Marcus rode off before heading over to the massive oak to get his horse. This old oak was special, and he would never have it cut down, as penance lay among its roots. A constant reminder of his mortal sin.

Jacob had always been a gentleman around him and his family, and there should be no problem with Adrien spending time with the young man. Yet Jacob must possess a violent, perhaps even a vicious, streak if he was capable of treating a human being the way he treated Gabriel and others before him. Negroes were considered by many to be no different from animals, though Paien would never treat an animal in such a manner.

Paien tightened his stallion's saddle girth and took up the reins. Why did Adrien seek out Jacob, who was young but years older than him? Settling his weight on one foot, Paien stretched his arms against the saddle, and lowered his head between them. Adrien, his head full of books and poetry, was ripe for some sort of hero. Young Jacob—fit, good-looking, an excellent shot, and tearing about the country on that wild stallion of his—would attract an impressionable young boy like Adrien. Though Adrien was a bit past the age of hero worship, he was late in developing a man's responsibilities. Madeleine's fault, keeping him so close to her. *And my fault for letting her and not keeping a tighter rein on the boy.*

His hands became fists, and the muscles in his arms tightened as, eyes closed, he planted both feet solidly on the grassy ground. The stallion shifted, lifting and swishing his tail. Anger rose that Madeleine was gone from him, before admitting to grief, to how much he yet missed her. His lower lip quivered. God, he missed her. He leaned into the stallion, pressed his forehead against the saddle. He could almost feel his beloved Madeleine in his arms, her warm breath against his ear.

He breathed in the soothing odor of leather, of horse. Exhaled.

A jay scolded from the oak above. Paien raised his head, gathered the reins, swung into the saddle and turned Max toward the south barn. From here on, he would pay more mind to Bernadette and Adrien. He had been neglectful; that must cease.

$$\maltese$$

A cold rain blew in from the southwest, and by evening Paien noted with satisfaction the warmth of the supper fire and his two youngest to his left. Lucien was visiting the Camden family west toward Brenham and wouldn't return until tomorrow afternoon, ostensibly to help with their new barn-raising. There was an additional reason—eighteen-year-old Joanna Camden.

Paien glanced to his right at the painting of Madeleine and their children. Paien had wanted her painted with her beautiful hair down around her shoulders and, after some cajoling, she had obliged. After his promise to remove the painting if anyone but close friends and family came to supper, as it was not proper for one and all to see a married woman with her hair down.

He lowered his head. "Bless us, O Lord, and these your gifts, which we are about to receive from your bounty, through Christ our Lord. Amen."

His family's voices joining in the "Amen" gave him comfort, which he found endearing with the response of his two youngest. *How have I overlooked them for so long? Thirteen-year-old Bernadette is practically a woman—she is becoming as beautiful as Madeleine. How many young bucks have already noticed her?*

Esther entered with a large tureen and dished soup into his bowl with a silver ladle. He breathed in the wonderful aroma of pork, onions, tomatoes, and spices. Mmm, one of his favorites. Esther was a treasure. She moved on to Adrien when Bernadette said, "Is he asking her tonight, Papa?"

He couldn't resist. "Is who asking what?"

Esther caught his eye and smiled as she finished dishing out Bernadette's soup.

"Papa-a-a."

"He better. There will be barely enough time to post the banns and have a wedding before transplanting." The taste was every bit as good as the aroma. Just the thing to take the chill out of his bones.

Bernadette laughed. "Even a wedding must make way for tobacco."

He glanced at her over his soup spoon. "This is our life, as you well know."

"Yes, Papa," she said grinning.

Mintie removed emptied bowls as Simon and Esther brought in plates of beans, corn, cornbread, baked squash, venison in a spicy tomato-and-cheese sauce, and pitchers of buttermilk.

"Save room for two kinds of pie comin up," Esther said, "apple and custard." She stood back rather imperiously wiping her hands on her apron.

Simon came around pouring buttermilk while Paien served up the plates. "Who took the deer, Simon? It's a buck?"

"It is, sir. Your son got it at dawn."

"Before he left?"

"Adrien, sir."

He glanced at his youngest, who lowered his glass.

"You took a buck?"

"Yes, sir." He wiped his mouth with a linen napkin. "One shot to the heart."

"Your first, isn't it?"

"Yes, sir. I found him south about a mile from the Brazos. Just me and Courage, but Courage was good—stayed close and quiet. We were downwind. I was lucky. I did not expect to find anything, but there he was, like out of some dream. I mean, well. It was all so perfect. I almost did not, shoot, I mean. But it was like he wanted me to take him. So, I did."

"How did you get him back here?"

Squirming in his chair, Adrien studied his plate. "That was the hardest part. I fetched Jackson." He looked up. "He was working in the south field. Jackson helped me hang him, but I drained him, and the rest. Colt Alvaro showed me how. I went hunting with him and Jacob a few times . . . before. I—" he considered the plate again. Swallowed. Took a shuddering breath and wet his lips.

Paien could imagine what happened with that buck, his sentimental, dreamy son cutting up a buck that was as big as he was, his son who hated killing things, even rabbits when he was little.

He looked Paien in the eyes. "I thought it was time." He reached for the glass of buttermilk. Took a long swallow and put it down.

Paien forked a piece of venison. Adrien would be fourteen in August, six months away. Fourteen was past time for most Texas boys. "This is excellent. I wish I could have seen that shot." He *did* wish he had been there. Damnation. His children were growing up in front of him.

He pondered Adrien's bent head as he picked at the beans on his plate. The boy looked like Madeleine, but for black hair and eyes that were like his own, even to high cheekbones his own mother said came from his Cherokee grandfather. And Bernadette, sitting next to him, was the same, enough alike to be twins, except in temperament. She constantly wanted to be where the action was, to be the sun, the fire to Adrien's unassuming moon. How did he end up with such two contrary children? She was likely wishing she had seen that shot, as well. She was smiling, the little minx.

The venison truly was delicious.

Bernadette daintily wiped her mouth with her napkin and placed it on her lap. "Adrien has been working the cows too. He can rope them."

"I hope you haven't frightened them off their milk," he said.

Adrien dropped his fork on the table. "Oh, no, Papa. She means the beef cattle. Charlie has been letting me ride with him and practice roping, as long as I do not rile them into running."

He had hired Charlie Woods as head wrangler soon after he purchased his first white Criollo cattle.

"Rile them, you say?"

Adrien picked up his fork, his face flushing. "Yes, sir. That is what Charlie calls making them run so they lose weight. He says running will make their meat tougher."

Madeleine wouldn't have cared for her son picking up Texas ways of speaking—fetched, rile. Soon, he will use contractions. Can't be helped. "It would appear I've been remiss in knowing what has been going on around my own plantation."

"I am doing my best to contribute where I can," Adrien said. He sounded so earnest. Paien brought his napkin to his mouth, smiling behind it. "I realize I have been of little help in the past," Adrien continued, "but I intend to change that. And Bernadette has been practicing her Chopin. Wait until you hear her play. She is absolutely amazing."

So. The two were teaming up on him. Madeleine once commented on how they supported one another in all things, and he was experiencing that support first hand.

"Very well," he said, sitting back in his chair. "Simon?" Simon stood to the right of the hearth, keeping the fire lit and waiting for instructions. "Please tell Esther we will have our pie and tea in the parlor."

The Jacob problem would have to wait.

Chapter Twenty-Three

Grace

The boss man seized her dress and apron the first of March when he locked her in a coffle with the other eighteen slaves in Houston. Before he put her on the boat that chuffed downriver from where she was born, before the white folks took her from her mam, before her mam gave her one good slap for crying so.

"Stop your fussing," Mam said, standing proud-like beneath moss-draped oaks. "I taught you better, and there's no place for you in this house. Less you want to become one of them field coloreds, you must find a house and mistress of your own."

In this warehouse that stunk of fish, she washed and put on her dress and apron again. Boss inspected her in a way she knew; she forced her arms to her sides and stared straight ahead.

"I got a likely buyer for you. You impress him and we'll both do well. You understand me?"

"Yes, suh." She understood, all right.

"You must assure him you came straight here from upriver."

Boss took her into a different room containing a desk, two chairs, papers, dusty shelves with books, colored bottles, odds and ends she hadn't time to name, and where a gentleman stood looking out a paned, cracked, and dirty window at ships bobbing in the breeze. Thankfully, one of the two south-facing windows was open and let that breeze into the stuffy, cluttered room. Somewhere out there was the boat she had arrived on. The gentleman turned and, my, how tall and handsome in his black wool coat, brocade vest, and so-white shirt with perfectly ironed cuffs. Such shiny leather boots. He reminded her of those refined yet hot-blooded men who often visited back home to buy her massa's equally hot-blooded horses. Deep-set black eyes pinned her to the floor.

Gulls calling out that window reminded her where she was. Galveston.

She curtsied ever so nicely; the way she had been taught. She smiled the littlest bit, not so much as to seem impertinent—the white gentlemen did not like their coloreds impertinent—but cheerful and ready to please.

"How old are you, Grace?"

Boss had surely told him, but he wanted to hear it from her. "I am sixteen, suh, and some months."

"I need a companion for my daughter, three years younger than you. I not only expect you to excel at the duties for which you were trained, I want a positive and cheerful disposition, particularly in the presence of my daughter. Do you think you can handle such a position?"

He *asked* her? Grace answered, chin up. "Yes, suh. My mam taught me to dress the young ladies and wash and do their hair, suh. I sewed this dress I have on, and this apron is my sampler. And I do love to laugh and have a good time, suh. We had lots of music and dancing back home, and my mam said I was always in the middle of it." She glanced down at her old leather shoes, the ones with holes in the bottoms. "When I had time from my duties, suh." Then peered up from beneath her lashes. Mam said she should look up toward the gentlemen from under her lovely long lashes. She wanted to please this one, mostly because he asked her a question. *Asked* her.

And listened to her answer.

❧

Some days after a trip upriver, the town of Washington was smaller than Houston. She rode in back of a wagon to her new home, where oak trees hung with moss lined the road just like her old home.

Oh my, this was one fine house, all right. Nearly grand as home in Houston, with two floors, high ceilings, double doors, and a deep, white-painted porch in front. And, oh, what glorious flowers and vines everywhere. She will be one big fool if she messes this up. The likes of her don't get more than one chance, and lucky for that one. That's what her mam said, and her mam was no fool. Such pretty, thick rugs so fine under her new shoes and made it that quiet she wouldn't know if anyone was in this room or the next. Such handsome chairs and polished wood and all those books—she has never seen so many books. Everything shiny and clean, even smelled clean—of cedar and lemons. Remember your manners and curtsy for the nice gentleman. Speak only when asked, the way you learned.

"Marcus will introduce you to Simon and the others, and you will meet my daughter and the rest of my family when they return this afternoon."

"Thank you, suh."

As she followed him down the hall, Marcus, who was darker than her, said, "If you have questions or problems, you must ask Betta."

He spoke good, just like Marse. She was relieved to meet Simon, Betta, and Esther, the cook, who were as expected, like her mam. It was Betta who told her where her duties lay, after they explored the house and entered the little miss's room upstairs where she was to spend most of her days.

"Now listen to what I say, chile. You is one lucky gal to have been bought by Marse Paien Villere, and that's a fact. He is a kind and good marse. You come to me if somethin not right here in this house.

"This house once full of love, now it full of sadness. Too many passed to the next life." Tears filled her eyes. She pulled out a stained but clean handkerchief from her apron pocket and blew her nose. "It be part of your job to bring happiness back to the two young ones, specially to little Bernadette."

"I will do my very best, ma'am. I surely will."

"You just behave yourself. We all get along fine."

She couldn't sleep that night because she was thinking so much.

"Grace Bodine." She whispered to the cedar boards of the ceiling. "You a long ways from that attic room in Houston." She had her own space, one she did not have to share. Her own bed. Her very own cabin. There was a chair, a table, and even a cupboard with three drawers to put things in. Tomorrow, when she had time, she would sweep out the cobwebs and dust and wash down everything. She would make a rag rug for the floor. How lucky no one else wanted this cabin because it used to belong to some hoodoo woman. She wasn't afraid of no hoodoo woman. Least of all one who'd been gone for years.

At first sight, she thought Bernadette would be nothing but trouble. White girls that pretty were spoiled things used to getting their own way. What a surprise. Grace would sleep in her own cabin rather than be at the mistress's beck and call like so many white missies required. This missie had "become accustomed" to her privacy. "Hello, Grace. I hope you are comfortable here and that we'll be friends."

Friends?

That Bernadette: "Not a lot of fuss, please. I do enjoy riding. Do you ride? No mind. I will teach you. I am glad you sew. I do not care for it. You may sew while I read."

Please? Thank you?

This would take getting used to.

The oldest boy, Lucien, had glanced at her down his long nose and busied himself elsewhere. Thank the Lord, she didn't want to get with a white man's child just yet.

She didn't meet the younger one until evening, when he came in the back door with a good-looking colored, both smelling of horse. If she hadn't had other plans, she might have set her heart on the young colored. Only he was a mite too dark, darker than her own coffee-with-cream self.

"This is my new maid, Grace," Bernadette said. "This is my brother, Adrien, who often smells like horses as he spends more time with them than he does with us."

"Hello, miss," Adrien said, nodding toward the colored. "This is Isaac." Then his eyes darted to his sister. "You only wish you were with us instead of being stuck here is all." He was on his way even as he added, "Excuse me, I have to wash for supper," and he and the colored fled upstairs, skipping every other step.

She shifted in bed and pictured him now, raven hair hanging over eyes as deep-set and black as his father's, high-boned cheeks flushed with exertion, slender and exuberant as a colt. And pretty. Lordy be, he was a pretty white boy. That one would make pretty white babies.

Chapter Twenty-Four

Simon

A fresh April breeze bestirred Simon from his accustomed place beneath the stairs in the hall. He stood from his rush-seated chair, stretched and sat down again, listenin to the new leaves flutterin from the open back door. From this place he could hear a summons from anywhere in the house and respond to visitors. He heard a great deal more'n white folks was aware, most of which he kept to himself. He had his own little table where Esther set a cup of hot tea, coffee, or a tall glass of water from the cistern, or a cold lemonade when he asked. When he grew stiff from sittin, he could step out onto the front or back porch, even as far as the outdoor kitchen, if he wasn't gone for more'n ten minutes or so. Unless he was needed for some job or other. Which brought to mind that turrible day in September when he failed to help the mistress.

That failure on top of the first sin. And so horrible?

He had worked hard to get his position as butler and headman of this house. Might he have got here without doing that one thing? The usual answer: he'd had no choice. Colored folk never had no choice. Which put the question away for another month.

"Oh, my achin bones." Betta lowered herself into the chair across the hall. She was sometimes able to get off her feet to swap information. She set her hands on her knees and stretched her back like a cat. "That new gal gone be the death of me. Mark my words, I see trouble comin from that one."

Simon felt a jump in his chest. "Nothin like—" *Rosanne*. Sayin her name out loud might bring her haint. Even the idea made him shiver.

Betta wagged her head. "No, no. Nothin like that one. Grace be a mite uppity is all. She used to them fancy places in Houston. She don't think she got to listen to nothin." Betta, hands on thighs, leaned forward and inspected his face. "You feelin poorly? You look a mite green about the eyes."

"I's fine. Jus don't like no trouble. All's jus startin to calm down, an thas the way I like it."

She stood. "Simon, you have got less years on you than me, but you is such a fuddy-duddy."

"A what?"

"Mistress called ole Miss Beechum that, afore—Speakin of, I gots to get that gal busy on hemmin Miss Bernadette's dress for the weddin next week. An you stop fussin. We gots plenty to cogitate on with Marse Lucien bringin home a wife. I takes care of that Grace. You see if I don't."

"Cogitate on?"

"Means think about. My boy's not the only one can learn new words around here. I gots" with a shake of fists and head, she puckered her face and murmured, "Drat, got to speak better to keep up with him and my man."

A young wife, a new Missus Villere. That'd be good. Good to have chilluns 'bout the house again. Little ones' laughter chased away bad thoughts. A smile pulled at his mouth picturing little feet runnin about the halls. Weren't bluebonnets coverin the hills same as every spring?

Chapter Twenty-Five

Bernadette

Journal - April 29, 1855: I was surprised, yet delighted, Joanna wanted me as her Bridesmaid.

I declare, I have never seen Lucien smile so in my entire life! A wife is just the thing. Joanna was so lovely in her Wedding Dress, and how she and Lucien kept stealing glances at one another! So romantic! I admit I was caught up in the entire affair. I ate with such abandon I feared bursting my corset, though the cake was not up to Esther's standards.

The Camdens do not own a single slave. Several cousins, Joanna's uncle's family, and her brothers help on their rather large farm.

The dancing continued until the sun rose. There was no ballroom, so they cleared out their new barn, and what glorious fun! My first time dancing with anyone but my brothers and cousins. My partners were: Joanna's brothers, Joe, who is ten, and Matthew, sixteen; Adrien's friend, Clay Thatcher; Jacob and Will Hart; Mr. Robert Camden, Joanna's Father; several boys whose names I cannot recall; Adrien; and Papa, who was the best dancer. Matthew Camden asked me to dance three times. He is quite attractive, if one overlooked the way the little bump in his neck bounced when he swallowed, which he did rather often.

The music was grand, no harps and such as the Harts have brought up from Houston for their New Year's Ball, but ever so glorious for all that. I declare, everyone moved with more vigor than I have ever seen. We were swung so fast our petticoats and lower limbs were exposed! Perhaps it was the barn, or because it was a wedding, or the music. I particularly liked the fiddle player, who was quite tall and had the *loveliest red hair and green eyes. He winked at me! Lily danced a waltz with him, though she won't be thirteen until September!*

I doubted I could sleep, as I am not accustomed to being crowded with a covey of girls. How surprised I was to languish until noon!

Journal - May 2, 1855: It was lovely being away but ever so nice being home with peace and quiet and no little ones screeching and running about everywhere. Were we like that when small? Of course, there were fewer of us. Two, I could abide. Perhaps three, if they were mine.

How confusing! I do not want someone telling me what my life shall be. I shall decide for myself. I daresay I do not wish to be inside a house all day doing nothing but sewing and planning meals and making sure the mantel is properly dusted.

What ever shall I do?

Journal - May 25, 1855: They have returned from their honeymoon to the coast, and, as I have been concerned about how we should get along, I have decided to have a conversation with Joanna as soon as Papa and Lucien leave for the fields.

I put my journal aside as I heard a discouraged Mintie disclaim, "All that unpackin and picture hangin, an she shoos me out, as she say my assistance unnecessary."

I must have a talk with the house people about Joanna. Oh, Lord, how am I going to phrase this talk? Do not do for her because she does not believe in slavery?

I tucked my journal in the drawer and discovered Lucien's new bride in the room off the south veranda that my brother had chosen for their own.

"Excuse me. Oh, my, this room looks lovely." It did. Especially with the yellow chintz curtains and Camden family pictures on the walls.

Joanna stood next to the bed, her arms full of blue fabric—the old curtains? "I hope you don't mind," she said, "my replacing some things, I mean."

"Of course, I do not mind. This is your room now, yours and Lucien's. You must do whatever you wish." I extended my arms. "I'll take whatever you no longer need and give it to Betta."

Joanna held the fabric, hesitating. I said, "Did Lucien tell you who Betta is?" Our house girl, woman, she runs the household, sort of, and—oh, pooh." I grabbed the fabric and flopped down in the chair next to the bed. "This is absurd," I continued forcefully. "I refuse to beat around the bush."

Joanna sat on the bed, facing me. "Let's not"—she gave a half smile— "beat around the bush." She leaned forward and placed a tentative hand on mine. "My dear Lucien was as close-mouthed as usual and didn't tell you a thing about me. I expect he still sees you as his little sister rather than as mistress of Blue Hills. Let me assure you I will not intrude on your running of this house."

I smiled. "Let me assure you I will not intrude on your running of Lucien."

I admit we chortled together like two happy hens. Joanna clasped her hands together. "Let me set your mind at ease on several fronts. I was raised Lutheran, as was my papa, who is originally from Pennsylvania. He is the youngest of eight sons and came to Texas with my mama, who is Quaker. It is the belief in God that is important to Papa, not the path to him. Lucien and I agreed to raise our children Catholic. Though my family does not own slaves, nor do we condone the institution, we noticed that your family treats your slaves with more respect than some of our neighbors treat their own families."

I had silently mouthed the words following: "does not own slaves" along with the speaker, as though to digest them more fully. "Treats your slaves with more respect," in particular, stuck in my mind. *I treat everything I own with respect. Things. Persons.* I had never considered our people this way. Not truly. How muddled.

Joanna was looking at me in the oddest manner.

"Oh. I am sorry. For a moment, my mind wandered. Yes. We shall be fast friends, I think. And learn from one another. I believe I am learning something new already."

Chapter Twenty-Six

Adrien

Secrets are terrible and lonely when you cannot share them, not even with your dearest friends. I told no one this dreadful longing for what I could not say.

One May during a school lunch break, Will, Clay, Henry, and I sat in the grass among a swath of white daisies. "Say, look at her," Clay said, leaning close, breathing into my ear and elbowing me in the ribs. Will glanced up.

I had noticed how pretty Faith Manning dressed to her best advantage. "She is lovely," I said, "the way her hair curls around her bonnet."

"I mean her bosoms, idiot."

"Well, yes, I suppose." Some girls were . . . getting those. Something vulnerable and soft made me want to lay my head there.

Not a soft bosom my head felt next, but a hard shove. "You suppose. Grow up, Slick."

Adele Gladstone's arresting figure produced the most appealing swinging skirts. Will had a fine visage. Sixteen-year-old Gideon Armitage did odd jobs about school and had the physique of a Greek god. Guilt filled me for noting the last two. What I noticed made fish wriggle in my gut.

I wanted to remain home and hide. What I wanted was not proper.

Sunday evening, Grace stood in my open door. I pulled the covers to my chin, wearing only a nightshirt. "I feel poorly," I said. "Will you tell Papa I am going to stay home tomorrow?"

She sashayed right in and laid her palm on my brow. My gosh, but she was pert with those dark curls dangling out from under her white cap and her neat, little figure.

"You are a mite warm and damp." Her bosoms practically in my face as she bent over me were the perfect size for my hand, like two peaches. *Please, God,* I slunk lower under the covers and closed my eyes.

The door gave a soft click as Grace left, but her alluring scent lingered. I pulled the sheet and quilt over my head, despite the rather warm room. I must burrow in the dark like a ground squirrel.

I grew up on a plantation around animals. *Would this misery end if I were gelded like Troy?* I scrunched under the covers and shivered. I discovered how to satisfy myself with trips to the privy—I never knew when Bernadette might knock only once and pop into my room—but that release was crude compared to how I felt when longing to caress such glorious hair and endearing skin, to holding warm bodies close like when I was little. No matter female or male, their enticing beauty left me with the same yearning. The books Jacob loaned me about Greece proclaimed that love among boys and men was acceptable, but I did not live in Greece hundreds of years ago. *I am here. Now. Why this torment?*

Why did Jacob loan me such books?

Holy shit, I am so dang muddled!

Hiding in bed would not solve this problem. I recovered enough to attend school by Tuesday. The following Saturday afternoon, Isaac and I lounged in cottonwood shade on the creek north of the house, our bare feet in cool grass, two ash poles dangling over a usually fish-generous eddy near our favorite swimming hole.

Isaac and I were the same age. He must have similar questions. We had explored when we were small, including who could piss the farthest and most accurately. Perhaps we could talk. About the feelings, if not all of it, exactly.

"Do you recall what we discovered about puppies?" I kept my voice low, so as not to frighten any fish.

"Which part?"

"The dogs playing." Focusing on animals was the best approach. Rather roundabout.

"You mean before puppies, making them?"

"That." He may get the idea and contribute . . . something.

Birds chirped, a jay squawked, water gurgled over the rocks, a whisper of wind fluttered the cottonwood leaves.

Isaac snorted into his arm, the one not holding his pole. His shoulders bounced up and down as though he were crying.

He was not crying. "What is so funny?"

Muffled, "Don't know."

"You are a big help." I grasped my pole tighter.

My only warning was a shuffle to my left and Isaac on me and we dropped our poles and rolled in the grass, grunting, laughing, cursing. Glorious. I loved this, and Isaac seldom jumped me first. The glorious pain of his knee in my ribs, his chest on my chest, curly hair against my cheek. His skull bashing my jaw flashed sparkles behind my eyes. Isaac's weight on me. I could not move, did not want to move and stared up at the sky, blinking.

"Get up." A deep, commanding voice from my left. My heart jumped in my throat and Isaac drew away. I turned my head and up through tall blades of grass saw: a horse, a familiar roan. I sat up, air spinning. Marcus in the saddle, mouth taut as pulled wire, regarding Isaac standing a few feet away, head down, all sweaty, grass in his curly hair.

"Are you all right, Master Adrien?"

I raised onto my knees, heart pounding, a little wobbly, on up, brushed at my trousers. "I am. We were only wrestling." *Dang.*

"Your papa sent me looking for you. Company has arrived from Brenham. Isaac will ride with me." He turned to Isaac. "Fetch those poles, boy, and climb on behind here."

Double dang. I had forgotten the Camdens' visit. I picked at my grass-stained shirt as I walked stiffly by the roan's nose to where I had left Troy in the shade of a cottonwood. "Isaac has done nothing wrong. Don't blame him."

Marcus lowered an arm for Isaac to swing up.

Chapter Twenty-Seven

Isaac

In the barn, Isaac rubbed down Troy, which normally Adrien would have, only Master Villere had commanded Adrien to hurry and clean up for their company. Everyone commanded them. Adrien was the only one who asked. When he was grown, Adrien would command him too. *I will command nothing. I'll be told what to do forever.*

"Lucky that horse is so even-tempered, else you'd get nipped for sending your wrath through the brush that way." Papa had moved up behind him. Papa, who must "yes sir, no sir," when anyone other than the family was about.

"Come. Let's sit over here on these bales. It's time we had a talk. Past time. I see that now."

Isaac sat and rubbed his nose with the back of his hand that held the curry brush. *A talk, huh.*

Marcus seated, hands on spread knees, glanced down, then looked hard at his son.

"I have seen how familiar you and Adrien are, your arms around one another's shoulders, the way you shove at one another. Fine behavior for two boys of the same color. Not for the two of you. If Paien were around more, he'd have corrected you both himself. You might think such conduct is harmless here at Blue Hills. But one day there'll be visitors and you'll forget because it has become habit."

Isaac's resentment had not abated, but a terrible sadness joined it.

"He's my friend." *And my brother, even if he is white. He said so.*

"I blame Adrien for not behaving as he should. I blame his papa for not teaching him. I could blame the world we live in, which is where the true blame lies, only that cannot be changed, not in our lifetimes. We must get along in the world we've been given."

"Why should I always take orders?"

"Do you not listen?" Marcus heaved upright, eyes large and piercing, body potent with suppressed emotion. "Look at Paien. He must live with this situation the same as us. He would like to set us all free, but how can he set us free, run this plantation, and be respected by his neighbors?"

"He would set us free—ha!"

"Years ago, before we came here, he set me free."

Isaac's breath wrenched from him. *Free? All this time, Papa was free?* "You're still here."

"Where would I run? How could I go with you and your mama, since Texas law doesn't allow a man to free his slaves?" His papa sat back and folded his hands in his lap. "Back in Virginia, when Paien and I weren't much older than you and Adrien, I taught him to grow tobacco. I've been saving what he pays me as overseer. Once I have enough, you and your mama and I will find life in a free state. Paien has been secretly working with those who would change the law, so we might go safely."

"No one here knows?"

"Only Paien."

It was Isaac's turn to lower his head. He considered the curry brush and ran his thumb along its bristles. *It is our secret that Adrien will buy my freedom when he can. Shall I tell Papa?*

Marcus rose, tenderly, as though he possessed tired bones. "You must let Adrien know how it must be, for he and his family would lose status, but you would lose a great deal more."

I better not. Leastways, not yet.

Chapter Twenty-Eight

Adrien

I had grown forgetful, my mind occupied with myself, with constant expectation of something unknown. I would lie in bed next to Isaac, ear against my pillow, and listen to my blood pumping. *Please God, help me to grow out of unnatural musings.*

As I was constantly tripping over my own feet, Bernadette took to calling me Lump.

I had finally become taller than my sister.

"I declare," Betta said, "I'm gonna have to let out them trousers again. Must tell your papa we need more cloth cause there be no more let-out left."

The Camdens left Monday morning after breakfast, which gave Betta an opportunity to catch up on her sewing. The three of us, surrounded by piles of fabric, crowded the workroom and kitchen we called the hive while our orange-striped cat contentedly washed on the sunny east windowsill.

I made a face at my sister, who stood inside the doorway waiting her turn to be measured for summer frocks. Until Betta turned me about and jerked at the fabric around my backside.

"Still mighty loose here. You got to eat more biscuits for more paddin if you gonna catch the eye of the ladies." She gave me a swat, and Bernadette laughed behind her hands.

"Skedaddle now, while I make Bernadette the prettiest little gal in this here county."

I plucked my hat from the peg in the hall. *Where will I find Isaac this hour of the morning?* Steps sounded on the front porch. Papa burst through the door in a swath of warm spring air, leather, and horse.

"Ah," Papa said, removing his hat, "thought I might catch you. I have a moment this morning if you want that discussion. How about the library?"

I rubbed a hand on my trousers and put my hat back on the peg. "Yes, sir." Papa had come home in the middle of the morning for our talk. In the library, which was also Papa's office, where he and Marcus, sometimes Lucien, and other gentlemen discussed plantation business.

I had entered the library previously to search among the books and left every item the way I found it. No one said I could not explore, but the family understood that the desk was Papa's and not to be disturbed.

I loved poring over letters on the walnut desk because they bore return addresses from such places as Savannah, Charleston, and even New York. The ones that interested me most were from Papa's sister in New Orleans, the only member of his family with whom he corresponded, and only once or twice a year.

I first heard of his sister years ago when I had been reading on the settee in the corner of the front porch. Virginia creeper climbed up the near column and spread across the southwestern edge of the overhang, creating an intimate, shady space. A languorous song of birds, hum of bees, and murmur of Maman's and Papa's voices among the nearby rose bushes had drifted through my consciousness.

"I will never go back, for any reason," Papa said.

Then Maman, "I don't understand why you must cut yourself off from your sister, your only family."

"You are my family, my dear. You and our children."

I had almost dozed off, but a fly tickled my nose, and I lazily waved it away.

"We have the same name. Is that why you married me?" Maman said.

"Coquetry doesn't suit you."

"I am vexed. I would like to know Madeleine Villantry. How could she possibly have done you such wrong that you refuse to see her?"

"Have I asked much of you? Leave this one thing be. I do not ask you to dwell on your family's past in France. Do not ask me to bide on mine in New Orleans."

I heard the sharp *snip, snip* of Maman's shears. "Very well. Here, these roses would look lovely in the blue vase on the hall table."

Maman had previously placed roses on Papa's desk, but there were none there now, not even an empty vase. Neither Simon nor Betta cut flowers for Papa's desk, nor would they believe it proper to do so if it had occurred to them. Where in spring and summer the library used to smell of fresh flowers, it now smelled merely of paper, leather, and Betta's linseed and lemon oil polish.

I perched on the edge of the chair facing the desk and glanced out the window behind Papa's shoulder where I could glimpse the pecan tree past the open curtains. My bedroom was above.

Each time I came in, I felt guilty. I yearned to tell Papa that I had noted his sister's letters and memorized the address. Instead, I sat in silence. Was what I had done so bad?

Papa leaned forward, elbows on the desk, hands clasped. "You mentioned you want more responsibility?"

"Yes, sir. Perhaps you could teach me about growing tobacco. Or whatever you think I should do." I fingered the edge of the desk, dropped my hands to my knees. "I have been little help around here. I would like to change that."

Papa gave me a close-mouthed smile. "I'm gratified to hear that, Adrien. I must admit, I was not sure what you were cut out for. Well, we'll see. But for summer only. I promised your maman that you would go to school, become an educated gentleman, and I'll keep that promise."

My heart thumped. *Yes, please, an education, books, unknown places, so much to learn.*

Papa sat back, his hands lingering on the desktop. "Our hope, your maman's and mine, was that you would take up medicine or the law, perhaps represent Blue Hills in Houston or Galveston. I'm sure that sounds far in the future, but it will surprise you how fast years pass once you're off to college. Any thoughts of college? Of where you want to go? Perhaps Chappell Hill, since it's so convenient."

Oh, Lord, not Chappell Hill. Convenient is the problem. "But Chappell Hill is Baptist."

"There are no Catholic colleges in Washington County."

"I would prefer to experience what there is beyond Texas, if possible."

Papa sat back in his chair, one hand stretched upon the desk, where he tapped his index finger. "You would, would you?"

I stared at the edge of the desk. "Yes, sir."

"Outside the state means additional cost. We'll see what sort of contribution you make in the next couple years and how well you do in your studies."

"Yes, sir. I won't disappoint you."

"I expect you to work the days you don't attend school. You can learn about growing tobacco from Marcus, but you'll be of greatest help with the cattle. Charlie Weeks is getting on in years, so I'll want you to learn what you can from him and assist as needed. I'll start paying wages, something you can put by for expenses when you leave for school. You may as well know that Lucien started earning profits when he turned sixteen; yours will go toward your education. You'll find Saturdays to be mostly work in decent weather, so don't linger at Hartwood."

I will not linger. I will work hard. You will see, Papa. You will finally be proud of me. My breath shortened. I leaned forward in my boots.

"Which reminds me. I understand you and Jacob Hart have been seeing one another."

My heart jumped. *Who told?* "Will and I are great chums. But Jacob, well, Jacob is like an older brother. I mean, you and Lucien, you're constantly working. I was always in Lucien's way. Jacob never minded us—me, Will, or even Bernadette and Lily. Often telling us stories, like Maman, only a little more, adventurous. He taught me and

Will how to swim and ride and helped us with our Latin and Greek. He's been teaching me how to defend myself. Perhaps you recall how I had problems with fellows at school? That ceased."

As I spoke, deep lines appeared on Papa's face, and his expression became one of serious concern, the opposite of what I expected.

"It sounds like he's done well by you, so far. Believe me when I say it's best you don't spend time alone with him. I want these lessons, or whatever they are, to cease."

"But, why?"

"I have my reasons. You can go to school with Will and join the family, but never attend Jacob alone."

"But—"

"Hold your tongue, boy."

This was so unfair. "Yes, sir," I said to the fists at my knees.

"You will find Marcus at the east field. He'll be happy for your help, and don't forget to have Esther pack your dinner. I'll see you tonight for supper. And take Isaac with you. I'm sure Marcus would like to see more of his son."

Stupid idea I had, to think I might work with my own papa. A familiar ache deepened in my chest, and I wanted to slam the door as I left. I closed it carefully, grabbed my hat and headed out the door to find Isaac. I was not hungry. *Now I'm not to join Jacob either, and there's no reason. Holy shit! Now I have to work twice as hard with the dang tobacco. I dare not fail, though. Not if I wish to go to a decent school.*

That afternoon Isaac told me about his discussion with Marcus and moved out of my room and in with his folks. What Marcus said was sensible.

Sensible hurt.

⁂

Unused to sleeping alone, I woke in the dark well before the birds began singing in the pecan tree outside my window.

Grow up. Isaac is still your friend.

"You can ride Shandy," I said to him after breakfast, thinking ahead how we would get about the plantation without causing undue talk from anyone. The mule stood inside the shade of the stable doorway, his white coat ghosting against the deep shadows. "He is smart and dependable, and I will not lose you in the dark." Our same old wiggery chatter.

"Sure nuff," Isaac said, looking at me pointedly, "that mule's got more sense than most horses and several folks hereabouts."

The way he looked at me when he said it made me uncomfortable, as though he meant me, in particular.

Isaac and I joined Marcus in the east field and began learning about tobacco.

The learning part was simple. Doing seemed easy at first, but after a couple hours of bending over weeding, growing blisters on my palms and fingers, and sweating in the scorching sun, I wished to lie down in the shade of the leaves. The only relief was a forty-five-minute meal break at noon beneath a copse of oaks.

Worse was to come.

The children's job was to collect and kill worms and pernicious insects, and they shrieked with delighted laughter when I gave an almighty grimace at a fat worm plucked from beneath a leaf. Several times a day, an older boy of ten or eleven brought around canteens of water hauled in barrels by mule from a cistern near the house. I had never drunk so much water in one afternoon, water that poured from me as sweat as fast as I could swallow it. Our people worked like this, day after day, all summer long, year after year.

The sun was slipping behind the far trees when Marcus called a halt. Isaac, Marcus, and I took to our mounts. The people sang while they walked the half mile to the quarters.

It ain't gonna a' gwine ter rain,
It ain't gonna a' gwine ter rain,
It ain't gonna a' gwine ter rain no mo';
It rained last night an' de night befo',

Rabbit settin' in de jamb of de fence,
It ain't a gwine ter rain no mo',
He settin' there for de lak ob sense
It ain't gwine ter rain no mo'.

I wished to join in the singing, but I wanted something else more, and urged Troy closer to Shandy and said, "Let's clean up at the swimming hole."

Isaac guided the mule to the side so Marcus and others could pass on by. "As you wish, sir."

I steered Troy over to bump into Shandy. "What are you playing at?"

"I'm not playing at anything. I need to behave properly toward my master. I'd be in a lot more trouble than you if we're discovered acting the way we were. If you *order* me to go swimming, I must. I must always do as you say."

How stiffly he sat on that mule with such anger behind his eyes.

I am to blame for this too. I stared at him, this sudden stranger, then jammed my heels into Troy's sides and galloped away. Away from these people, among whom I had suddenly become an intruder.

※

Saturday, I mounted Troy and rode up to the north pasture to help Charlie wean new calves from their mothers. *Poor little critters, I had half a mind to let out a good bawl myself.*

That evening after supper, I wandered over to the chicken coop out back, set my chin on crossed arms on the fence and watched the hens scratch around in the dirt for missed feed and bugs. Their low murmur was soothing after the desperate calls of calves all afternoon.

She was so quiet I didn't hear her until she was nearly upon me.

"I am sorry, suh. I hope you don't mind that I followed you here. You seemed so sad. I thought you might like some company." I turned to see Grace dressed in a yellow calico frock and white apron, her head wrapped in a matching scarf. She blinked her soft brown eyes and gave me a hesitant smile. The way she held her hands behind her back pushed her bosoms up against her dress.

"Um." *That all you have to say?* "I don't mind. I mean . . . you can walk where you like, I suppose. I was just, looking at the chickens." *Oh, Lord.*

She walked closer, up to the fence, next to me. "I've always liked hens. They're so soft and cuddly in your arms." She turned and looked at me. "Have you ever held one?"

Held one? "When I was small," I said. *She was warm and soft—the hen had been. Grace is older, but we are the same size, and she smells of spice, her being so close. Is she as soft as she looks? I could reach under her scarf and touch the curl peeking out there, lay my hand . . . Papa said never. Never to touch our people. Others do; that is where light colored folks come from. Light like her. Such a thing is taboo at Blue Hills.*

My hand was on the fence, and she leaned close and put her hand on mine. I slid mine out from under, stepped back. My head swam, my mouth dry, I could barely say, "I'm sorry." The words came out raspy, and I turned and hurried off to the house.

I'm sorry. Idiot. What are you sorry for? For the way I was sweating, for the thudding in my chest, for the pressure in my groin. I wanted to run, strike out; my blood boiled. I grabbed the column at the bottom of the stairs and nearly swung around into my sister coming down.

"Hold your horses," she said, laughing and holding both hands up in front of her chest.

I didn't look up, dodged and ran on up the stairs, leaving her in my wake—sure her eyes were boring into my back.

Next morning, Sunday, after prayers and breakfast, I saddled Troy and rode over the hills to Hartwood, hoping to see Will. Small matter that I would likely miss supper and have to get up at dawn tomorrow. I had to talk to someone about what was happening to me, to someone who might understand.

Looking back, perhaps I wanted more than talking. But what occurred changed everything.

Chapter Twenty-Nine

Adrien

Troy was no longer the young gelding Papa had given me years ago; our canter over rolling hills wore on him, and we walked the last mile. I turned toward the Hart stables to find someone to rub him down and give him a few oats before the trip home.

Fortunately, their stable hand Robey was walking Lily's mare beneath a copse of dogwoods near the barn. "Sure nuff, massa. I give him a good rub an not too much oats and water. I keeps him out here in de shade where he can take de breeze wid us."

I turned toward the house when Jacob appeared at the barn door. "Long time since we've seen you at Hartwood, Adrien. Catchfire's missed you. Come on in and say hello."

Papa would not know. What harm this once?

I followed Jacob inside the barn and walked past curious, snuffling horses to Catchfire's stall. The familiar smells of horses, hay, and leather were a comfort. Jacob went on in and raised the big stallion's off-rear hoof. I rested my arms and chin on the stall gate and recalled the first time I had been in this same stall years ago. Catchfire wiggled his lips at me, lifted his nose, and blew. Jacob dropped the hoof, stood up, and wiped his hands.

"Something wrong with his leg?" I asked.

"He's been favoring it a little. Can't see anything, but I'll let him rest a couple days."

"You'll rest, won't you." Troy was a fine horse, but he did not have the breeding of this animal who was as unflagging as the day he was born. I set my hand on Catchfire's velvet nose. He suffered my touch only a moment, jerked his head up, nodded several times, and rolled his eyes. He lipped at my hair, and I lowered my head to give him access to the top of my head. He had always liked doing that, and for some reason, I liked it too.

"You're lucky he doesn't take a bite out of you," Jacob said.

"Not me, he won't."

"No, I suppose not." Jacob moved along the stall, his hand lingering along Catchfire's back. He reached over to lift the latch and stepped out. "I've missed you, Adrien. Not a word about why you suddenly stopped appearing. I thought we were friends."

"I would have come if I could." I did not want to tell him Papa had forbidden me. "In fact, I am glad I found you here." I said it before I realized.

One of his hands remained slung over the top of the gate. He settled back on one leg, his mouth forming a smile of interest. "Oh?"

His look of pleasure set my heart thumping. "I need to ask you, about something private." I folded my arms in front of my chest, unable to decide which foot to rest my weight on.

"No one else is here this morning, but come to the tack room if it makes you feel better." He pivoted and headed to the rear of the barn. I followed, nerves prickling, and watched Jacob's shoulder muscles flex beneath his linen shirt. I drew my eyes away to glance at golden dust particles floating in a beam of sunlight from a high window.

After we entered, Jacob hauled the gray plank door closed. It protested with a low squeak. The ten-by-ten room reeked of leather and neat's-foot oil. Diffused eastern light fell through one small, dusty window opposite the door. Saddles on sawhorses and bridles, halters, hackamores, and harnesses looped over pine pegs lined two walls. Numerous bottles and blacksmithing equipment were neatly organized on a wooden shelf attached below the window. Faded saddle blankets lay piled on a bench beneath.

We were alone.

Jacob took the one stool, limbs spread, elbows on knees. My limbs suddenly weak, I slid down the wall to the straw-dusted pine board floor, arms on my raised knees. I looked across my hands at the stool rungs, the shadows beyond on the wall. *Why am I here?* I popped up off the floor, spun away toward the door. "I am sorry. This is stupid. I am stupid, I have to—"

I grasped the iron door handle; Jacob clutched my arm. "Hold on there. You got me in here with something to say. Now say it. We both know you are not stupid."

I leaned my forehead against the door, perhaps to bang my head against the wood and hide the sound of my heart pounding in my ears. "Remember last winter when we talked about feelings? About how Papa was always gone and, all that." I spoke to the grains in the pine.

"Of course." His hand relaxed a little.

"I think I missed Maman and was jealous of Lucien. Because Papa wanted his company more than mine."

"I understood."

I slowly turned. His grip slid down my arm, fingers slipping through my palm, making me shiver. I looked into his calm face. His intense eyes dark blue in shadow. "You did?"

"Of course. Especially after your mama died. Your papa was so caught up in his own loss and taking care of his land, he wasn't attentive of your needs or your sister's. The situation hasn't changed, has it."

"Am I selfish, wanting so much?" He was only an arm's length away. I breathed him in—musky, of horse and leather and—

"Certainly not. I'm aware of what it's like to not have an understanding papa, which is more difficult when your mama has passed."

I reached out and grasped his arm, where he had held mine. Only his was larger and harder. "Of course, you do. I *am* selfish, not to consider that. You always seemed so—"

"Strong and above all that? Everyone needs love. Even those of us who manage to appear we do not."

Jacob. Who had always understood everything I needed, who had never made me feel . . . less, or weak, or strange. He and I were alike.

He accepted me. Lord, how natural to step into him, to wrap my arms around him and let him wrap arms around me—to hold and be held. His hand in my hair, the other caressing my back. God, I wanted this. It had been so long, and the warmth of another person was so good. An overwhelming desire to please him arose in me.

Then . . . his mouth, hot, tender, possessing mine, the tip of his tongue . . . entwining mine, shooting delicious tremors between my thighs. This was not what I meant, was it? Jacob's probing lips, his searching hands, lifting my shirt, caressing my chest, sliding low over my back. Should I stop him? Jacob would never hurt me, never. He loved me—he had said so. I loved him. His hand moved down over my trousers, covering, then stroking the most private part of me. Was this love?

How good, but, *God. Wrong. This is wrong.* I pushed, then my hands in his hair, pulling him away.

"Jacob," breathing his name. Disgusting, Papa would say, disgusting. "No," I said, deep in my throat, but did I mean it? "Stop. Please, stop."

"No more games, Adrien." In an insistent voice I never before heard. "You came here for this. It's time you grew up and realized what you are."

What I am. What am I? How strong he was. He reached around to lift me up against his chest and pressed kisses to my eyelids, my cheeks, my neck.

He had loosed my trousers and was on my flesh and Lord, I did not want him to stop, but I had to make him stop. Oh God, he was on his knees, I was on my back, and Jacob solved my confused longing in a few brief minutes of hot, slick mouth and persistent tongue, of moaning, convulsive pleasure while I dug my fingers into the floorboards.

I had no control, not even over that.

"I love you, Adrien. You see, don't you, how wonderful it can be? You have so much to learn, and I will teach you. No one need know, no one but us."

Us? God would know.

Unable to speak, I gathered myself together with trembling hands, legs quivering. I could not bear to look at him, but turned, opened the door, and shuffled my shame through the barn and outside to where my horse waited, swishing his tail at flies.

Did he think I would come back? He turned what we had into this . . . perversion of love. Hands on the saddle, the familiar odor of leather, of my horse, my Troy. I pushed up into the saddle on limbs as weak as a newborn colt's. Did not glance back, only forward, out across Troy's flopping mane, between his flicking ears, past the waving, dry grasses, over the rolling hills and away toward Blue Hills and home. I stood on weak limbs in the saddle, leaning on my arm, hand on the saddle horn, not wanting anything to touch me down there, that place that burned like fire. The entire ride, my mind repeatedly recalled the delicious agony of my desire to surrender when Jacob had lifted me, pinning me against his chest as though I weighed nothing.

I could never get away from myself. It was my fault. I had wanted it, but that did not make it right.

Something was wrong with me to want such a thing.

Chapter Thirty

Bernadette

Journal - July 1855: *It is so hot in the house. I came down here to the cool creek to catch up. What would it be like to wear only a light shift similar to field colored? Some days I am tempted to lie about in bed in undergarments only, but upstairs is hotter.*

Only three months, and it seems as though Joanna, who is pious and clever, has been with us for ages. I believed she might better accustom herself to her new home absent my constant presence; therefore, I spent a week with Lily in June.

We visited Hartwood constantly when Mrs. Hart and Maman were alive. What fun we had dressing up, doing plays, and making up stories. Their house is enormous, with so many rooms we might run from one to the other without fear of giving offense. At least when Mr. Hart, Sr., was not home, as was often the case. I daresay he frightened me a little.

My name day is next week, and Aunt Charlotte has invited me to visit her and Uncle Charles in Galveston at the end of August. Lily is joining me. We are going to a coast resort at Velasco for two entire weeks and can loll on the beach beneath palm trees while being served tall glasses of iced lemonade. Lily wants to share a book she is reading entitled Moll Flanders and swore me to secrecy. I can't imagine what sort of book Lily would read that must remain a secret. One of our neighbors, Mrs. Alcorn, who was educated at Piedmont Female Academy in Virginia, reads romances.

At any rate, I shall be happy to be away. It is disheartening the way my once cheerful brother has turned solemn and distant. He is reserved with Isaac, who has become servile and no longer in jest. Something has set Adrien to brooding again, and he insists he is merely tired from working all day. He cannot fool me.

I am not the only one aware something is wrong. Poor Simon, our butler and man-about-the-house, has always been rather sensitive and skittish, and Adrien and I treated him shamefully when we were little. He is usually posted on or near the chair in the center of the hall and ever made a tempting target. We learned he wore a charm around his neck to ward off evil spirits and found every opportunity to sneak up and tease him about it.

When I approached him from behind last night, he nearly jumped out of his skin. He is younger than Papa, yet I feared he might have apoplexy there in the hall. I expect Papa may have said something that set him off concerning Adrien's Rosanne question. I must take extra care of Simon in the future.

"Why such doleful dumps, Adrien?"

"I'm tired, that's all." He stalked away down the hall and out the back door. I was left standing there, never having felt so summarily dismissed.

Papa suspected long hours in the fields, as my brother had taken on extra work. The extra effort was the result, not the reason for this grim attitude. But, as usual, I was not consulted. Betta declared, "The boy a trial at that age, but he straighten out soon enough, you see." She gave me a knowing smile and a spark in her eye as though I might know what she meant and should not ask any further questions.

Adrien could be as Villere stubborn as any of us.

As if that were not enough, I have been puzzling over conversations I had with Joanna, as well as studying other writings, including a book I found in Papa's library by Frederick Douglass. Dare I ask Papa why he has such a book?

Adrien is one of the few, perhaps the only individual, besides Papa with whom I might discuss such reflections. In taking a rational view of the South's entire situation, I fear I have come to the conclusion that slavery is a monstrous system and utterly wrong.

Chapter Thirty-One

Adrien

Once home, I found splinters in my fingers.

On my knees in my room, arms laid across my bed, I begged God for forgiveness.

I can't lie to him any more than I can myself or Jacob. I wanted what happened. I want it again. *Take this from me, Lord, please.*

Lucien was right. I am a nancy.

Summer wound on, and I dragged my miserable, guilty self through sweltering days and nightmare-filled nights. I worked at any task imaginable to keep from thinking and slept little as my thoughts would not give me peace.

I could not return to Hartwood for fear of seeing Jacob.

In August I turned fourteen. My smiles hid lies. Papa noticed and asked if work was too difficult—was I ill? No, I said, I was fine. The truth went unspoken.

"Growing pains," Betta said, "he's grown nearly two inches," and put a mustard plaster on my chest at night.

Bernadette knocked on my door, but I refused to let her in.

We topped flowers off tobacco under sweltering sun in August, Marcus's expert crews of four men each cut long stalks in September, and the rest of us strung them on sticks in the field for a day before hauling to one of the drying barns. One morning I was so lost in my misery I forgot my gloves, and Marcus sent me scurrying back home to fetch them. No one, he said, certainly not Paien's son, was to go near the sticky, pernicious leaves without protection. The crop must get in, but he's proud not a soul on this plantation has ever come down with the tobacco sickness or fallen while hanging the leaves.

I could no longer sleep in the same room, bed, or pallet where Isaac and I once shared innocent, childish pleasures. After the family slept, I padded downstairs and curled up with Courage on the back porch. Sleeping outside relieved a small measure of weight from my soul, of dreaded guilt that suffocated me within the four walls of my room. As Courage flopped against my feet, I closed my eyes and pretended to return to the previous fall when I was still innocent of this contemptible affliction.

Late one night, as October color crept over hills and into hollows, Grace found me.

"I seen you out here, young master. You catch your death for it'll frost tonight. You come with me, come on." She grasped my arm, pulling me, hauling me up from the cold floorboards.

Chilled and miserable, going with her was easier than not, for what should I fear considering my . . . predilections? She led me toward the house people's quarters, to the first cabin on the left. The ground froze my bare feet, but I hardly noticed for her surprisingly sturdy grip on my forearm. Courage followed and, though Grace held the door open, my dog would not come in and settled outside on the threshold.

She closed the door and led me to her bed. A gibbous moon shining through the panes of a window bathed pale objects in a soft blue glow: the pitcher on a whitewashed side table, a coffee can full of dried field daisies, the thin linen shift that barely hung to Grace's calves—thin enough to outline her form. Every part was framed in solid muscle; no wonder she felt sturdy when she took my arm. She sat down beside me on the bed, and I had to push on my right foot to keep from leaning into her, because of the mattress, the way it sloped where we perched close together. I pulled my eyes away and stared at my hands twisting around one another in my lap. I wore an old pair of flannel trousers and an oversized flannel shirt for warmth in the night air.

I am not here. I had been disconnected, ever since—

"You been powerful unhappy, Master Adrien."

Of all people, how did she know?

"Something is wrong with me." *Could I tell her? After all, she's, she could not . . . I have to tell someone. This dark inside, constant, I cannot—*

"I've known many people in my life, and I believe I know you," she said. "I've seen how you are, how you are with us folk, and I believe you're a good man. Whatever you think is wrong, you're kind, and that's what matters most."

I could not credit it. *She thinks I am kind, a good man.* Tears burned my eyes. I closed them tight. "I am not a good man." *My heart will surely leap out of my chest if I do not say it, if I do say it. Will she tell if I do? Oh, God, I must tell someone, or I will choke on it.* "I am perverted. I love other men." I shoved a fist to my mouth. *I cannot retch on her rug.*

She looked confused, had no idea what I meant. Then I saw when she did. How her black pupils widened like a cat's in the dark. She brought her free hand to her mouth. I nearly leaped off her bed, would have if she hadn't clutched my arm tighter.

"That may be," she said with a gasp, "but love is better than hate, any way you look at it. I've seen how you look at me, my handsome young master, and I think it'll take more than other men to satisfy what you have inside." With that, she took my head, put my face between her bosoms and rocked me. I breathed in the spicy scent of her and knew from what happened between my thighs that she was right. Relief flooded me, so strong that my tears poured onto her, but she paid no mind, only licked them off my cheeks and continued licking my lips, neck, and chest.

I had come apart, but Grace put me back together that night and each night afterward that we met. *Oh, Lord, thank you for bringing Grace into my life!*

I again heard the wind flutter the leaves, smelled the rich earth following rain, and enjoyed the taste of eggs and coffee in the morning. All because of her. She taught me how I could love a girl.

We never met more than once a week. "Not just your family," she said, "but someone might be up and see you coming or going. They would tell Marcus, and he would surely tell Marse."

I wanted to tell everyone what she had done, but what remained of my good sense kept me from doing so. I ignored the feeble cry inside my head that said our meeting was wrong, that Papa would disapprove. That cry was much weaker than the relentless yammer that had railed at me previously.

I loved her. I told her so, again and again. She never reciprocated the sentiment. I presumed she wouldn't allow herself to say it because she was colored and I was white. *And she does not believe me because I am fourteen.* No one believed Romeo and Juliet either. Or Tristan and Isolde. Love like this made all else insignificant. It made one quivery and silly, greens greener and blues bluer. All I read had new meaning, deeper meaning. Even Lucien's taunts meant nothing, only made me laugh.

Grace raised an eyebrow, gave me a smile, and ran her hand up my inner thigh. I soon forgot all else but her body urgent against mine.

⁊℣

December again. Surrounded by pieces of fabric and ribbon on the floor in my room, I wrapped a piece of blue gauze left over from Betta's sewing around a small box and tied around it a darker blue bow of silk. Surely Grace had never received such a fine Christmas gift, nothing as nice as the little silver heart locket inside. I had bought a long chain so she might wear it beneath her blouse where no one but the two of us would know.

A tap on the door behind me. I hastily pushed the box under my bed. "*Entrez.*"

"You are wrapping," Berni said as she swooped into the room. "I daresay it was that or a book." Our latest calico cat came sauntering after her and found a sunny ray on the counterpane. Berni dropped to the floor before me, her lavender taffeta skirt ballooning, and plucked a piece of green velvet ribbon from the pile on the carpet. "I thought you might have this. I have had my eye on it for a month. May I have it? For Papa's gift."

"Take it. Take what you want. I'm finished. Except for yours." Berni's was a delicate silver chain strung with lovely tiny freshwater pearls of cream, pink, and lavender I had purchased from a merchant who had come upriver from Galveston. I leaned back on my elbows and gave her the most ambiguous look I could manage. She returned a steady, unwavering gaze.

Her lips crept up into a smile, and she laid a hand on my knee. "This will be a good Christmas. Better than last."

Last Christmas? The first without Maman. A thump in my chest. I placed my hand on hers and squeezed. "It already is, Berni."

"Make it better for Isaac, too, will you? Whatever happened between the two of you has left him doleful," she said. "He is not himself."

A rush of anger. I tightened my jaw. *Isaac's fault.* "*He* rebuffed *me.*"

She sat back, primly straight. "Rebuffed you, did he? I wonder how he felt, being told his place."

Whap. She might have slapped me with a glove. I heaved upright. Left her sitting there and hurried to the window, folded my arms, and looked past the branches of the pecan tree.

Purposeful silence behind me. She waited for me to calm. The same as I would an unruly horse. She made me feel . . . foolish. This thing with me and Isaac *was* foolish. Why had we let what others thought come between us?

"I'll talk to him," I said.

"Now?"

I must have been waiting for someone to give me a push. I turned. "All right. Now."

"I saw him walking toward the creek with a book."

"One you loaned him."

"Of course," she agreed. "When was the last time you loaned him a book? Would it suit you to spread a little holiday cheer to your most loyal friend?"

Could I refuse Berni's request when put in such a manner? I was not yet entirely forgiven for my earlier behavior toward Isaac.

I had a good idea where no one would disturb his reading. Our special place.

My heart jittered as I leaped the rocks across Oak Creek. I crawled through the tunnel where we once walked upright through the underbrush. Rainwater fell from the leaves and dribbled through my hair and down my face. My hands, arms, and legs were soaked in gooey mud and leaf litter. I wiped my hands on wet leaves to remove most of the mud.

On an old, folded blanket, his back against the sycamore, Isaac glanced at me from over his book, an unreadable expression on his face.

I sat in a sunny spot on a fairly dry, sun-drenched rock next to him. Shivered in the damp chill. Birds chirped; the creek trickled behind me. A woodpecker drummed. The air smelled of green, moist earth and wet stone.

Isaac lowered the book to his lap. "You look a mess," he said.

"The tunnel is a bit overgrown."

"Expect we are too."

I peered at my hands. Rubbed them together, to brush off what remained of the mud, but mostly rubbed it in. Raised my face again. "This is a damp place to read in winter."

"It's private."

"So is my room. I could leave you alone if you wanted."

"I don't," Isaac took a deep breath. Exhaled. "I'm sorry, Adrien. About what I said. About everything."

"I am too. About everything."

"My blood was up about everything."

"So was mine."

Isaac leaned forward over his book. "We'll have to be more careful. We can't go on as before."

"I know it. I've learned some things since then." *Grace taught me how to be circumspect. Or was the more accurate word: devious?*

The side of Isaac's mouth turned up. "I'm freezing. Can we find a warm fire somewhere?"

"Fine by me."

How easy when we admitted we wanted the same thing.

❧

How perfect that holiday until Isaac spoiled it two days before the new year.

"Would you say I know you better than anyone, Brother?" We were saddling up Troy and Shandy. Isaac continued tightening the cinch without looking at me. "Maybe this is none of my business, being only a poor colored boy speaking to his master. But I reckon two certain someones are gonna rue the day they tried to catch a weasel asleep on this here plantation."

The first time I had heard about catching a sleeping weasel was when he and I were boys and attempted to snitch an entire warm berry pie from under Esther's nose.

My blood rushed. "Do not call Papa"—I stopped.

Isaac stilled, looked at me. "You do get my meaning."

How did he learn of us?

"Only a matter of time afore others realize, and soon enough, my papa and then—"

"You haven't . . ."?

"Course not."

"Shit."

Isaac smirked, reached up, stroked one of Shandy's long ears. "You sure can pick 'em. Or should I say, be picked by?"

I narrowed my eyes and leaned from my saddle. "What do you mean by that?"

"Don't get your dander up. I'm acquainted with her kind, and you're pretty naïve when it comes to, well, some things. Otherwise, how do you think I'd take it with you canoodling with one of us? Never mind your papa."

I had not thought, as usual. I stammered, "She, she—"

"Yeah, you think I didn't figure it was her idea? You can be a fool, Brother. End this before it's too late."

"I cannot. I love her."

In silence, Isaac stared at me, rolled his eyes, mounted, and rode off.

Chapter Thirty-Two

Grace

After an entire week of March rain, the sun summoned spring by flooding the hills with bluebonnets, white daisies, and red paintbrush. New Criollo calves and colts romped among the fresh green grama grasses and bluestem their mamas fattened up on. A pair of scrub jays, ever watchful for nest-building materials, dove past the cattle and cut across fields to the pecan tree next to the house and out of the wind, where it stayed warmer at night. The male landed first with warning chatter to any bird that might be nearby—any bird not his mate.

Behind in her chores, Grace was in the hive ironing out ruffles on Miss Bernadette's cotton pinafore.

The months had passed quickly since she had retrieved Adrien's curled up and shivering form from the back porch with that dog. Something had happened that made him sneak out to sleep out there alone. Believing he was a fancy boy. She had soon proved him wrong on that score. He needed somewhere to put all that hot energy was all. They spent many nights together before he became easy in his skin, before he quit startling when she touched him below the neck.

She smiled to herself. *We have learned ways of pleasing one another since.* He was butter for her churning and would agree to anything she asked.

"What you be doin, gal?"

Betta, snooping. Grace slammed the iron down, push, push. "I am doing my job, same as always."

"I know what job you been doin all right, young missy, and you best end it right quick. This house not like others. Marse does not care for such goin's on, an you know it."

"Marse Adrien doesn't mind, and his papa won't if you don't tell him."

"You believe that, you one stupid gal. An it not be young Marse that lose his place here."

Maybe she should listen to Betta. Only she is enjoying herself so. She had not planned on his being so accommodating.

She spit on the iron, and it sizzled. Grace grinned to herself. Sighed. Worked her way around a ruffle. *Ah me. Why must that boy talk of love? We doing fine without such talk.* She set the iron to heat again. Wiped a forearm across her damp brow.

Two weeks later, shortly after breakfast, she had finished making Bernadette's bed when the young mistress came hurrying into the room.

"What have you done?"

She remembered to curtsy. "Miss?"

"I have never heard Papa roar so. He is in the library with Adrien, and I could hear him from the hall. It is about you!"

"Miss, I don't understand."

"You do. Oh, Grace, you have turned this family upside down."

"Me?"

Bernadette was fourteen. Fourteen-year-old girls of her time and place were cloistered and naïve. Bernadette was neither.

"My brother would never force you."

"Miss Bernadette, he did not have to."

"But you are so much older."

"Excuse me, miss, but now you are being silly."

Taps on the door. Bernadette turned. It was Betta, head lowered. "Marse wishes to see Grace in the library, miss."

When she arrived, Adrien was no longer inside. She closed the door carefully behind her. Marse stood on the far side of a desk, his back to her, hands crossed in fists at his spine. He turned.

"I am exceedingly disappointed, Grace. Tomorrow morning, Marcus will deliver you to a man in Washington who'll arrange for your sale far from here. Be assured it'll be to someone who will take good care of you; you have nothing to fear on that account."

There was no point in denial. "Sir, may I speak?"

"If you wish."

"I am carrying his child."

"Blazes!" He pounded the desk. She was afraid he would come around and strike her. He shook and was so red. Instead, he placed both fists on the polished surface and slowly sat. "Does he know?"

"No, sir. I only just became sure, myself."

"You are positive it is his."

She dared let her anger into her voice. "There has been no one else."

His eyes bored into hers. She would not let him stare her down for long seconds, then she looked over his head, lifting her chin. Waited.

"So," he said, stretching his long fingers across the edge of the desk. "I'll arrange for someone to take you to"—she watched his eyes move about the room— "New Orleans and stay with you until the birth. If it is my grandchild, you will be freed and given funds for a fresh start."

"I would rather go north, suh."

"How dare you!"

She had gone too far, and he had made her jump.

He stood, strode to the window where he looked out, twisting his hands behind him. Then he turned, face in shadow.

"The North is not the paradise you think. I am acquainted with people in New Orleans who can help get you started in whatever you wish. You will receive funds on one condition. You never tell my son."

Oh, my. Of course not. She could imagine the row, knowing Adrien. He could be a fool about such things. "I accept," she said, blinking hard to contain her joy.

Chapter Thirty-Three

Bernadette

Again, I urged my fingers, if only the blasted things would cooperate. Chopin must be played lightly, with proper attention to the expression of the piece. In this case, a nocturne in C sharp minor. Only my mood was of a Beethoven symphony, with blaring horns and banging drums. As Betta had taken down the drapery for spring cleaning, the sound would crash delightfully against the bare windows. Papa's withheld anger seeped out unexpectedly. Better to be like Adrien, who erupted into a storm that quickly spent itself and left a rainbow. Papa simmered for days. He would likely simmer for weeks after this. Fooh! Dratted keys; dratted fingers.

"Berni?"

I slapped my hands on my lap. Behind me, the cause of this strife. Half of it, anyway.

Adrien sat carefully next to me on the bench, as though it might explode once he landed. He lifted one hand, his finger lingered lightly on a single E, which echoed.

"Talk to him, will you?" He turned his head to me *after* he asked.

How can one so guilty appear so innocent? Because he loves that, that . . . seducer? Or thinks he does. "What good can I do? Papa never changes his mind once it is decided."

"He will listen to you. You are his favorite. You know you are."

"I know no such thing."

"You are the only girl. You remind him of Maman. He will not listen to me—I am anathema." He looked down again, squeezed his knees together. "This is all my fault, not Grace's. If anyone is sent away, it should be me, not her."

"He did not tell you?"

His red-rimmed eyes, so miserable. "Tell me what?"

"I heard him planning with Marcus. You must leave for school this fall. I daresay he fancies you will get the discipline you lack here. He blames himself for not knowing what is going on in his own household."

"He *would* blame himself."

"I believe it runs in the family, at least in the males." I could not help but grin.

"I am to go away to college? He said that?"

That took some glumness from his face. "You must pass the entrance exams, but that will be no problem."

He was gazing off across the room. "I wonder where he has in mind. Will he give me a say, I wonder? There is Baylor, and that new one starting in Chappell Hill, but I mentioned last year I would prefer Centenary in Louisiana."

"At fifteen, I doubt he will send you too far."

"Will is the same age, and he is leaving for Europe."

"That is different."

He turned to me, one arm stiff, his hand clasping the bench between us. "How is it different, Berni?"

I sighed. "I do not mean what you suppose. The Harts can afford to send guardians with Will. He goes nowhere alone. You are too touchy, Adrien. It is not Papa's fault he had to raise us by himself. You must give him time. One day, he will realize you are as much a man as Lucien. Besides," I folded my arms, tucked my chin, and blinked at him from beneath my lashes. "I expect you have shocked him into realizing you are no longer a child." How fun to see his neck flush pink, watch color creep into his cheeks. Served him right.

"It is improper for young ladies to speak of such things."

"Pooh!" I pushed him with both hands, and not like some dainty maid, either. He needed to brace himself with his foot to stay on the bench. Then he upended me over his left shoulder. "Put me down! Lump, put me down!" Only my cry came between laughter and half-hearted beating of fists on his back. "Adrien!" He carried me across the room.

"Into the flower bed with you."

Thankfully, we were caught in the hall by Betta. "What in the Lord's name be this commotion! Put that young lady down, Marse Adrien. That's no way for young gentlemen to behave. I have none of these shenanigans goin on in this fine house!"

He did as she bade him, and I brushed at my skirts, and we were both grinning, trying not to.

"Shenanigans?" Adrien said. "Why, Betta, where did you hear such a word?"

"Never you mind, you not be the only one learn new words, young sir. You not too old for Betta take a switch to if need be. Now git and behave like the young gentleman and lady you be."

"Yes, ma'am."

Adrien and I parted at the bottom of the stairs. My brother likely went up to his room to dream about college, while I made my way to the corner settee on the porch where I could muse in private. *Men can be such fools, but Papa is not one of them. Adrien is so entranced with this college idea that he will not have time nor inclination to worry about Grace. Grace brought it upon herself. She was willful and too clever by half for a girl in her position. Though I will miss her lively gossip and keen wit, I will miss Adrien more. Even Lily has gone East to boarding school. I do like her, in spite of her overly romantic nature, her head a little too full of frivle fravel.*

No one considers I might wish to attend college. If I marry, my hus-band must not metaphorically hang me for what I know—a great deal too much for a lady.

Which brought to mind that book of Lily's, *Moll Flanders*. Lily refused to say how she came by it. Besides the one by Frederick Douglass, I have read nothing that left me so conflicted, astonished, and resentful all at once. Written by a man about a woman. I ache to discuss it with someone knowledgeable, but who would that be? I am desperate to read similar books. Lily has promised I might.

Chapter Thirty-Four

Adrien

I entered the library and remained standing. "I love her, Papa."
"You love her, you young fool? Did you expect to marry her?"

Marry? "I . . . ." My voice faltered.

Papa spread his hands on the desk, as though holding it down. "You planned on keeping her as your whore, then."

"No." The answer jumped out of me. Whore—what an awful thing to say.

"What, Adrien? Did you think at all?"

I was stuck to the floor like a fly on honey. I had not thought. Not a whit.

Papa sat back, stretching his arms against the desk. He sighed. He relaxed. I saw disappointment in his face, in how he drooped in the chair. He gathered himself. His entire body stiffened, and he pinned me with his eyes.

"She told me the truth," he said. "She hoped to get a child from you, a child who would pass for white, so when it became old enough to pass as her master, they would run north. She used you is all."

I will not consider such a thing. Not after what I shared with her. It was a sham? Troy might have kicked me in the gut.

Papa stood, came to the front of the desk, and faced me. His entire demeanor softened. "We've all been through a difficult period since your maman passed away. I see now, perhaps you have taken her death harder than I realized. I never forget you are my son, Adrien. You are a Villere. Have you any idea what that means?"

What? What do you want?

"I owned little before I came here. I am trying to build something to leave those who come after us—your children, my grandchildren. Lucien will get this plantation, but you have an opportunity for an education, a chance to build something of your own."

Someone else stood in Papa's place, someone I had never seen before. His eyes glazed over as if gazing somewhere into the past, his breath hitched, and his familiar features distorted.

"If you had any idea what I did to get this far. Don't throw it all away. Please." Confident, unapproachable Papa with anguish in his face practically begging, begging *me*? My heart raced; my legs turned to water. I grasped the back of a chair, could barely breathe. Could I speak?

"Whatever you want, Papa. Tell me and I'll do it." *I would do anything to make Papa right again.*

His right hand gripped me by the upper arm as his other hand settled on my shoulder. I felt a quickening inside, an unbearable longing, and raised my arms to grasp him, but his hands slid away.

He moved back behind the desk. And picked up papers from on top. "These are from Centenary College in Louisiana. That is where you wanted to go, isn't it?"

Relieved, am I not? Back to normal. Then why do I feel this . . . disappointment? "Yes, sir." *Those papers had been on the desk all along.*

"You better fill them out as soon as possible if you wish to attend this fall."

"Thank you, sir. I won't disappoint you." *I dare not, ever again.*

Papa met my eyes. "I don't think you will."

I got myself into the hall, which was empty, thank God. I began with a shuffle halfway down the hall, walked with purpose to the back porch, and stopped, eyes on the little cabin. The empty cabin now. I would like to ask her if what Papa said was true, but Papa never lied.

I might saddle Troy and race after her and Marcus, catch them up. I had played the fool long enough. And I needed to fill out those papers.

Face the truth. She never said she loved you. My eyes burned. Heat flared to my head; I was practically standing on my toes as though about to take off across the yard.

Then a wet, familiar nose pushed at my dangling fist. I took a deep breath and exhaled. Caressed the soft muzzle. *I loved her like a dog loves. I will never let my feelings override my common sense again. I swear. And I will not let Papa down. Anything to avoid that look. I promise, Maman, I promise.*

Footsteps behind me, followed by a familiar presence on my left. "The cattle yonder have been dropping a bumper crop of calves these last days," Isaac said. "Charlie mentioned he could use help keeping track of them."

I slipped my hand under Courage's ear and absently scratched, as the dog leaned into my thigh. "I suppose we ought to get at it."

"I spose."

Chapter Thirty-Five

Isaac

Isaac didn't learn of the "incident" until evening after washing up. Mama always supervised supper in the main house first. Even so, food was on the table when he entered their cabin, shadowy and dim this late on a June evening. They got the same vittles as the big table, only later. All the people ate well here at Blue Hills from vittles the women fixed when they left early from the fields to make their families' dinners—vittles the older folks had tended from garden plots among their cabins, plots their men had helped dig and tend on Sundays, holidays, and other times set aside for such. That was another difference from other plantations where field slaves often ate nothing but slops. Such contrary goings-on at Blue Hills made him uneasy. Particularly when he was reminded of that talk with his papa.

Papa looked up from his chair where the lantern light caught his face—left eye nearly swollen shut with a purple bruise that sent blue and red tendrils across his nose.

Isaac halted, mouth half open, gasped, "Papa"?

Two things happened at once: Marcus lurched up, staggered a bit, caught himself, and came around the table toward him. Mama hurried from the stove to Papa's side, taking his arm. Whereupon he removed her hand and gave her a brief nod. "I'm able," he said. "I'm able," he repeated firmly, standing straight and tall and smiling at his son. "Come on in and sit with me while your mama finishes putting supper on the table. I'll answer your questions while we eat."

He turned and moved without a hitch back to his chair, although

Isaac saw how tightly he held his hand at his side and how gingerly he sat.

Papa uttered not a word until Mama found her place.

"I figure you will be off your feed if I make you wait until after eating," he said.

"You figure right."

After their brief thanks to the Lord, Papa took a bite of chicken and swallowed. "I went to town for the mail and was attacked by a couple strangers. Strangers in town, I mean. They had no idea who I was, that I belonged there. They'd been drinking and declared I had 'no business striding about town on my own hook.'" Papa mimicked a broad, drawn-out accent and gave him a grin which appeared more like a grimace, considering his bruised face.

His papa was bigger than most men, and stronger. "Did you bash them good, Papa?"

Papa lowered his spoonful of peas. "You know better than that, Son. Fortunately, Mr. Hawkins, the postmaster, interfered, along with several other folks who knew me. Seems those fellas were from Kansas and were riled because of something an abolitionist John Brown did." He wiped his mouth with his napkin. "Paien was about to light out and give those fellas short shrift until your mama and Miss Bernadette put some sense into him. Takes a lot to get his blood up, but he can get mighty riled."

Isaac watched his papa eat. His papa hadn't defended himself. Wouldn't even consider it. Had to depend on that scrawny white postmaster to defend him. And he didn't dare speak a word to Papa about how he felt cause Papa was doing the best he could.

Isaac was about to choke on his meal, he burned so inside. But he got it down all right. A person never wasted good food, not when you worked hard all day. Not when your mama and papa expected you to act normal despite what had occurred. How tired he was of what was expected, but he would do so for Mama and Papa. But one day, one day.

Chapter Thirty-Six

Bernadette

"This is monstrous, Papa, utterly monstrous!"

I had stood on the back porch watching my papa turning terribly red, his fists trembling at his sides, and had worried he might have a fit of apoplexy holding onto his temper. Marcus placed his large hands on Papa's shoulders, looked him calmly in the eyes, and whispered something only Papa could hear. I watched while Papa helped Betta take a limping and bleeding Marcus to their cabin.

I had followed Papa down the hall and into the parlor before exclaiming.

He had his back to me and slowly turned. I was shocked by the tear that ran down one eye and by the control and soft voice with which he said, "Be silent, my girl." Then he collapsed in his favorite chair as though he could no longer hold the weight of it all upon his shoulders.

I perched on the sofa across from him, waiting. After some time, it became impossible for me to wait. "I read *My Bondage and My Freedom* by that man Frederick Douglass. We are doing wrong. Slavery is wrong."

Papa met my eyes with his dark ones. He sat back in his chair, gave me this ghost of a smile, and said, "It is. That is why we are helping the enslaved hereabouts find their freedom. But never speak a word of this, not even to Adrien."

How did I not know?

"But, but, you, we own . . . people. They are our slaves, Papa, no matter you call them *our people*." Eyes threatening tears, it was so terribly difficult to say as I fisted my skirts and wished to flee but dared not.

Papa grasped the arms of his chair when he lifted his head to look up at me, partly with shame, yet not entirely.

"If there was another way, I would have taken it. Yes, I wanted, desired, land. And the only place I could afford to get it was under Stephen Austin here in Texas. We made a go of it, right in the middle of where these people needed help. This is a place of safety, Bernadette, in more ways than one, where I do the best I can. I freed Marcus years ago before we came here, and he agreed to support me at his own peril. He believes in what we are doing. There are others here who believe the same, but I can't, won't tell you their names for their safety and yours. Don't ask me anything further. Please." He had begun wearily, but his words became more firmly and earnestly spoken as he went on, even unto the last.

My papa. I saw him differently. I hurried over, sank to my knees at his feet and wrapped my arms around him as far as I could reach. My dear papa. I loved him so.

"Don't look at me like that, dear daughter. I am no hero. I, I don't deserve such."

He pushed himself up, out of my arms, and shuffled to the fireplace, placed his hand on the mantel, stood there, his back to me, then turned, head down, a hand on his brow.

I could say nothing. I was afraid to speak. The room, the air had become thick and burdened like that of a gathering storm.

He spoke, head and hand remaining in place. "You may despise me after what I am about to say, but I must, as you may be the one person in this family who I can tell. I did not speak the entire truth about that woman, Rosanne."

Papa shakily made his way to Maman's armchair and settled, clasping its arms. The chair angled toward the front window, and he gazed there, as though replaying what he spoke of. "We, Marcus and I, meant to send her downriver, but she refused. You would have to have known her, how strong, how determined she could be. She had retained a good deal of hate, and it all came out in furious invective, in screeching curses. She threatened your mother, all of us, my entire family with her curses. Over and over, screaming. I lost it, lost my temper, struck out to stop her, shut her up. I . . . hit her just right—or wrong. I broke her neck."

Papa folded his hands together against his forehead as if in prayer, elbows on knees. Moments of silence. He sighed and raised his head and looked at me for the first time since he began.

"Marcus, Simon, and I buried her under the oak tree by the north drying barn."

He rose from the chair, ever so slowly. "Perhaps someday you will be able to forgive me. Not only for murdering that woman, but for choosing you to unburden myself upon. I fear this will always be your lot, Bernadette, as you are the strongest of us."

With that, he left.

Chapter Thirty-Seven

Isaac

At dawn, Isaac and Adrien saddled up and rode into the ground fog without a word. Isaac simmered beneath a stiff exterior. He had exchanged Shandy the mule some weeks past for a decent cow horse, and it flicked its ears and pulled at the bit.

Shandy had been a fine mount, but he had two worrisome predilections. That mule despised snakes and cows. Everyone knew about the snakes. At first sight, the mule would trample any reptile and, once mashed, grab the thing in his big teeth and fling it at least ten feet. No one learned about cows until Isaac rode within five feet of one. Then Shandy let out a magnificent bray, turned, lowered his head, and whacked the cow one great thump with his hind legs, knocking it to the ground. Isaac was nearly flung over Shandy's head.

"If we work cattle, best you ride a horse, anyway," Adrien said.

A year later, Isaac saw old Shandy moseying around the quarters with six small children clinging to his back. He was a calm, obliging old mule as long as no snakes or cows lurked near.

They were rounding up strays that had wandered onto Hartwood land. It would not do to have an angry rider and nervous horse chase cattle across Hartwood cotton fields, but right now, he didn't give a damn.

"I cannot imagine how you feel," Adrien said.

"You bet you can't." Isaac faced forward, left hand gripping the reins, right in a fist at his thigh.

"How about you tell me?"

Isaac pulled up. Glared at him. "You really want to know?"

"I asked, did I not?"

"Imagine a couple no-accounts beat on your papa. He could probably take either, maybe both, down, but he wouldn't dare. He let someone else do it for him. He drags himself home, all beat up to tell how someone else took care of him. You tell me. How does it feel?"

Adrien gazed at his friend, unblinking, his hand curled stiffly at his thigh.

"Know this," Isaac said. "I admire my papa. But I can never be like him. A man strikes me, I swear I will strike back, be he dark as night or pale as day. I hang. So be it."

"You will not hang. I would never let you hang." Isaac saw righteous indignation in his friend's face, in the firm set of his mouth. "We will do what we dreamed. When I finish school and have money of my own, I will buy you from Papa and we will leave Texas together. Somehow, I will free you. I swear. You have my word on it." He reached across the saddle and offered his hand.

Isaac hesitated, then took the offered hand with his own and grasped tight. It felt good to speak what he had been thinking. He could depend on Adrien. Weren't they brothers? Brothers who had chosen one another, better than born.

Chapter Thirty-Eight

Bernadette

Journal –August 1856: I admit this is a difficult, an extremely difficult effort writing this on paper, though Maman said it helped to do so when one is troubled. I do not believe I have ever been so troubled in my life.

I consider the "thing" over and over and over. Forgive? I find it so impossible to imagine. My papa. I practically tiptoe around him now. Look askance. Find I do not know him. It hurts him so. I can tell. Dear Lord, help me.

Chapter Thirty-Nine

Adrien

The night before I left for college, I slipped out of the house to say goodbye to Isaac and his family.

Betta and Marcus sat on cane chairs on the front porch of their cabin, enjoying the evening breeze. Fireflies flitted among the trees, and I heard the thin, buzzy call of a nighthawk. Isaac came from inside with glasses of lemonade for his folks.

"Want some?" he said.

"No, thanks."

Isaac squatted on the floorboards, and I joined him. "I just came by to say goodbye." I was all quivery inside. I had been to Galveston visiting my aunt and uncle and once to Austin, but never as far or for as long alone.

"It's a mighty trip you'll be taking tomorrow for one so young and inexperienced," Marcus said.

"Papa gave me instructions for practically every step of the way."

"Did he warn you of pickpockets and such?"

"He said to hide most of my money in my boot."

"The riverboats will be most dangerous, full of scams and outright thievery. You may not want to wear that fine new suit Betta made, either. No point in looking like the prosperous, easy mark you are."

"I am?"

"Dress down and hang on tight to your bags. Beware of gamblers and fancy women on that Mississippi boat. They'll be after your money. The fancier and prettier they are, the more they'll want. And will give you nothing *you* want, no matter what they say."

Oh, *that* sort of woman. Last summer we had discovered that sort sashaying about on a particular street in Washington. Henry and Clay often whistled at such women, and sometimes received a wink back.

I had never mentioned Grace, though I suspected our people were aware. As far as I knew, she had kept my terrible secret. *I could not stop thinking of her, of the moments we shared.* Though I no longer blamed her for her deception. Not after reading that book Berni had loaned me, *Moll Flanders*. If anything, I was now *more* aware of possible dangers.

Berni would not say where she got the book.

Next morning, the entire family saw me off at the dock in Washington for an uneventful riverboat trip down the Brazos to Galveston. On the ride overland to Port Arthur on the coast, I was disappointed our group was not attacked. I would have liked to have seen a fierce, wild Indian or two, rather than the few thin, flea-bitten creatures that wandered the streets of Washington begging for liquor.

The rest of the journey became a blur, a drowning in fresh experience with scattered moments of coming up for air. I saw New Orleans from on deck—a forest of masts, schooners, barges, and steamers bobbing at their moorings on the Mississippi. On the wharf: piles of cotton bales, oranges, green bananas and other mysterious fruits alongside hogsheads of tobacco and molasses; horses, wagons, sailors, dock workers black and white, their bare backs gleaming in the sun; top-hatted gentlemen in fine frock coats with lace at their throats; ladies with feathered hats and silk parasols mimicking the bobbing boats.

The din was deafening: barrels rolling, crates banging, cranes squealing, men whooping and hollering orders, bells clanging, horses clopping, and carriages squeaking. Another steamer arrived and let loose with a magnificent blast of its smokestack. Booted and bare feet, big and small drummed and thumped on the dock and gangplank.

So many smells flowed up from shore—rank, sweet, spicy, smooth, and sharp.

Papa had made me promise not to enter that den of iniquity.

The *Sultana*, the grand sternwheeler that would take me upriver to Jackson, nodded at its dock like a floating affectation of one of Esther's fancy tiered cakes. All her gilding and scrollwork every bit as elegant and, judging from the advertisements, the food would be just as delicious.

Two hours later, after a hasty trip across the damp, slick boards of the wharf and up the boarding ramp, I leaned far over the second deck rail to watch the gigantic paddlewheel throw brown Mississippi water into glittering gold plumes in the setting sun.

Night on the river, legs dangling over the bow, eyes closed, I listened raptly to the rhythmic splashing of the wheel, the frogs and nebulous, wet plops and mysterious screeches from the distant shore. Scent of fish, turtle, snake, of ponderous rich mud, drifts of magnolia blossom, of jasmine on the capricious breeze.

Twice a woman attempted to get my attention. One was so bold as to take my arm and ask me to promenade the deck with her. I stammered, "I have no money."

She said, in a drawl slower than cold molasses, "That's all right, hon."

It took me nearly a complete circle of the deck to escape and make my way to the nearest privy, where I lost my supper.

Returning to my cabin, I looked at myself in the gilded mirror and considered slashing my face with the little knife I carried in my boot. *I am too pretty for a man. People believe they can use me for whatever they desire.* Jacob's strong yet tender hands tormented me in unwanted dreams, and Grace might slip into my consciousness in any relaxed moment, leaving me angrily flustered and filled with and longing for what I couldn't have.

I held the blade along my cheekbone, lightly ran the point down the edge of my mouth, leaving the tiniest trail of blood. The sting was . . . engaging. I took a deep breath. Exhaled. Might I cut deeper, enough to leave a scar?

Maman's face appeared before me in the mirror. Was that what stopped me? Or did I merely lose my nerve?

In Jackson, I rented a second-floor room tucked beneath house rafters for $3.50 a week, including breakfast and supper—well within my budget. My landlady, Mrs. Crane, with her blinking dark eyes, gray wisps of hair lining her cap, and constant fidgeting, reminded me of the little fluttering sparrows that hopped along the ground searching for grubs and seeds.

The first night, I lay awake staring at the ceiling leaning close over my head. *What am I doing here?*

It was a short walk to the college grounds where I was enthralled with the magnificent Greek Revival white-columned buildings of Centenary College as well as the French Creole homes of Jackson and the surrounding countryside, their galleries and colonnettes, their pink, yellow, and turquoise facades.

Books lined the college library's walls, more than I could read. Once classes began, stimulation from novel ideas and new accomplishments flooded my mind: calculus, biology, theology, literature, art, history, Greek, and Latin. A fresh, unexplored world spread before me like Esther's most sumptuous holiday dinners, and I might gobble up all I desired. Exhaustion sent me toppling into my lumpy little bed each night, to rise eagerly with renewed enthusiasm at dawn the following morning.

So much to do, I almost forgot to feel lonely.

Surrounded by so many men and boys, I was spooky as a colt brought in from pasture. I was afraid to get close to anyone, for what I might feel. The exuberant charm of my fellow students left me aching. When they spoke to me, I returned a brittle smile, a brief answer, and turned away. In a few weeks, no one bothered. I was best alone. More time to study.

Until a blustery November morning, when I was crossing the cropped grass of the commons.

Eyes half closed, except now and then a glance at my feet to not stumble, I was reciting lines from Emerson's "Ode to Beauty," to myself: "Thou eternal fugitive / Hovering over all / that live, / Quick and skillful to inspire / Sweet, extravagant desire, / Starry space and lily-bell / Filling with thy roseate smell. . . ."

I hesitated, tried to recall the rest, and another voice continued—

"Wilt not give the lips to taste of the nectar which thou hast?"

I stared into the face of the auburn-haired boy who grinned back at me with such white, even teeth and flushed cheeks.

"I do not believe he meant to end in a question," I said. For nothing more—engaging—occurred to me.

"My error, then. My name is Roger Broadhurst." The fellow offered a hand.

I transferred my texts to my left arm and took the pale hand in mine.

"I doubted you were quite as cold and aloof as fellows said. I'm the grandson of a lord and ought to know. I'm not proud, as my father is a younger son and had to take ship for the colonies—pardon, I mean the States—in order to make his way. He sent for my mother, my sisters, and me five years ago after making a go of a plantation outside of Baton Rouge. We have a home there, in Baton Rouge, I mean. You don't talk much, whilst I can talk enough for both of us. Rather obvious, isn't it."

"You do, speak quite fast." *I am cold? A lord? Baton Rouge?* We continued walking side by side. My heart beat against my chest, half in fear, half in expectation, of what, I did not want to consider.

"Yes. I have found it necessary, with three older sisters, in order to get a word in edgewise, as they say. Also, I tend to run on whenever I am the slightest bit nervous."

"Nervous?" *He is nervous?*

The fellow hugged his books, three of them, tight to his chest. "Indeed. It took some, well, urging, on my part to come over here like this, force myself upon you, as it were. We have classes together. Perhaps you noticed. I've been spying upon you."

"Spying?" I had noticed him. There were not so many first-years that I had not.

"These one-word responses do tend to make conversation rather difficult."

"I am sorry. I do not mean to be difficult. It is only that you, surprise me, I guess."

"I'll likely surprise you a great deal more. For example, I love to listen to you. Your recitations are well-prepared and to the point. You have the most wonderful long, drawn-out sound to your words, as though warm honey was coming out of your mouth."

I turned to get a better look at this unusual fellow. Such pretty green eyes. "Good Lord, we all sound the same here."

"But you combine it with such fine diction and that odd bit of French accent. I find it exceedingly . . . sensual."

Which stopped me, one foot poised to step forward, and I stumbled. This was quite enough.

"I'm sorry. I shocked you, didn't I? That's me, always saying the first thought that enters my mind. The sister thing, again. Hesitate, and all is lost. I can be an excellent study partner. After all, who knows their way around English history better than I? I hope to be an engineer one day and am quite good at mathematics, yet I love the arts."

We stood facing one another, and he leaned toward me a little, a look of earnest expectancy on his pale, refined face, an auburn curl bouncing above his left eyebrow as he nodded his head in agreement with his own statement.

I smiled. How fine to have a friend and study partner who was British as well. Besides, I had friends my own age at home. I should have such friends here.

The first few weeks, Roger's impulsive habits unnerved me, the way his arm wrapped around my shoulders, his hand on my arm. No one else seemed to take it amiss, and it appeared part of Roger's personality, a naturally occurring outgrowth of his bonhomie, perhaps a peculiarity of upper-class young men in England. I admit I liked the contact, which reminded me of home, of when I was little. Of how

Isaac and I were formerly. As weeks passed, what thrilled me most was the discovery of a kindred soul. No one had ever expressed the same enthusiasm over lines of poetry or sunlight sparkling on dew. Not anyone of my own . . . sex.

And I was tired of running from what made me happy.

I spent Christmas and New Year's holidays with Roger and his family in Baton Rouge, where I was not only welcomed but treated like visiting royalty, especially by Roger's sisters, who were pretty and fun and not nearly the problems I had been led to expect.

Chapter Forty

Bernadette

Journal - November 18, 1856: Life goes on as usual, though I miss Adrien terribly. Joanna and I have become close; it is wonderful to have her about the place, and I am learning a great deal from her. Who would have thought?

Unknowingly on her part, our discussions have aided my feelings regarding Papa. I expect it was the shock that threw me. I have been able to "let him down from his hero's plinth" and begin to love him as the courageous and caring man he is. I must leave behind the child in me who was frightened by his reveal and embrace the new strength I find in the woman who sees him as human. He needs me.

Chapter Forty-One

Adrien

I first learned of what I years later considered the unfair decision that affected so many lives, including my own, near the end of February the following year.

I bent over a book at a long study table in the new Centre Building library and heard them across the table and a couple chairs to my right. Two upperclassmen, I surmised, were discussing the law in excited whispers. They spoke of a current case before the Supreme Court concerning a Negro who declared he was free, as he had lived for several years in free territory. Might this case affect Isaac? I had to find out. I pushed up from my chair and leaned toward them.

"Excuse me. What case are you discussing?"

One fellow frowned, the other raised a brow and said, "You mean you haven't heard?" He glanced at his friend and back at me. "Why, *Dred Scott v. Sandford*. It's the most important case in the courts at present. Don't you read the paper?"

I felt a fool, and stammered more foolishly, "I barely have time to read what I am assigned."

"Wait till next year when Campbell expects you to read *The Advocate* every morning, as well as the text and biographies." The fellow tugged at his waistcoat and raised his chin officiously.

I had been put in my place. I grabbed my books and hastened out of there. I must learn all I could about *Dred Scott v. Sandford*.

I returned that night after a brief supper. The library would close early because of the high cost of kerosene, but it took only a few minutes to find back issues, as the case had been making front pages for the past few days. I was even more of an idiot for not being aware of such an important issue happening in my own country. One that might well affect my family.

I read that Dred Scott was the slave of a Dr. John Emerson, who took Scott and his family to the free state of Illinois and, afterward, Wisconsin Territory. Years later, when he lived in Missouri as a slave, Scott petitioned the state court for his and his family's freedom, since he was originally from a free state. In a series of trials, he first won his case, though later the decision was reversed and, finally, rejected. With financial assistance from the son of his former master, he took his case to the Supreme Court.

No sooner had I learned of *Dred Scott v. Sandford* than the entire campus was up in arms over it. Everyone had an opinion, and most were against Scott's freedom. I kept silent, listening to all sides of the argument. What might I, a first-year and not even a student of law, contribute?

The decision eventually came down against Mr. Scott.

One cloudy afternoon Roger and I were comfortably ensconced in my room on the third floor under the rafters where it was fairly warm in winter, certainly in March, as the main chimney ran up the middle of the west wall next to my bed. Roger had been giving me sideways looks as news of the trial drug on, as though waiting for me to give my opinion on the matter.

"What do you think?" he said.

I let my temper get the best of me and spit at him like a surprised snake. "You are the outsider. What do *you* think?"

By the startled, abused look on his face, I saw I had hurt him and became even angrier at myself.

"I am sorry, Roger. It is only that I find myself with contrary feelings about this case. I wish the dang thing had never come up."

"I merely noticed you have been rather glum of late. Though most of our classmates are cheering the decision."

"Yes. Well, I am not most. That is the problem. I am not sure what

I am." It struck me that I meant this in more ways than one and sat on my bed, suddenly weary.

"You may tell me. Indeed, we are bosom chums, and I will keep what you say close to my heart. No one shall hear a word. We in England abolished slavery in 1833, you know."

I knew, all right. Emancipation was never mentioned in class, but everyone was aware all the same. Sometimes the fact was brought up derisively, as in, "Why do you suppose England must buy our cotton? Without slaves, the fools can't afford to grow their own."

I peered up at him. "I have told you of Isaac, whom I love like a brother. I would set him free if I could." My hands, my arms, took off of their own accord, flapping in the air like some two-bit orator. "I would free all our slaves, but then what would happen to us? To our land? And where would our people go? What would they do? They know nothing except how we raised them." All hollowed out, I dropped my arms. "Maybe that is our fault, but there it is. They have no land of their own, nothing to live on."

"I thought we were talking about this Dred Scott decision."

"You are not stupid and neither am I. We know Supreme Court decisions have far-reaching consequences."

"You reached farther than most, eh?"

"I doubt it."

"Your father pointed you in the right direction if he considered your being a lawyer."

"I do not think I want to be a lawyer."

"What do you want?"

I shrugged. "I have no idea. Yet."

❧

A wet winter passed into a glorious Louisiana spring. New life burst forth everywhere, from bees humming the golden air at our feet and about our heads to schooners of white clouds in the ocean of blue sky high above. Studying inside? Exceedingly difficult.

"Did you notice that web? How do you suppose such an insignificant creature can create something so intricate and glorious?"

I had not noticed. I was using the trunk of the willow we were under as a backrest and reading *An Essay on Man* by Alexander Pope. The text was requiring all my attention, which was somewhat difficult with Roger's head on my thigh continually flopping this way and that.

What the hell. I lowered the dull book and had to move it to glimpse Roger's green eyes peering up at me, a silly grin on his face. "All right, where is it?"

Roger pointed up, where a spider's net stretched among the thin, draping limbs of the budding willow. I leaned forward to see better. Fine luminescent threads woven in the most delicate circular pattern danced with each breezy movement of the dangling boughs.

Roger's hand reached the back of my neck and pulled down, a few inches only, and naturally I lowered my chin to peer at him. Our lips met.

I jerked. My throat went dry. We breathed the same air. I blinked once into his face, waited for an answer to an unasked question.

"I didn't plan that, but I have thought of it, lots," Roger said. His hand was in my hair, his fingers fondled the strands at the back of my neck.

"We must not," I said, and sat up.

"I love you, Adrien. 'I know perfectly well my own egotism, and know my omnivorous words, and cannot say any less, and would fetch you whoever you are flush with myself.'"

"What?"

"Walt Whitman. *Leaves of Grass*. I don't suppose you have read it. You ought. I'll lend you mine. He says it all. But I love you. No more kisses if that is what you wish. I don't care. I do care, but don't look at me like that. Don't turn me away. I couldn't bear it."

"I will not. I should, but I could not bear it, either."

Roger sat up, grasped me, his arms about my shoulders, his lovely, soft hair against my cheek.

This was true, pure love. Our love would not be ruined by my past with . . . Jacob. Or Grace, for that matter.

I pushed Roger back, rose, and stepped away. I brushed the grass from my trousers, straightened myself, refused to look at him. For the moment. "No more of —that," I said, my hand flopping in the air like a wounded bird. I peered at the other boy, reached up to brush hair from my eyes.

"All right." He gave me a quick smile, looked aside, back again, fingering his own tousled hair.

This time would be different. Like David and Jonathan in the Bible, with no shame attached. No matter how insistently that devil knocked at my door, I would not open it. Dared not.

The school year passed too quickly. I was overcome by surges of affection for my new friend, for everyone on campus, for golden spring when it arrived. Roger sent me love poems, and I attempted a watercolor of the bluebonnet-covered hills of home for his birthday.

At a popular café, we found a cozy corner beneath a fringed table lamp where we might hear one another over the raucous carrying-on in the room. During the dark hours circling midnight, we discussed Sophocles, our tutors, society, religion, and God. Roger had been raised Anglican, I, Catholic. "I am a sinner," he said, his eyes turning wet. It must have been the ale we were drinking. Perhaps the ale made me say I was the greater sinner. For that sin of which I could not speak and had not been confessed. That night, despite the drink and our damp eyes, we neither confessed our sins to one another.

Our mutual delight in one another was obvious, and other first years teased us with good will. They were gratified the "cold fish" had feelings, after all. Love of the romantic sort between young men was an accepted and beautiful thing, as long as it was spiritual only.

I finished the school year near the top of my class. Roger and I made plans to room together in the East Dormitory next fall and said our farewells with hugs and thumps on the back.

The new year began with such contentment before 1857 turned around and bit me like a Brazos snapping turtle.

Chapter Forty-Two

Bernadette

Journal - January 30, 1857: I must admit I am poor at keeping a journal. I have been busy with Holiday preparations, as Joanna was in the family way with her First Child, born on January 5! We were in a state of suspense that we might have a New Year's Day Baby. Alas, it was not to be.

Father Isidro came by on his rounds, baptized newborn Renée, and I confessed to reading Lord Byron's Don Juan—which made me feel better, though I believe Father Isidro had no idea who Lord Byron is or why I should confess to reading him. Does the Father's lack of knowledge make my confession moot? I do not believe so, as he is but an intermediary between me and God, and God knows, surely.

Journal - June 14, 1857: Adrien has been home a whole week!

He is thin, but Betta will soon solve that. He had a little hair on his chin, which he called a beard. Betta helped me convince him to shave it off. She was so funny. "What is that?" she declared. "Why, a flea couldn't hide in there."

Though Lucien now has a short beard, Papa has always been clean-shaven, but for a mustache he grew after Maman's passing. A little gray has arrived at his temples, which appears quite distinguished.

Adrien seems more content, dare I say, happier? We hear a great deal of his Special Friend from England, the one with whom he spent the Holidays. It appears that College and his friend Roger have nearly turned Adrien back into his former self. I write, nearly, because he carries about him a reserve, lacking the enthusiasm he had only two years past. Perhaps this is merely what occurs as one grows older.

He will help me with any of his books I wish to attempt. I cannot read the Plato in Greek, but I may attempt Pliny in Latin. We will take parts and read Candide by Voltaire in French together. Adrien said I shall see what an excellent Candide he will play as they are the same sort of Fool. I can barely wait to begin. Though there are parts the Church considers scandalous, those parts hardly matter considering Lord Byron's book. I admit to teasing him unconscionably about his being a perfect Don Juan.

Chapter Forty-Three

Adrien

High in the loft above the stalls was a fine place to pass Sunday afternoon reading. I sprawled on the floor, my back against a bale of hay, *Leaves of Grass* open between my knees. Isaac lay gazing at the canted ceiling close above, ankle on an upraised knee.

"Listen to this," I said. "'I believe a leaf of grass is no less than the journeywork of the stars.'" I closed the book, exposing its finely embossed leather cover.

Isaac chewed on a piece of hay, waved off a fly. "It's not subversive like some of the rest. How did he put it, 'taking care of the kept woman and sponger and thief and heavy-lipped slave?'"

I looked down at the book, ran my finger along the embossed flowers and leaves. "He says everyone is deserving of love and compassion." I found myself leaning forward expectantly.

Isaac tossed the chewed hay aside. "He can afford to *say* it, can't he? I also read the part you skipped."

I opened my mouth but didn't know what to reply.

Isaac sat up. "When you went to take a piss." He closed his eyes and recited: "'You settled your head over my hips and gently turned upon me, and parted the shirt from my bosom-bone, and plunged your tongue to my heart,' or near enough."

"You memorized that?" My heart throbbed as though it might break through my ribs.

"I recall what I read." Isaac lifted his chin, peered down his nose. "I am one talented nigga."

184

I threw a handful of hay at him, then threw myself, knocking Isaac onto his back. In the hay-dusted air, I turned my face away and sneezed, sat up and turned my back for another sneeze. "Dang."

Isaac raised onto his elbows, grinning. "Saved by hay."

I wiped the back of my hand across my nose, sniffling.

"I read to the 'Voices' part," Isaac said. "'Interminable generations of slaves, of prostitutes, of deformed persons, diseased and despairing,' et cetera. I don't care for being in such company. I got as far as the voices of sexes and lusts part, and that's when you came back."

"You know what he meant by it."

Isaac placed a hand on my shoulder. "Don't go guilty on me. Can't you take a hint? I want to read the rest."

"I don't think we should."

"Now I *really* want to read it." Stretching, he lifted the book from the floorboards. He leaned against the wall, upraised knees supporting the open pages, and flipped through them. "They *are* like leaves, aren't they," he murmured. "The pages, I mean. *Leaves of Grass,* clever metaphor."

Isaac would make a better student than half the fellows I met the past year at Centenary. He would appreciate the chance more than most of them.

"Here it is." Isaac raised the book up a little higher and began to read to himself.

I scrunched down. Fiddled with a piece of hay.

"I see what you mean. Glory be." He read on. Hooves shuffled below. "Oh." He dived the closed book between his knees. Looked at me, wide-eyed, and took a deep breath. "This white man is mad to publish this. Have they tarred and feathered him?"

"I don't believe so."

"Maybe people don't realize what they're reading."

"How can they not?"

"Here." He handed me the book. "I have work to do." Isaac was up, hurried past me to the ladder and down.

"Isaac?" He had no work on Sunday. I started to rise, did not, flopped onto my rump, book dangling. I lay on the hay and gazed into the rafters.

I remembered well what was on the following pages. Not the exact words in order, like Isaac, but I recalled them: *firm masculine coulter, tussled hay of head and beard and brawn it shall be you, fibre of manly wheat.* Written and published, right there on the page for all to see. As though a man loving, lusting for another man were acceptable. This Walt Whitman wrote that anything to do with love was acceptable, was beautiful.

Did *I* believe all print was true? What Whitman said in these "leaves of grass" *felt* true and beautiful. True and beautiful the way the world ought to be. Only it was not.

I knew the truth and dared not speak it.

⁂

Most days Isaac and I sweated in the tobacco fields. As before, we worked among the leaves the same as our people. I had not earned the right to supervise from horseback, as did Papa, Marcus, and Lucien.

Two days a week, more often when necessary, we worked cattle in the north pasture with Charlie. I began to glory in developing muscle and newfound energy and rediscovered that falling into deep sleep after a hard day of physical labor was immensely satisfying.

I had just cut, roped, and tied off a yearling calf, holding it down so Charlie could brand it, when I felt eyes on me. I twisted my soft rope into my back pocket, began winding my lasso, and turned. A horse and rider cast a long shadow off to my right. I removed my hat to wipe sweat from my brow with my forearm and looked up.

"Thought I'd take a gander at what y'all were up to out here."

"Lucien?"

"Does me good to see you sweat, Brother."

I ambled over close enough to catch his amused smile. I watched him lift the reins, turn his horse and trot off.

That was the first time Lucien called me brother.

※

Bernadette was nearly fifteen, a young lady. My little sister, but in some ways she had caught up to me, perhaps passed me by. I sought her opinion on all sorts of matters.

I told her more about Roger than anyone, as she asked so many questions: "What do you have in common? What do you like most about him? What do you do together besides study? What are his sisters like? His parents?" Discussing him almost made him present, helped make the hot days without him pass more swiftly.

July brought afternoon rains, adding to humidity. I put aging Troy out to pasture. Several springs ago, Papa had told me to choose a colt to train for my own. Roman was now a deep-chested, three-year-old gelding who would go all day, flick his ears at any new thing, but never spook. I saddled Roman every Sunday and rode about the countryside with Clay Thatcher and Henry Carlyle. I did what Papa wanted—reconnected with neighbors, learned their views on politics, crops, and social doings. There was talk of a new mail route from El Paso to California that would make far west territory closer. Would I see it one day?

Will continued his studies in Europe. At first, he sent letters once a week, then every couple weeks, eventually once a month or so. Lily was back East at some fancy lady's school.

In August, I finally received a letter from Roger, and the family was in the parlor when I opened it. Letters signified family occasions. I had not received a response to two previous letters until now, which was not like Roger.

Roger was not returning to Centenary as planned but going to England to continue his education. He wanted me to keep *Leaves of Grass* as a remembrance.

I excused myself and headed upstairs to my room, lay on the bed, and stared at the ceiling. I was tired and heavy; all air had left me. *Roger had spoken of love. Now this short farewell? No explanation?*

What is wrong with me? I expect too much. I am Candide, a fool who believes life is full of love and beauty and truth.

Life is a joke. A big joke on me.

Tapping on my door. Dear Lord, I knew who it was, who it had to be. What if I ignored her? Would she go away? I pictured her out there, standing in the hall. I had told her too much about Roger.

May as well get it over with.

"Come in, Berni."

What a lovely figure she cut, hesitating there in the doorway. She gave me a tentative smile, but the turn of her lip was a warning. I had best sit up. "If you must know, I am finished feeling sorry for myself. I have had practice at getting over disappointment."

"Oh, pooh. And here I was, all prepared to give you a shoulder to cry on." She scurried across my room and landed on the bed next to me. Hands folded in her lap, head turned toward me and tipped in order to continue at closer quarters. "You left rather hastily. We were keen to share news and you barely read your letter before disappearing upstairs. Papa had no idea what your escape was about. He is likely still wondering and worrying."

"Some shoulder."

She looked at her fine fingers that now picked distractedly, and might I say, angrily, at her skirt. "Yes. Well. I am somewhat peeved."

"Do tell."

She poked me in the ribs. Only Berni would do such a thing.

"I am gratified," she said, "to see you have ceased being disheartened. You can be such a trial."

"I thought you loved me." At this juncture, I was finding it difficult to keep my face and voice solemn.

"You know I do."

"I love you too, Berni."

We looked at one another, mere inches apart. Several dark curls had escaped from her upbraided hair and one dangled over her brow. I squinted and peered closely at her face, turning my head, searching.

She raised her hand to her cheek, opening her mouth slightly, copying me. "What?"

"I was sure I saw one of those beauty marks on your cheek."

"Do cease being capricious. Now go downstairs and apologize to Papa."

So much for Roger Broadhurst. I would be more careful next time. Next time? There would be no next time. If anything came my way, I would dally with affection like everyone else, but love? Forget love. No more fool, me.

In fact, it was years before his memory took its proper place in a far corner of my heart.

Chapter Forty-Four

Adrien

My new roommate in the East Hall Dormitory at Centenary was a tall, long-faced Creole from New Orleans by the name of Phillippe Gascon.

"I must spend one year at this miserable place before continuing my education in Paris. And you?"

Oh, Lord. Gascon's French Creole accent was much stronger than mine. "Adrien Villere, Washington, Texas."

"Texas," he pronounced with a sneering lip. "Yet you have a proper French name."

The fellow took my offered hand, and his was warm and dry when it emerged from his starched lace cuff.

"Papa was originally from New Orleans," I said.

"How fortunate! *Grandpère* was apoplectic when he learned I might have to room with an *Americain*, but you must be French Creole as well."

"Maman was French."

"You speak French from the old country?" Both brows jumped in unison.

"*Assurément.*"

"*Merveilleux!*" His entire face beamed.

What a marvel, I was acceptable.

I arose at five every morning and three days a week borrowed a horse from nearby stables and explored the countryside and sugar plantations to exhaustion, then rubbed the animal down until my arms ached. I buried myself in my studies. Engaging my mind saved me. I could pick up a book and disappear into its pages, into research or some problem. Discussions with fellow students were especially invigorating. I wrote letters home weekly to Berni and Papa, describing my progress.

Roger, well, Roger was in the past.

Phillippe was fine if one ignored his idiosyncrasies: the scent he patted on his cheeks and neck each morning, his condescension of anything not French or Creole, his air of absolute and total boredom. On the other hand, he shared the most excellent coffee sent every week by his maman. One weekend he led me to a restaurant in Baton Rouge that served the best red beans and rice and introduced me to beignets at the local bakery. For such culinary wonders, I could forgive him for everything.

"But you must come home with me to New Orleans!"

I had promised Papa I would not enter that "den of iniquity." Could it truly be so bad?

Six weeks into term, I learned something that made me temporarily forget about New Orleans, food, and my studies.

The mammoth Centre Building had been completed the year before, and I planned to spend a couple hours in its new library before Professor Gourdin's rhetoric class. Fellow second-year Sumter Milledge halted me in front of the arched entrance.

"Did you hear about Broadhurst?"

"No. Heard what?"

Milledge took my arm and maneuvered me from the doorway and into the shadow of one of the four-story Grecian columns.

"Why his father sent him away." Milledge glanced about furtively, as though expecting someone to interrupt us at any moment. "He was discovered last summer in a compromised position with another fellow. He's a sodomite."

Wham—my chest clamped. I grabbed a breath.

"Did you suspect? Last year you two were so close; then this fall you never mentioned him, not a word. Everyone wondered, you must have suspected. You might have said something but didn't. You didn't want to slander him, did you, with no proof."

Such a wary, dubious look he gave me. I must be extra careful with my response. "I . . . no. I did not. I mean, there was nothing." On a cool October morning sweat trickled down my neck, my back, dampened my armpits. I hugged my books tighter. *God help me.*

"Lucky, then. Lord knows, you wouldn't wish to be seen with him now—not as a close friend."

"They are sure? There is no mistake?" *Please, no.*

"Someone saw him, someone dependable, I'd guess. His father sent him off, didn't he? Can you imagine how this must have hurt his family? I wouldn't wish to be in his shoes for all the tea in China."

"No," I murmured, gazed down at my books, shifted a little to lean back against the white, fluted column. My limbs turned watery. *Hold on. Not now.*

"I *am* sorry." Milledge dropped a hand on my shoulder. "He was your friend, wasn't he? Must be a bit of a shock. Why don't you come with us tonight after supper? We're going to meet in Burnett's room before snatching the freshman flag. It'll do you good to raise a little hell."

"Sure," I said. "I will." Thank God. *Thank God I never let our love go too far. All the same, I might have.*

There dared be no caution in me that night when I threw myself at the other boys, the poor freshmen who tried to save their flag from the second years.

"I had no idea you were such a devil, Villere." Milledge and the rest, all winded and muddy, trotted behind the East Dorm with the captured flag. My nose leaked blood, and I was mindful of numerous pats on my back. I had lost a shoe somewhere. "Me and George have invited a few fellows to our room for a little libation." He poked at me with his elbow—some things never changed. "And I don't mean tea, either."

"I lost my shoe, I—"

"All the more reason."

A reason? To disobey the no-alcohol rule? Why not? I am, must be, one of them now.

In November, I received a letter from Papa saying he expected me home for the Christmas holiday. I had made no plans to the contrary, not like last year with Roger. Roger, whom I had loved. Will still studied in Paris. I would not think of Roger. I dare not.

※

On a rainy evening two days after Christmas, Papa requested that Marcus's family and all house servants join our family in the parlor. The room was cozy with the warm glow of a crackling fire and scent of beeswax candles on the decorated fir. But the grave look on Papa's face gave me pause.

Standing with his hands gripping the back of his favorite chair, Papa said, "I don't know if you have heard of the financial problems up North, of bank failures and gold lost at sea. What you are not aware of is that I had investments in those banks and have lost a great deal of our family's savings."

Lucien made a strange noise, a groan, quickly cut off. I swallowed, not yet realizing the full impact of Papa's revelation.

"I will have to sell many of our people and nearly half the land."

The fire snapped. We all knew what our people and land meant to Papa. Our situation was truly dire.

He looked at me, and I became stuck in my chair, breathless, dreading what Papa would reveal next. "We can no longer afford to send you to college."

What could I say? What was my fate compared to our people who would be sold? My fingers dug into the arms of the chair.

"We will manage, Papa," Bernadette said.

"We surely will," Betta added. "Times been worse an we did jus fine. Don't you worry none."

I said, "Isaac and I always did want to be cow hands."

Isaac joined in, and they all crowded around Papa, which gave me the opening I needed to slip out back, though cool air could not keep my supper from coming up over the edge of the porch. Rain soaked my head where I bent over beyond the eaves. Water dribbled down the middle of my back when I straightened.

Holy shit. So much for a college education. For travel. I cupped my hands to catch water pouring off the corner of the porch roof and hawk the aftertaste from my mouth.

How many of our people must be sold? Papa had never sold anyone of whom I was aware. Except that one woman, Rosanne. Marcus had told me that even Grace had been given her freedom and funds for a fresh start, although I had no idea where.

Papa must feel terrible. I never imagined he made investments in the North. What had possessed him to do such a thing? Had Lucien known? Marcus?

And the land. God. How much would go? To whom? Lucien's inheritance. And part of Bernadette's dowry. What right had I to complain?

There would be less tobacco and fewer people to work what was left. Surely, he would keep the cattle.

I must be the best damn cow wrangler Papa had ever seen.

Lowering my head into a raised arm against one of the porch posts, I smelled soaked cypress, rich, sodden earth, heard rain thudding on the roof, the distant roll of thunder.

Damn. Damn.

Chapter Forty-Five

Bernadette

I pulled on a shawl and found him under the eaves in the rain. He might never know how truly difficult selling a single slave was for Papa, and I must never tell him.

My first urge was to share as we did when small, so I walked over and tucked into his side where he put an arm around me. Courage flopped at our feet, and Isaac came and warmed the other side of me. This was as it had always been from the beginning. Somehow, this way, we and Blue Hills would be fine.

PART II

Chapter Forty-Six
Blue Hills, 1860

Adrien

I should never have returned to Hartwood Plantation—swore I would not. But by no means could I refuse my sister. The Hart picnic celebrated the return home of Will and Lily.

It had been five years since the incident. My thoughts slid away from that thought like a slippery fish. What would happen if I met Jacob? Could I behave . . . normally?

I had hoped an early morning ride would settle my nerves. Rambling over Blue Hills among oaks, meandering creeks, and rolling hills often brought problems into perspective. But here I stood, frozen by disordered thoughts in the downstairs hall.

During Father Isidro's visit last year, I had finally confessed, hoping my sin would recede into my childhood rather than continue to haunt my present. He took my confession in stride, as though such a story were not as shocking as I had supposed. Dare I imagine he had heard such things before? Fifty Hail Marys supposedly lifted my guilt for desiring such depravity, along with a promise never to act on such again. The other individual involved? It was up to him to confess, and Father did not care to hear the man's name. Since he was not Catholic, there was no point.

I dreamed an old childish dream that night—one from before Troy. Papa had given me a horse, but it was so small my legs hung over both sides and dragged on the ground.

"Adrien, is that you? Come here. Help me, please?" Berni

summoned me from upstairs. A glance at the grandfather clock in the hall told me I was late.

※

I kept a light hand on the reins as our two-wheeled shay passed swiftly, wheels singing, over the grassy road between spreading green fields of Hartwood cotton—as yet too early in the year to show white boles. A good deal of East Texas was planted in cotton, except for Blue Hills, where Papa grew tobacco much prized by our neighbors as well as buyers farther east. Papa's Kentucky-bred filly pulled us along at a fast pace, her high trot too fast for easy conversation, for which I was grateful. I would have enjoyed the ride but for our destination, and my thoughts churned like the Brazos in flood.

Over a rise in the distance amid green grass and oaks stood Randolph Hart's Greek Revival house, a rectangular edifice white as the cotton that would surround her in a few months. My heart gave a thud.

The drive formed a grand circle around back to the side yard, where other carriages parked beneath a copse of live oaks. I could not help but glance at the stables as we passed. The stables looked the same. My mouth went dry.

I had hoped to slip in quietly, but the filly created an unavoidable flashy entrance—head, tail, and legs lifted high as she trotted across the lawn as though the shay were a feather. One of Hartwood's people took her head as I secured the reins, hopped down and presented a hand to Berni, ready to burst with mirth by her grin and twinkle in her eyes.

"My," she said, "I had no idea."

"You did not, did you? Whose idea to hitch up Fair Melody?"

"Not mine."

I bet our overseer was behind this. Marcus Holland had never cared for Randolph Hart, and often attempted to prove Papa the better man—owned a finer plantation, finer horses, and happier and healthier Negroes—the last was easily proved.

No help for it. I gave Berni my arm and escorted her across the lawn toward the house and the gathering of local gentry. Several onlookers smiled our way. I would not be surprised at an offer for Fair Melody. "You must admit," Berni said, "the ride over was rather exciting. You enjoyed it."

"I expected her to settle down by the time we arrived."

"Rather the opposite, don't you think? One would suppose she, rather than I, hoped to catch a suitor today." Berni flipped her fan open to cover her smiling mouth, but not her flashing eyes.

Half the people in the county envied Randolph Hart's house. It was too ostentatious for my taste. Though, as children, we had relished charging about and hiding from one another in its numerous rooms and hallways. Ten two-story columns surrounded the building in support of the deep veranda where the picnic was taking place on the shadier, north side.

I might get through this farce as long as I behaved according to Maman's teachings. Act the gentleman.

Then I saw *him* coming toward us over the grass. Breath left me. All receded, muffling sound. I must take hold of myself.

Chapter Forty-Seven

Jacob

Jacob Hart had been on the lawn meeting and greeting since the first carriage arrived over an hour past. As eldest and heir, playing host was his job when the old rooster had not yet deigned to present himself. Probably up there having a cigar, overseeing his kingdom or some such. Let him. Not many more years and it would be Jacob's turn to rule the roost.

The old fool. Like those steamboats, his time is nearly past, and he doesn't know it. Jacob had warned Randolph Hart and his cronies of the importance of the railroad, but they hadn't listened. They refused to pay what the railroad requested to place its tracks through Washington, and the tracks had gone farther west through Brenham instead. *Well, now those fossils regret it. Washington is sinking fast in Brenham's rising wake.* The railroad brought goods and services up from the coast safer and faster than riverboats. Flood season did not delay trains.

Jacob recalled the last time his father had beaten him with his fists, the morning Randolph slapped Jacob's mother against a bedpost. Fourteen-year-old Jacob, nearly as tall as his father, swore he would do the same to Randolph one day. His mother was beyond reach now, passed away in the yellow fever that had taken so many others in the summer of '53.

Jacob strolled across the lawn to greet Adrien and Bernadette, and what a pair they made. Perhaps he should have waited for Bernadette to grow up, despite the trouble she might have given him. And Adrien, absent since Jacob overstepped himself. That business was one of his biggest mistakes. His emotions had gotten the best of him, and never would again. At six one, he stood gratifyingly taller than Adrien—it wouldn't do to look up at the boy. He gave him a sly smile before bowing and taking Bernadette's hand.

"My, but you are lovelier every time I see you. I almost wish I were single."

"You own a velvet tongue, Jacob." She smiled and retrieved her hand.

Jacob turned, straightened, cocking one knee, the picture of southern manhood.

"Hello, Adrien. I don't believe we've seen you since before you left for that college—Center something, wasn't it?"

"Centenary." Adrien straightened as well, weight equal on both feet, chest and chin slightly raised, eyes narrowed and bright.

God. He must be eighteen. It was beneath him to bait the boy, but he couldn't help himself. "Centenary. Our local Baylor unworthy. I suppose you're a man now, aren't you?" he said, raising a brow.

"I don't need two children to prove it."

Ho. He's developed a sharp tongue as well as a man's frame and height.

"Must you two bicker?" Bernadette tapped Jacob on his left biceps with her closed fan, moved forward, and took Adrien's forearm in one hand. "We were such devoted friends. As children, you were a dear older brother to us, like Lucien."

"You are right, my dear. I apologize," Jacob said. "William and Lily will want to see you; come up to the veranda." He gave her his arm. *I was never like Lucien, who paid as little attention to his siblings as did their father to his children.*

Chapter Forty-Eight

Adrien

I let Jacob maneuver Berni from my arm. She could scarcely walk between us, as space must be allowed for her ample skirts. Hands clasped behind my back, I followed like a skiff in the wake of a grand ship. My fear and anger subsided considering the picture she made, the glances she received from the young and old men we passed. She was, by far, the loveliest lady here. I managed the introduction; I might make it through the rest, despite feeling as weak as a mouse between the paws of our house cat.

We climbed the four whitewashed steps of the veranda and turned left toward welcome shade. Who was that rising off the porch swing beyond the well-groomed shoulders of so many gentlemen—a glorious smile of rosy lips and flushed cheeks, and wide welcoming eyes? Her face lit with expectation.

"Bernadette! Oh, Berni!"

Lily? Silly little Lily? Sapphire eyes were soon lost behind my sister's dark curls.

"I missed you so." Lily's hands grasped my sister's.

"I missed you. Look how beautiful you have become," Berni said.

"Look at you! Oh, Berni, we must find time to ourselves."

"Yes." Berni leaned closer and whispered. I hadn't heard my sister giggle like that since before Lily left. Before Maman—

Lily glanced up, past Berni's ruffled shoulder. Our eyes caught. "Adrien." Her face softened, the smile fled, returned, only differently.

My chest tightened. "It's you," she said, her voice a butterfly's flutter that nearly blew me over. *This can't be.*

Berni slipped aside, and Lily and I moved toward one another. I took her hand, such a tiny hand, raised it to my lips, warm, soft, graceful fingers, smelled apricots. I looked into her blue eyes. "Lily." I held her palm inches from my lips. Her mouth opened a little. The corner of one of her front teeth was chipped. I wanted to touch the place with my tongue. *Dear God.* "Your tooth."

"What?"

"Your—"

"Oh. That." Her lips widened.

I lifted my thumb, and her hand slipped away. Mine hung singularly suspended before slowly dropping.

"I fell from a horse. Aunt Willa was furious. She was mostly frightened, I think. Proper ladies do not go fox hunting, not at jumps, anyway."

"I imagine you were glorious."

"Falling from my horse?"

I lowered my head. *God, had I said that?* Surely heat was not climbing my neck. "Jumping. On horseback, I mean."

"I've enjoyed watching you make a fool of yourself over my sister, Adrien," a masculine voice interjected, "but I must put any critter out of its misery whenever the situation calls for it."

Yanked back to reality like a horse with a bit in its teeth, I had forgotten about Jacob, who stood between Lily and Berni.

"My goodness." It was Berni. Stepping in front of Jacob, her skirt smothering his boots on one side and mine on the other, she took my arm and one of Lily's. "I am melting of thirst. Shall we fetch glasses of Callie's famous punch?" We three were moving off before I could open my mouth. Or close it.

At any moment I expected Jacob to come forward, make some comment, some gesture, but he did not. My admiration for my sister went up another notch. Whatever fellow won her had better be worthy of her.

Gentlemen neighbors impeded our passage, all vying for the attentions of two lovely young ladies. One more boisterous than the rest sidestepped his fellows and laughingly armed his way to us.

"Excuse me, if y'all don't mind, I'd like to reacquaint myself with an old friend and his lovely sister, whom I've not seen in years. Holy Ghost, Bernadette, if I'd known how beautiful you'd become, I'd not have stayed away so long." He flashed a smile from beneath warm brown eyes. Sideburns draped his cheeks in the latest fashion.

"William." Berni smiled, arms wide and accepting. "Why, you have become a French gentleman. I warrant you had all the ladies in a tither."

He bent low and brought both her hands to his lips. "Not a one compared to you."

She laughed and swung to me and Lily. "Hear what those French folks did to our William!" She turned back to him. "Come here and give me a proper hug."

A second of surprise registered on William's face, followed by relief. Then they were in one another's arms, and he lifted her off the ground, set her down, again grasped her hands and smiled so big that a dimple showed in his cheek. "Now I truly have come home." He gazed at her for an almost uncomfortably long time, then turned. "Adrien."

"Welcome home, Will." My childhood friend had become a young man.

We hugged with hard pats on the back and gave my solar plexus a quick punch. "You're hard as a field hand. Father said you've been working alongside your people and had to leave school."

Randolph Hart would mention that. "Yes. Papa had to sell some of our land and our people after '57. We kept the acreage that produced the best leaf." The Panic had happened mostly up North to northerners. I was repeating what Papa had said. Defending. I should not have to. Not to Will.

"We were more fortunate," Will said.

"Yes, fortunate." *Smarter than Papa is what he meant. We should have kept to our own and not meddled in northern stocks.*

Lily took my arm, sending a warm surge through me. "Let's sit under the oaks like old times. I'll send Mae for a blanket, and we can take our drinks and eatables out there."

"I don't believe your father will approve," Berni said. I saw Randolph Hart approaching from the far end of the veranda, dragging along Lawrence Dobbs, heir to a cotton plantation farther south.

Lily's right hand slipped from my forearm as she raised it for the introduction to young Dobbs. Clearly, I was no longer welcome here, not in the way Mrs. Hart had accepted me years ago. Since losing half our assets and the abrupt end of my education, I now had nothing to bring to anyone such as Lily.

See the beautiful woman she has become. Life has played this joke on me. I wanted to leave so much display and pretense. Instead, I remained tenuously present and folded my arms, watching her, curling my toes within my boots.

I beheld only that lovely girl, her eager blue eyes, that dear, chipped tooth.

Chapter Forty-Nine

Lily

Lily's affections for Adrien had changed—she had loved as a child. She wanted love as a woman.

When she was four, Adrien had gazed at her as if she were a mirror in which he sought his own reflection. She yearned to run her fingers across his lashes and make tears. He turned away. She cried when he teased her.

She had watched him and Will and Jacob playing with the dogs, taking apart rifles, riding off before dawn to go hunting some animal they hauled to the back kitchen and handed over to Nancy, the cook. Boy things, dumb things, mostly. Despite the smile on Adrien's dirty face, he didn't care much about those things, either. He went because Will and Jacob did. She saw him stroking the fur of dead rabbits they killed, and once caught him being sick behind the spring house after their slaves drained the blood from a hog. She never let on she knew. She also did things or did not do them because they were expected.

Then one day, he had defended her. Without Bernadette asking him to. She would never forget the afternoon he climbed down from the tree to sit beside her. Never.

When she grew older, she read of undying love and other less romantic realities in those books Jacob gave her—beginning before school in Charleston and continuing long afterward. She discussed more acceptable tales with her cousin Mary, with friends Julia and Frances. But not the novels Jacob sent her. She mentioned those to no one. Except Jacob—and Bernadette.

In Charleston, she, Mary, Julia, and Frances met in one another's rooms, giggled and planned and invented stories about the young men to whom they were introduced, or the older, more interesting, gentlemen.

She spoke of Adrien.

"A childhood sweetheart!"

"No, he doesn't realize," she said.

"A secret! How romantic! Tell us! Tell us!"

She told a little, not all. Such whispers, exclamations, stifled giggles, and crinolines shushing across quilted, canopied beds. She told how Adrien had teased her, made her cry, and was sorry afterward.

Bernadette made him sorry. Bernadette defended her; she wanted to be strong like Bernadette. It frightened her how Jacob took Adrien everywhere on the back of that stallion. How Adrien laughed when he and Jacob rode across the fields together, scrambled down banks and jumped gullies and fences.

Jacob, not Father, put her on her first pony when she was seven. When their mother died three years later, it was Jacob who kept her and Will, as well as Berni and Adrien, busy with games, riding, and reading books right through winter. He never treated her as though she were stupid.

"You are like me, Lily," he said. "You have a sharp mind that is not meant to be buried by hypocritical, prudish society."

She was no overprotected city girl. That same summer, she became aware of neighboring boys' scrutiny. She followed Will out to the stables to watch Jacob breed Catchfire to one of his mares. Will indicated she should leave, but Jacob said she could stay if she wanted. They brought in the stallion, neck arched, snorting, prancing high and hooves landing with thuds that echoed in her ears. She had never realized how beautiful he was, how primal and majestic. He could easily shake off Jacob and the man grasping his halter, but his attention was on the mare.

Afterward, Lily spoke to no one. *I am not ashamed of what I feel. I am not like Susanne Carlyle or those other pious girls. I will never be like them. I am changed*, she mused and hugged herself with a delicious shiver.

An exciting world opened to her in those books, and she desired it.

She desperately wanted to attend school in Charleston. No one realized how fear of leaving Hartwood descended upon her the night before—how she cried. No one, save Jacob.

Jacob was privy to everything.

❧

Father told Porscha not to invite Adrien to the Hartwood ball. He was no longer eligible.

On a warm, breezeless evening the last Saturday in May, Mrs. Hooper, whose husband ran the First Bank of Washington, appeared at the ball with her hair curled and twisted on top of her head in a most amazing manner. William said it was the latest style from France. Perhaps she should try it. Would such a thing matter? In only a month, it had become obvious she could have any man she wanted. Any but the one she preferred.

She wore a new watered-silk gown from Charleston, the one that showed her décolletage to such advantage. Jacob raised his wineglass in salute from across the candlelit ballroom.

This was all so dull. She would choke on such dullness. Recent talk of slaves revolting in Texas bored her. Such horror hadn't happened here in Washington County. Who cared if Douglas and Breckenridge split the Democratic Party? Men would make such decisions without her. She snapped open her fan and turned back to Artemas Montgomery from Blossom Run.

"I suspect you haven't heard a word," he said, smiling, eyes only now returning to her face from lower quarters.

"Something about horses, wasn't it?" A safe guess—it was always horses, dogs, hunting, or politics. She felt her heart thumping. The room was a drum, and she stood inside.

"Ha!" John Moore hovered, wineglass in hand. "She has you. It's always about that mare of yours."

"I am sorry, will you gentlemen excuse me?" She brought her fan fluttering to her eyes, blinked over its lace edge, gracefully grasped the folds of her skirts in one hand and, with a sweeping turn that sent nearby candles flickering, made her way across the room to the double French doors. Through the parlor she rushed, down the hall past gilt-framed and glaring visages of her ancestors and up the rear servant stairs, stairs she had not used since she was ten or eleven. What the devil did it matter? The narrow corridor squished her hoop, and she heard a distinct ripping as she pushed the thing behind her.

She pushed the door so hard it slammed back against the second-floor wall and she stumbled, bubbles of hysterical laughter choking her throat and tears in her eyes. Someone was outside smoking on the rear hall balcony—he spun at the commotion.

"Lily? What the devil?" It was William. She stood there, grasping folds of her gown in both hands.

"Oh, William, I can't stand it."

"What? Has someone—I'll kill him, I swear—"

"No, no, nothing like that." She grasped the lapels of his ivory linen coat, her cheek against his silk cravat. He smelled of shaving cream and tobacco, but not so rank as Father's.

"I, I." She stuttered like a fool. Dear, sweet William.

"You are all glowing and pink. It's quite pretty, but please don't faint on me."

Faint. She was hardly the fainting type.

He led her to one of three old armless wood chairs from which green paint had peeled in ragged strips. They had long been relegated up here for use by house slaves.

"Here. Sit. Tell me why you are upset." He sat in the other chair, leaned on his knees, and mashed the tip of his skinny little French cigar against the floorboards. "You know you can. You always have, if you will recall."

She forced a meager smile for him and regarded her entwined hands in her lap. It was a terrible lie on her part that he assumed she had told him all. She had told him a good deal, but hardly all. Dear

Will. She would not enjoy using him, but he was all she had. After all, he would surely get what he wants.

"Why are you up here alone, William?"

He sat back. The chair wobbled a little beneath his weight. A man's laughter drifted up from the porch below.

"I came up here to concentrate, gather my thoughts." He gave her a bemused smile.

Only six weeks home and I expect he's decided. "About Berni?"

A soft lilac breeze rustled the oak leaves.

"Yes. About Bernadette." He crossed an ankle over knee, an arm over the back spindles.

"You have been over there often enough since you arrived home. Are you courting her?"

"Yes, I told Father earlier and received his approval. I'll ride over there next Saturday to see Paien. If he approves, I'll see Bernadette."

"Why not tomorrow, on Sunday, when you will catch everyone at home?"

Her brother glanced down. *Oh, of course. How much more difficult to face the entire family at one time.*

"What about Adrien? Will you call on him?"

"Yes. I hope to, after Bernadette. I don't expect he'll mind. We were such splendid chums growing up. He generally agrees with whatever Bernadette wants, if you'll recall."

"Yes, he does." She leaned forward, clutching the fabric at her knees. "I love him, William."

He blinked at her. "Which one?"

The look on his face nearly made her giggle. She lowered her head, a hand to her mouth. "Oh, Adrien, of course."

"You can't." Both feet hit the floor, hands flat on knees.

"Why not? I have always loved him, since we were children."

"He has nothing to offer you. You hardly know him."

"You are being ridiculous. I know him as well as you know Berni, who has no more. Do you love her any less?"

"That's different, and you know it. I can support Bernadette. It's unfair Adrien lost his education, but without it, he would be the first to admit he has nothing to offer."

"The others are vain, dull, and disagreeable. All I think of is Adrien."

"Is he aware?"

"I doubt it."

"You see him from when you were children, Lily. You must stop."

"Stop! I must stop. As if I could snap my fingers, say it, and do so. Help me. Let me talk to him. Let him tell me he doesn't love me and set me free of it." She grasped his hands, her eyes full of tears. One dropped right onto her finger, and another licked *his* finger. Did he notice?

"Oh, Lily, you mustn't."

"Help me, William, please." Another tear; she sniffed. He slipped his hands out from under hers, patted her with one hand, and reached in his trouser pocket for a kerchief with the other—to wipe her nose; she reached to take the cloth. He drew back, tried again, confused, hesitated, let her take the kerchief. He glanced at his lap as she dabbed her eyes, her nose. His eyes lifted to her face.

"I'll arrange a meeting."

"Yes?" She crushed the cloth in her fist.

His eyes narrowed; he peered over the railing toward the trees. "I should be there."

"No, you mustn't. It will be difficult enough if, when, he says he doesn't love me. To have you present. I would be mortified. And say nothing to Daddy or Jacob. You can imagine."

"I can. If it was anyone but Adrien, if we hadn't all been children together, and I didn't trust him as I do." He took a deep breath. "All right."

She stood, skirts rustling. When he rose, she rested her hand on his sleeve.

"William. I love you so. You are the best brother. I will be sure to remind Berni how fine you are." She hugged him, her tattered skirt lifting behind. He was so much better than she.

Chapter Fifty
Blue Hills

Bernadette

Journal of Bernadette Villere - June 1, 1860: *Will Hart, of all people. I have always considered him a brother. I should say, *had* considered him. For the first time, I have an idea what those books are saying. Desire. Oh, my. Will? I want to laugh, but this is truly not the least amusing.*

I am all in a muddle. What happened to never getting caught up in such a thing? To be caught by someone so near, or so familiar? Perhaps he does not feel the same? I fear he does. I fear he does not. This is disheartening. I may desire Will Hart. There. Truly? Oh, I do. I want to run my fingers through his hair, which I am sure must be soft. When his eyes look into mine. No. I will write no more of this nonsense. Bad enough to consider it. I believe he has a good heart. He made me laugh so yesterday. At himself, actually, and that is a fine quality in a man. He hurried to help Esther when he saw her struggling with a heavy pot.

Will is a man I can love. But do I want to marry him?

Do I? I think best in the early morning before breakfast, before I've taken coffee. Pros: He is a fine man I expect I know rather well, and the prior reasons. Yes, I could do those things I read of in books with Will. My goodness, yes. It would make Papa happy, and Adrien, and it would save Blue Hills. Cons: I am not in love with him. But that will grow, as I am so very fond of him. Most importantly, I believe he will let me be myself.

What do you think, Maman, shall I marry William Hart?

Chapter Fifty-One

Adrien

Midmorning June sun beat down hotter than blazes. I moved through heavy, sodden air down rows of tobacco plants, most of which had grown so high that the hats of field hands dipped among the tobacco like straw islands in a sea of green. Brown resin covered my gloves. The sticky stuff stuck on anything that rubbed the damp leaves.

I dropped to my knees, lifted leaves, and peered beneath. Last year we nearly lost this field to blight. I had been a mite careless and left checking lower leaves to children. Only two fields remained since Papa sold the north portion, which cut our yield in half, and that barely managed.

Completing my rows, I ambled to the trickling creek—and shade of oak, hickory, and sweetgum trees. Roman, flicking his tail at flies, showed no awareness of my arrival except the turn of one slow, brown ear.

"Lazy beast." I tucked my gloves into a back pocket and ran a hand over his rump. Upon reaching the water, I dropped to my knees in cool, green grass, dunked my hat, and splashed enough water over my head to soak my shirt. Squatting back on my heels, I watched tiny striders skate back and forth over the glittering surface above reeling strands of brown, green, and red water plants. Cicadas whirred loudly from above. The buzzing trailed off, and others answered from across the creek. How nice to lie here awhile and do nothing.

Hat in hand, cool water dripping down my face and back, I combed fingers through my wet hair. I walked to Roman, scratched under his mane where he liked it, peered out and admired the sun-soaked hills dotted with white star-shaped blooms and green leaves. Plenty of work from dawn till dusk, year after year. And Blue Hills would go to Lucien. What was I doing here, besides earning my share of the dwindling profits at the end of each season?

I fancied distant places of which I had read, of mountains so high the snow stayed on them in the middle of summer. Of deserts where stars were so close you could practically touch them. My Centenary education had left me aching for more than tobacco fields. Discontent was my constant companion—to love a place yet want to be gone from it. This land was not mine. Never would be.

Papa held the family together to keep Blue Hills going. They did not need me. I had saved nearly every coin and paper in a tin box beneath my bed. Roman and the saddle were mine. I owned a rifle, a shotgun and a fine pistol given to me by Papa. I could leave.

Did I have enough to buy Isaac's freedom?

What would become of Berni if more were lost?

Now, Lily, whom I had no business contemplating. I had promised myself I would not get caught up again, yet in one glance, her innocent beauty had captivated me.

Avoid her—in that way lies safety. Besides, her father will keep her busy meeting every eligible bachelor in Washington County and beyond, and I am far from eligible.

Roman shifted under my hand, raised his head and ears, and snorted. I shoved my hat on, squinted into the sunlight. Saw a wavy outline on the sun-drenched horizon, floating against the flat, cloudless sky below shimmering leaves of cottonwood shading me and Roman. I knew that sorrel gelding, as Randolph Hart had given it to Will upon his return home.

I waited until Will rode into the shade, then stepped forward and placed a hand on his mount's neck while its rider dismounted. "What brings you out in this heat?" We smiled and grasped one another's forearms in greeting and turned to enter the deeper shade, leaving the sorrel to shake his head at a fly.

"I saw your father this morning," Will said. "I'm courting Berni."

"Ah. You found your courage." I sank to the ground, my back against a downed cottonwood. If she agreed, Berni would be taken care of. I tore a blade of grass lengthwise and handed half to Will, who sat down beside me. We chewed the ends while gazing off across the fields, arms on upraised knees.

"You guessed," he said.

Cicadas buzzed from somewhere behind, louder than our voices. We waited until the sound settled.

"With all your visits and heart-sore looks, I would have bet on it."

"I wasn't that bad, surely. Was I? You don't think she felt sorry for me."

I chewed my grass and could not hide my grin.

"Pshaw!" Will punched me in the biceps. I leaned away and snorted.

"What do you think?" Will said.

"More important—what does Berni think? She was concerned you would return all puffed up and fattened on French cooking. When you did not, she considered you might be the best of a rather poor lot. If you had the nerve to come forward, that is." The cicadas started up again, long rattles.

"You can be a real pig, Adrien."

"I prefer a goat, as it climbs anywhere and enjoys eating anything."

"You stink like a pig."

"Mine is a righteous stink. I am a working man, whereas you sit on your rump all day and dream of my sister."

"I love her. And she said yes."

"Berni has never been one to dillydally. You better take care of her, or this pig will stomp you good." It took all I had to keep from jumping up and cavorting like some mad clown.

"You know I will." He turned to face me, dropping what remained of the mangled grass.

Our eyes met. "I know, Brother."

I smiled. We grasped one another, hugged. "Shall I kiss your cheeks like the French? *Mon ami.*" Posthaste, I did. "Now you have a green smear on one cheek."

Will slapped at his cheek, rubbing frantically. "Christ, we're in Texas, not France."

"We certainly are."

"Yes, well, I'm sorry. I remember how we talked of going to France together. Damn shame about those stocks, the flood, and—"

"That is past, Will." Our losses were the last thing I wanted to be reminded of, or discuss. "What are your plans?"

"We'll live in Brenham. Wilkes and Barnes are opening a shipping office there, and I'll manage it."

I might hug and kiss this man again, for Berni would be well taken care of . . . and loved. "Fast work. Congratulations."

"While I was gone, I made contacts in France and England, also Richmond and Houston. Father will use us and ship our cotton by railroad from now on."

"Like everyone else."

Will picked at the grass between my feet. "Sometimes I feel like a traitor."

"It is not your fault Washington's councilmen looked no further than the steamboat trade. The town was never your responsibility, nor your family's."

"Regarding my responsibilities." He removed his tan planter's hat and dangled it in one hand. "I have a favor to ask."

"What may *I* do for *you*?"

Will regarded his hat as he turned it by the brim. "I would like you to speak with Lily. Mae will accompany her, of course."

Dear God. I intertwined my fingers, peered down at them. "Why?"

"She fancies . . . she has this childhood fantasy about you, can you imagine? You recall how close we all were when we were little, growing up together, always at one another's homes. She loved Bernadette and you. You were the only boy near her own age. She formed an attachment, and you, well, you are aware of how you are."

"How I am?" *I am a fool, is what I am. A terrified fool at present.*

"Must I say it? Your dark good looks, with a way about you. You conversed with girls when the rest of us couldn't."

I dropped my head, exhaled a drawn-out breath. Then I turned to look at Will, forcing a grin. "I dare say, it was because I enjoyed their company when you all considered them stupid nuisances. It is amazing to me that any of them put up with you insufferable dolts."

"Your sister doesn't think I'm so bad."

"Berni is strong-willed. I am sure she believes she can make something of you."

I watched Will's eyes, his entire face, soften. "I love her so much, Adrien. I have loved her ever since she insisted on climbing that tree with us when we were ten. We sat up there for at least an hour, do you recall?"

"I do."

"This thing with Lily. If you talk to her, that will likely be the end of it." He ceased turning the hat and looked at me. "Will you do it?"

I had become engrossed in rubbing the tips of my thumbs together. "Yes." I raised my eyes to meet Will's. *Heaven help me.*

"I was hoping to rely on you. I would have heard no end of fret from Lily otherwise." Will pushed his hat on. "She often rides early in the morning. Is there somewhere you can meet?"

"How about right here? We'll be working this field for the next month or so. We can ride down the creek."

"Her girl, Mae, will be with her on Sam. You remember Sam."

"That gray mule. Still going strong, is he?"

"Old but hearty, like Father."

"That is an apt comparison if ever I heard one," I said.

We walked together toward Will's horse. "I had hoped Father might mellow as he got older." He took the reins and mounted.

"Not yet, he hasn't."

I slapped the sorrel's flank before Will could respond, and the animal cantered off, soon slowing in the heat.

I watched the rear of the horse, its tail swinging, Will's back rocking. *My fine friend. Is it God or the devil who planned this?* Turning to

Roman, I gathered the reins, placed both hands upon the saddle, and lowered my head between my arms. Will was correct. Lily did not know me. Hers was a child's fantasy. Christ. *I am not prepared for Lily Hart.*

I knew nothing of her, except the little girl that used to follow us around. I saw her face, her sweet smile, and my chest clenched. It was her innocence, the same innocence I had lost years ago, that drew me. Lust drew me. *I will not do that to her.* I swung into the saddle, pulled Roman's head up, and we were off. Maryanne might be free. Maryanne DeLeon and I had had an affinity for one another for nearly a year now. Perhaps, after spending an evening with her, when I saw Lily I would be able to use my head and not give in to my baser instincts. Which brought to mind what I considered my baser instincts, from which I immediately shied as a horse would from a nest of rattlers.

❧

A muggy morning two days later the mule team barely needed a tug on the bridle from Ash to move to the next row. At this rate, we should finish harvesting a quarter of the field by noon. If we were lucky—no rain, nothing unforeseen—by August, this entire field would be in the curing barn. Yesterday Charlie Woods had told me it was time to castrate the calves; the cow barn roof and fences needed mending.

Hovering over it all like an unforgettable tune was my last image of Lily Hart. Her voice, her smile with the chipped tooth.

"You gonna put those leaves in the wagon or stand there lovin them the rest of the morning?" Isaac stood before me, holding the end of a strung tobacco stick and eyes sparkling with mirth.

I grabbed the opposite end of his stick and lifted. "Heat must be getting to me."

"Something is. You've been dreamy as a new bride these last weeks. Maryanne find somebody else to warm her bed?" Maryanne had plenty of men to warm her bed. She never mentioned them, nor did I for fear of losing our current arrangement.

"I should not have told you about her."

"You had to tell somebody." Isaac grinned. "I told you about Molly."

Hoofbeats approached from the hill behind us, and Isaac's expression made a good bet who it was. I was expecting her, after all, and grabbed the clean shirt I had previously thrown over the side of the wagon. I hastily pulled it on, heart beating too hard and fast for a mere greeting with a neighbor. Isaac, folding his hands and bending in his usual parody, said, "Best I be off, Masta," and hurried down the row. I turned.

Lily's black, white-stocking mare nodded her head and pawed the ground. Clearly, the mare did not care for this unaccustomed halt in her morning exercise. Lily was pert and pretty in a dove-gray riding habit, her gold curls pinned up and dangling beneath one side of a sporty hat with a blue feather. She perched on one of those English sidesaddles, of all things.

Mae, Lily's servant girl, sat on the gray mule behind on Lily's right.

"Good morning, Lily." I touched the brim of my hat.

"Good morning to you, Adrien." The mare flung her tail.

"Morning, Mae."

Sam, the mule, stretched his neck, pulling Mae's arms. "Mornin, Marse Adrien."

"Will you spare a few moments to ride along the creek with me?" Lily leaned forward, patted the mare's neck. "Star doesn't like halting, and there's a trail under the trees. Do you remember?"

"I do, and I can make time for you, Lily." I turned to where I had left Roman beneath a copse of live oak. Did I say that? Christ. I felt her eyes on my back, which made walking difficult, as though my legs had become rickety. *She is not watching, you inflated goat.* I did stumble at the last, but hopefully hid it by leaning against Roman and picking up the reins.

Chapter Fifty-Two

Lily

Riding out to meet Adrien was the bravest thing she had ever done. She had dreamed of him while away at school and pictured him as the hero of novels. When they were children, when he hadn't ignored her, he had been . . . felicitous. Except for the teasing that had driven her mad. It had surprised her that day on the veranda, how grown up he had become.

She kept glancing at him, then down, away, her eyes constantly shifting. He will know, he will feel it. How can he not, if their eyes meet for long? She will tremble, make an unseemly fool of herself. When he faced elsewhere, she stared. His sleeves were turned up above his elbows, and the faintest trace of dark hairs arched on tan forearms. The muscles of his shoulders and back rolled under his damp shirt.

The big bay shambled along, and Adrien relaxed. She signaled Star and cantered past him. How long would it take him to catch up? The rutted road was clear of debris and potholes; a short run should be safe. She heard his horse come up on her left and risked a peek. Adrien smiled at her, right hand lazing on his thigh. He could be in a rocking chair. She was reminded of childhood and wanted to strike him with her quirt. Then she laughed.

They settled to a walk and turned down a hill, past a group of white cattle, toward a snaking line of trees to the creek: dappled shade, flickering bright green of cottonwood, sycamore, hackberry, and willow. A squirrel chirred a warning from above. A jay answered, *check-check-check.* The cooler air caressed her face and limbs where she had pushed up the arms of her blouse, making her shiver. Green water gurgled over oval stones and smooth, moss-covered rocks. They rode to the center of the stream, where Adrien lifted one foot from the stirrup and hooked it over the saddle horn while both horses drank. The creek was six to seven feet wide this far north but only five inches in the deepest eddies. By mid-August, it would be nearly dry. Nearby trees were "old as Moses," over eighty feet tall and full of chirping birds. They waited for Mae to catch up.

"I'm glad you didn't sell the land along the creek," Lily said.

"It would be the last to go, though Papa could get more for it." He was leaning forward, arms crossed over his leg, hands dangling. His shirt was open at the neck where his exposed skin, red from the sun, glistened with damp. His horse took a step, gently rocking his rider from the hips down, and blew a big, noisy fart. Adrien smiled.

Her thoughts were unseemly.

"Adrien?"

His eyes opened wider, brows raised. Her heart beat furiously. "We are no longer children," she said.

He sat up. "We are not."

Mae rode into the trees behind them.

Adrien lowered his leg, and they moved on across the stream.

She was glad Mae had arrived. And furious.

They rode side by side at a walk, and Mae followed at twenty feet or so.

"Lily, will you listen to me with an open mind?"

What does that mean? "Of course."

"When I saw you a couple weeks ago on the veranda, I thought you were the loveliest girl I had ever seen. I still do."

Oh, God.

"I thought you were a pretty little thing when we were children, a bit of a pain sometimes." He turned in the saddle and grinned at her, adding, "But pretty, nonetheless."

Star tossed her head. Her skin quivered as though flies tickled her.

"You are aware Will arranged this meeting. He told me why." He glanced at her.

"I thought he might. I never asked him not to." She could not look at him; she gripped the reins because Star was trying to take the bit and jerking at her arms. Adrien leaned across and took the near rein close to Star's mouth.

"Do you want to dismount?"

"No. I've got her; just give me a minute."

This was her own fault. Settle down, settle down. "There, girl, there." Pat her neck. "That's better." *A nice, quiet walk.* "Father said she's a bit high strung, but I like her that way. She takes a firm hand, is all."

"I can see that," he said. They smiled at one another.

She's okay now, she's ready.

The sound of the creek was lovely, and the birds.

"Listen," he said, and she heard—*tsee-tsee-tsee*— "there," he pointed left to a flash of yellow among the green.

"A warbler, how delightful." They stopped to listen. The song went on and on, as if the little thing's life depended upon it.

"He is telling the other males this is his territory, and they had better stay clear." He gazed into the trees.

"You mean it's not for his lady love, and how do you know it's a male?"

"He only sings that song in the spring and, among birds, only the males carry bright plumage to attract females." He gave her a satisfyingly vulnerable smile, then glanced away.

She was sure he blushed. It gave her courage. "You learned about birds at Centenary?"

"One thing." His horse moved forward. "This is another thing I am learning."

"What?"

"Who you are now."

Who am I? Sometimes I hardly know.

"You do not know me either, Lily. I am no longer that boy who teased you so unmercifully."

"So, you are aware of the teasing."

"Afterward, yes. Berni reminded me."

"You never said why you ceased visiting so suddenly. We suspect it had to do with Jacob, as you haven't gotten along since."

He looked directly at her, his gaze intense and unwavering. "We?"

"Me and Will, of course. Not Father. He never paid much attention to us when we were little."

He turned away. "It does not matter, Lily. What matters is that perhaps you feel love, but it is not for me. What you feel is for that child I was, or for something you think I am. If you truly knew me, all my faults and desires and foolishness, you would see I am just another man, like all others. Likely less, for I have nothing to offer you, who deserves so much more."

"How do you presume to know what I deserve?"

He grinned. "See, I have already put my foot in my mouth."

"What an absurd picture that makes; the odor would be quite dreary, to say nothing of the taste."

"What a strange sense of humor you have."

"Strange? You bring out humor in me, which is far more pleasant than dull weeks spent heretofore. Perhaps we should meet again, to make one another laugh."

"Only if I may tease as I used to."

"You forget. I studied at Madame Talvande's French School for Young Ladies and learned how to conduct a return sally upon assault from any quarter."

"That remains to be seen, Miss Hart."

"It does, Mr. Villere."

⁂

Like any man concerning a woman, he is sure he has the upper hand, she mused, riding home under the weight of heavy, bronze Texas heat with Mac at Star's heels. Sweat trickled down the center of her back, pooled in private places. *He does not know me. In that, he is correct. But we shall meet again—and again, and again. If I am careful. I did not study the French arts for nothing, even if my books were not all from the school library. I will not be some planter's wife, old before her time from bearing children, or locked up in some mansion with a fat, old, lusty politician. I will have the man I love.*

Normally, she despised the heat. She rejoiced in it now, gave Star her head, and closed her eyes, contemplating his dark, deep-set eyes and how his beautiful, firm hands so easily guided that big horse.

Chapter Fifty-Three

Adrien

Rain beat a staccato tap on the roof of a square, snug house three blocks south of Bonham Street on the edge of Washington. Water gurgled down the drainpipe. A damp draft crept through the draped window, flickering the flame of a glowing kerosene lamp on a marble-topped table. Turned hardwood, satin, and burgundy velvet completed the room along with a carpet that pictured maroon peacocks strutting amid a garden of azure and citrine foliage.

Satin sheets sighed from a massive four-poster bed. A female voice, surprisingly husky on the left: "Are you going to tell me who she is?"

Me on the right, her left: "Hmm?"

I was too young at the time to know any better. So many of us were. I should have listened to those, like Maryanne and my papa, who knew.

Maryanne DeLeon pushed herself up against the pillows, dark hair tumbling about her bare shoulders and full, exposed breasts. She reached to the night table for a thin French cigar, picked up a gold-trimmed porcelain lighter, and flicked open the top with her long, polished fingernails. The flame cast red highlights dancing in her tangled locks. She raised her chin, blew a thin stream of smoke, and returned the lighter to the table.

"The one who sends you to my bed every week, dear boy. Neither of us are fools. Indeed, I am not. Your visits have doubled, though I am aware tobacco has not ceased growing."

I sat up, and the sheet slid down across our laps. I carefully rearranged the emerald necklace that had become twisted around her neck. "One of these nights you will set us afire."

"Isn't that my purpose?" she said.

Maryanne's lustrous hair was the color of a prime beaver pelt. Her deep brown eyes were invariably full of mischief, often passion, and always intelligence. Tall for a woman and voluptuous as a Renaissance Venus, if even half the adventures attributed to her were true, she must be in her late thirties. She had retained the skin and body of a much younger woman, certainly the stamina of one. Men adored her. She discussed politics with governors and senators and held her own at the finest table. A scandal had caused her to leave Richmond, for the sake of a senator or someone similar, and she now hid out in Washington, Texas.

"You are attempting to change the subject." She blew a puff into my face.

"You are correct."

"Miss Hart won't be riding so often in the morning since the rains have started." She had pulled up her knees and dangled her hands over them.

My chest thudded. "How did—"

She leaned toward me, placed two fingers against my lips. "It is my business to know what goes on in this county. Don't fret. No one else is aware, certainly not Mr. Hart, senior." She slipped her fingers down my chin, my neck, my chest. "You likely will not take heed of my words, yet I will say them. You have no prospects, nothing but a gentle heart and an uncommon beauty, which will get you women, but nowhere in this man's world." She poked my temple with her finger. "And a mind you refuse to use."

She leaned closer. The aroma of spice and tobacco on her breath made my breath catch with renewed passion. "You do recall I once told you Flora is not only my paid girl, but my confidante. That slaves hear and are privy to all, including everything their white masters get up to behind closed doors—or on long rides across the county.

You may be considerate, but like most wealthy southern men, you are self-absorbed and think yourself special."

"I am no longer wealthy, Maryanne, as you are well aware."

"Ah, so you admit the self-absorbed and special part."

There went that. Nothing like being told you were self-absorbed, etc., by the woman you were in bed with to make one limp. Particularly if one suspected she was correct.

Pulling away, she took another draw from her little cigar and let the smoke drift from between her lips. "You grew up wealthy, and such habits are not easily lost." She came close, again placing her palm on my stomach. "This is a foolish game you play, Adrien. It goes nowhere. You know this is true. Lily Hart is not for you. There will be tragedy at the end."

I had never seen her so serious. Peering into my eyes from mere inches away, her warm palm pressed against my clenched middle. Perhaps if she would—drat, she continued with her lecture.

"There is a much bigger game afoot with which you should be concerned, and it will have considerable impact upon both your families."

"If Lincoln wins the election—the talk of secession?" It must be what she meant; it was all everyone talked about. Talked? Many were yelling, declaring they would shoot "that monkey" if he became president. But I did not want to discuss politics.

"If he wins, and I fear he will, the North will never accept secession." She stroked my stomach; I would return the favor and reached to do so.

"Why not? Why should they care? We have the right; it is—"

Her stroking hand punched—hard enough to make me cough.

"Think! Think, you stupid boy!" She pushed my thigh with first one, then both her feet. "Out," she declared, her voice raised and snappy. "I was looking forward to more pleasure, but you have ruined it. Don't come back until you have used the brains God gave you."

I have ruined it? I have? I had to catch myself, grab at the mattress or I would be on the floor. Bad enough getting tangled in the sheets. Holy Ghost, it was cold out of bed; the fire was nearly out. I had tossed my clothes over a chair, and they were cold as well. At least the rain had stopped. I glanced at her while pulling on my trousers. She watched me from beneath lowered eyelids, one arm crossed over tucked-up knees under the quilt. Her elbow rested there, her hand gracefully holding the cigar, its smoke trailing toward the ceiling. She made me feel *I* had been bought. I never bought her favors; I could not afford her. Our relationship was one of mutual pleasure.

Flora sat sewing next to the fire in the front parlor. She jumped up to get my hat and coat hanging on the rack by the door, held the coat open for me, held out my hat. "Thank you," I said. "The fire in the bedroom needs tending. Goodnight, Flora."

"Night, Marster Adrien." She gave a little curtsy and opened the door before I could. I started out, halted, turned, reached into my trousers pocket for a coin and placed it in her hand.

"Thank you, suh."

"Thank you, Flora."

Maryanne had never kicked me out before; my departure had always been mutual. At least it had seemed so. On such a cold, wet night, too, with a long ride home and no stars or moon to light the way. Damn her. She was only a high-priced adventuress, after all. She accepted my meager gifts with grace, as did Flora, but I noticed the expensive jewelry that newly appeared on her throat, in her ears and hair.

I found Roman in the shed out back and gave him his head, depended on him to stay out of the worst puddles and sucking mud.

What had she meant—the North would never accept secession? Would southern states actually leave the Union? Would Texas? People talked, but people always talk. The southern papers and every red-blooded Texan believed Yankees were godless, hypocritical destroyers of the Constitution and, if faced with southern moral conviction, would back down at the first opportunity. Would they? I could not imagine fighting for a government like the North, where so many immigrants worked day after day inside a dark, smelly factory like some dumb animal. Texas had its own Irish and German settlers. Would they fight for secession? Fight, sides, what was I thinking? That it would come to that.

Maryanne's fault, putting me in such a mood.

Henry Carlyle and Clay Thatcher were secessionists. As was Will.

What held me back?

Damn this rain.

⁂

The following evening, my family gathered in the parlor where we shared the light of two kerosene lamps. Lucien's two young boys were upstairs in the nursery. I recalled how Berni and I had often lain awake for hours up there whispering and telling stories.

Papa chewed on his pipe stem from his favorite chair next to the fireplace. He smoked, he chewed, he smoked. He was first to read the *Texian*, two or three days old by the time he brought the paper from town with the mail. Sometimes he read a book—often reread the last couple years. Tonight, it was Sir Walter Scott. Now and then his dark eyes rose over his reading spectacles and gazed around at us, his head unmoving. *Does he get satisfaction that we are all here? I expect he misses Maman.*

My heart still clutched each time I thought of her, saw her sliding from her horse to the ground, calling my name. An insect bite, the doctor said. Not your fault. But I had been with her.

At least she did not experience our losses. Half our land gone and more than half our people. Simon, who had arrived as a young man with Maman, remained. Papa would never sell Marcus, Betta, or Isaac. They were family. Betta had taken over the cooking, sometimes with Joanna's and Berni's dubious help. Horace and Esther, who were brother and sister, had been sold to Uncle Phillippe in Galveston, who would take excellent care of them. My uncle and aunt had admired Esther's cooking for years.

The second kerosene lamp lit the circular table where Berni and Joanna sat across from one another, working on a quilt for Berni's trousseau. The quilt took up half the oak top before it cascaded in a heap onto the worn carpet.

Lucien rattled his newspaper together, stretched, and rose from his armchair. He bent over Joanna's chair, one hand on the back, and kissed her on the cheek. "I'll warm the bed."

She gave him a smile. "I just wish to finish this piece."

"Goodnight, Papa, you two," he said.

"Goodnight, Lucien."

I watched him leave. *Is this what I want—a home of my own? A family? A pipe, newspapers, and quilts? Why am I flirting with Lily?* I could no longer deny that was what I had been up to, meeting with her once a week. We did nothing beyond talking, but I ached for more. Maryanne had caught me out. The only others who knew were Isaac and Mae. It must be Mae who told, which meant it was possible all the Hart servants knew. The people kept to their own; their white masters counted on it. I ought to have known better.

I should no longer see Lily. Maryanne was right. She was likely right about everything.

"Papa, do you think Lincoln will win the election?"

Papa peered over his spectacles, only this time he lowered his book and removed the pipe from his mouth, tapped it to remove dottle into the cut-glass ashtray Maman had given him years ago. "We Democrats are about to split our votes between Mr. Breckinridge and Mr. Douglas. I am afraid nearly everyone else is going to vote for Mr. Lincoln. What does that tell you?"

"Many are for secession."

"What do you think?"

His questions sent me back into class at Centenary. Having mulled over this issue for weeks, by no means was I unprepared. "The North has no right to tell us how to live our lives. The Constitution guarantees states' rights. But I think we should do whatever possible to settle matters without breaking up the Union."

Papa relit his pipe with care. Berni and Joanna's needles made the tiniest popping, in, out, in, out. Neither looked up, but I was sure

Berni was listening. A log on the fire shifted, and the smell of burnt oak blended with Papa's tobacco.

I swallowed, gathered my thoughts. "I have been reading *Harper's* and Lincoln's speeches. He is heavily supported by abolitionists. If states should attempt secession, there will be trouble, and it will not be merely an argument in Congress." *Trouble*. I was not sure what I meant by the word and did not care to consider it too closely.

"I have come to the same conclusion," Papa said.

"Is there nothing we can do?"

"We can hope and pray that logical minds prevail. Other than that, a man can only educate himself and follow his convictions."

Berni stopped her needle in midair. "Those people would not actually fight over such a thing, would they, Papa? I mean, if a state seceded."

"I do not believe there would be only one," Papa said.

"But we all fought England together. Virginia and South Carolina leaders practically won the war," Berni said.

"That was a long time ago and a different world," Papa said. "No fine gentlemen such as Washington and Jefferson as president."

"Both were southern men from Virginia. What would Virginia do if Lincoln became president?"

Papa sent a trail of smoke to the darkened ceiling. "I am afraid the differences are greater than who is president. I don't think a fight with the North will be easy."

"But, why?" I could not imagine those soft northern city people standing up to anyone from Texas, or anyone from the South. After all, we were in the right.

"Surely, at Centenary you studied the Greek and European wars. Did you learn nothing? Learn what you can of our northern neighbors, then look at our entire country objectively, without the blinders of southern romantic idealism."

This was my papa? Southern romantic idealism? Lord. I was reminded of Maryanne's words.

"When you have reached a conclusion, let me know." Papa shoved his pipe back between his teeth and lowered his head to his book.

Joanna and Berni stopped sewing and looked at me as though I had created a major disturbance of some sort, as though I had brought this discomfort to our parlor.

I suppose I had.

Chapter Fifty-Four

Bernadette

Journal - October 1860: Poor Mr. Houston is no longer our governor as he is against secession and refused the oath of office. Most Texians are for it.

I do not believe states should secede. Secession is the same as running from a problem because you disagree and solves nothing.

Since that horrid incident with Marcus, Papa goes to town for our mail and papers. His attempts at avoiding a grim face when he returns are unsuccessful. Charlie Woods said there was an awful "ruckus" between our cow hands who want secession and those who do not. He let two of the most volatile go, so Adrien and Isaac must take up the slack.

Someone shot Mr. Brown, the undertaker, in the foot last week. The national elections are next month, and our sheriff felt it was necessary to hire three more men. Men are proving what fools they can be.

Will and I must discuss secession and other concerns. I fear we may not see eye-to-eye on several subjects that must be aired before we are husband and wife. I pray I will not give offense by expressing myself, but I simply cannot keep silent. I do wish Maman were alive to advise me. Surely, she would say I must follow my heart. If Will is the man I trust him to be, I have nothing to fear. Only why this apprehension?

We sat side by side on the front porch swing, watching a gray cloud advance from the gulf. A cool breeze licked at my hair, and I drew my shawl tighter about my shoulders. Will dropped his arm from the back of the swing to pull me close.

"Cold? Shall we go in?"

"Not yet. I wish to discuss something with you before supper."

"Adrien told me of your learning to cook. Father's giving us a girl for that. And she can clean and take care of the house." He took one of the hands I had curled in my lap. "It's sweet of you to consider helping, but you needn't—"

Why do men assume they know all? "Will, please."

He was taken aback by my interruption, as though struck by a heavy wind. "What?"

"This does not concern my learning to cook." I spun the lovely engagement ring on my finger.

"What then?"

He gazed at me so sincerely. I must speak quickly before losing my nerve. "It concerns my reading and how I feel about secession." I squeezed his hand in both of mine and he smiled.

"Your reading? I don't mind your reading. It's grand you're educated—"

"I have read DeFoe, Fielding, Voltaire, and Shelley and will continue to read the like, and I do not think any state should secede from the Union." There. I made short work of it, all in one breath while looking into his eyes, so he appreciated my sincerity.

His mouth, not quite closed from what he had been saying, closed now. He looked at me, his lovely brown eyes blinking. He must be contemplating what I had said. He took me seriously, at least. Yes, dear Will, I am cognizant of politics and what is happening in the world.

"You are against secession?" He was disappointed. Secession was more important to him than those books.

"I am sorry, Will. Our ancestors fought for our United States, and I believe we should do what we can to stay united. We will never settle our differences by breaking apart. We elected representatives and if they are doing their jobs correctly, there should be no need for secession."

"Obviously, they aren't doing their jobs." His dander was up, I could tell by his tone.

"Then people should elect someone else. Perhaps if women voted, we would have representatives with more sense." I had become louder and withdrawn my hands. I lifted my chin.

"Vote?" Brows raised, big eyes—such a thing as women voting had never entered his mind. I should have known.

"Yes, vote. Women should be allowed to vote. Though I expect that is in the future. Once we are allowed the same education as men, I daresay—"

His expression drove me to a halt: confusion, open-mouthed surprise. I may as well be some, some unknown something or other because he did not see *me*. I would have laughed were I not so offended. He was not the man I thought *he* was, either.

"Oh, Will." My disappointment made me stand and hurry inside and upstairs to my room. I sat on the bed, bent, hugged myself in misery, stared at the carpeted floor—and held tears that threatened. I should have said how I felt earlier. I could never be false. *Can I love him?*

Adrien found me some hours later, in bed, having eaten nothing. I was attempting to read but read the same words, the same sentences over and over without understanding a word.

"Betta wanted to rouse you for supper," he said. "But Papa and I expected you needed time to brood." He sat on the edge of the bed by my feet.

"Brood? I am not brooding." How dare they imagine I was brooding, like some silly hen. I returned to my book. "I am reading."

"I talked with Will before he left—without supper."

"He did not eat?" He rode all the way here and back without eating? I could not help but be concerned.

"He lost his appetite. The same as my sister, it seems."

I set down the book. "We . . . had a disagreement."

"According to Will, you did not give him much chance to disagree."

"He did not have to. I could tell by the look he gave me. I told him who I truly am, and he was horrified."

"You never told him before today about what you read or your feelings concerning secession, and you did not expect he would be surprised?"

"Of course, but. . . ." But what? But he had been too surprised?

Adrien leaned toward me, one hand on the quilt. "Look, Berni. I have been a coward, not saying a word, not knowing, really, how I considered this whole" he exhaled, glanced down, up "mess. But I told Will, tonight, that I pretty much agreed with you. He was shocked, but he listened to what I had to say and understood. He's going to keep quiet about it. We remain friends, and he still loves you." My brother straightened. "Despite our treasonous impulses." He smiled. My heart was thumping in my throat. "Thus, consider this your first lovers' quarrel and forgive the fellow, all right? Talk to him?"

Didn't matter I was in my nightclothes. I pushed forward and threw my arms around his neck. "Adrien, I love you dearly. Of course, I will talk to him." Now the tears. How silly.

Chapter Fifty-Five
Hartwood

Lily

Lily met Adrien in the abandoned north drying barn on the portion that her father had bought from Paien Villere. The barn was a determined forty-five-minute ride over hills and across several creeks from her home, but she didn't mind. Sneaking away without Mac had been the most difficult.

Iron-hinged cladding boards had been left open for air circulation but would soon be closed against winter rainstorms.

Something untoward had happened since the last time they met. He was sullen, unreachable. Was he considering ending their rendezvous? He didn't yet know her, didn't appreciate her determination.

Horses were tethered inside where they wouldn't be noticed; they sat facing one another across the hard-packed and leaf-dusted surface of the barn floor.

"Did you hear?" he said. "Lincoln has won, and several states are threatening secession."

"Secession, secession, I am tired of the word. Speak of something else."

"It looks like rain," he said.

"You will talk of the weather?" If he kept this up, she would slap him. Good Lord, his testy mood was affecting her.

"Your family will be suspicious of your riding in the rain," he said.

"Everyone is busy with one thing or another."

"How long have you got?"

"All morning."

"All morning riding in the rain?"

"It's not about to rain. See? The sun is coming out." She raised her chin and closed her eyes, warm sun on her face—cool on her nose where a slat created shadow.

He didn't answer, so she peered from beneath her lashes. He sat with his arms around pulled-up knees, watching her.

"You are trying to make me nervous, but you won't succeed," she said.

"Why should I do that?"

"To get the upper hand."

He smiled. She liked it when he smiled like that. He appeared rather impudent. Perhaps it was because his mouth lifted a little higher on one side, and his eyes slanted partially closed, like a sleepy cat's.

"Then you shall have the upper hand, for I see you are a clever girl."

"No, you don't. You see me as a delicate piece of porcelain, alluring but useless and breakable if touched."

"True. But you can also be amusing."

He turned toward her, shifting his limbs, one tan palm near her smaller one. His hands were slender, the fingers fine and long, the nails filed. She was aware of the calluses on the pads of his fingers, on his palms, and a deep scratch across the upper surface of one hand. What if she licked that scratch, sucked the calluses? What would he taste like?

"You should be amusing me," she said. "After all, I am the one with money and power."

"You have neither, save by the good grace of your father."

"We are all like that, we women. Even Berni, as much as she would deny it. Everything I am or will be is what my father desires. What about me, Adrien; what about my desires?" She leaned toward him on one arm, the other lying along her skirt, her thigh.

"What could you desire that you do not have?" His face was partially veiled from the glare filtering between the slats behind his back.

Fathomless eyes, fine-boned nose, partly open mouth, the indigo shadow that defined his cheekbones and chin that might prickle against her fingertips, or any part of her that might brush across there.

He drew the word from her. "You."

What did he think, staring at her like that? She thought to reach with her free hand and place it around his neck. She did and felt the warmth of his skin, the cool damp collar against her smallest finger, the wonderful softness of his hair. Would he have her make a fool of herself? She need do no more, for he leaned close, and she inhaled his difference from her brothers and her father, horse and leather and something all his own. The tip of his nose touching her cheek was as sensuous as the touch of his warm lips brushing hers. His tenderness would drive her mad. He pulled away and stood—she held nothing but air.

"We will not meet like this again," he said. "This is wrong. I am sorry. We should not have begun."

She looked at her hand spread on the dust of the barn floor, reached for the pale-yellow kid glove lying there with its dirty creases and sweat stains. "Then I will come here and wait for you." She stood, and he did not reach to help her—she rose gracefully, without his aid.

"No, Lily, you must not."

"Will you come to stop me, then?" They faced one another close enough to touch if she should only raise her arm. She saw anger in his narrowed eyes, in the thin pale lines that formed around his mouth. Shadow settled over them as a cloud hid the sun.

"You know as well as I why we can no longer meet," he said. "There is no future for us." His fingers curled so tight his hands trembled at his sides. "And you will find it much colder here in December and January." He turned on the pad of one boot, grasped his horse's reins, and shoved the door open before she could muster a response.

The door was still swinging when she reached it. She would not watch him ride away but stayed inside until he was gone, until she no longer heard his horse thudding the damp earth.

He would not have been so angry or run so fast if leaving her had been easy. He would not have kissed her at all. This was not over. Her father had taught his children that when you wanted something bad enough, you didn't quit until you got it.

Chapter Fifty-Six

Adrien

Nearly every morning I turned Roman toward the north-quarter barn where I waited hidden beneath a copse of live oaks. Her behavior only proved her a spoiled, childish girl. To continue riding out alone, rain or shine, merely to make a point. What was her point? That she might make me do whatever she desired? As Will's sister, Jacob's sister, I must never see her alone again.

Thank God, Will and Berni found one another again. Their temporary rift made me come to my senses. A man had a moral obligation to do what was right. Sneaking around and lying to everyone I loved was wrong.

On a cold, dreary afternoon two days before Christmas, Will cantered into our yard with shocking news—South Carolina had seceded! Lucien grinned and took Will's hand in mutual congratulation. Joanna gasped, a hand over her heart. Berni collapsed into the nearest chair.

I got the strangest notion, like urging your horse down a steep decline. No slowing down; there was no stopping until you reached the bottom.

&

Christmas was practically a secondary affair compared to news of secession.

As usual, our family was invited to the annual Hart New Year's Eve Ball. When Maman was alive, she and Papa took the entire family to the ball. Though we youngest were supposed to be in bed, we spied on the older folk from the second-floor balcony. This was the first year Berni and I were old enough to attend as adults. Joanna was too far along in her third laying-in, and Lucien decided to stay home with his wife.

My sister and I were on our way upstairs when I told her.

"I have decided not to attend," I said. "Papa will take you."

"Why are you staying home?"

"Why not? I am not affianced to one of them." I dared not face Lily or her older brother.

Berni grasped her skirts high and nearly tromped on my heels right down the hall and into my bedroom. I had hoped to avoid her ire; foolish me. Scattered about the floor were dirty boots, a pair of trousers, and an outdated copy of *Leslie's Illustrated. Ivanhoe* lay open upon the haphazardly made bed. What did she expect when one must take care of one's own room? I heard her disgusted huff.

"I did not ask you in," I said, fetching the filthy trousers from the floor.

"You cannot hide out among tobacco plants all your life."

I wanted to laugh at such an image. I shoved the tobacco-stained trousers into a basket in the corner and mashed on the lid. Turned. She looked so serious, standing there with her fists on her hips.

"Go away, Berni."

"We must talk."

"We must not."

"It is not fair what Papa and Lucien ask of you."

"No one has asked anything."

"They do not ask, they assume."

"Berni, you are not helping."

"I do not mean to help *them*. Papa has had his life. Lucien has made his, and I am going to get mine. I shall not leave here with you enslaved to Lucien's needs."

"Enslaved? Hardly." I flopped onto the bed, snatching the book before it slid to the floor.

"This land will not only support tobacco. Lucien can grow crops that are far less labor-intensive, ones with which he can feed his growing family."

"Picture that: Lucien Villere, gentleman farmer."

She stomped her foot. "We can no longer afford that sort of stupid pride!" She flung her hands up in fists as though she would punch someone. She was pretty in her pink-flushed fierceness. When facing an angry creature, it was best to keep as still and quiet as possible.

"This family can be so vexing," she said, "and you are the worst, playing at martyr."

"You must like it, for you love me best." *What? Martyr?* "What do you mean, martyr? Do not be ridiculous."

"You are too much like Maman."

I threw myself from the bed and took a step toward her. "Do not say that, Berni. Maman was virtuous, kind, and loved others above herself. I am not like her; I was never like her."

"She loved you best of all. I might have been jealous, only you were oblivious. Maman was not perfect. She came between you and Papa, and she will forever be between you and Lucien. Look at me that way if you must, but it is true. I saw it each time Papa rode off with Lucien and left you behind. It was not Lucien's fault, nor Papa's."

"Stop, please." I stood on a cliff, and the slightest breeze would blow me over.

She stepped close and held me tight, an ear in the hollow of my shoulder. "I love you, Adrien. I love you so, and I do not want to leave you here this way."

I palmed her delicate shoulder blades, lowered my cheek against her hair that smelled of lemons. I loved her more than anything in the world.

"This is not finished," she murmured into my chest.

"Leave it until next year, at least."

"Which is two days away, and you must attend the ball."

"I will not, Berni. Let it be."

She leaned back in my arms. "What is it, Adrien? Why do you dislike going there? Won't you tell me what happened between you and

Jacob? He can be a pompous villain at times, but he was grand to us when we were little, like an older brother when Lucien was too busy."

If only I might say. But I could not bear her look of disgust.

I sighed. She would not let it go. I sat her on the bed. *To assure her, I decided to reveal part.*

"I have done something stupid, Berni. I put an end to it or am trying." I risked a glance. She sat on the bed so pertly, brows raised, amber flecks in her eyes in the afternoon light. *No wonder Will could not resist and Lily adored her. She is the best of us.*

"I was meeting secretly with Lily."

She pounded fists into her lap. "I knew it. I knew it was something like that."

"*Was*, I said; I am no longer. We have ended it."

"Do you love her, Adrien?"

Do I? "Does it matter? We can never marry; Randolph Hart would never allow it, and I would not blame him. I own nothing to offer Lily."

"You have yourself."

"Not enough for Lily Hart."

"You might leave and make something of yourself."

"Ah, you are trying to get rid of me again. Even if by some miracle I made my fortune, Randolph would marry her off long before." I studied the rag rug beneath my feet. Since I began working outside, Betta decided I needed one to cover the finer carpet. "No. It is best I keep my distance. Eventually, she will tire of waiting in that drafty barn by herself."

"She waits in one of the barns?"

"Yes." My voice was low, nearly a murmur. "Once or twice a week."

Berni cocked her head a little; a dimple appeared in her cheek. "She has more nerve than I thought."

"She has nerve, all right. You should see her ride, even on sidesaddle. That mare of hers will take any jump, and she will go anywhere Roman will. She was frightened once or twice, but she did not let it stop her. She is amazing."

Berni looked at me with a peculiar, knowing smile.

I gave a brief snort, shifted my feet, and ran fingers through my hair.

"You have not—" She searched my face.

"No." I paced to the wall, turned. "How can you ask? A fleeting kiss, once."

"I did not think so, dear one." She stood, placed her palm on the side of my face. "You are much too comely. I fear you will always find women easy."

"I am sick of feeling that is all I am." I stood up, leaned my forehead against the wall.

"You are much more, full of unsatisfied desire and too intelligent for a tobacco farmer."

"Sometimes I feel as though I am the younger one, Berni, not you."

"Women grow up faster than men. We must in order to take care of you."

I turned from the wall, tipped my head, and raised my brows.

"You heard me," she said. "You cannot forever avoid what you find unpleasant." With that remark, she gave me a quick smile, spun, and flounced out of my room.

I forced myself to sit and think. Did I dare speak to Papa and Lucien about switching crops? Tobacco was too labor-intensive. There weren't enough workers, and the tobacco we grew did not produce adequate income to make the work worthwhile. Each succeeding year, we were further behind.

I had promised Isaac one day we would leave together. We would go north or west where he would be free. I spoke three common languages, plus Greek and Latin, could read and write and sum, which should bring a decent paying job. I would find work and save enough to finish school.

How quickly I jumped at Berni's idea—like a starving fish at a baited hook.

Berni, you know me well, yet not well enough. You do not realize how depraved I am. I lowered my head, elbows on knees, and fisted my hands in my hair.

She had asked me to speak to Lucien. Perhaps the time had come.

Chapter Fifty-Seven

Bernadette

The mere idea that I planned a secret assignation with a Negro in one of our people's cabins made me want to giggle. Oh, the look on many of our lady friends' faces! Until I considered other men and Isaac, himself, which sobered me considerably. I am eighteen and we were no longer children, as much as I might wish it.

Dusty cobwebs diffused any light made by low November sun through the doorway from the rear west window. Fortunately, I had brought a lantern with me, and set it on the table in front of the long-dead fireplace. It was cold and musty in here, but I dared not light a fire. Pulling my wool shawl tighter about my shoulders, I perched on a chair next to the table, and held my hand to my nose to resist a sneeze.

Three soft taps on the door sent my heart beating hard and fast, and Isaac stepped through and closed the door behind him. Fresher air, his horse, leather, and personal scent entered with him. He removed his slouch hat and pulled up an old wood chair opposite me. We gazed at one another for a moment, and then he gave me that same old mischievous smile.

"When Mintie said you wanted to meet here, I thought she was making a joke on me. Till I figured it was no joke, and it had something to do with Adrien."

"You always were a step ahead of us, Isaac."

"Nah. I just keep my eyes open is all. While y'all's got plenty time to let your emotions run you about."

"Then you are aware my brother's been meeting with Lily Hart."

He dangled his hat from his knee. "I reckon he is a mite reckless when it comes to that lady, regardless of what me or anyone else has to say."

"I dare say, he declared he has done nothing amiss, but I fear Lily is no more levelheaded than my brother. Neither is Jacob one to be ignored in such a situation."

"No, miss, he is not."

"Indeed, perhaps I am merely assuring myself you are keeping an eye on Adrien where I cannot. I am aware there is little you can do." Of all things, my voice cracked, and I squeezed my shawl tighter, as I had let it loose while we had been talking.

Isaac looked up sharply. "No need for you to fret, Berni. Haven't the three of us together always made out just fine?" He hastily switched to another subject.

"You picked a fine place for a meeting," he said, glancing about. "I expect you aren't aware this cabin used to belong to my folks, but they abandoned it when a conjure woman put that mark on the front door. No one else would live in it since but that girl, Grace, and you know what happened to her. Folks believe it's cursed."

"I don't believe in curses. And you are right about the three of us." I reached forward and laid my hand on his knee. His silly grin disappeared. He sat back a little and blinked.

"You should know, Isaac. I no longer believe in slavery. I am aware of Papa and Marcus's doings here at Blue Hills."

His hand slid away, nearly dropping the hat. "Doings? What doings?"

Oh, dear, I thought sure he knew. What have I done?

My fingers closed into a fist. "I have said what I ought not. Ask your papa."

"Rest assured. I will."

"You sound more like us every day."

His gaze dropped to the floor as though he had been caught at something.

"Adrien swore to take me when he leaves here. If he ever does."

That sounded like my brother. "I will pray he goes for both your sakes. But you must promise to write to me, from wherever you are."

He flashed me that familiar, white-toothed smile that lit up his entire face. "I shall write you an entire book, Miss Bernadette. And I will keep an eye on Adrien, though I fear it won't make a hooter of difference in what he does or does not do regarding Lily Hart."

Chapter Fifty-Eight

Isaac

Evening after supper was one of the few times they were alone together: him, Papa, and Mama. Papa told Mama everything, even if he didn't tell Isaac. After a full stomach, Papa would be in a better mood for confrontation, if that was what this turned out to be.

Plus, an entire day of hard work gave Isaac time to settle his own self.

The aroma of stewed chicken and greens hung about the cabin along with mixed live oak and mesquite from the fireplace as Papa settled himself with last week's paper in his stuffed chair. Dishes done, Mama took up her latest sewing project.

Now or never.

"Papa, what are these secret doings you and Master Paien have going on here at Blue Hills?"

Mama halted her needle. Papa slowly lowered his paper. Silence but for the crackling of the fire. Isaac heard an owl hoot somewhere off behind the cabins. *Hoo hooo, hoo hooo.* He always liked that sound, though some thought it meant an imminent death.

Papa, as thick through the shoulders as ever, had neither gained nor lost weight over the years, and was yet a man to be reckoned with. The look he now gave Isaac reminded him of this fact. Then he appeared to shuck off whatever lay over him like he would shuck off a coat and said, "First tell me who mentioned such?"

She would surely be prepared for this. "Berni believed I already knew."

Down went his chin. "Hmm. I expect she was correct in thinking so. Though Paien and I never discussed it, so I never did say. The fewer who knew, the safer for everyone. But now, it seems, the cat is out of the bag." Papa's eyes bored into him, his expression reflecting calm assurance of the seriousness of what he was about to say.

"You must never repeat this to anyone, not even Adrien, for it is his papa's right to do so if he wishes. I have stayed on here at Blue Hills all these years because Paien and I have been helping colored folks to escape bondage. Do you understand?"

"But, but—"

"Yes. Paien owns slaves; he must in order to remain here on this plantation. You know how he treats our people."

"Yes, sir." This one fact explained so much.

"Better Paien than some."

"Yes." A whisper this time.

"You realize what would happen if we were found out?"

"I do."

"Then you realize why we must retain a proper front at all times, including how you behave with young master Adrien."

"I've been doing my best. Do you have any complaints?"

"Not at all. I appreciate your efforts. I know how difficult such a thing can be."

"Papa."

Papa stood from his chair. So did Isaac. It had been a while since they had come to such an understanding, since they had grasped one another close.

Chapter Fifty-Nine
Hartwood

Porscha

Jacob's wife, Porscha, was queen and undisputed general of her household army, and none dared interfere, including Randolph Hart. Determined this would be the finest New Year's Ball over which Hartwood ever presided, she assigned two slaves to beating brocade, velvet, and lace draperies on an outside line until all within range were hacking from dust; three to polishing wood and two to silver. By afternoon of the big day, all seven fireplaces burned merrily, chasing away dampness from a morning storm. Bouquets of evergreens, berries, and poinsettias graced every mantel and table. Wall mirrors reflected light from nearly one hundred candles set in gleaming silver sconces.

Ham, venison, quail, and turkey were taken from ovens and placed on shining silver platters along with bowls of candied and brandied fruit, sweet potatoes, squash, pumpkin, and pickled beets. Strawberry and pear preserves, quince and apple jelly, along with gleaming silver bowls of Irish potatoes, rice, and delicate corn biscuits covered the lace top of the walnut sideboard. Terrapin, redfish, shrimp, and oysters docked by riverboat from Galveston early this morning now lay on beds of ice on the center table surrounded by fresh evergreen boughs. The glorious, sinful smells of rum and brandied cakes were heady enough to knock one silly.

Guests arrived all the way from South Carolina, Alabama, Louisiana, and Mississippi. They would see that a Texas board matched the best of any in the South. She had even arranged for a small string group from Houston to play waltzes. Every room gleamed to a fare-thee-well. The coloreds would have their own entertainment and an entire barbecued hog.

Porscha had done herself proud marrying into the Hart family and did them proud as well. Her father-in-law was pleased, her husband satisfied. She might have wished for more, but she was a realist, not a romantic dreamer like her sister-in-law. She was the last of four daughters and, if not considered beautiful, she was attractive enough. It surprised family and friends—and her—when handsome Jacob Hart came courting. He soon made clear what he expected in a wife, and she obliged. She gave him a boy and a girl that yet survived. After one more boy as insurance, he would let her be. She ceased wishing his advances were anything more than duty. Fortunately, her temperament suited their arrangement. If not attentive, he was not cruel, like some.

In fact, she might call her life nearly perfect. Will would soon marry, and then it would be Lily's turn. Lily would be the most difficult—her father and brothers pampered the girl. She was headstrong and something else; she demonstrated a tendency toward arrogance, a lack of restraint. The girl read too much, novels and such. She should marry as soon as possible.

Chapter Sixty

Lily

The terrible storm that raged throughout the morning blew itself out by late afternoon. Mae had brought Lily breakfast in bed while she watched thrashing trees through her west window. She and Will had played chess in his room after a light lunch; then she had taken a short nap. The sun never showed itself until dusk, when it threw a last glorious orange below pink and purple clouds.

She felt strangely sad, standing at the window. She wasn't entirely awake—afternoon naps put one in such a pensive state. More news from the East had thrilled the family but left her melancholy. Mae was poking the fire behind her, and Joseph would soon bring up hot water for her bath. She would feel much better afterward. Adrien would arrive tonight with Berni and their father. She must look her best.

Three hours later, Lily stood at the bottom of the stairs, twenty feet from the house's grand entrance. Angry words and taunts bounced throughout the parlor and hall. The gentleman from South Carolina was daring everyone to follow their state's noble example and secede. Dr. Hoover, the Baptist minister, cautioned restraint. Judge Mallory, who espoused a wait-and-see attitude, fiercely supported him. The other gentlemen joined in.

Mrs. Wigfall, wife of their Texas United States senator, approached from across the room. "Our men have not yet sampled the eatables, and they are already behaving like wild turkeys arguing over field grain. Come," she said, placing gloved fingers lightly upon Lily's forearm, "let's see if we can't secure the two worst offenders and guide them toward the tables. I shall snatch our fire-eater, Mr. Barnwell, and you take Judge Mallory." Lily liked Mrs. Wigfall, but now she wouldn't be able to keep her eye on the front door. Anyone might arrive without her knowing.

After nibbling on shrimp and sipping a glass of champagne, Lily took a turn around the floor with the judge, then another gentleman whose name she forgot because she kept telling herself to stop looking toward the double doors, to cease caring. Then she saw Will hurrying toward the entrance. There could only be one reason. She begged off from James McPherson's approach, waving her fan because the room was so warm, and it was true she desired a rest.

Will was kissing Berni's cheek—she was so pretty in gold silk that set off her dark hair and eyes. Paien was with her. Not Adrien.

The air went out of her. The devil, if he imagined she would pine for him. She took a deep breath, clutched her fan, lifted her chin—stepped forward, faster and faster, smiled, opened her arms. "Berni, Mr. Villere, how wonderful to see you again." A hug for Berni, a curtsy for Berni's father.

Even at his age, Paien was a fine figure of a man. If he still had his fortune, he would be the perfect catch. What fun to be Berni's mother! What an idea to turn Washington County heads, especially Adrien's. That would show him.

"Lily, you look positively radiant," Berni said.

"Why shouldn't I? It's the New Year with much to look forward to. I do believe this is the best New Year's Ball ever. Surely, in Texas. We'll be part of the same family."

"We certainly will," Will said, circling Berni's waist with his arm.

Lily's father appeared at her side and extended his hand. "Paien, it is far too long since you have been under my roof."

"Thank you, Randolph. I hope to get reacquainted, since we are about to join our families."

"Yes, one family, and I couldn't have asked for a better addition to mine. Come, I would like your opinion on a fine old brandy I recently acquired from Virginia. We must make a toast. If you youngsters will excuse us?"

"Behave yourself with my girl, William." Paien grinned and placed a hand on Will's shoulder before he and Randolph headed toward the libations table.

"The music sounds wonderful," Berni said.

"Yes, I must allow, Porscha does know how to throw a party," Lily said. "Let's go in; I fancy you two can hardly wait for an excuse to be in one another's arms." With a flourish, she snapped open her fan with one hand and lifted her voluminous lavender skirts with the other.

You assume you have bested me, Adrien Villere. You shall soon realize you do not know me at all. But you will.

Chapter Sixty-One
Blue Hills

Lucien

The fire in the bedroom hearth had burned down to coals by the time Lucien's wife was abed. He hung the vest and blouse he'd worn for dinner in the wardrobe and shrugged into one of his favorite old flannels. Another year gone, another season of barely realized profits. Hardly enough to maintain the place and purchase what they didn't produce. A button popped off his shirt. *Shit.*

"Lucien?"

"Yes?" He'd wear it, anyway. What difference did it make for an hour of reading the paper before bed?

"Will you sit a moment before you go?"

He closed the cupboard and turned. "Certainly." The quilt was pulled up nearly to her chin. He smiled at her roundness, at contemplation of their third child due next week. He crossed the room and took her hand.

"You've been worrying about the crop," she said, squeezing his hand. "Of how we'll get on next year. Especially with another child and each year worse than the last."

"How do you do that?"

He sat beside her. He hadn't spoken of his concerns.

"You cannot hide what is obvious to someone who knows you," she said. "Bernadette and I have discussed this—problem. My goodness, look at your face. You think that because we are women, we are blind to what is right in front of us. We needn't inspect the books.

Tobacco can no longer sustain this family. The question is, what to do about it?"

"You make it sound simple."

"Isn't it?"

"Papa has spent his life and heart on tobacco. How do I tell him we can no longer do so?"

"Your father appears to be a reasonable and intelligent man. He can no more be blind to what is happening than we are. And your brother?" She tipped her head, looking down at their hands. "I don't understand him at all. There is nothing here for him but a dwindling share of profits." Placing her remaining hand on top of their three, she looked him square in the face and declared, "Family loyalty is one thing, but do you think he will stay once your sister is married and gone?"

She was right. There was nothing here for Adrien. If they stopped growing tobacco, his family would have to subsist on producing their own food, and there would be no such thing as profits.

He felt the same old anger. It would not do to let such seep out upon his wife.

"Tell me, Husband, what is this business between you and your brother? You have anger between you I have never understood."

Lucien lowered his head. How could he discuss what he had buried deep for years? "It's childish, I suppose, from long ago when we were small. I worked hard with Papa while Adrien did nothing but learn poetry." He looked away and shrugged. "My stepmother spoiled him."

"You have mentioned little about your childhood."

"I never considered it important. I told you our girl, Rosanne, raised me after my mother died."

"You said nothing about what she was like or what happened to her."

Lucien searched her face. She gazed back at him, unwaveringly. He absently stroked the back of her left hand with his thumb, exceedingly aware of her soft right palm on top of his rough and calloused one. "I'm aware it's difficult for you sometimes, living here with our people, as Papa calls them."

"I knew what I was getting into when I accepted you, as did my family. As did you when you learned how my family feels about slavery."

"As a boy I wasn't conscious of Rosanne as a slave. She ran this house and everyone in it, sometimes even Papa. She surely ran me." He could see her now, the red scarf wrapped about her head, her strong, brown hands.

"Did you love her?"

"Love her?" Love a colored? Absurd. But he had cared for her. What happened wasn't her fault. Or was it?

"What happened to her, Lucien?"

He had never spoken of that time. Recalling it now, the incident had been of major importance. He had been a child before and become someone else after.

❧

Paien Villere had brought Rosanne Hayes with him from Virginia as part of Lucien's mother's dowry, along with fifty field enslaved and nine bags of tobacco seed. When his own mother died shortly after arriving in Texas, Lucien took the place of the child Rosanne had lost to illness. Death was not uncommon in those days of hard work, bare sustenance, and animal predation, particularly for women and children.

Rosanne had plenty of work after Madeleine and her slaves arrived, but without her previous authority. But she had power, she told him, a secret power she kept hidden in a tiny bag hung around her neck. Negroes from all around the county came to her for love charms and charms for casting out devils and illness.

Only later he found out there were some who believed she used her power for evil.

Madeleine lost two babies in two years. The house came under ever-increasing tension. Someone broke a plate. A silver spoon went missing. A fox got into the henhouse, eggs were found with bloody centers, and an owl flew into the outdoor kitchen in broad daylight.

In January 1841, Madeleine announced she was with child for the third time.

On a warm early morning in midsummer, Lucien and Papa were at breakfast when they heard screeching from outside behind the house. Papa closed his eyes and stopped chewing, fork halfway to his plate.

Betta, eight months heavy with her and Marcus's baby, came hurrying into the dining room to Papa's chair. "Marse, suh, I can't take this no more. I knowed it was her. You gotta see." She bent over him, fists grasped together in prayer.

Papa sighed, stood, and took her by the shoulders. "All right, Betta. Take a breath, settle down, and show me what you must. Go on now." Lucien followed them out the door and down the porch steps, along the path through the grass toward the house slaves' cabins—to where Betta and Marcus lived—where Betta stopped eight feet from the door. She stood, all atremble and pointed.

Lucien would forever remember the sight and stench. In the middle of the cabin door hung a red flannel bag tied with a piece of snakeskin, a black chicken feather sticking from the knot. Blood soaked the bottom of the flannel and ran down the cedar boards of the door.

"It's evil," Betta said with shaking voice. "She done it. We all know she has the power. She hates me and she bad for this family. She will do to this new chile what she done to the others. She hate Mistress Madeleine and me ever since we come here cause she no longer rule this house."

Papa's jaw clenched. He shook his head as if denying such a thing could happen, and said, "I'll have Simon remove this"—he flapped the air with his hand— "and have the door cleaned. And I'll take care of Rosanne."

Lucien met Papa at the door to the front porch. "You don't know Rosanne hung that there."

"Others have come to me with complaints of her, and I didn't want to believe them. She has been given pardon after pardon, and my patience is at an end. I don't believe this nonsense about charms, but our people do, and I must have peace in this house." He ran a hand through his hair and gestured toward a wood chair behind Lucien. Papa pulled up a chair from the opposite wall, sat down before him, and leaned forward, elbows on his knees.

"I am aware that Rosanne was your wet nurse. I am aware of all she did for us before Madeleine arrived. But that was her job. With the grace of God, a month from now, you will have a new little brother or sister, and I must do everything possible to ensure this child arrives safely."

"But, it's not her fault." He could barely breathe. His head, his entire body swelled with fury.

"Several of our people relate how she sells charms and potions. We are Catholics among Baptists and Methodists, and I cannot let word get around that neighbor slaves are visiting some conjuring woman here. She and Betta do not get along. Simon is afraid of her, and he is not the only one. She has become the rotten apple in the barrel, and we can no longer afford her."

Lucien flung up from the chair, hands in fists. "It's not right. She was here first!"

His papa stood. "Do not speak to me again in that tone."

Rosanne was sold, and the baby lived. Lived and thrived, and Maman and Betta and cook and everyone doted on that little mama's boy.

⁂

He was shamed by how such memories tormented him and passed a palm across his forehead and through his hair.

"Do you know what happened to her?"

"No. I sometimes wonder if she yet lives."

Lucien gathered himself and gave his wife a tight-lipped smile.

"So there it is. I've told no one before. I was too attached to her, and—"

"Shush." Joanna placed two fingers on his lips. "Don't say it, dearest. You were young, and she took care of you. She was the only mother you had until Madeleine arrived. You needn't take that away from your memory of her."

Rosanne had been a mother to him. Joanna would infer such a relationship. Maybe he had felt that way too.

"What would I do without you?"

"I expect you would do just fine." She drew her hand around his neck. "Kiss me goodnight, will you? And consider speaking to your father about changing crops."

She pulled the quilt up. "Now go read your paper." He kissed her gently. She patted his hands, settled back into the pillows, and closed her eyes.

Worry crept deeper into his bones as he looked at his wife. What if he couldn't make a go of this place? They were barely making ends meet, and next year would be worse. And now this secession thing. He must do something.

Chapter Sixty-Two

Adrien

I poked at the flaming logs, though the fire scarcely needed it. I had been alone in the parlor since Papa and Bernadette left for the ball and Lucien and Joanna retired to their bedroom in the new wing. Lucien always returned to the parlor once Joanna was settled. I stepped to the window, held the drape aside, and peered out into the dark.

Lily was at the ball.

I dropped the heavy fabric and paced twice around the room before flopping into a chair and clutching the arms hard, so that one of Maman's lace doilies fell to the floor. I leaned down to snatch it up, fingered it, and a wave of something unexpected. Not sadness. Oddly relieved I felt . . . fine. Fine with missing her. I placed the lace carefully back on the arm.

Stared into the fire. How the flames danced. Lily was dancing with every man in the county and beyond. I pictured her there in the flames.

Footfalls from the porch and the front door opened. Had Lucien and I been alone together since we were boys?

Lucien entered, hesitated, as though surprised at my presence, settled on the sofa, its green velvet now crushed and shiny with age, and reached for the newspaper folded on the cushion.

I leaned forward, elbows on knees. "How is she?"

"Sleeping. She is more tired with this one." He spoke to his paper.

"Another boy then." I had heard that somewhere, about boys

making mothers more tired. Stupid remark, but it filled the silence. I tapped on the stuffed chair arm. Lucien turned a page, the paper rattling. A log dropped on the fire with a thud and a minor burst of light.

I grasped the chair, hard, released. I must find a way to begin this conversation. "I am sorry, Lucien."

For long moments, only the crackle of the fire. Then my brother lowered his paper. "Sorry? For what?"

"Being," I wanted to say being born, but, no, that would be childish, and get me nowhere. "For being jealous."

"Are you joking? Did you plan this, attempt to make a fool of me without Bernadette's and Papa's interference?" Red-faced, he crushed the paper in his fist.

"What?" I pushed myself back, recovering from an invisible blow.

"Oh, come now, don't play stupid with me—it doesn't suit you. You may have pulled the wool over everyone else's eyes, but not mine. Jealous! While I worked, you stayed home and played little lord of the manor. I sweated in the fields while you went on picnics and read books. You and your pretty face and exaggerated manners. Your mama's perfect little boy."

"I never . . . but, you had Papa. You had all of Papa."

"You wanted him too, did you? Figures. He only kept me with him because she didn't care, because of you. If she had been my mother, I might have had a chance. He married your mother in rather a hurry, as I recall." Lucien yanked open the paper, now mangled and torn, then tossed it onto the cushion at his left, cocked his head and observed me, much as he would one of the dogs, curious to see its reaction after he had taken away its bone.

Contrary to what I had planned, to make things right, I wanted to hit him for such a remark. To slam my fist into the center of that arrogant face. "Stand up."

"Oh, God." Lucien turned his head aside with a dismissive shake.

I lunged and jerked him up by the collar. Furious and unaware before a fist bashed my jaw—flashing stars, then all-encompassing, muffling black.

"Marse Adrien? Please, dear Lord, Marse Adrien?" A female voice above me, somewhere.

"He's all right, Betta. See, his eyes are fluttering. You may go. Go on. I've got him."

Lucien?

The ceiling spinning, supper coming up. I swallowed it back down, blinked, swallowed again.

"Holy Jesus, Adrien, Betta was afraid I'd killed you. Can you see me? Say something."

"Mmmf."

"Something I can understand. Do you know who I am?"

"Lu-cien."

"Good enough. Sit up. Deep breath, that's it."

Lucien's arm around my shoulders, pulling me up. I was sitting on the floor, legs flat out, Lucien's arm holding me. First time for everything.

I hung my head between my knees and dripped water onto the carpet. My face, hair, dripping wet?

In a rush, all I had learned regarding temper and smart fighting had been forgotten and I had paid the price. *Learned one more lesson from my own brother.*

"Betta must have been snooping in the hall," Lucien said. "She ran in here screaming. You would have thought the house was afire. She ran to the kitchen and returned to dump a pot of water over you. Seems to have worked." Lucien sat on the carpet too, leaning his arms on drawn-up knees.

The room appeared dim in the lowered firelight, or maybe it was my eyesight—my ears rang. "You pack quite a wallop." The words came out strange. My mouth would not bite the consonants. I moved my jaw around, gently.

"A life of hard work."

I peered up from the corner of my eye. Lucien gave me a smirk from one side of his mouth, a look of shared complicity.

"I meant it about being sorry." At least, I thought that is what I said. *Though I am damned if I know what I was sorry for.*

"Did you now? We are a pair, aren't we." A statement, not a question.

"Are we?"

Lucien's jaw shifted, then he looked me in the eye. "I didn't realize, until I saw you lying there and Betta screaming I'd killed you. It hit me. I don't want you dead. You're my brother. You weren't even born when—never mind. I mean it this time. About all you've done sticking around here this long. And I apologize for the past and for hitting you." He held out his hand.

I hesitated, then took it. Caution, certainly, on both our sides, but this time we began with honesty, and it was worth Lucien's having the first and last punch if it settled this. If I ever figured out what *this* was.

"Though I needed to hit you, I think, to get it out." Lucien smiled.

"One day, I may have to pay you back for that."

"If you can." Our eyes held one another, in agreement for now, even some sort of respect that might last.

"Do you hate the work, Lucien? This place?"

"Not really. I did, sometimes growing up, when it seemed you had all the fun."

I had all the fun?

"But I love this land, and I want it for me, Joanna, and our children. If we can hang onto it."

"I wanted to talk to you about that."

"If you left, you mean?"

No point in my remaining, as he well knew.

"Joanna and I have discussed that," Lucien said. "She said I couldn't expect you to hang around here like some hired hand, especially not for what you were paid. Even if you stayed, we aren't making enough to keep growing tobacco, not with the few people we have left."

"What if we no longer grew tobacco? Oats practically grow themselves, and if we enlarged the cattle herd, and there is wheat and corn—"

"And rye and sweet potatoes. I've thought of that," Lucien said.

"Have you talked to Papa?"

"About replacing his precious tobacco? Not yet."

"We can talk to him together?" I looked at Lucien across our knees. Curious, how we sat on the floor together, the same way.

"Let's wait until tomorrow evening, give him time to recover from the ball."

"All the victuals and New Year's cheer?"

"The cheer, mainly."

I was thinking about the few "people" we had left, the slaves.

"Here," he said, holding out his hand as he stood, "let me help you up."

I took it. "Thanks."

Chapter Sixty-Three

Bernadette

Journal - January 30, 1861: *I previously wondered what it was like to live in important historical times, and now I know. It is dreadful. Papa says little or nothing, but the look on his face reveals his unhappiness concerning this uproar since Lincoln was elected President. Southern states have been seceding from the Union like falling dominoes. This month, Mississippi, Florida, Alabama, and Georgia joined South Carolina, and we just learned that our neighbor, Louisiana, seceded. Only last year I had no idea what secession meant or that states could do it. Now that word is in everyone's mouths and is all we read of in the newspapers. The violence that has arisen from everyone I previously believed normal is the worst part.*

I am shamefaced thinking this, but I cannot help myself. My wedding is ruined. How can I smile, plan for guests and gowns? Why are friends galloping across the county with the latest news as though the Revolution had begun again? Most astonishing is that Will is one of them. He tries to remain calm, but I see the excitement in his eyes, in how he can barely sit still.

Will apologized for the other evening. He declares he seldom knows what I shall say or do from moment to moment. Then he turned serious and stated that he admired me for more than my beauty. You have substance, he said. Dear me. Fancy that? He will be happy to purchase any reading material I want under his own name, to protect me from gossips. Though he insisted on reading the same books, to be sure they did not lead me into evil ways. How we laughed!

Adrien does not speak of secession any more than Papa, but he said he would stand up to anyone from the North "who came down here to tell us how to run our lives."

Where will it all lead?

Journal - April 21, 1861: Horrors! We are going to war! A General Beauregard fired on a Union fort in South Carolina. The paper said Texas General Twiggs surrendered his generalship of the 14th Army in order to join the Confederacy, and states who seceded are called the Confederate States of America.

We received word today that the Great State of Virginia seceded. Many of the heroes of the Great Revolution were from Virginia, including our First President. Surely if Virginia is with us, we are in the right.

A boy came by from the Alcotts' informing us that local women are gathering there on Saturday to sew secession and company flags. Brenham has formed Company E, but no one has seen an actual military person. Papa recalled that a particular number of companies make up a battalion, but where is this battalion and who is its commander?

Will said not to worry, the war would be over before Christmas. Papa made no comment, but hastened off, murmuring to himself as if someone might overhear him speak to the contrary.

I overheard Papa and Marcus discussing what Marcus should say to our people about all these carryings-on. Papa does not believe as many do, who consider the Negroes blind and deaf to what we white folk are up to.

Joanna provided me with pamphlets on the intelligence of the Negro race written by her abolitionist friends. We must be circumspect about such things, especially now.

Chapter Sixty-Four
Hartwood

Lily

February blew in on a cold northwest wind, followed by three glorious sunny days of unusual, blustery warmth. Lily was in the parlor playing chess with Will when she heard a commotion in the front hall. Porscha, on the velvet settee before the window reading, looked up as Father and a windblown and dusty Jacob threw open the double French doors, sending a chilly breeze across the floor that stirred her skirts.

"Texas has seceded," her father said. "Representatives are meeting in Montgomery to write a constitution and elect a president." Will sprang from his chair and dashed to Jacob. They grabbed each other's arms, slammed one another on the back, and laughed.

Lily jumped Will's pawn with her white knight, putting his queen in immediate peril. Checkmate.

Nearly every day of March, a rider galloped up to the veranda shouting news that made Lily feel as though some mad joker were pulling the carpet out from under her feet. Lincoln was inaugurated president of the Union. Jefferson Davis was elected president of the Confederacy. Soon after, many congressmen, governmental officials, and military officers resigned. Back East, the Washington Congress called for a constitutional amendment prohibiting congressional interference with slavery in the states. "Too late," her father said. "Those no-account northerners should have stood up to the damn abolitionists while they had the chance."

She had sent two messages to Adrien without response. How dare he not reply? She planned to tell her family she was going to Blue Hills to talk to Berni about the wedding. Adrien was always working in the north field or with those cows. He couldn't ignore her forever.

She had come from her room when Porscha sauntered down the hall. "Your father wishes to speak with you in the library." He sent Porscha, of all things. She looked as though she had sucked on a lemon, eyebrows so high they nearly reached her hairline.

Surely Father hadn't discovered her meetings with Adrien. She had not seen him since November. Mae had told her about that woman he visited in town, that . . . adventuress. Too many nights she had lain awake thinking about what they must do together.

"Close the door behind you," Father said when she entered. "Sit down."

"No, thank you, I prefer to stand." Her heart was beating too hard and fast to sit. He was behind his desk, and she wanted to peer down at him for a change.

He leaned back and picked up a pen, though he did nothing useful with it and rubbed his forefinger along its length.

"I have arranged a marriage with Andrew T. Garrison. You may recall dancing with him at the ball. He was quite entranced with you. I checked his background as well as his habits. He lost his wife and three children in a shipboard accident some years ago and has been looking for someone to dispel his loneliness and give him an heir. He is older—fifty-three, to be exact—all the better, as he has no living children and has agreed to leave his estate to you and any children you give him when he passes on. He is on the board of directors of the Houston and Texas West Central Railway. His death will leave you a woman of independent means." His eyes had fastened upon hers during this entire discourse, and she had willed hers to blink calmly back.

"And a son-in-law on the board will do you no harm." How convenient. She clasped her hands together. Growers shipped cotton on the railway, which was faster than steamboat.

"Intelligence in a woman is fine, as long as she is circumspect and obedient. I have done my best for this family, and that includes you."

"Yet, I have no say."

"You may be clever and educated, but you must never make such an important decision. You think I didn't notice the calf eyes you made at young Villere? You don't know him. For over a year, he has been the bed boy of an infamous woman in Washington. And while you were in Charleston, uncountable Nigra bitches succumbed to that pretty face of his. You, my dear, are not about to become his latest conquest."

Her nails dug deep into her hands. How dared he speak of Adrien's liaisons, when she suspected who Mae's father was and why a number of light-skinned slaves abided in this household. Did he think she was blind? Did they have a choice? Did she? She knew her father. She would lose a head-on confrontation.

"Have you planned the date, as well?"

"No. I leave that up to you. Only Garrison requests it be before winter, and I agree. Of course, the wedding must wait until after William and Bernadette are married in May."

"Very well. I'd prefer it here, not church, and in October when the weather is cooler." Never a church wedding, for such a farce.

"Excellent. I confess, you are taking this better than I'd thought."

"I want to enjoy my freedom this summer and study the marriage documents myself. I must be assured I will be left with all you say once Mr. Garrison is gone." Was dead, she meant. He had said it, and she would leave nothing to chance. A woman of independent means. One day.

He smiled. "Good girl. I see you're my daughter, after all."

No more than an hour later, Jacob leaned against the doorframe of her room, his arms crossed at his chest. He smelled of the stables.

"I tried to talk him out of it, the old reprobate."

Lily sat at her dressing table and turned her back to her brother. She could still feel him there; his presence could never be ignored. She picked at the jewels in a butterfly brooch lying on top of the table.

"Did he tell you of the special clause in the contract? The old goat's got to provide for you as well as any children, even before he kicks the bucket."

She raised her head. Looked at him in the mirror. Saw his sly grin. "That was your idea?"

"I'll always look out for you. Count on it."

She should have taken his words to heart.

Chapter Sixty-Five

Adrien

Blue Hills on an early spring morning was the most beautiful place on Earth. I generally woke up before anyone except Betta, wrapped the breakfast she prepared in a cloth, and rode out to fields in dark silence while mist lay soft across the hills and curled in the ravines. Dawn sun revealed silhouettes of deer rising from dew-covered grass and wild turkeys nesting in trees. I would sit on Roman, unmoving, barely breathing, feeling time had stopped. It had, for those few moments.

Inducing Papa to agree to grow less tobacco had been easier than either Lucien or I expected. "I've been pondering over growing more food and grain," he said. "Our military likely needs grain for horses more than tobacco."

Consequently, I would spend more time with cattle, as our troops would need meat.

Will came by three or four times a week. On Sundays, the family left him and Berni alone within ten minutes of his arrival. I did not.

"Be an excellent brother, Adrien, and fetch us some lemonade," Berni said.

"I'll call Betta." I leaned into the hall and yelled, "Betta, would you—"

I laughed as Berni shoved me out.

Teasing Berni and tending fields and cattle were preferable to my qualms regarding Lily.

On a Sunday in late April when bluebonnets covered the hills,

Will arrived with personal news. He took Berni's hands and turned to the family. "There is to be another wedding in October. Lily is engaged to be married."

It felt like Roman kicked me in the chest. Lily was bound to be married. I wanted nothing to do with that girl.

Why was I panicky, needing to rush down the hall and out the door, hell-bent for leather—to do what?

In the west field Monday morning, I headed to the wagon for another box of seedlings. As I reached into the wagon, the muffled sound of a horse's hooves on damp grass made me turn. The ground fog was a foot high, and the approaching black horse seemed to float above it, a bright outline in the rising sun. My heart raced. Lily checked her filly not two feet from me. *God, pile on the agony.* I grasped the bridle. Star breathed hard, all hot and lathered.

"That is no way to treat a horse," I said, sounding angrier than I meant.

"I had to see you alone, before others arrived."

"Here I am then." Star blew and shook her head, jangling the bridle.

"Help me down." Her foot was already out of the stirrup, both arms reaching toward me. She was so light, her waist so small. I should throw her back on the mare and swat her out of here, but Star needed to walk off that run.

Lily began walking away, holding the reins. It was a measure of how hard she had pushed Star that the horse followed her quietly, head down, nodding. "I am to be married."

"I know." I crushed my hands into fists.

We continued across the dew-covered spring grasses and wild-flowers: blue, yellow, red, and white. Her skirt hem became soaked as it swung above the ankle of her polished black boots. I had tucked my gray trousers into my boots to keep them from the worst of the mud.

"From the dirt on your boots it will be obvious you have been walking in the fields," I said. I barely stood her presence for the raw ache inside, and the strain shot out in my voice.

"I don't care," she spat. "Our dirt at Hartwood is the same as Blue Hills. Dirt is dirt, and I learned of yours."

I halted, heart thudding.

She turned to me. "Father told me about the woman in Washington and your other doxies. He expected to shock me, which shows how little he knows."

I turned away, took a deep breath, exhaled. Hart had been spreading the typical sort of story most men found acceptable. I would laugh if the idea were not ludicrous. "There are no 'other doxies' as you call them."

Her hand grasped my biceps in a surprisingly strong grip. "You suppose I care? What do you think I am? That eleven-year-old child I was? You never gave me a chance to be anything else."

I faced her. "I know you are not that child, Lily. I know too well."

"Then, for once, be honest with me. Why do you hate me so?"

"I do not hate you, and you know it. You play at love and have no idea what you do or do not care. You take no responsibility for yourself and leave the consequences to others. You always have. In that way, you *are* still a child."

She took a step closer, so close I saw purple flecks in her dilated blue eyes. "I am absolutely aware of the consequences. Especially now when I am bargained away to a smelly, old oaf. I may never know what it is to be loved by a man I love, to be touched in a way that makes my blood sing."

"Love is not poetry and silly romance." *If my own blood would not sing when she was close. I smelled mint and something else on her breath.*

"It can be if you wish it badly enough. With the right person. It is the consequences I want, Adrien. Need I speak the words? Take me. I want to run my fingers over you and feel your hands on me. I desire your kisses, to run my tongue over every part of you."

"God, Lily." I stepped back. Had to. Blood was beating in my ears, and the crotch of my trousers was tight.

"You see, I do know."

"You have been reading what you should not." *Damn, she and Berni have been sharing those books.*

"You will change your mind once we begin." She had such a determined look, as if she were cognizant of what she was saying. Chin up, arms stiff at her sides, and booted feet planted as though rooted in the dirt. At that moment, she appeared more fierce and more dear than I had ever seen her.

"Such a thing cannot last. If discovered, you would be ruined. Ruined, regardless, if your husband realizes you are not a virgin."

"We will not be discovered, and I can manage the other. You may be all I ever have, and that is worth everything."

Where is sweet, naïve Lily? Sweat trickled down my back. "Do not ask this of me. I cannot. You are Will's sister. There are things about me you do not realize."

"I *have* asked. I want no others, but others want me."

"Do not say such a thing; you will not do it."

"You trust not? Look at me and see how determined I am." *She stared at me. Surely, she would never carry through with such a threat. Although anyone would be eager to oblige her, certainly Art or Clay would—they have as much as said so. I will put a ball into anyone who tries.*

Minutes later, I stood in the shade of an oak in an admiring daze, slapping a switch against my boots and watching her ride off. We had arranged to meet in the abandoned north drying barn again. She would explain to her family why she rode in the heat of the afternoon—she loved the creek with its birds, and it was cooler under the trees. Early afternoon was the only time I could get free. Everyone worked in the fields at first light until the worst of the heat, rested, started up again around four and continued until dark. Will's and Berni's wedding preparations filled the mornings, and Lily was an eager helper. Their wedding would be at the Methodist Church in Washington, and Randolph had convinced Paien to have the reception at Hartwood, which provided accommodations for all those from out of town, mostly Hart people.

She had planned the entire operation beforehand, right down to my objections, and I was right where she wanted me. Our military could learn a thing or two from women like Lily and my sister.

I may be all she ever has. Such responsibility. She was a virgin and likely expected some sort of momentous unveiling. My desire was not what Maman meant when she spoke of love. If Lily were in trouble, I would do anything to save her. Any man worth his salt would do the same. I admired her pluck, her intelligence. Best I did not love her, because she was marrying that railroad man in October. I would try to please her, though, with all I had learned from Maryanne, and there had not been so many as Lily assumed. Only Grace.

I was no longer acceptable for marriage and was not interested in that other sort of woman. Until Maryanne. Maryanne was highly paid to please men, and when we met, she had wanted a young man who was willing to learn how to please her.

Such a relationship worked for both of us.

I already regretted agreeing to meet with Lily, but how could I end it once begun?

Chapter Sixty-Six
Hartwood

Lily

That evening, Lily sat at her dresser while Mae wove curls into her hair. Earlier, Mae had helped her wash off the afternoon perspiration and change for supper. Mae chatted away, but Lily paid no attention. Something else occupied her mind.

A shame Adrien wouldn't see her in this satin gown and this hairstyle. After all these years, he was under her thumb. Or soon would be. She couldn't stop the trembling of her hands in her lap beneath the dresser.

What would the act be like? She had read about it, but reading wasn't the same as doing. When she imagined him without his clothing, she felt warm and . . . wanting. But when she imagined herself without her own clothing, she wanted to hide.

Several of those books indicated women enjoyed the act. Some gave themselves pleasure. She had never attempted that, though she had considered it, once or twice, contemplating Adrien. The idea seemed ludicrous. The sex act itself, animals, all that, was rather ludicrous, when one considered it.

Dear Lord, what have I done?

She ought not think of that part. Only holding Adrien in her arms and him holding her. Touching him, there and there, his kisses and his hands—

"Please, miss, you mustn't wiggle so. I cannot do your hair if you do not sit still."

Lily opened her eyes. "Of course, Mae. I will be good." *I will be excellent.*

※

He had told her to bring Star into the barn, redolent with the odor of tobacco leaves. Afternoon sunlight streamed in beams between the wallboards.

Lily wrapped the reins around an upright post and raised a hand above her eyes to peer up into the rafters high above. The high ceilings and sunbeams made this similar to a church in one of those old religious paintings.

She had decided upon this course, though her thoughts fluctuated like a wind-whipped kite on the end of a string. *What am I doing here? A girl with my upbringing, my education, aimed toward one future. Yet here I am, prepared to abandon it all. How am I so different that I dare do this? What part is mine and what can I blame on Jacob, who gave me those books to read?* Apprehension tangled with her love for him—an older brother willing to educate his sister in such diversity, in subjects a woman of her station had no business being privy to.

She heard a horse approaching. Her blood rushed.

Adrien stood in the doorway, face in shadow beneath his hat, his horse behind him. His linen blouse revealed moisture in the hollow of his throat. The bottoms of his trousers were tucked into high boots covered in mud.

Here and *now,* in this counterfeit cathedral of sparkling sunbeams and pitter-pattering mice.

He came forward to the soft shuffle of his horse's hooves and creak of leather. He tied the horse next to Star and untied something from behind the saddle—unrolled a red, cream, and gray Indian blanket he threw open at her feet. "My lady," he said with a hesitant grin. How considerate. Hands at his sides, he cocked his head. Looked at her. Removed his hat.

His black hair was damp and crushed in a circle at his temple;

sun-blessed skin above his shirt collar was shiny with perspiration. "We can stop here if you wish. I will leave."

She unbuttoned her short jacket. A first step to show her determination. *I am not afraid.* Despite her pounding heart. She carefully removed, folded, and laid it upon one side of the blanket.

When she looked up, he had removed his blouse and undershirt. Her hand went to her mouth, a burst, an unladylike snort. She glanced away, then back, and the muscles of her inner thighs tightened. She had never seen, only imagined. The smooth chest, taut stomach muscles above low-slung trousers.

"What is so funny?" he said.

She could barely breathe, had lost all reason. "Nothing."

He hung the shirt on a post and approached, kneeled at the edge of the blanket. "You will tell me one day, *ma femme.*"

He was giving her a bemused smile and speaking French. Again, she wanted to giggle. She had never been near a man lacking an undershirt, not even her brothers. She wished to touch him. Was it possible? Merely raise her hand, like this, and—the tips of her fingers touched unyielding hardness in the center of his chest, where lay a circle of dark hairs. Her fingers stroked right, left, seemingly of their own accord. He trembled. She had such power?

"You think so, *mon homme*?" Her voice came throaty, nearly didn't obey her. His flesh was warm, smooth, and she spread her fingers so that her palm lay there and raised her eyes to his, where she saw an intensity, an intimacy she had never imagined in all she had read, in all the hours she had lain dreaming in her bed. He saw what no one man ever had, and she perceived no judgment, only longing. How did she know this? He fondled a curl at her ear.

"Is this who you are, Lily Hart?"

"Yes." She wanted it to be. She was filled with the damp scent of his hair as he bent to place his lips, soft yet firm, to her cheek, her temple. His fingers slowly worked down the buttons of her blouse and guided it off her shoulders and down her arms; the light brush of his calluses made her shiver. He leaned close, held the back of her head, his fingers in her hair. She grasped his upper arms and breathed in the earthy scent of his skin. Ran her hands down his smooth, muscled back, placed her lips on the slope of his shoulder and tasted the salt of him on her tongue.

She pushed him, stood, and undressed. So many layers of protection between her and what she wanted. He took her cue and did the same, watching her.

"You need not rush," he said, smiling.

"I do," she said, "or I shall lose my nerve." She was down to her unlaced corset and pantaloons when his trousers fell about his ankles. His linen drawers left little to the imagination, and she felt herself blushing. He stepped forward and took her in his arms.

Tears flooded her eyes. She didn't know what to say. She was a frightened idiot. Her heart was beating too fast, and she couldn't catch her breath. This wasn't at all what she'd planned.

"Sit," he said, and walked away to his horse. She pulled her corset close beneath her crossed arms, wiped at her face. How ridiculous she must look, sitting here in corset and pantaloons. At least her feet were small. What if they smelled from the hot ride over? She could smell only straw and horses.

Having returned, he settled down before her with ankles crossed, knees open, and—goodness, obviously uncaring about whether she noticed bulges there—and she felt an urge to laugh.

"Here," he said, holding out a perfect red apple.

She took the apple. She had not eaten an unsliced apple since she was a child. The first bite was tartly sweet, and the juice ran down her chin. She wiped with the heel of her hand. Adrien was eating one of his own and smiled at her. She smiled back. Bite, chew, bite. Grin at one another. His lips were wet with juice. He took a bite and held the piece delicately between his teeth. She leaned forward, placed her teeth on the near end, their mouths barely touching, pulled. She was disappointed when he let go. They played the game again, only the second time he followed the apple, and she forgot about her open corset when his warm hand cradled her breast, and she was glad she forgot. She forgot everything except here and now and this man, and what she had thought would be difficult became simple, elemental, a moth to light. She was engulfed by adoration, by this male creature who worshipped her with every caress of his lingering lips, his stroking fingers, every glide of his warm flesh across her flesh. She was deliciously shocked by what he did with his mouth, his tongue, when he spread her thighs and she grasped his hair, arched from the blanket and squealed his name alongside the name of God.

They lay side by side, her head cradled in his right arm.

"Was that . . . did I—?" she said.

"I believe you did," he said.

She could hear the smile in his voice. She might call him on such self-satisfaction, but not now. She was much too content.

He caressingly circled her belly. Her face was inches from his chest; she saw clearly one nipple, the color of dark molasses. *What would happen if I—?* A touch, a tentative stroke and circle, so small, so, reactive; he shuddered. And ran her hand in ever-widening circles, over his ribs, over the sleek muscle and bone of flank and hip, up and into and over all the planes and hollows of him. She rose, pushed him flat onto his back, and continued with both hands.

"Lily," he said.

"Don't talk. Turn over."

From where such impulse, such nerve? He has seen her at her most wanton. What did anything matter now. Men wore such baggy trousers; one would never realize they had such divine bottoms. *And we hide behind hoops and skirts and—no wonder, we might be like animals in the yard.* She dared caress that delicious roundness, bend over and bury her face in his left buttock, leave a kiss and nip the soft flesh there.

He lifted himself on one elbow. "Lily, it is rather difficult to lie here while you are doing that."

"You expected the same from me."

He was about to say something more and changed his mind. It

was all in his compelling, black eyes. He turned onto his back, raised on both elbows. Obvious what her ministrations had done.

"You are right," he said. "You surprise me, is all. I did not expect this, so soon, from someone so . . . inexperienced."

"Inexperienced, yes. Unknowledgeable, no. I have read a great deal."

"Those books—nuh!"

She had begun fondling his member. What a delightful way to shut a man up! His mouth fell open and his eyes fluttered as she stroked and caressed this smooth thing with skin as delicate as . . . a rose petal. His wonderfully tight stomach clenched, breath came in short, gasping bursts, his eyes closed, head dropped back, fingers clawed at the blanket. How it grew even more in her palm, firmed with a little curve, saluting her. *Goodness, look what I am doing.* A low sound escaped his lips, a moan. He squirmed. *Oh my.*

"Please. Faster. Harder. Please." In between breaths, he was practically begging. He *was* begging. Begging her, Lily Hart. Oh no. Not this way. She released him.

He had never looked at her like this. Lost, his eyes glittery with need.

"Take me now," she said.

"Wait. I'm not—" He stretched across the blanket, scrambling for his trousers, pulling something out of a pocket.

She sat back, feet tucked beneath her thighs, and watched this rather awkward interruption. Oh, so *that* was a rubber. She was staring. She looked into his face, and he looked at her with hesitation, like the little boy she once knew. "Can you teach me to do that?" she asked.

His eyes, large and lustrous, brows raised. "You would?"

She smiled and leaned forward, reaching, sliding her cupped fingers down the smooth surface to where it ended, to caress the taut, hot skin of him beneath and between, to press there and make him expel a sharp breath. "I would."

She was shameless. She had waited for the reality, after years of reading and dreaming and planning, and in this she would be queen and no one's pawn.

Webbed rafters above, she saw, felt, only him, and he was entering her, slowly, carefully, backing out, in, panting. He tongued her nipple, rocked forward, and fire shot up her quivering thighs. "Now, Adrien, now." Didn't he know this power has made her frantic? He will do anything she asks. A sharp, glorious pain injected her core, and she grasped his buttocks and pulled him into her farther. Clutch and release, the strength, the sweat, the man scent of him. She clamped her teeth against his collarbone and bit down when he gasped her name, shuddering, collapsing in her arms.

Everything was different because she was different. No matter what her father did, no matter what her brothers thought, from now on she would be sublimely herself, right under their noses. She would never belong entirely to the old man whose wife she would be. She would continue to imprint herself upon Adrien Villere, and none of them would be able to touch that in any way.

"I never thought you would be such a fierce lover, Lily."

She kissed the forming bruise of her bite; she had broken the skin.

He stood, began gathering his clothes.

"So soon?" She should not have said it. She will not ask him to stay longer.

"I have been too long already. Isaac will wonder."

"Isaac." She reached for her pantaloons—that needed washing or they would stain.

He was much faster dressing than undressing, already had his trousers on and was bending for boots and taking the blanket.

She was standing in her open corset again.

He had his unbuttoned shirt on when he led his horse to her. He dropped the reins and took her face in his marvelous hands. "I do not mean to dismiss what happened here lightly. I am only concerned that we will be found out, that *you* will be found out. There must be no sign of what we do. Not here and not at either of our homes. You must not be ruined. Can you do this?"

"You underestimate me." Of course, she must not be ruined, as if she were some fine horse or piece of furniture.

"I hope never to underestimate you again," he said, looking down into her eyes. "Leave nothing of yours here."

"I won't. I can get away four days from now."

He closed his eyes, placed his thumb against her lower lip, and left a kiss there. "Four days then," he said, leading his horse out the door.

The fire in her was even higher now. She inhaled the scent of her fingers where he had left a trace of dew before putting on the . . . thing. Her eyes closed, she brushed her fingertips across her mouth and exhaled.

She took her time dressing, as it was difficult by herself. Next time, she would be sure he stayed long enough to help her dress.

She rode home along the creek bed, as she had said she would. She was no sooner in the front door than William told her that Confederates had taken Fort Sumter in Charleston Harbor from the Yankees.

"That is who we are," he said. "Confederates."

Father and Jacob walked in, and Father had a newspaper in his hand. "If I'm not mistaken, we will have a war, my girl, even before your brother can be married. Now that Texas is in it, we'll likely have them licked before you're Mrs. Garrison."

"I'm going to join up," William said, "right after Berni and I are married, before it's all over with."

"You better take your honeymoon first," Jacob said.

"A short one. I don't want to miss my chance to get a lick in."

"You are an idiot, William," Jacob said.

"Jacob," their father said, "your brother feels strongly about serving—that does not make him an idiot."

Jacob said nothing, but she could see his hands grasped behind his back, the white knuckles. He will not argue with Father, not about this.

She had been anxious all the way home, had prepared to talk of birds seen and happenings upon the trail, but nobody was paying her any attention. She ought to be relieved, not disappointed. She was relieved. She headed upstairs to her room to order a bath and change clothes. Will there truly be a war?

Chapter Sixty-Seven

Adrien

I had ridden off as though she hardly mattered. As though our meeting was of little consequence. I would not get caught up in some semblance of love again. I did not love her and never would.

I was determined to meet Lily no more than once a week. No matter her insistence we meet more often. "One of us must remain circumspect."

She was in my head when I rode out in the morning. I was afraid to sleep at night, for dreaming of her.

I could not get enough of her, of her smell, of the animal moans she uttered, of how she made me more alive. Each time I left her, I was determined to stay away. But I returned. No woman had provoked such intense desire in me, not even Maryanne.

I rode to town to see Maryanne, hoping for release from thoughts of Lily, but Lily was all, and somehow Maryanne knew.

"I will not be part of this," she said. "You are deceiving yourself and risking the reputations of yourselves and your families." Her face was flushed with anger as she drove me to the door. Once there, she held a palm to my cheek. "I understand the impulse that leads one of your age to such foolishness but dislike seeing it happen to you. Use your head, Adrien. End it while you can, before it is too late." She stepped back, holding the door open.

I thought to drown my shame in a beer at the Alejandro Hotel and caught a glimpse of Garrison at a table drinking with two other men. I ached to go over and murder the man. I slammed my glass down and strode out.

How cheerful I was with Will and Berni, playing the fool. Surely one or the other would find me out. Or Papa would or Marcus or, more likely, our people, who discovered all eventually.

✤

By the middle of May, our tobacco was ten inches tall. Grain, black-eyed peas, peanuts, and the kitchen garden thrived in the sun and intermittent rains. We had a bumper crop of field corn coming up, and Isaac and I were busier than ever with calving.

On a warm Saturday morning in late May, we two ambled down a row in the peach orchard, the sound of our voices rising and lowering on the breeze that sent blossoms fluttering about us like pink snow.

No matter how often Isaac and I had talked of going north or west together, such a thing was now impossible.

"I could never, in all conscience, ride off until this upset is settled," I said. I refused to think of the problem as war. The word was too strong. Too encompassing. "We might leave by next spring." I peered at my boots. "I am sorry. With folks up in arms all over Texas, practically the entire country."

"It's the way things are. Only if the Yankees win—"

"You cannot be serious."

"If you were in my place? I love you, Brother, but if I were able to leave here, to be my own man, do you not think I'd do so? Am I any different from you? Except for this?" He grabbed my hand and held it against his own.

"No different, except, in many ways, you are better."

Isaac dropped his hand. "I am. I have more sense than you." He halted, folded his arms at his chest, and glared at me with a knowing eye from beneath the shadow of his floppy hat.

I understood that look. I rocked back on my hind foot and turned. "Shit."

"I swear I've known no man who could get himself into female trouble like you. You find the worst possible situation and latch on."

"You ever think it might latch on to me?"

"You ever try to run?"

"Guess I'm not the running type."

"Christ almighty, Adrien."

"Who else knows?"

"A few. Mae won't say a word to the Harts. Thank the Lord word got to me and not Papa. He'd feel bound to tell your papa. But you're dealing with a hot powder keg here."

"I know." I turned away. Grasped a limb and gazed north through the trees. Murmured, "I know."

"Then do something about it this time."

"I cannot."

"I have one powerful urge to bust you in the head right now."

I let go the limb and faced him. "Then do it. I won't stop you."

"One day you'll wish I had. Hard enough to knock sense into you." He spun and strode off.

Perhaps he could have knocked sense into me. But I doubt it.

Chapter Sixty-Eight

Lily

"The blanket's quite dusty." She removed her yellow riding gloves first, as always.

"It is to be expected." He tossed his boots in the corner.

He appeared distant, as he often had lately. But that attitude didn't last long. Not once she touched his hand, his arm, or any other part of him.

"We must see one another in public at the wedding next week," she said as he bent on one knee to pull off her boots. It was the only time she saw the top of his head, the way his dark hair fell in layers, like feathers on a duck's back. She longed to hold him between her breasts.

"Are you worried?" His fingers caressed her cheek.

"No. I was only making a statement."

He was unlacing her corset. "I have become accomplished at this, you think?"

"Almost as good as Mae."

"Better." His long fingers opened the cotton folds as he might a treasure; he ghosted his tongue over her nipple. Murmured, "More finesse."

She cupped his privates through his fine stockinette drawers. "Mm. This is . . . nice. Isn't it strange how it all fits so nicely, in my hand, I mean?"

"You think God planned it that way?"

"Of course. All those 'begets' in the Old Testament." She snuggled closer, fondled him, and licked the saltiness along his breastbone.

"If you keep that up, I will not fit in your little hand for long."

"I want to be on top this time," she said.

"Getting creative, are you?"

"You have no idea. But you will."

Afterward, they gazed up through the rafters.

He was distant again. His mind was somewhere else.

"Will you ask me to dance at the wedding?"

"If you wish."

"If I wish."

She picked at the blanket, pulling off tiny pieces of wool.

"Lily," he said, "of course I will dance with you."

She dropped the wool, piece by piece, onto his bare stomach.

Chapter Sixty-Nine

Adrien

Crystal vases held white and pink roses that sagged in the late afternoon heat, despite ceiling fans spun by numerous slave children on the surrounding balcony. The mammoth, yet delicate, Austrian chandelier glittered in sunlight thrown from open balcony doors and shimmered from the sound of violins and harp playing a Viennese waltz.

Virginia and Arkansas had seceded, adding to the wedding celebration. Champagne poured from crystal bowls into goblets and down throats like water from a cold mountain stream.

"You have only requested two dances on my card," Lily said as I turned her around the floor.

"Your gown is too revealing. I could not manage more," I said.

"You already know what is beneath."

"That is the problem." I guided her into a wider swing. "Do you feel, a grand *teneur* at all this?"

"Why, what do you mean? What have I to be satisfied—"

"In the midst of all this, and no one suspects, not—"

"Stop. You are being tempestuous. It is too warm in here," she said. "Let's go onto the veranda."

"Your future husband may not approve."

"He is not my husband yet, and you are now my brother-in-law. Will you fetch me a glass of champagne first?"

I took her fingers in mine and bent at the waist. "Whatever you wish."

I had no sooner reached the silver bowl holding iced bottles of champagne than Will's hand was on my shoulder. "Have you seen Lily? The family must have their photographs taken."

"Whose idea is this?"

"Porscha and Father arranged it. Right here at the house."

"I hear you have to pose without moving. It is no wonder people look peculiar."

"Peculiar or not," Will said, "you'd better get used to pleasing those two now that you're part of this family."

"I believe the only way I can please either is to remain as invisible as possible."

Will stepped closer and took my arm. "Don't mind my father, and Porscha—"

"I mind neither. It is only your opinion and Lily's that matter to me. Lily is on the veranda."

"Will you fetch her? Bernadette's waiting."

I grinned. "She has you hopping already."

"Go on. Wait until you find the right woman and fall in love; then we shall see."

I hoped I turned away fast enough. That my face showed nothing. Was I getting better at deceiving those I loved?

Lily was leaning on the porch rail fending off Samuel Parker, who had drunk too much champagne. "This should be fun," she said, once I explained the proceedings. She took my arm. "I have never had my photograph taken."

I attempted to extricate myself before we slipped inside by pulling my arm from hers. "Leave me out of this. I will not behave like a mummy in front of a stranger."

"Adrien." She refused to release me. "We expect you; we are all part of the same family now. Berni will be crushed and your father disappointed."

"You do not know that."

"I do, as do you. You plan to leave one day. What if it is years before we see you again? What if—?" She closed her mouth. Her expression fell and, for a moment, I saw how she might look years from now. She grasped my arm tighter with both hands. "You must come. I will never forgive you otherwise."

"Very well. For you. And Berni and Papa." Besides, a gentleman should not shake off a lady's hands as if he were some trapped animal.

It was such a silly ordeal, the two fathers sitting on chairs in the center, the rest all crowded around, posing, attempting to hold still for innumerable seconds in the heat, staring at a black box. I kept wanting to laugh, constantly fidgeted. When the photographer finally finished, Jacob maneuvered through the others, and I turned and escaped through the parlor door. Surely Jacob had too much pride to follow. I had almost reached the end of the hall and the ballroom door beyond where I heard a muffled waltz.

"Are you always going to run from me?"

Whose pride now? My hand was on the door handle. This would never end, not until I stopped and faced him. Heart thudding furiously, I released the handle and turned. "I am not running now."

Subdued light fell on us from the cut-glass doors at opposite ends of the hall. Jacob came toward me with the same long-legged confident amble, the same lazy authority.

"We're of one family now. For Will's and Berni's sakes, we should put any enmity behind us and love one another like brothers." That attenuated smile on his face. He offered his hand. Blue eyes stared at me without a blink, daring denial.

I wanted to slap down that hand and put a fist in that face. "For their sakes, I have come here today. Do not speak to me of brotherly love."

Then Jacob showed a different expression than his usual superior smirk, one I had seldom glimpsed. "I regret what was done and am heartily sorry."

"What was done." I could not stop the memory or the heat that began about my neck. "Stay clear of me, that is all I ask." I spun and shoved open the door, nearly slamming it behind me.

It took years to realize that all that anger covered my fear. Fear of myself more than of him.

When the photographs were framed and set on the mantel in the parlor, everyone exclaimed over William and Bernadette's portrait. How handsome he was, and she was beautiful. I thought they looked like stiff ghosts of themselves. Berni had wanted one of Papa, and that was the only picture I liked. Papa was relaxed and gazing away somewhere, as though considering the future, . . . or the past. The group photograph was as I expected: a collection of strangers with no souls, my face a blur.

Chapter Seventy

Bernadette

Journal - July 1861: *Armies are forming around Washington City and Richmond as word of war passes faster than our local newspapers print it. Everyone hopes we can bring England and France in on our side. Surely, they need southern cotton as much as ever.*

I should be writing of the joys of marital bliss. Instead, I am writing of these terrible circumstances.

Many young men are rushing to Brenham to catch the train East to join up. Adrien said Clay Thatcher, Clay's brother, Henry Carlyle, and both his brothers left yesterday. They are afraid the war will end before they can get there.

Will is determined to go East to join the army, only he must complete his shipping connections first. I am grateful he is not rushing out to join one of the local companies. Papa is concerned these companies are too hurriedly put together and that they are not well-equipped or led.

Our lovely house in Brenham is near Will's office. The girl Mr. Hart provided is quite biddable and a fine cook, though not so fine as Esther, and I have ceased gaining weight. We will not remain long enough to turn this house into a home, as I plan to return to Blue Hills after Will leaves. I don't feel guilty about Cassie as she is better with us than she would be with Mr. Hart, who I understand treats his people shamefully.

Adrien visits once a week and reveals nothing of his intentions. I am torn between wishing him and Will together to keep an eye on one another and wishing one of them safely nearby. I read that in England, boys of nineteen remain in college. Must war take boys so young?

Chapter Seventy-One

Lily

Three weeks later, Lily and Adrien rode down the creek for relief from the stifling barn. Though chancier, they should be able to hear anyone approach.

Cottonwood leaves pattered in the tiniest breeze. She never imagined being outside unclothed, even on a blanket, and she huddled close to Adrien. He stood and offered his hand.

"Come, Lily. Get acquainted with how refreshing the air is on your skin, and you will love the cool grass under your feet. We will be Adam and Eve."

She took his hand. "What if someone—?"

"Roman will let us know long before."

She stood and wiggled her toes in the wonderfully cool grass. She was not so sure about Roman, over there half asleep, swishing his tail at flies. How could she be so brazen, walking about like this in the open?

She slid her hand from Adrien's and moved slowly off toward the creek. Each step was immense; she had never been so exposed. She frightened herself and, at the same time, cherished the shivers that rose on her torso. He stayed behind, waiting. She stopped in the sun, heat on her shoulders and the top of her head. Weeds tickled her. Touching the toes of one foot to the chilly water, she nearly lost her balance. The slightest change of air caressed every part of her body. Had she ever felt so alive? She turned.

He stood in the shade, weight on one limb, watching, reminding

her of one of those Italian marble statues in books she was not supposed to read. Would she be able to marry that old man now? She
had thought these months would be enough, but if Adrien asked her,
would she leave everything behind, everything she had ever known?

He held out his hand. "We are running out of time."

"Yes." She stepped forward and left the grass for the soft blanket.
"We mustn't miss our sexing."

He raised her chin. His injured gaze met hers. "Lily."

"I'm sorry. Time, you see. It is not enough."

"I know. We need not do anything. We can sit and talk."

"That is not what I meant." She wrapped her arms around his neck,
pressed against him with her entire body. How exciting to feel every
part of another's flesh and inhale his scent, the parts warm from the
sun and the parts that had remained in shadow, like a solved mystery.

"Here, in the grass, now," she said.

One of the most glorious things about being a woman was to
make a man yours, to make him lose himself in you. She would never
have believed this in the beginning. She craved the things he did with
her. The memory of them most often returned upon waking and had
her tossing and touching herself for release. But it was unexpected
moments during the day—her memory of his open mouth, his stu-
porous moans, his straining glorious body—that gave her the most
satisfaction, that caused her to turn her face away so no one asked
what made her smile.

Chapter Seventy-Two

Adrien

I arrived in the barn before her. The afternoon heat was nearly unbearable—even here in the shade, sultry air stifled breath and movement. She would not come. Has had her fill, was tired of riding in the heat. Surely the excitement of her own daring has worn off. She has become disgusted with my poor treatment of her. I must wean myself from her as I did calves from their mothers.

I should have taken up smoking; it might help the waiting.

I would never smoke in a barn.

This was a mistake. It had been from the beginning. She was late. I decided she was not coming when I heard her horse.

Chapter Seventy-Three

The newlyweds drove their four-wheeled buggy east from Brenham every other Saturday and spent the weekend at Hartwood or Blue Hills, bringing the latest news.

Near the end of July, Will told them that General Beauregard faced Yankee General McDowell at a place called Manassas Junction. Surely Beauregard would give the Yankees what for in short order. The Yankee General McClellan was winning battles in Virginia, and someone should do something about it.

A couple of fellows named Terry and Lubbock had gone to Richmond to persuade Congress to let Texas form her own regiment. God help them.

Will said all his contracts were signed, and he would soon be off to Richmond.

While walking in Porscha's flower garden after dinner Saturday afternoon, Berni told Lily that, after Will went east to Richmond, she would return home to Blue Hills and help Joanna with the children.

"Can't you make him stay?" Lily said. Will was being selfish, running off to play soldier so soon after being married.

"Make him?" Berni gave her a peculiar smile, blinked several times, and one slow tear escaped. "I told him I did not want him to go, that I feared this war would last longer than he assumed." Turning her head and considering a nearby rose bush as though she might find an answer there, she continued, "He must prove himself." Her sister-in-law spoke in a forceful, urgent tone that Lily had never heard from her before. "He must stand for what he believes, could never forgive himself if he did not. I cannot deny him that, can I? If so, tell me how. I wish someone would tell me how. I would listen to the devil's words if he would say them, if they would keep Will home, and he would not grow to hate me or himself later."

"Oh." Lily didn't know what to do with her hands; her corset was too tight. She wanted to run down the path away from this intense, serious woman who had made her heart beat so. She clutched her skirts.

"Berni, come inside out of the sun. It is much too hot out here. We must get some iced lemonade." She was turning away, glancing back. "Come along. Everyone will wonder where we are, especially Will. You know Will, he can't stand you out of his sight. He adores you so." She would not look to see if Berni followed. Berni would feel better inside with the others. Will and Jacob, the children, would cheer her up. Berni loved children. Lily loved them too, when they weren't screaming or carrying on.

That night, heat kept Lily awake. She finally drifted off, only to wake up from a horrid dream she couldn't recall. If this continued, she must ask Porscha for a little of the laudanum she kept in a blue bottle on her dresser.

Peepers pulsed outside her window amid a distant roll of thunder. Mae said the frogs were calling for rain. Rain would be welcome to cool the air.

She would write Will every day. Surely, her brother would not be gone long. Adrien wouldn't leave before next year. She would be married by then and in her own house, able to write to whomever she pleased.

In August, at Will's farewell party, Berni took her aside and told her of Will's and Adrien's private farewells over whiskeys at Gorham's in Brenham.

"I wish you could have seen them." Berni smiled and surveyed the room before continuing. "Will engaged a suite for us and a room for Adrien, which was excellent planning on his part. I have never seen either so soused. Adrien was more hindrance than help in putting Will to bed, so I took my brother out. We got no farther than outside the door before he slid down the wall and fell asleep there in the hall. I should have been mortified, but he was such a caution. I managed a blanket so he would not catch cold from a draft." Berni put a hand to her mouth, and Lily thought it was to keep from laughing. Until Berni's brows drew down, her gaze turned sad, and she laid a hand gently on Lily's arm before declaring, "Adrien will be nineteen tomorrow."

Chapter Seventy-Four

Adrien

I was awakened by giggles. Two dark-skinned maids stood across the hall, arms full of linens, glancing down at me. Me, on the floor.

I pushed up, unwinding myself from a blanket. Lord, the smell and taste. Thank God, my room was merely a few steps away. Now for a bath and breakfast to clear my head and escape before the Hart family arrived en masse to give their fond farewells at the train station.

Hungover in a steaming hot bath allowed me thoughts I had avoided. Why was I not leaving with Will? He was my closest friend next to Isaac. But Will and Isaac were on opposite sides of this—this war. Abolitionists in the North say it's a war to free the slaves of which Isaac is one. But the northerners would change our entire manner of life—Papa's and Berni's. Would they take our land from us?

I would have to leave Lily. I must find a way for the good of all.

After a hearty breakfast, there it was, newly tacked right outside the hotel as though waiting for me. A beautiful new flyer: "Mounted Rangers, Terry and Lubbock's Regiment for Virginia During the War. A company of not less than 64 nor more than 100 privates is now being organized for the above service."

The mustering date gave me plenty of time to get Berni settled home at Blue Hills and one last meeting to say goodbye to Lily before riding to Houston.

❧

Informing Papa of my plans turned out to be easier and more difficult than I had imagined.

I had risen early in order to catch him alone in the front hall before he left with Marcus and Lucien for the fields, before we were all to part for our various duties. Was it relief or disappointment I saw in his face?

"It's for the best you have come to a decision, as straddling the fence only causes problems from both sides of a question. Have you told Bernadette?"

"I will tonight. I do not want some sort of grand fuss over this."

"She and Betta will want to prepare a special meal before you leave, at least," he said with what appeared to be a small grin from the side of his mouth.

I could not help but shuffle a little and lower my head a second. "I would appreciate that, as I likely will not get that sort of food in the future."

"Take one of the shotguns and grain for Roman. You have funds?"

"I do."

We stood there a moment before he stepped forward and grasped me by my upper arms, squeezed, released, and walked away.

Chapter Seventy-Five

Jacob

J acob was prowling the stables when Colt Alvaro came down the stalls in his swift, rolling walk. Jacob preferred horses to cotton, although part of the proceeds from cotton enabled him to raise horses. He had always loved a fine horse between his limbs and never tired of watching choice horseflesh running across a field, particularly brood mares and foals.

He had brought Flora Mac, one of his favorite mares, out in the aisle where he walked her prior to a good brushing. He clipped her halter to a nearby ring.

"I have found where your sister goes," Colt said from behind him.

Jacob stroked the back of the chestnut mare.

"She rides into that old barn on the new field. The youngest Villere boy meets her there."

Jacob picked up a curry brush and worked on the mare's neck. Their colored could do this, but he'd always found it relaxing.

"They were there a while. I went closer—looked inside through the slats."

"And."

"They were . . . face-making."

"You mean having sex, fucking."

"Yes." His voice was barely audible.

Jacob continued brushing the mare; she lifted one hind foot and lowered her head. "You're only reporting what you saw. You didn't linger?"

"I came here."

"Tell no one. You and I will solve this."

"As you say."

"Leave me."

Jacob waited until Colt left before he curled his empty hand into a fist, before he turned and hurled the brush into the stable wall, making the mare and two nearby horses jerk and fling their heads.

Chapter Seventy-Six

Adrien

The breathless, cloudy afternoon threatened rain. I would urge Roman faster, but my loyal horse should be dozing in the shade somewhere, not obeying his foolish master by crossing miles of muggy fields in August heat. Sweat trickled down the middle of my back. I stopped at the top of a rise, and the north barn beckoned on a high flat beyond a drainage ditch. Roman's ears shot forward. He lifted his head. A light breeze bent the grass north. I removed my hat and ran my fingers through my hair to let the air get at it and cool me. A storm would create a break in the heat, and the cycle would begin again until winter rains.

This would be the last time I would see Lily. The only way to stick to my guns would be to leave Washington County, leave Texas. Waking up on the floor alone in that hallway brought me to my senses. And contemplation of Will about to do what he believed in, even if it meant leaving my sister—my dear Bernadette.

I would ride south to Houston and join up. *For once, I will do what is right.*

She was waiting. Urgency pumped my blood, and I urged Roman to a trot. I heard the threatening rumble of thunder as I placed a hand on the grayed wood of the barn door and pushed, saw Star in her usual place and Lily, her hands braced behind her on the blanket, ankles crossed.

"I had begun to think you decided not to come," she said.

"When have I not?" Without the usual sunbeams, the barn was all shadow, and a breeze snaked its way in between the slats, lifting bits of straw and leaf from the floor.

I wanted to grasp her to me. I dropped to my knees on the blanket.

She seized my arms, her eyes glistening. "Show me how much you love me while there's time, so I will have something to remember."

She remained such a mix of reality and romantic notions. She ripped my shirt open, popping the buttons. I fingered a dangling thread. "How do I explain this?"

"However you can." She pulled my shirt from my belt.

"Wait. This is the last time, Lily."

Shirttail in hand, she stared up at me. "It's only the first of August. I won't be married until October." With that, she began unlatching my belt and, damn me, I let her. I wanted her fingers where they searched. I didn't want to interrupt, though I must, before we went any further. She pulled at my trousers before I managed to grasp her hands.

"Lily, listen. I will be gone well before then."

"Gone?" An incredulous expression on her face, turning to—

A loud bang! The door slammed open against the wall. She fell against me; I clutched her in one arm, reaching for the pistol hanging over my saddle with the other—too far—ten feet to where Roman and Star had both startled, jerking on their tethers.

Jacob, feet spread, backlit in the doorway, holding a pistol. Colt behind him to his left. Lily turned in my arm.

"Jacob." Surprising how strong, even angry, her voice was. I helped her stand as she said her brother's name and felt her tremble—which kept me from doing the same.

"Get your horse and go home," Jacob said.

"We—"

"Don't lie to me. Do as I say. I may yet save your future and the Hart name. You aren't with child, are you?"

"No. I don't think—"

"I would never—" I began.

"Shut pan! Do as I say, Lily. Now."

She stepped toward her brother, between him and me. "Please. I will never forgive you."

"You will never forgive *me*—if that doesn't take the cake. I won't hurt him, much. Too hard to explain a dead Villere. Unless you don't do as I say."

She reached Jacob and placed a hand on his arm. "Promise me."

"I doubt he will kill me," I said. I dared not look at her, not with Jacob holding my eyes.

"I won't even maim him. You have my word if you go right now."

She and Star passed through the doorway without a backward glance. I was both relieved and hurt. I heard Star canter off amid the sound of thunder and rain on the roof. A gust of cool, wet wind blew in through the open doorway. Colt closed it.

I took deep breaths to quiet my thudding heart, made fists to keep trembling hands still.

Jacob handed my pistol to Colt. "He won't need this." In a lower tone, "Watch the door." Colt turned, his back to the interior.

My mouth went dry.

Jacob stepped closer, stopping two feet away.

"My sister did that?" He reached toward my torn shirt and open belt. I knocked his hand aside. "Touchy, aren't you?" he said.

I wanted to step back but dared not show fear. Jacob was bigger than me, stronger. Always had been.

"You cannot run away now, can you? You had to go after my sister. Did you prove yourself a man? Was it to get back at me?"

"Not everything is about you."

"This is, and you know it."

"It is not."

Jacob's backhand nearly knocked me down; his fist would have knocked me out. He did not want me unconscious, for then I could not fight back and prolong his pleasure in thrashing me.

"You never have learned, have you," Jacob growled. "You should have expected that."

I learned to never back down from a fight, even one I was bound to lose. I had fought no one seriously since those days this same man taught me to defend myself from schoolmates.

The few times my own fists landed solidly surprised him, and I was thankful for hard work in the fields. But he had not taught me all he knew, and for each hit I landed, Jacob landed two—on my head, my ribs, spinning me and punching my kidneys.

Jacob pushed the side of my face into the trampled dirt and straw. Rain drummed on the metal roof, and I sneezed from dust covering the floor. Ridiculous. Jacob pulled both my arms up my back—shoulders about to pop.

"Hold still. I don't want to break you."

I spit, mouth driveling blood and bits of bloody straw. "Get off me then."

Jacob bent low, huskily sighed, "I'd rather not," close into my left ear, in an old, familiar way.

A flash of traitorous response sent me bucking, nearly got me a dislocated shoulder until Jacob smacked me across the back of the head, making my ears ring and collapsing me against the floor. I was tired, years of tired. One of Jacob's hands tangled in my hair. His voice in my ear, "I could take you now, however I wanted, and you could do nothing." He held me there, innumerable moments to prove his point, let go, and the weight lifted.

"I suppose I should have taken into consideration your Catholic upbringing. And your hero worship of an ever-absent father. There's no such thing as a hero. You'll discover that one day."

"Like you?" An exhausted gasp into the floorboards.

"Me? Definitely like me. I never set myself up as a hero. That was all your doing. I followed my nature as I always have. I was besotted with you and let it run me. You came to the barn that day wanting what you got. Don't tell me you didn't."

I staggered to my feet, spread to keep a tottery balance, wiped the back of my hand across my bloody nose. "I was fourteen." I peered at the floorboards, holding my nose.

"Old enough to know."

"I was only beginning to. I loved you like a brother." My hand curled into a fist. All the years of running it through my head, of misguided belief, of betrayal, of wanting to forget and being unable to.

"Our relationship was more than that, and you know it. You knew it then."

"Only that it was special. I trusted you."

"I loved you, Adrien."

I glared at him. "You love no one but yourself." The memory was too terrible. Humiliation had been the least of it.

Jacob stroked down the corner of his mouth, observed his bloody fingers with disdain. "I have grown too old for love, thank God." He glowered at me. "Damn your hide. You have ruined my sister's one chance to get away from here, from that old reprobate. I could kill you for that."

"So she can marry another old reprobate?" I couldn't keep righteous anger from my voice.

"The man's got heart problems and won't last long. You think I didn't check? He'll leave Lily a wealthy widow. But I know her. She'll be sneaking out of his bedroom and into yours."

"Not if I am gone."

Jacob narrowed his eyes, fists clenched, cautiously hopeful.

I had gotten enough breath to straighten, despite the pain. "Fellows named Terry and Lubbock are forming a company in Houston. I was about to tell her I planned to join them before you interrupted us."

"You'd do that?"

"It is best, is it not?"

We locked eyes. I had never, would never outright lie, and he knew it. "I accept, for her and for me," Jacob said. "But go now. Tomorrow morning at the latest. If I ever catch you near her, I won't hesitate."

Jacob stepped back, turned, and strode from the barn, Colt close behind.

I wiped blood from my nose, wobbled to Roman, leaned against him, arms over the saddle. Fitting, this aching misery was what I deserved.

Perhaps a Yankee ball will find me, and no one will discover how depraved I am.

I took a cloth from my back pocket—still there, fortunately—wiped my face and nose, waited for my head to stop spinning, then led Roman through the barn door. Lord, I hurt all over, could barely walk, but must focus on explaining this to the family, as well as what gear I would put together—

Holy! Isaac stood in a drizzle of rain to the left of the doorway. "I was near Owl Creek when I saw Lily Hart riding like the devil for home." His eyes narrowed, head cocked. "You are one bloody mess."

Too much—images, words, questions—tore through my mind.

"I rode here, saw their horses and slipped in close to make sure they didn't slit your throat."

"You heard—"

"Enough."

According to the penetrating look in his eyes, Isaac meant all of it. Both shame and relief flooded me that Isaac had been the one to learn of that particular history.

"You think I didn't know? We grew up together, remember?"

"But you—"

"We were children, and children grow up and find other outlets. I had to. Lord, you know why. Bad enough for you, but me?" He shifted uncomfortably. "You were on your feet when I got here. Though I nearly busted in when I heard." His face twisted, his hands became fists, then his expression softened. "That summer I suspected something bad happened, but you said nothing."

I was speechless. All those years of mental isolation when I might have shared what had consumed me nearly beyond reason with Isaac.

Isaac studied my face, and the rest of me; he straightened, weight on both feet. "You'd better take me along if you expect to get there."

"What? To Houston?"

"Lots of men take body slaves and, at this juncture, you need this one."

"You belong to Papa."

"You think Paien will let it be known that his son ran off with one of his slaves? More important, my papa and mama are free, which means I am free, as well. Ask your papa."

Dumbfounded and speechless, that was me. Was this another of Papa's secrets? I was in such a state as to believe almost anything of him.

"Why go to war with me?"

"I won't. I'll continue to Mexico." Isaac barely breathed and stared into my eyes. Ever since we were boys, I had promised to take him with me when I left.

"You could be killed trying to cross the Rio Grande," I said. Texas paid a bounty for runaway slaves, dead or alive. The rain stopped. The sun peeked from clouds behind him; a drop hung glittering from the front brim of his hat. Isaac said nothing. He had not moved a muscle. His eyes told me all.

"I had planned to wait until morning, but we better go now. Get what you need and wait across the creek from our secret place." I felt deep in my aching bones that this was the correct decision. All paths were coming together, and I was meant to leave with Isaac by my side.

❧

Once home, I washed off in the creek next to the house, hoping cold water would keep the soreness from swelling more than it already had.

I slipped in through the back door. No sign of Simon in the hall; he was likely in the outdoor kitchen helping Betta prepare supper.

Hastening upstairs to my room, I cautiously changed out of my torn and bloody shirt and packed my saddlebags. I took half my past years' earnings from the stash beneath my bed. Downstairs in the library, I left two notes on Papa's desk. Berni would be furious I did not stop to say goodbye. So little time. What would we do if someone stopped us and asked for ownership papers?

One last glance around. Would I ever see my home again? I flung my bags over my shoulder, flinched, gasped, and cursed at the pain, then turned—to see Berni standing at the entrance.

"You are leaving now," she said. "Without saying goodbye."

Oh, my soul—the expression on her face. How could I have considered merely leaving a note? The dearest person on Earth. My bags slid from my shoulder to the floor with a thud.

"Sakes alive, you look . . . terrible." She closed her mouth, lower lip trembling, eyes glowing with unshed tears. So few steps to take her in my arms, inhale the aroma of lemon soap, feel her soft hair beneath my chin. My Berni, my beautiful, dear sister, whom I must memorize with every moment.

"I am sorry," I said over the top of her head. "I was not thinking, as usual." I held her back to take in her face. "I was afraid to let you see me like this. To have to explain—"

"I will not ask more than you can say. Only tell me what you can." Her dear chin trembled.

I seized her hands. "I am afraid I took up again with Lily. Jacob discovered us, which is why I am in this—absurd condition. Isaac is going with me. Jacob has forced me to leave sooner."

She lightly laid a finger beneath my cut and swollen lip. "Give me a proper farewell before Papa arrives home, and you have to recite a much longer explanation."

"And I would not commence before morning at the earliest."

"And Betta would fill your saddlebags with food that your horses could barely carry. You would need a packhorse, and she would carry on about Isaac leaving and—"

We were hugging again (lightly, being careful of sore ribs, etc.), and stifling our tears. I grabbed my saddlebags from the floor, limped out of the office to the front doors, and hurried across the yard past the oak without looking back. I dared not.

Late afternoon sun drenched the barn where I had left Roman.

Marcus waited next to the horses.

"Your papa sent me for a wagon wheel, and I ran into Isaac. He would not lounge in the shade when there is so much to be done. Not with a full travel pack."

"This was my idea."

"I know whose idea it is, and you are both foolish." His eyes narrowed. "Who have you been fighting?"

I glanced at Marcus's boots, then up. "It is nothing. You will not—please—"

"I said you were foolish, not that I didn't understand or that I would stop you." He pulled out a thick wad of bills from a shirt pocket. "Give this to Isaac. Be assured your papa won't send anyone after you."

I stared at the greenbacks in Marcus's hands, wondering whence they had come.

"Your papa pays me wages. You and Isaac take the risks. He'll need this for expenses. And remember what I said about keeping your money in a safe place. And give him this." He pulled a pistol from the back of his belt and cartridges from his front shirt pocket. "Your papa purchased this for me, and my son needs it more, considering where he's going."

"He told you?"

"About Mexico, he did. And he must go through the Nueces Strip to get there."

"He knows how to use that. We practiced together with the pistol Papa gave me."

"Another of your secrets." His grim smile told me he was glad of this one.

I reached for the pistol, and our fingers touched. This might be the last time I saw Marcus. I clasped him close, breathed in the familiar horse-and-leather scent of him and let go, mounted Roman, and rode out of the barn and the yard leading the other mount with the pistol and cartridges in the saddlebag toward Oak Creek where Isaac waited.

I reflect upon these moments I made myself hurry through. Those goodbyes. My sister. Marcus. Not Papa. Dear Lord, I had not been able to say goodbye to Papa.

At the time, I felt their importance and could not bear them drawn out.

How quickly Lily had left.

Chapter Seventy-Seven

Bernadette

"I doubted he had it in him."

"Lucien, you have a way of making yourself disagreeable at the most inopportune times." I stared at him, as if eyes might shoot arrows.

"Enough," Papa said. A last afternoon sun filled the parlor with hazy light. The room was warm despite the breeze from the open hallway door.

Lucien looked properly abashed, as well he should, considering Adrien was gone to war. Thank the Lord Joanna and the children were visiting her family, so they could not see the strife in this one.

"Marse?" Betta stood at the parlor entry, Marcus next to her.

"Yes, Betta?"

"Marcus?" Papa raised his brows and his shoulders hitched ever so slightly. *Oh dear, he must be here to tell Papa about Isaac.* I had not been able to. The rest had been difficult enough.

Marcus took a step forward. "Isaac is gone." He glanced at me, at Lucien, then back at Papa. "He went with Adrien."

Dear Betta, whose eyes glistened as she clutched her hands at her waist.

"I will give you manumission papers," Papa said, "if ever the time comes. . . ."

"I understand. Thank you, Paien."

I had never heard Marcus call Papa by his given name before. But Papa took no notice.

They headed for the library, leaving me and Lucien uncomfortably alone.

"I am sorry if I upset you, Bernadette."

I attempted to maintain a serene countenance and made rather dreadful work of it, mashing my skirts between my fingers and biting the inside of my lower lip. "You are?"

"Yes. I am." He moved toward me and stopped, with the little marble-topped table in front of the sofa between us. "I realize how close you and Adrien are. Were. I spoke without thinking, which I am inclined to do." He hesitated, glanced down, and scratched the side of his beard. "I spend all my time in the fields. Not in polite company, female company, as such. For years, I was resentful of Adrien." He faced me again, brows together, his right hand gestured as if to present me with what he said. "I don't know if he told you, but we, talked. I guess he was envious of me too. Ironic, each of us wanting what the other had. What I'm trying to say is, I've got what I want, and I hope he gets what he wants."

What did my brother want, besides an education and Papa's love and respect? "He has always wanted to leave and see the world."

"He will, now," Lucien said. Then he pushed his lips together as if he were trying to take the words back.

Chapter Seventy-Eight

Adrien

We rode, slowly at first, as Isaac insisted because of my recent pounding, south then west on the Atascocita Road, avoiding others as much as possible. Those we met assumed Isaac was my body slave accompanying me on my way to join up, and we said nothing to disabuse them of the notion. If not for the throbbing in my temples and my aching ribs and kidneys, I would have enjoyed the trip immensely, as the journey across the rolling hills and green valleys reminded of our previous shorter jaunts when we were boys. Here we were, finally off on the long-awaited adventure we had always planned.

Only we must part at the end.

We avoided that subject while we rode and in the evenings around our little fires. Rather, we went over the route, what had occurred during the day, and what might occur the next. Or:

"Fine shot to the head," Isaac said. "Course those Yankees aren't gonna have big ears like that rabbit and might be a mite harder to put a bead on."

"Since I do not plan on eating them, a ball in any old place is good enough, just so it keeps them from coming on. I expect I will miss your cooking, though. It does not match Esther's, but it is mighty tolerable out here under the stars."

"I can't imagine eating anything you'd cook."

"Me neither."

By the fourth morning, I had begun to relax my arms against the constant sway of the ride and stop clenching my teeth—the pain had lessened, and the swelling was down. I rode like a normal person, not minding rocking in the saddle. Enjoying it, even.

"What are you smiling at?" Isaac peered at me from under his hat.

"It is a splendid morning, do you not think?"

"I think you look better."

We rode side by side, and I urged Roman on. "I can ride faster now. Once we cross the Colorado at LaGrange, we must push harder to get to San Patricio in time."

Isaac made no answer. San Patricio was a small town not far from the border on the near, east side of the Nueces Strip. There was no law there of any kind—a place for wild cattle, wild horses, and wilder men. That night at our fire, he let me know what he thought of my continuing on with him.

"We will part ways outside of Victoria," he said as he heated a pot of beans over the coals. "You accompany me any farther and you won't make it back in time."

He had waited until I returned from the nearby creek with our little coffee pot of water and set it over the grill at the edge of the fire.

"Sides, I doubt I can take your coffee any longer than that," he added.

He crouched, stirring the pot. I stood and could not imagine him riding alone across Texas and the notorious Strip all that way. "Isaac—"

"Don't."

Only once before had he spoken to me in that voice. It was not one to which I was accustomed. He stood then and studied me from a foot away. Looked into me. The authority in those eyes did not belong to the boy I had known, but to a man. A man in his own skin with his own plans and risks that had nothing to do with mine.

I recall little of what we did or discussed the rest of that evening. Isaac had decided the plan for our parting, and no more was said about it.

After five days of riding across open grassland dotted with mesquite, yucca, and springing deer, we made our way down into the thick, sodden air of the swamps south of Victoria. Night beyond the fire became as dark as the inside of an upturned bowl and swelled with the sound of creepers. Crouched in the firelight, our faces were masks in a morality play—all planes and deep valleys.

I rose to my feet.

"I wish I knew how accurate this was." I scratched the back of my neck. "You have a long way to go. I ought to come with you."

Isaac stood next to me, folded the map, and stuffed it into the pocket of his faded shirt. "No. We've been over this." He dropped his arms to hang loosely at his sides. "You've done plenty already."

I crossed my arms in front of my chest, lowered my head, and made a low noise in my throat. All our words had been said. On the western horizon, lightning crackled the sky like some mad spider web. A distant rumble.

"I'd better go," he said.

"Take Roman." Roman was Isaac's best chance at getting across the river safely.

A deep breath, a sigh. "You'll need a good horse where you're going." He copied my folded arms. "Besides, I know how you feel about that animal."

"Precisely. He will be better off with you than blown to pieces by Yankee cannon."

A breeze from the west stirred the coals, lighting our boots and trousers. I looked at the fire, not Isaac's face. Had I memorized it well enough?

Isaac shifted his feet. "We said our farewells last night."

"We did."

Isaac spun and strode into the dark where I heard soft shuffling, creaking leather, and the slap of a saddle on a horse. I rocked back and forth, clutching my biceps. Isaac came fast out of the gloom leading Roman, dropped the reins, and stepped into my open arms. We clutched at one another's shirts and whispered in an ear, before Isaac pushed away, swiped his slouch hat from the ground, mounted, and was swallowed by blackness.

I gazed a while where Roman had disappeared, hands rolled into fists at my sides. I breathed in long and slow, hoping to remember the last brisk scent of Isaac in my arms. I returned to the fire and sat cross-legged, staring into the coals, trying not to think. Not wanting any stray image to get between those last moments. My dear friend. My brother.

The sky to the west continued to break with heat lightning. A breeze lifted my hair. As the fire darkened and cooled, I added small sticks, leaned low and blew, added larger pieces, though the night was not cold, not here in South Texas this time of year so near the coast. Saddle and gear lay at my back; dark shrub cozily walled me in. Looming oak trees draped with moss cast elongated shadows that twisted and waved over the circle of firelight. Lulled by the rhythmic song of frogs, I succumbed to exhaustion, and my chin dropped to my chest. The pumping belch of an alligator woke me.

A sound of bugling hounds came from the north, then circled to the east.

I rose, snapped off a leafy twig, and swept detritus around the campfire and over the area where Isaac had ridden off. I made my way through the shrubbery to relieve myself. A large log caught, and the ensuing light revealed the other horse tethered to a small chest-nut oak. Ears forward, he gave a snort at my approach. I caressed the soft nose. "I expect you miss Roman." I held his head to my chest, rubbed his nose with one hand, and passed my other behind his ear. The baying swung to the southeast. As the cries moved nearer, I patted his neck, returned to the fire, and added another log.

Hearing approaching horses, I half-pulled my rifle from a leather stock by the saddle, halted, left it. Moving a pile of coals to one side of the fire, I placed a well-burned grill on them and picked up the coffeepot. I was crouched with it in my hand when the first riders pushed their way through the bushes into the firelight to much stomp-ing and shuffling. There were five, all armed, horses sweating, leather creaking. One kicked his horse forward, nearly over the fire where he shied, and the rider reined hard.

I set the pot on the grill and stood; hands clear at my sides. "Heard you coming. Thought I had best put on a pot of coffee."

The front man spit to the side. "What you doin out here, boy?"

"I found myself lost and decided to stay put until daylight."

"Lost." He glanced at his fellows and a couple sniggered. "Where you tryin to be?"

"I mean to join up with Terry and Lubbock's outfit in Houston."

"You and that horse aim to join the cavalry, eh? Too bad the horse don't know where it's goin or you might be there by now." More sniggers. A guffaw. "Your name?"

"Adrien Villere, from Washington County."

"Oowee! We got us a Frenchie plantation boy here, fellas. Lost and probl'y away from his daddy for the first time. And he wants to jine the cavalry!" Much slapping of thighs and whistling. The horse jumped again, was hauled back hard, and the man leaned forward, eyes narrowed and spat again, hitting the toe of my right boot.

"You see any niggers come through here?"

"No, sir." *No niggers, never any such, you ill-bred dunderhead.*

The fellow kept staring, then straightened. "Houston's at the ass end of your horse, boy. See you're out'a here at first light." He didn't wait for an answer, kicked his horse in the ribs and they tore off as fast as they could in all that shrubbery—northwest, following the dogs. Following the trail of some other poor soul.

Not west, thank God. Not on Isaac's trail. He is truly gone, and I am alone. Alone and going to war. I had not let the word enter my consciousness until then. I stared into the flickering fire. No sound but the crackle and snap of wood burning, the dry scent of wood smoke. The peepers started up again.

Military life will not be like Centenary, the only time I had been alone among strangers. How is Will getting along? Fine, I expect. Lord, I miss my family already. Hard ride to Houston tomorrow. What have I done? Right choice to leave Lily, but joining up? To fight for a way of life that sends Isaac to Mexico for freedom?

Again, I am on that horse lurching down a steep ravine and have no choice but to hang on.

Acknowledgments

Heartfelt thanks to:

My best friend since first grade, Mary Curtis Kellett, without whom this book would never have been published.

Fred Bissell, whose unwavering support never failed for over fifteen years of research, frustration, and writing.

My Critique Circle buddies who helped me through those first, second, and third attempts with their focused attention and suggestions, especially Toni Morgan, Ben Zehabe, and dear Casey Robb who took the time to edit the final manuscript.

Elaine Platt and Star of the Republic Museum in Washington, Texas, for their assistance and allowing me into their stacks to accomplish research.

My diverse sensitivity readers, especially Drew Hubbard of Pride Reads, whose suggestions and encouragement meant so much to a woman writing a male character.

Brooke Warner and She Writes Press, the only publisher willing to support a book with a debut author writing about such subjects.

All those folks who give their time and support to victims of child abuse.

Last, but definitely not least, those authors like Frederick Douglass, Alex Haley, Octavia E. Butler, and Toni Morrison, who dared to deal squarely with the theme of the horror of slavery, no matter the discomfort it might cause. It is only through learning from them and others like them that I humbly submit that you have reached this writer. Thank you.

About the Author

Karen is a sexual abuse survivor who completed her formal education at Kent State University and San Diego State, entered several years of group and one-on-one therapy and pursued knowledge about psychology and spirituality. Her love of nature led to four decades of wandering the West and parts of Mexico and Central America hiking and backpacking before settling in Tucson, Arizona, with her cat buddy Dickens. Although she enjoyed minor success as a watercolor painter, she discovered her true passion when she began writing fiction at the age of sixty. Her interest and experience in psychology and therapy inform her writing about persons who overcome their fear to be who they truly are.

Karen believes in taking risks, for this is how we grow. With over fifty years of overcoming her own fears and challenges she hopes to help others find their own true selves, to not only survive, but to thrive.

Her web site and blog are at www.karenklink.com.

The following is a preview of *War and Preservation*,
Book 2 of The Texian Trilogy

Chapter 1
August 1861

Ethan

If a fellow asked Ethan Childs how a man from Louisiana ended up in Terry's Texas Rangers, he would say it was because he lost his Houston enterprise in a card game. Truth: his partner caught him in an indiscretion that meant he must sell his partnership in the saloon and leave town. *Indiscretion, my great-aunt's fanny*—he mentally kicked himself in the behind. He had let desire overcome caution.

He would put a decent piece between himself and Houston, and his mouth watered for the taste of a fresh beignet.

In Galveston, he discovered there weren't any ships bound for New Orleans, as Galveston ports were under Union blockade. The long-faced man at the ticket counter winked and spit three feet into a brass pot.

"Come back next week, and maybe I can get you on a ship to Nassau. You can prob'ly get a ship to New Orleans from there. No guarantees, though." The fellow laughed like a pig squealed, coughed, slapped his knee, and turned red in the face. Ethan walked away to the sound of fading coughing mixed with spasms. What the hell. He wasn't the sort to let a little war ruin his life, not with his pockets full of silver.

Back in Houston, he treated himself to a good meal of expensive blockade-run shrimp, oyster stew, and a couple drinks. Got in a game, got out of it, had a few more drinks. Maybe more than a few.

When he crawled out of bed the next evening, an entire day was gone. He barely recalled signing up with Benjamin Terry's cavalry. The girl with him—being circumspect this time—Ginny, or Jenny, he was never sure, thought he was a hero. He recalled drinking with a hell of a bunch of jolly fellows.

He later discovered some of the rowdy Texas recruits couldn't read, but there were plenty of educated clerks, lawyers, and other such who proved they could sit a horse better than average, and shoot. Many fellows from surrounding counties had been turned away before the remaining thousand or so were split into companies of a little over one hundred men each. They were to be sent in two groups, one after the other, to join the army in Virginia by way of New Orleans, which must have been why he joined. He could not recall. That was the trouble with mixing bourbon and beer. Even what happened *before* he started drinking faded into oblivion.

He became part of the first half of recruits to be sent overland from Houston. The rest would follow a few days later.

Ethan's group, along with their horses and gear, rode in boxcars to Beaumont, Texas, where they boarded a steamboat up the Sabine River to Niblett's Bluff. In Beaumont, there was no room for horses on the boat, and they were told every animal must be left behind.

"But we're cavalry," a fellow said.

An older bearded recruit to Ethan's right squinted from under his dusty flop hat. "You're in the army. Get used to such goings-on."

Upon arrival in Niblett's Bluff, they were crammed into two-wheeled oxcarts, standing room only. Ethan leaned his elbows on the side of the cart and ruminated on Texas cavalry being treated in such a manner.

"I'd rather be on my own two feet than janked along by a pair of dumb cows," the grizzled individual next to him said, and held out his hand. "Name's Crane Forbes."

"Ethan Childs." Forbes, who was older than most, conversed some on the surrounding territory, but not too much, so turned out easy to be alongside. His knowledge of birds and plants they passed was nothing short of astounding. "Been through Louisiana a couple times afore," he said. Ethan was too embarrassed to admit he'd passed his childhood in Louisiana and didn't know half what Forbes did of the flora and fauna. Ethan had been born in New Iberia, wandered her streets and levies, then finished his growing in New Orleans, never exploring much beyond the houses. He had turned fifteen before mounting a horse, and that occasion caused him to learn right fast.

Forty miles later, Forbes got his wish about walking on his own two feet when the ox carts and their Cajun drivers abandoned the recruits. If the men hadn't been so miserable, they might have laughed at the idea of cavalry trudging one hundred miles across Louisiana on foot in rain.

Ethan figured this was what a person ought to get used to in the army—things not being logical. When his father had gone off to fight Mexico, he'd said the same. And that having someone you trusted at your back was essential. A professional gambler, Ethan planned on being careful whom he called friend. A man rarely remained a friend after you took his money. Ethan would watch the goings-on, test the waters before he decided whom he would trust at his back in this coming fight.

Test the waters, he smirked as he splashed his way through another muddy creek, or hole, or damn whatever. Fast and accurate judgment remained a prerequisite of Ethan's calling.

He noticed a well-dressed young fellow as they trudged past miles of cane sugar through Louisiana mud. His smooth-combed canvas trousers were double-seamed. The fawn-colored deer hide jacket, though worn at the edges, covered a finely tailored cotton shirt. Silent beneath his wide-brimmed hat, the boy rebuffed no one's friendly advances but was stingy as a banker with his responses. He was soon limping along like the rest. Hand-tooled leather riding boots were not made for walking mile after mile; neither were riders.

Perhaps this mark—how quickly they became marks—might be interested in some sort of diversion from this daily murk and toil.

That evening after supper, he joined seven others huddled around a campfire. No colored servant accompanied the men at this fire, including the young gent he had noticed earlier. The soaking rain slowed to a drizzle, then stopped. The young man's hat projected low over his face as he sat on a stump cleaning a .36 caliber Colt revolver.

"That's a fine piece," Ethan said.

"My papa presented it to me."

"Appears you've taken good care of it. Used it much?"

"Enough to hit that at which I aim." The oil rag stilled. Poking from beneath the hat was a straight, refined nose above a sparsely whiskered chin. "Tin cans, mostly." The rag was off again, no less busy for the interruption.

Ethan was too tired for a game, anyway. Everyone soon collapsed on their bedrolls, complaining of the usual—they joined the cavalry for this? He tossed a coin and won a somewhat dry spot beneath one wagon.

As tired as he was, he had never been one of those gents who could nod off soon as he closed his eyes. Had he heard right? He had lived in New Orleans with his mother until sixteen, and he knew French Creole, even if mangled by Texas drawl. Did a kindred soul present itself this way? Old Mamsy Dee would tell him so. He recalled her dark, wrinkled face, her bright red tignon with the crow feather stuck in its folds. The other boys had feared her piercing black eyes and gravelly voice. His favorite Sunday afternoons comprised visiting her in the cottage near the wharf, though he quit believing in her spells and pronouncements when he left other childhood fancies behind.

Two days later, he saw the same youth again, much changed.

They had arrived late the night before at Spanish Lake on Bayou Teche, a glorious encampment of cropped grass, spreading oaks, gum, and cypress trees. Palmettos rattled in the soft breeze. Ethan slept well until after the sun rose. They washed by finding a partner, soaping up and pouring buckets of cold water over one another. Not everyone washed, which soon determined who slept near whom. Followed by a breakfast of ham, spicy Cajun sausage, cornbread with butter, scrambled eggs, and coffee—rich, black coffee, coffee he remembered.

He spied a big log near the water, in warm, morning sun,

unoccupied, no less. The perfect place to eat what looked like the best breakfast in weeks. How happy he felt among all the familiar smells and sounds—the nattering of so many birds, the soft breeze redolent with the smell of flowers. He'd left home to get away from anything that reminded him of his childhood. Yet here he was, looking forward to being home and seeing it all again, even his mother.

A young fellow was heading the same direction. Ethan would know those boots anywhere. It was the same fellow who'd been cleaning his pistol that night. Cleaned up and without the hat and scruffy semblance of a beard to hide behind, he appeared younger than Ethan first believed.

Ethan ambled forward with his biggest grin.

The boy turned, a look of hesitant anticipation in his eyes—deepset black eyes that met his, slightly slanted and set above prominent cheekbones. Ethan was reminded of Louie, a boy he'd known years ago in the Quarter—the son of a French cotton broker and his beautiful quadroon mistress.

Ethan offered his hand. "Never introduced myself. Ethan Childs, Houston. Before that, New Orleans."

"Adrien Villere, Washington, Texas." Something melancholic hovered about his face; then he smiled with a hopeful look and a curious twist to the corner of his mouth. A fine mouth it was, too, made sensual by a full lower lip. And that delightful inflection again. It had become a habit, the way Ethan's speech adjusted to that of the other person. A good habit to acquire when you wanted someone to relax, to trust you more than he ought before a game.

Ethan nodded toward what appeared to be their same destination. "Will you join me at this fine log?"

They dug into their cooling eggs and spoke between mouthfuls.

"Are you glad to be going home to New Orleans?" the youth said.

"I'll surprise my mother, a few old friends."

"I have never been, but I hope to find family there."

"I thought I recognized your accent."

"Maman was French, though she grew up in Savannah. She loved the way Papa spoke, which was familiar and different from Texas. He came to Texas through Virginia but was originally French Creole from Louisiana. She insisted all of us converse with what she declared proper diction." His spoon hung suspended above his plate for a moment of silence, as though his mind hovered somewhere beyond where they sat at present. He continued eating.

"I don't recognize the name Villere," Ethan said. "But I have heard the name Villeré, with the accent at the end. You might ask for that name if the other doesn't work."

"I have an address where Papa wrote her."

"It's a woman you're looking for, then."

"Yes, my papa's sister."

They talked, off and on, into the afternoon. He learned the youth had an older brother and a younger sister, and a little of life on a Brazos tobacco plantation. Adrien made nothing of it, but Ethan was familiar with those Texas families who colonized the Brazos River. They left Louisiana, Tennessee, other southern states, and nearly all came from wealthy plantation families. What the devil brought one of their sons to join up as a lowly roughneck horse handler instead of using family influence to gain a commission? *I better discover the fellow's inclinations up front.*

"You may as well know my father was a gambler, and my mother runs a fancy brothel on Rampart Street. I grew up in the place. It's where I learned to read and speak properly and play a little piano. If my breeding doesn't suit you, say so now."

"You suit me fine, Ethan. *Maman* played piano. She taught me, yet I could never play as well as my sister."

He lost years from his face when he smiled like that. He also looked . . . innocent. So many of these country boys were. *How many will be alive six months from now? Is this a mistake, getting so friendly? But I can't go into this thing without pals.* His father had been damn frank about his own experiences fighting under Commander Scott in the war with Mexico. Never volunteer, Son, he'd said. So why had he? Hell if he knew. Being full as a tick at the time didn't seem a good enough answer. But if you're in, find someone to watch your back. He'd said that too.

Maybe he'd figure it out before this thing was over, and it being over in a month or two wasn't likely. He knew too much about the North to be so fanciful.

He chanced a glance at Adrien as the boy took a gulp of coffee. Fellow was from a first-class family and was educated, so that would keep him from being bored in the weeks ahead. Kept himself clean and didn't smell like dog roll. *Maybe I won't displace him of everything he's got, after all.*

SELECTED TITLES FROM SHE WRITES PRESS

She Writes Press is an independent publishing company founded to serve women writers everywhere. Visit us at www.shewritespress.com.

This Is How It Begins by Joan Dempsey. $16.95, 978-1-63152-308-3
When eighty-five-year-old art professor Ludka Zeilonka's gay grandson, Tommy, is fired over concerns that he's silencing Christian kids in the classroom, she is drawn into the political firestorm—and as both sides battle to preserve their respective rights to free speech, the hatred on display raises the specter of her WWII past.

Who Are You, Trudy Herman? by B. E. Beck. $16.95, 978-1-63152-377-9
After two years in a German-American Internment Camp in Texas, teenager Trudy Herman's family moves to Mississippi, where Trudy comes face-to-face with the ingrained discrimination—and has to decide whether to look the other way or become the person her beloved grandfather believed she could be.

Estelle by Linda Stewart Henley. $16.95, 978-1-63152-791-3
From 1872 to '73, renowned artist Edgar Degas called New Orleans home. Here, the narratives of two women—Estelle, his Creole cousin and sister-in-law, and Anne Gautier, who in 1970 finds a journal written by a relative who knew Degas—intersect . . . and a painting Degas made of Estelle spells trouble.

The Green Lace Corset by Jill G. Hall. $16.95, 978-1-63152-769-2
An artist buys a corset in a Flagstaff resale boutique and is forced to make the biggest decision of her life. A young midwestern woman is kidnapped on a train in 1885 and taken to the Wild West. Both women find the strength to overcome their fears and discover the true meaning of family—with a little push from a green lace corset.

The House on the Forgotten Coast by Ruth Coe Chambers. $16.95, 978-1-63152-300-7
The spirit of Annelise Lovett Morgan, who suffered a tragic death on her wedding day in 1897, returns in 1987 and asks seventeen-year-old Elise Foster to help her clear the name of her true love, Seth.

The Great Bravura by Jill Dearman. $16.95, 978-1-63152-989-4
Who killed Susie—or did she actually disappear? The Great Bravura, a dashing lesbian magician living in a fantastical and noirish 1947 New York City, must solve this mystery—before she goes to the electric chair.